The Li Continues

The Light Continues
Copyright © 2025 by Lin Stepp
Published by Mountain Hill Press
Email contact: steppcom@aol.com

This is a work of fiction. Although numerous elements of historical and geographic accuracy are utilized in this and other novels in the South Carolina Coastal series, many other specific environs, place names, characters, and incidents are the product of the author's imagination or used fictitiously.

Scripture used in this book, whether quoted or paraphrased by the characters, is taken from the King James Version of the Bible.

Cover design: Katherine E. Stepp
Interior design: J. L. Stepp, Mountain Hill Press
Editor: Elizabeth S. James
Cover photo and map design: Lin M. Stepp

Library of Congress Cataloging-in-Publication Data

Stepp, Lin
The Light Continues: Fourth novel in the Lighthouse Sisters series/ Lin Stepp

ISBN: 979-8-9877251-8-4
First Mountain Hill Press Trade Paperback Printing: April 2025

eISBN: 979-8-9877251-9-1
First Mountain Hill Press Electronic Edition: April 2025

1. Women—Southern States—Fiction 2. South Carolina- Fiction
3. Contemporary Romance—Inspirational—Fiction. I. Title

Library of Congress Control Number: 2024926781

The Light Continues

4th Novel In The
LIGHTHOUSE SISTERS SERIES

LIN STEPP

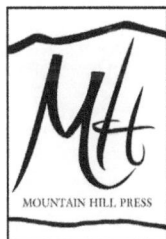

MOUNTAIN HILL PRESS

DEDICATION

This book is dedicated to all my fans and readers who loved my Edisto Trilogy of books set in the Lowcountry of South Carolina and who asked for more!

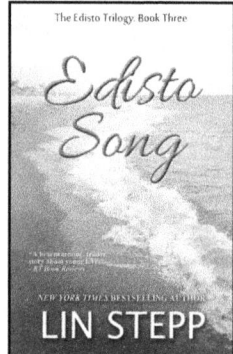

ACKNOWLEDGEMENTS

"Living in a state of gratitude is the gateway for grace." – Ariana Huffington

Thanks so much to everyone at Edisto Island, South Carolina, who shared their memories and stories, making the island, its people, and its history come alive as I worked on planning this book and the others in The Lighthouse Sisters series. Special acknowledgement to the lovely plantation homes and historic sites on Edisto that are mentioned in *The Light Continues*. J.L. and I especially appreciate the kindness shown to us by Colby and Jane Broadwater at Crawford Plantation for allowing us to visit and feature their lovely home and property in this story.

Thanks to Wey Camp and his wife Anne, at Trinity Episcopal Church on Edisto, for offering their kind hospitality to both J.L. and myself on our visits to the island, letting us tour the church and grounds, sharing information, and sending me the church's newsletter to continue adding ideas for my new Edisto books. You will find Trinity featured in my books.

My appreciation also to the many restaurants and shops around Edisto you will find mentioned in this book, each unique and individual. A special thank you to Russell and Robert Hughes, owners of the Edingsville Grocery Restaurant for their kind hospitality and good food, too.

When visiting at Edisto, you will find all my Lowcountry books and some of my Smoky Mountain book titles as well, at the Edisto Island Library on Hwy 174 and at the Edisto Beach Library at 71 Station Court, closer to the ocean. Thanks to both libraries for carrying my books.

Final thanks to the Lowcountry bookstores carrying my South Carolina titles and many of my other books in their stores ---- Barnes & Noble Bookstore at Sam Rittenburg Boulevard in Charleston, Buxton Books on King Street in Charleston, Beaufort Books on Boundary in Beaufort, The Edisto Island Bookstore, and many others.

Acknowledgements to all those who helped with this book:

_ Elizabeth S. James, copyeditor and editorial adviser
_ J.L. Stepp, production design and proofing
_ Katherine Stepp, cover design and graphics
_ And ongoing gratitude to the Lord, who helps me with all my books.

A BRIEF EDISTO HISTORY

2000 BC	Archaic cultures inhabited the island
1550s	Edistow Indians lived on the island
1663	SC Colony founded by King of England
	Lord Proprietors granted lands from Charles II
1700-1770s	Plantations grew, exporting rice and indigo
1775-1783	Rev War; planters fled; property destroyed
1780s-1860s	Plantations thrived growing cotton
1800s	Edingsville Beach formed for wealthy planters
1861-1865	Civil War years; slaves freed; property destroyed
1870s	Many families returned; cotton still a big crop
1893	Hurricane destroyed Edingsville Beach
1920s	Boll weevil ended cotton production
	Drawbridge to island replaced Dawhoo Ferry
	Intercoastal Waterway dredged, linking rivers
	Truck farming and fishing grew on the island
1925	Resort development on Edisto expanded
	Early cottages built, no electricity or water
1935	Edisto Beach State Park built with CCC help
	Palmetto Boulevard paved for cars
1940	Hurricane destroyed most all homes on Edisto
1941-1945	WWII slowed growth; military patrolled island
	Coast Guard patrolled park; reports of spies
	Edisto S.C. Hwy 174 straightened and paved
1950s	Development on Edisto Beach resumed
1954	Big pier built near park entrance; later burned
1959	Hurricane Gracie did heavy damage
	Groins built to hold sand, stop erosion
1970s	Edisto tourism grew and expanded
1973	Oristo resort and golf course opened
1976	Beach changed fr Charleston to Colleton Co
	Remaining Island stayed in Charleston Co
	Many businesses and beach homes built
1976	Fairfield Resorts bought Oristo Ridge
1993	McKinley Washington replaced drawbridge
2006	Fairfield Resort bought by Wyndham
2008	Botany Bay wildlife preserve opened
	Growth continued with beauty remaining

DEVEAUX BANK

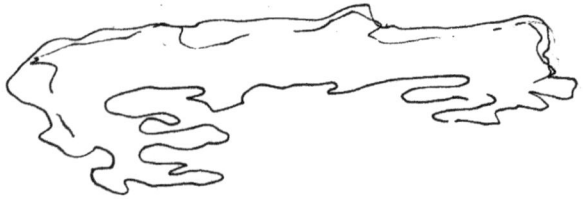

ATLANTIC
OCEAN

WATCH
ISLAND

MAIN BEACH

CABANA

LIGHTHOUSE

INLAND
Cottage

GUEST
COTTAGES

Pavilion

GIFT SHOP

STOR

DEVEAUX
INN

FOG
HOUSE

Lighthouse Road

GAZEBO

The
LODGE

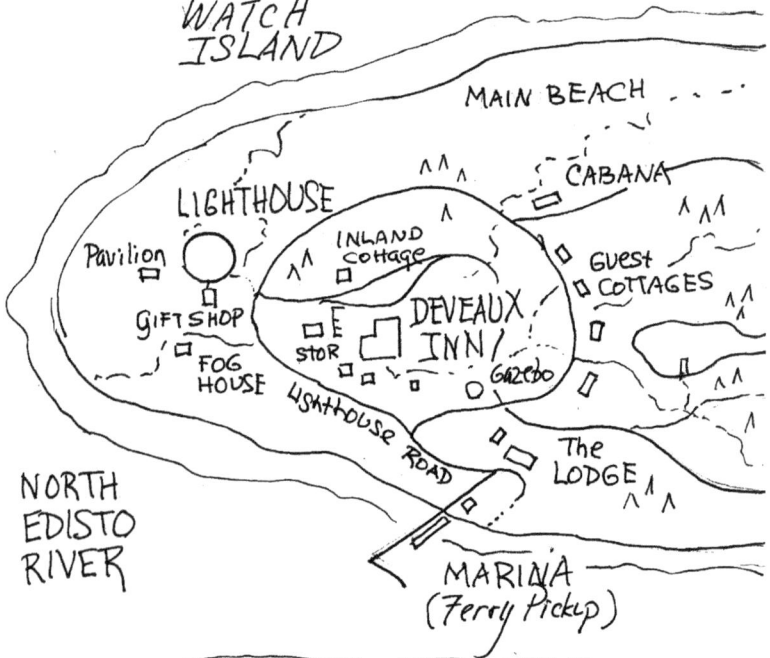

NORTH
EDISTO
RIVER

MARINA
(Ferry Pickup)

MARSH AREA
- Estuary

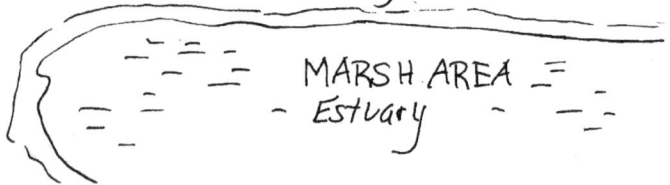

MAP for
WATCH ISLAND

EDISTO ISLAND

Townsend INLET

SOUTH BEACH

MARSH AREA

INLET

ISLAND LOOP ROAD

TWIN LAKES

TOWNSEND CREEK

MARITIME FOREST

BOAL'S HOUSE

BOAT HOUSE

MARSH

GEORGE'S HOUSE

RAMP

OCELLA CREEK

BOAT DOCK

SCOTT CREEK

FIG ISLAND

CHAPTER 1
March 2018

"I *so* agree it's time for a rest," Gwen said, laughing and sitting down beside Lila in a lawn chair. "You'll be happy to know I told the kids this is the last batch of Easter eggs we're hiding, too."

Lila grinned, watching her sister's children, Chase, nine, and the twins, Rose and Leah, six, racing all over the lodge's yard, giggling and searching for the colored eggs she and Gwen had hidden.

"They've had so much fun today," Lila said.

"Yes, but it's getting late and I need to head back to our place with the three of them. They'll need baths and an early bedtime with Easter church in the morning."

Lila leaned back in her chair. "It's wonderful we're all here together this year for Easter again, isn't it?"

"Yes, and these are happier times." Gwen smiled at her. "My life was a real mess this time last year."

Lila nodded, remembering that difficult time last Easter with so much unrest for them all.

Gwen leaned forward. "Listen, Lila, I'm sorry Chase said all those dumb, disparaging remarks about your being a nun, thinking they locked you up, made you wear black robes, eat gruel, and stuff. I have no idea where he got such crazy notions, probably from a TV show or kids at school. I've always told him and the girls you were an Episcopal sister in a community and not a nun."

"It's all right Gwen," she interrupted. "I explained things to him and the girls. We had a good talk. Remember, they never visited me.

It's hard for them to understand what they don't know about. Kids their age don't even like the regulation and structure of school most of the time, so they can't imagine anyone voluntarily selecting a life with a lot of built-in rules and obligatory mandates."

Gwen made a face. "Maybe, but I hate to think they hurt your feelings." She paused. "You are happy back home, aren't you?"

"Yes, I am, Gwen, so don't worry about me." She glanced around at the shadows of the evening deepening. "I'm going to head to my place, too, to get ready for Easter. Tell everyone I'll see them in the morning."

After waving at the children, and giving Gwen a hug, Lila walked up the quiet winding road from the lodge, where Burke and Waylon lived by the marina, to the small home where she lived. Inland Cottage, a cute red house trimmed in white, sat a short distance behind the Deveaux Inn. The big bed-and-breakfast Inn, once the old lighthouse keeper's home long ago, was now a sprawling white two-storied structure with multiple wings and inviting porches. The Inn's deep crimson roof matched the red stripes of the tall Deveaux Lighthouse that rose high on the hillside above it. All the roads on Watch Island, at the Deveaux Light Station, were little traveled and private, with the 500-acre island surrounded by water on all sides.

The island was a lovely, idyllic place to live, facing the beauty of the Atlantic Ocean, and every inch of it familiar to Lila, who had grown up here with her three sisters. They were all here together for the Easter weekend now, with their spouses and children, an annual family gathering they looked forward to every year.

Around keeping up the business of the inn today, they'd visited and shared meals, hid Easter eggs for the children, and enjoyed catching up on their lives. It was always a sweet and blessed occasion to share time together at the holidays, but Lila, a little introverted by nature, felt glad to finally slip away from the lively noise of the family to head back to her own place.

Inside, she changed into gray knit slacks and a matching long-sleeved shirt, putting her other clothes away. The evenings were still chilly here at the end of March, although tomorrow, Easter Sunday and the first day of April, promised to be sunny, fair, and warm. Rummaging in her closet, Lila pulled out the blue dress she'd worn at Burke's wedding last June. It would be a nice choice for the Easter service at Trinity Episcopal in the morning, and she still had the white pumps Celeste and Gwen insisted they all buy.

At the Community of St. Mary, where she'd lived for two and a half years before coming home, Lila possessed few clothes. The sisters all dressed basically the same, except for minor differences related to their position in the community. Of course, Lila had bought new clothes since coming home, but familiar disciplines were hard to leave behind. She still lived simply in many ways. A wise quote Lila remembered said: *"You are what you repeatedly do."* She'd grown used to a very different and structured routine before she returned home, and, truthfully, it had taken time to establish a new pattern. Old habits still called to her, like now, the usual time for Compline, or evening prayers, at St. Mary's.

Prayer, so much a part of a sister's life, was something Lila had enjoyed though, quiet, special time with God. She settled down now in her favorite chair with her Bible and Book of Common Prayer to spend a little time getting ready for Easter.

"Alleluia. The Lord is risen," she spoke into the quiet, crossing herself and then beginning the words of the Daily Office, so familiar to her. "O Lord, open thou our lips. And our mouth shall show forth thy praise."

A voice from the door said, "I guess I'm interrupting."

Lila looked up to see her sister Celeste.

"Is anything the matter?" Lila asked.

"No, I just came to deliver a gift I forgot to give you earlier." She pushed the door further open. "Is it okay if I come in?"

"Of course."

Celeste walked into the room, dropping a box on the coffee table, and then settled on the sofa across from Lila. "I do love your little cottage," she said, looking around. "It's so cheerful with all the red touches and red-gingham everywhere. I remember when Mother redecorated it, she used mostly white with splashes of color here and there. You've added to the cottage to make it more personal since you've been here, your paintings, plants, books, and more red touches, like the porch furniture you painted red."

"That old metal furniture needed paint."

"It did." Celeste propped her feet on the table. "I love the studio you created upstairs, too. It's fabulous."

"That well-lit room with all the windows drew me to this place, and I love the screened porch in back. I like to work and paint there when the weather is fair."

"That porch looks across one of the garden areas, with its pathways, flowers, benches, and statuary. You work a lot with Clifford there, keeping the garden weeded and beautiful."

Lila smiled. "Only in the ways Clifford permits. It's like working at St. Mary's for the head gardener and caretaker. We were very much aware it was more his territory than ours. He supervised all our interns and volunteers, too."

"Do you miss it there?" Celeste asked.

"There are things I miss. Good people. The beauty of the mountains around Sewanee, the difference in the seasons in Tennessee. It was a glorious place, nestled amid incredible scenery. You came to see me once."

"Yes, I did, when performing nearby." Celeste wrinkled her nose. "I didn't feel happy somehow to see you living such a rigid, scheduled life. Look at all the beautiful art you've had time to do since coming home."

"Yes, but remember that all things work together for good. At the Community of St. Mary and in college at Sewanee nearby, I learned the discipline I needed to use my talents wisely and well. Talent and work aren't about mood. Practice and persistence develop gifts and talents."

"You have a point," Celeste conceded, studying a nail.

Lila smiled at her. "It seems obvious you and Reid have made a happy marriage. You seem well-suited, and it is clear how much you care for each other. Are you happy?"

"Yes, I am, and as you would say, I have been blessed. God was good to bring Reid and me together again. You told me last year you saw changes coming for all of us. Do you remember that?"

"I do."

"I remember it was right after Easter last year that Burke and Gwen came looking for me in Nashville and found me battered and beaten by one of Dillon's senseless attacks. They brought me home and a time of healing came for me here. You encouraged me to stay open for new opportunities then, and those came to me, even amid all the sorrows. I am grateful for your love and prayers, Lila."

"You are welcome. God is good and wants to shower us with his love and favor," she replied. "If we are willing to walk with Him in His best way, He can more easily do that."

"I'm sure that's true. You know I've been trying to grow in faith; Reid has, too." She rubbed her neck. "However, I could not choose the rigid life of a religious community you did. I'm too independent, and there would be no space for my talent to develop there." Her mouth quirked in a smile. "Additionally, I do love men, romance, and passion. I think I will pray for you to know more of that."

Lila knew her mouth flew open. "Bridle your tongue, Celeste."

Celeste wrinkled her nose. "You need to read the Book of Solomon more attentively." She pointed at Lila's Bible. "God created love and passion just as He created all good things. It isn't wrong to recognize His goodness in doing that and to be thankful for it."

Lila tried to think what to say.

"Creative people are often passionate people, Lila. Perhaps that is something you have left to learn about yourself." Celeste glanced around. "Those who love red tend to have a passionate nature, too. It is the color of love, you know, and love and passion are intended to be enjoyed in reality as well as in décor."

Lila rubbed her neck, glancing around, uncomfortable with this conversation with her sister.

"I've been thinking how all these changes you've seen for us have come to pass," Celeste continued, moving the conversation in a new direction. "Gwen's change was in getting back together with Alex, don't you think?"

"I do," Lila agreed.

"They found forgiveness after hurts and difficulties, and they seem happier than before—their children, too. Alex loves being back at Trescotts, his family's business and restaurant in Beaufort, and Gwen loves teaching in Port Royal. She says you were a help to her."

"So were you, Celeste, but God was the sweetest help. He always has the best plans for our lives." She paused. "Even at St. Mary's we were taught the best vocation for any person is the one God intends exactly for that person."

"That's a good truth," Celeste agreed. She hesitated, thinking before continuing. "I believe the change you saw for Burke was, in part, her reconnecting with Waylon. Isn't theirs a great story with a happy ending? Waylon has brought so much laughter, joy, and companionship to Burke, and now they have their beautiful new baby, too."

Lila nodded agreement. "I love that they named him Lloyd Andrew, after Daddy, and are calling him Drew. I think Drew Jenkins is a good name, don't you?"

"I do," Celeste agreed. "And he is a dear. I admit, he makes me wish for one myself."

"He is precious—strong, smart, and so easy-natured." Lila leaned forward smiling. "Drew was born on Sunday, March 11th, so he'll be three weeks old tomorrow. Waylon and Burke are purposed to take him to Easter church."

"Will he be baptized?"

"No. It's a little too soon. Pentecost Sunday next month in May will be a better time. I think they plan Drew's baptism then."

"Reid and I will plan to come." Celeste glanced at the box on the coffee table. "Speaking of church, open up your gift now. I bought you a new Easter dress for service tomorrow."

"Oh, you shouldn't have done that. I have my blue dress from Burke's wedding I planned to wear."

Celeste shook her head. "It's always nice to have a new dress for Easter, Lila. Before you fuss at me, know I bought new dresses for Gwen, Burke, and Mother, too."

Lila began to take the string off the box.

Celeste smiled. "Your dress is white. I know it's one of your favorite colors, and it so suits you. Don't worry. It's very tasteful in design, falls below the knee, has a lovely boat neck and sweet puffed sleeves, and it's made of a soft dotted Swiss fabric. I think you'll love it."

Lila pulled it out of the box. "Oh, Celeste, it's beautiful. I do admit, it will be fun to have a new dress to wear." She stood up and held the dress against her to admire it. "You honestly have the best taste. Look how pretty this dress is! Getting into the retail world, along with your singing career, was such a perfect fit for you."

Celeste walked Lila back to her bedroom where she could see the effect better in the long mirror on the closet door.

Lila smiled at Celeste over her shoulder. "What color dress did you get for yourself?"

"A dramatic, rich coral but it's tasteful and Easter-perfect."

Lila laughed. "What about for Gwen?"

"I bought her a sunflower yellow dress, a fun and joyous color, perfect for her. For Burke, still getting her figure back after having Drew, I picked out a patterned navy dress with a slightly high waist."

As Lila hung her dress up, Celeste continued. "For Mother I chose this lush champagne sheath dress with a pretty jacket. She'll look so beautiful and sophisticated."

"You are truly kind to think of others as you do, Celeste," Lila observed as they walked back to the living area.

Celeste's glance met Lila's. "If God favored you with rich prosperity, you'd do the same. Many wouldn't, but you would."

"If great prosperity came to me, I would see it as God's wealth and not mine. However, I can imagine He would love me to help and bless others often as you do. I am sure God is pleased at the generosity you share and that He will richly bless you back for it."

"Give and it shall be given," Celeste parroted, smiling back at her.

Lila frowned. "Yes, but not giving foolishly or for wrong motives. And always giving prayerfully. I am sure people frequently try to take advantage of you, lie to you about their needs, present philanthropies or charities in a wrong light. There is so much greed and evil in the world. I don't want to see your good heart hurt."

Celeste laughed. "That's why I employ excellent attorneys and accountants to look into things for me. You are right though. There are so many who do not have a good heart."

After returning to the living room, Celeste said, "I need to go back to the Inn to Reid. I left him talking with two couples from Cincinnati, Ohio, staying at the inn for the Easter holiday, and all eager to explore Charleston this coming week. They were pummeling Reid with questions, learning he is a native."

Lila gave Celeste an impulsive hug. "Thank you again for the dress."

Celeste stroked her sister's cheek. "It is your turn for some beautiful changes to come into your life, Lila. As you once told me: Stay open for opportunities. Be flexible. See options, and be brave enough to take life by the hand and run with it. God will open the doors, but He won't push you through them."

CHAPTER 2

Edward walked up one side of the double staircase at his home at Indigo Plantation and down the hallway to his mother's bedroom.

"Mother, are you ready? I brought the car around to the front." He glanced at his watch. "We need to leave to be on time for church."

"I'll be there in a minute, Edward," she answered with a cross tone to her voice.

Edward stood for a few moments in the doorway watching her tie the belt of her pink suit, straightening the jacket, smoothing down the skirt. His mother, Clarice Alston Calhoun, was still a beautiful woman. His father had once called her, his "trophy wife." Edward didn't like remembering that or most of the memories of his father that had swept through his mind since coming home on Friday.

His mother sat down to pull on her high-heeled shoes. "You look very nice today, Edward, so much more a man than when you left home for college those years ago. You have a distinguished bearing like your father, too."

He frowned. "I was eighteen then. I'm twenty-six now. Eight years makes a big difference for anyone."

She stood to walk to the mirror to check on her make-up again and to arrange her silvery white hair, falling in a perfectly styled cut to her shoulders. "You've become a fine attorney, too, like your father wanted."

Edward felt like adding, "It's not like I had any choice," but he checked himself before the words came out. Instead, he looked at his watch again. "Mother, we do need to leave."

"I'm ready," she replied, reaching for her purse on the bed. She came and tucked her arm into his. "I am glad you finally came home to help me figure out what to do with this plantation and everything else since your father died. You know I've told you if you don't want to come back here permanently to handle it all, that you should sell it. I want to move to Charleston to live with my sister Eula. She's also widowed, you know, and lives in our family home in the city, and we've always been close."

Edward well remembered his mother went to his Aunt Eula Heyward's whenever his father traveled and often at other times, when clubs and events gave her any excuse at all. She'd never really loved the plantation, had never gotten involved in it beyond being the lady of the manor, ready to entertain whenever his father Sam wanted. She'd been rather a distant mother, letting others see to his upbringing. Frankly, there had never been a genuine, loving closeness between his parents either. Not like with Lloyd and Etta Deveaux, where he'd spent so much time growing up, showing him what family was really all about.

They walked down the stairs of the big plantation house to the wide entryway and then out to the broad covered porch. It was a gracious and elegant home, sitting on over one-thousand acres of land bordering the North Edisto River, and it had been in the Calhoun family for generations.

Edward opened the car door at the bottom of the steps for his mother, helping her in. Good Southern manners were second nature to him and always expected, too.

"Do you think you will stay here now or go back to Nashville, Edward? I know you stayed on at length after graduating from Vanderbilt with your law degree, not even coming home for the summer, working in that legal clinic and doing teaching and supervision for them. Even after your father died, you stayed on."

"I like working at the clinic," he replied. "However, Father wasn't happy I didn't come home right after graduation."

His mother straightened her skirt, crossing her legs. "It did cause some discord," she admitted. "However, your father said a little more time working at the clinic would better prepare you for work at the Maybank-Calhoun firm here on the island. He also said if you were foolish enough not to see it your responsibility, after graduation, to come home and to begin to handle what was yours with gratitude, you probably needed more time to see the advantages in doing so."

Edward almost laughed, remembering the very different, angry and threatening words his father had lashed out at him, telling him he had a year to get himself straightened out. Then, of course, his father died unexpectedly, dropping dead of a stroke out walking in the field this fall, checking something on the property.

"What will you do, Edward?" his mother asked again. "Since you didn't come home right away after your father died, there have already been people coming to talk to me about buying the property. Interested in it. Of course, it isn't mine to sell, it's yours. Your father always told me I could stay here as long as I liked though. He wrote that up in his will, but you know I don't want to stay on here any longer."

He tried to think how to answer. "I didn't come home right away after Father died because I wanted to finish out time I'd honorably committed to the legal clinic and the college. In honesty, I stayed on longer because I wanted more time to think." He paused. "I still don't know yet what I want to do about anything. I have a lot to look into before I can make any decisions. However, please know I'll talk to you about any choices I consider."

She waved a hand. "Do what you will, Edward. I already know what I want to do, and you know your father left me well provided for. I think I'll go to Charleston to Eula's at the first of the week. One of my groups meets on Wednesday and my sister and I are invited to a luncheon I don't want to miss. You'll be fine here. You know the help will take care of you. I don't need to be here. You won't mind, will you?"

Edward bit his tongue on a reply, to avoid mentioning she seldom had been here for him in any way that really mattered for as long for as he could remember. The Jessup family, that she called "the help"—and he hated that term—had been more a family to Edward than his own parents growing up. They also ran this plantation skillfully and competently. His grandfather had known that, loved and valued all the Jessups, saw them as equals. Edward's father knew their expertise, too, but with his inflated ego, he hated acknowledging it.

When Edward didn't answer his mother, about going to Charleston, she smiled and added, "I'll leave you some phone numbers so you can reach me if you need to."

The drive from the plantation house took them down a long shady lane under ancient oaks draped with Spanish moss. Now at their property gate, Edward headed into Point of Pines Road that wound through rural farmland and marsh, and past almost hidden driveways, to meet the main Highway that ran through Edisto Island. Trinity Episcopal Church wasn't far up the road from the intersection. Edward hoped they got there in time not to walk in the door after the service started.

Inside the church, crowded on Easter morning as usual, they found their way to two seats near the back of the sanctuary. He'd missed hearing the ringing of the old church bell before the service but at least they were seated before the first hymn began. Several around them nodded, recognizing he was visiting with his mother today.

Wey Camp, the Rector, opened the time of worship next, reading from the Book of Common Prayer. As the service moved on, Edward found his attention wandering. He could see the Deveaux family near the front of the church. It looked like all the girls had come home, as they often did for the Easter holiday. With their spouses and children now, they filled two pews instead of only one.

It hurt him not to see Lloyd Deveaux with them. He missed the big man and knew they did, too. He hadn't been able to leave work to come to Lloyd's funeral, but Lloyd's wife, Etta, along with Burke and Waylon, had come to pay their respects when his father died later. They had been kind and he'd enjoyed seeing them. Sitting with them today, Edward could see Celeste from the back. She always stood out, the only blond among the sisters. He recognized Gwen, too, and remembered his mother told him she, her husband, and children had come back to South Carolina from Arkansas.

Beside Etta he saw another dark headed woman. Was that Lila? It looked like her. Did they let Episcopal sisters out to visit family at holidays? It looked like she was wearing something white. Was that what they wore when not at their own services? He knew he'd seen photos on the internet of the sisters at the Community of St. Mary, with their long, navy habits.

He tuned back in, trying to attend to the service, feeling guilty for his wandering thoughts and inattention.

"Is that Lila beside Etta?" he whispered to his mother.

She glanced toward the front of the church and nodded.

At some chiding looks in their direction, Edward didn't say more, turning back to his hymnal to join in the next hymn, but he kept glancing in Lila's direction. What would she be like now after all this time as a sister? They'd grown up together, always been best friends as the two youngest of the kids. Would she act different now? How should he act toward her? It still felt like a betrayal to him, in some way, that she'd gone off to become a sister and not even talked to him about it when once they'd shared everything.

When the service finished, he spoke to the rector, who welcomed him back with warmth, and then he and his mother stood outside the church building greeting friends. She introduced him to anyone he didn't already know and then drifted off, waving at an acquaintance across the church yard and leaving him standing alone to wait for her.

As the Deveaux family came outside, Waylon and Burke spotted him and came to greet him and show him their new baby.

"He's a fine, handsome boy," Edward said, watching the baby's eyes brighten as he leaned closer to him, snuggled in Waylon's arms.

Gwen rushed in to give him one of her exuberant hugs. "Oh,

look at you, Edward Calhoun, all grown up and so handsome," she said. "How long will you be here on the island?"

"I'm not sure, yet," he answered honestly.

"We're sorry about your father," Celeste added, moving to join Gwen and giving him a hug, too. "I regret I couldn't get to the island for his funeral. I was on tour then." She drew a tall man forward. "This is my husband, Reid Beckett." She gestured toward the other man standing with them. "And this is Gwen's husband Alex Trescott. I can't remember if you met Alex, before he and Gwen married in past, but they're back and living nearby in Port Royal now." She pointed toward a group of children giggling and running around in the yard. "Three of those children are Gwen and Alex's."

"Time brings a lot of changes," he replied, happy to see them all.

"And here comes Mother with Lila," Gwen added.

Edward tried to keep his expression neutral and congenial as Lila walked up, dressed not as a sister or a nun at all, but in a pretty, girlish white dress with a flirty full skirt that drifted around her legs in the Sunday breeze. Her long dark hair lay spread over her shoulders, most of it pulled back somehow behind her head in a clasp, and she looked beautiful. He knew he sucked in a breath.

"Hello, Edward," she said to him in that soft lyrical voice he remembered, coming to take his hand. "It's good to see you. I'm sorry about your father."

He searched for a reply, but then blurted out, "I thought you were a sister in that religious community at Sewanee. Do they let you dress like this when you leave for a visit somewhere?"

Celeste laughed out loud. "Catch up, Edward. Where have you been? Lila left the Community of St. Mary and came home last December. She's been home almost a year and a half now. I know you didn't come home last summer but we were all here. Didn't you even hear she was back?"

Etta stepped closer to them. "Be kind, Celeste. Edward has been away a long time and he lost his father not long after your father died."

Edward felt his face flush, and he saw Lila attempt to hide a smile.

Waylon slapped him on the back fondly. "I think the last time you were at home was for your father's funeral. Lila hadn't come back yet. I'm sorry no one told you she came back home to stay later, but I'm surprised your mother didn't."

His mother, Clarice, walked over to join them. Hearing Waylon's comment, she shrugged and said, "I assumed Edward knew, friends with all of you as he was. I guess I never thought to mention it."

She smiled at Etta. "Isn't it good to have our children here with us though?" She walked over to Waylon. "Let me see your new grandchild, Etta. Isn't he a pretty little thing?"

While his mother made on over the new baby, Edward managed to sidle over toward Lila, who had walked a few steps away from the family to admire some jasmine in the church garden getting ready to bloom.

"Why didn't you tell me you'd come home?" he hissed at her.

"Spring is coming and the jasmine will soon be blooming out in full," she said, before turning toward him. "Should I have contacted you, Edward? It's not as though we've kept in touch much in the years since we left Edisto."

He scowled. "Well, I thought you were in that religious Community at Sewanee. We've always been friends. You could have let me know you'd left."

She studied him for a moment before answering. "As I recall, our friendship drifted apart over the years, but it is good to see you again. I remember you once said you thought you'd never come back to Edisto."

He frowned. "Well, I hadn't expected my father to die so young."

"I see. Will you stay now?" she asked.

"I don't know," he told her honestly. "I have so much to think through that I hadn't expected to consider before." He let his eyes move over her. "I am glad you are home, though. We've always been friends. I hope we can be again. Will you come to ride with me? We always rode horses together, and Levi has complained the horses haven't been ridden enough over the years with us both gone."

He could see Lila considering how to answer.

Celeste walked closer. "I actually believe Lila will be at the plantation frequently over the next few weeks. She's working on illustrations for a new book for a history professor at the College of Charleston. She's visited several of the other island plantation homes already, doing sketches and paintings, but I remember she said Indigo was next on her list."

Burke joined them, too. "The professor Lila is working for is Morgan Richards. He's a colleague of Myron Andric's. Myron is an ornithologist and also a professor at the College of Charleston. He spent a large part of last year staying with us at the inn, while working on a book about birds. Lila illustrated his book."

"Did you know Lila was doing work like that?" Celeste asked. "She's incredibly gifted. I've been carrying her paintings and gift cards at my shop in Charleston and she's making a name for herself now in the art field."

Edward felt stunned. "I guess I have a lot of catching up to do."

Lila's soft eyes, studying him, made him nervous. He had not kept up with her like he should have. But life had been complicated. He wished now, with her eyes on his and with the breeze ruffling her hair and dress, that he had.

He saw Celeste give him a small smile laced with a touch of amusement. "I imagine Lila could work in a horseback ride after she finishes her sketches at the plantation tomorrow."

Lila sent Celeste a glance of annoyance at her words, which Edward didn't miss.

"We'll see." Lila replied. She hesitated a moment and then added, "I have missed riding."

"Didn't you go to the plantation to ride when you were at home other times?" Edward asked. "You know you could have."

"No, I didn't go." She looked away, with a pained expression in her eyes.

Edward's mother walked over to take his arm in hers. "We need to go back to the house, son. Annamae said she left lunch for us to heat up."

"The baby is getting fussy and we need to head home, too," Waylon added. "Come over to the island when you can, Edward. Don't make yourself scarce. Maybe we can go fishing one day."

"I'd like that," he said, before trailing his mother to the car.

In the car, as they headed back to the plantation, he asked, "Why didn't you tell me Lila had come home?"

She shrugged. "It never came up, and, like I said, I assumed you knew. I seem to recall you and that girl spent a lot of time together before you left home for college. Why didn't you keep up with her more yourself if you wanted to know about her life and what she was doing?"

He made a face. "I don't know. Sometimes when you go away, you make another life, and you begin to let your past life go."

A little silence ensued and then his mother added, "I know you had problems with your father. Sons often do, and your father was a strong man with assertive opinions and an aggressive personality. However, in his way, he loved you, Edward. Perhaps now, back at home, you'll find ways to see that and to remember the good about your father as well as the difficult."

He scowled at her words. "How did you cope with some of the things he did, Mother?"

"That is personal and not a subject I care to discuss with you," she replied primly. "In life, you learn to live with things and people as they are and you focus on your blessings rather than life's small problems and disappointments. If you have not learned that yet you need to."

CHAPTER 3

Watching Edward leave the church with his mother, Lila felt grateful she had learned in the last years how to maintain a calm serenity regardless of the experiences life brought her way, thankful, too, she'd grown in temperance and patience. In truth, she had been shocked to see Edward again and stunned at the tumult of feelings that swept through her simply being near him and talking casually with him again. She thought she'd put all those old feelings and memories behind her. She'd certainly worked hard enough to do so.

"It was nice to see Edward again, wasn't it?" Celeste asked with a smirk, taking her arm as they walked toward the family van.

Lila turned her eyes toward her sister. "Celeste, don't be interfering and matchmaking in my life."

Celeste shrugged. "Well, it was obvious Edward noticed you. I rather enjoyed seeing his discomfort."

"You shouldn't enjoy seeing anyone's discomfort," Lila answered. "Keep in mind Edward is a long-time friend of our family's. You should be kind to him as I will be. And don't be pushing other feelings or ideas that are inappropriate on either me or Edward."

Gwen, joining them added, "Oh, come on, Lila, you have to admit Edward did seem more than simply surprised to see you. Looking back, you and Edward were always rather sweet, chummy friends growing up. Was there more between you that we don't know anything about?"

"Nothing I know of," Waylon put in. "And quit quizzing Lila. Don't make it more awkward for Lila and Edward to be friends again with your little manipulations and interfering comments. Edward had a difficult relationship with his family, and now he's come home to deal with what is to be done about Indigo Plantation."

He paused, thinking for a minute. "Dad said he inherited the plantation and all the estate as the only son. That comes with a huge responsibility. I doubt it was one Edward expected to take on so soon. He's only twenty-six, and Dad said he heard Edward didn't really want to come home at all. He stayed on in Nashville after graduating with his law degree and credentials, working in the legal clinic, teaching college classes. He and his dad had disputes about it, I heard. Additionally, if you remember, Edward came home very seldom over the years after he left to go to college. He could use some friends at this time."

"That's true," Burke added, as they climbed into the van to start back to the island. "We all need to be a support to Edward. I doubt his mother Clarice will be any help at all."

"I think you can count on that," Waylon agreed.

Lila had ridden to church, as she usually did, in the Deveaux Inn's van they kept at Jenkins Landing, with Waylon driving. Lila's mother Etta sat up front with him today, while, she, Burke, and baby Drew, snuggled in his little car seat, sat in the back.

Celeste and Reid had driven from the landing in their car, and Gwen, Alex, and their children in theirs. As everyone split up now to settle in for the ride back, Lila felt glad when the conversation shifted to other subjects.

At the landing a short time later, they all loaded into one of the Deveaux ferries to head back to the island. The noise of the boat kept conversation limited, and Lila felt grateful for the quiet. She had a lot of things to pray and think about. Had she sensed in some way earlier Edward would come home? Was she meant to be a help to him at this time, like Waylon said? Could she even be a good help to him with other matters about Edward's family still troubling her? And with her own feelings so ragged and restless? It was certainly a situation that needed a lot of thought and prayer.

Back at the Deveaux Inn, life got busier and noisier. The Inn's dining room was full of guests staying at the Inn and in two of the rental cottages. The Inn's meals, always buffet style, were served at the same times every day: breakfast 9:00 to 10:00 am, lunch 1:00 to 2:00 pm; dinner 6:00 to 7:00 pm. Maggie Bouls, who always worked at the Inn on Sundays on Novaleigh's regular day off, had already been hard at work all morning getting the food prepared and put on the buffet, but Etta, Burke, and Lila kicked in to help as soon as they got back.

Yesterday, Etta had worked with Novaleigh to bake a ham for Easter lunch today and helped to make sweet potato casseroles, carrots, and green bean dishes that could be heated up easily. Maggie had made a fruit salad this morning, between the breakfast and lunch shift while they were at church, and she'd also baked two pretty spice cakes with cream cheese icing for dessert.

As the guests all began to come into the dining room now, Lila took freshly warmed French bread, drizzled with garlic butter, out to the buffet to add to the other dishes already there. Sunday lunches at the inn were often of simpler fare, but for Easter Sunday, there was an expectation for something special. Even the tables were decorated with Easter decorations and colored eggs Lila and Gwen's children had helped to dye yesterday.

After all the Inn's guests were settled in the dining room, the extended Deveaux family went through the buffet line to get their own lunch to carry to the big family porch. Here in early March, the windows of the big Arizona room were still shut, but as warmer weather came, they could be opened and the long outdoor room with its big table enjoyed as a screened porch.

"There's a lot of us today," said Chase, looking around with a big grin.

"I counted eleven," his sister Leah added.

"We'll have twelve when little Drew is big enough to sit at the table," Rose put in.

Drew was sleeping now inside the family apartment in his crib, content after his busy church morning and a feeding from Burke.

Lila sat, somewhat quietly, through the meal, as she often did, while her big family ate their dinner, chattered and laughed together. After everyone finished, Lila helped her mother and Maggie clean up from lunch, while Burke tended to Drew. Alex and Gwen went to pack their belongings at the Seaside Cottage to head home to Port Royal, and Celeste and Reid left with them on the ferry to get their own car and head home to Charleston.

All the guests, staying at the Inn this Easter weekend, had opted to travel on the ferry to Jenkin's Landing after lunch, as well, to where one of the area tour buses was picking them up and taking them to visit and tour Middleton Plantation and its historic grounds in Charleston. The Deveaux Inn often worked with local tour companies to take its guests on tours offered to different Lowcountry sites, an arrangement advantageous to the tour companies and a perk for guests staying at the inn.

Lila, weary from the day, draped her kitchen apron on a peg and headed for her own cottage for some quiet time. Back at her place, she hung up her new Easter dress, changed into something more comfortable, and fixed herself a cup of hot spiced tea before settling down in her favorite chair to put her feet up.

She searched in the Book of Common Prayer then for the Prayer for Guidance, knowing it something she needed right now. She read the words and then offered her own personal prayer. "Lord, it always seems so much easier to help and counsel others in what they should do, when they face uncertain situations, than to see your own answers clearly. I ask for Your help for myself now. Help me know Your right path and way ..."

A little peace settled over her as she prayed, not for herself alone, but for Edward and for others she lifted up, too.

She heard a tap on the door after a time and looked up to see Burke opening the door to look in. "I'm sure I'm intruding, but I was checking the lighthouse and thought I'd stop by."

With Gwen reunited with Alex and living in Port Royal and with

Celeste married to Reid and living in Charleston, Burke and Lila had grown close again. Their six-year age difference mattered little now that they were grown, and in truth Burke had always been like a second mother to Lila. They'd shared a room growing up, and with Etta often busy with their father at the inn and lighthouse, it had often been Burke who took care of Lila.

"Do you and Mother need help at the inn?" Lila asked.

"No, it's very quiet there with all sixteen of our guests on that tour. Mother said we should work with these tour groups more often to take our guests places. She's reading a book in her room, and I just fed Drew and put him down at the lodge for a nap. Waylon is keeping an eye on him while enjoying a basketball game on television."

She came to sit down on the couch opposite Lila. "Are you okay after that situation of running into Edward again this morning? I know Celeste and Gwen didn't make it easier for you, teasing you and Edward." She sighed. "Edward was obviously shocked to see you. It's hard to believe his mother or someone hadn't mentioned to him you'd come home from the Community."

Lila didn't answer, closing her eyes for a moment.

"Listen, you don't have to talk with me about this if you don't want to," Burke said.

"No. It's just been upsetting and confusing. I guess I should have realized Edward would come home at some time, at least to visit. I simply didn't imagine it would go as it did."

"I probably shouldn't say this," Burke began, "but I couldn't help noticing, the summer before Edward went away to college, that it seemed like more than friendship was going on between you two. You wrote a lot to each other in that last year when you were still finishing high school. When Edward came home that summer, after his first year at Vanderbilt, you spent time together, too."

Her sister paused remembering. "Then it seemed like everything changed. Edward left abruptly. You left not long after for Sewanee for college, and it seemed the two of you quit communicating much at all. I noticed you never went to Indigo when you came home anymore, even though I remember the Jessups encouraged you to come ride any time you wanted."

"People change when they go away to school. Edward did, and he had serious problems with his father before he left. That's why he hardly ever came home for summers or holidays anymore." Lila knew she hadn't fully answered all Burke's questions.

"And?" Burke finally prompted.

"Perhaps some young sparks kicked up between us back then, but it was a long time ago."

Burke raised an eyebrow. "It did seem like sparks kicked up for Edward again today. What about for you?"

"I don't know, Burke." She rubbed her neck. "My life since has been very different. I expected the church to be my vocation, but then I felt uncertain of that path as you know. Feelings of a romantic nature, other than dedication to the life of the church, were tucked away for me as a sister. It seems odd to feel them again now, if I even feel anything. I'm not even sure I want to. Edward is still full of anger at his father. He has a lot of his own problems to work through. I do, too. I don't want to go in another wrong direction."

Burke nodded. "That's honest." She smiled after a minute. "Feelings are funny things, though. I thought I'd buried everything I felt for Waylon and I had no idea he ever held any feelings for me. And then, well...." She giggled. "You can see where things ended up for us."

Lila couldn't help laughing. "Yours is a sweet story."

Burke glanced at her watch. "I'd better walk back to the lodge. Drew will be waking up soon. He's a very scheduled baby. Probably takes after Waylon and me in that." She grinned. "He wants to feed exactly every four hours. He'll start fussing about five minutes ahead of time and then really tune up if one of us doesn't go to get him. It's almost like he has a little personal time-clock built in."

"He keeps you busy."

"He does." She hesitated. "I know you are a really private person, Lila, but if you need to talk with someone, please know I'm here."

"I do know that, Burke, and thank you. One of the psalms, Psalm 32:8, I read earlier said *'I will instruct thee and teach thee in the way which thou shalt go: I will guide thee with mine eye.'* That comforted me. There are a lot of complicated issues here, some I'm not ready to talk about, some I'm not sure what to do about, and there are many difficult issues and problems Edward needs to work through, too. I think more than anything right now, like Waylon said, what Edward could really use is a friend. I've been that in past. Maybe I can be that again. We'll see. But everything feels awkward and strange. That doesn't give me much comfort."

"You'll find your way. When Gwen, Celeste, and I were struggling with our problems you reminded us that we had family that loved us. You do, too. You also said God would help us find the right way if we reached out to Him, and He did."

Lila shook her head. "I need to give myself my own advice."

"Will you still go to Indigo Plantation tomorrow as scheduled?" Burke asked. "I know you told us you planned to go there to sketch some of the scenes Morgan Richards asked you to do."

"That visit is already scheduled." She paused. "After Morgan gathers research and information and does interviews at a historic home, church or site, he paves the way for me to follow, sends me photographs, and gives me ideas of scenes and spots he'd like me to do sketches and paintings of. We've worked together like that well so far. We met for dinner at the Waterfront Restaurant on Jungle Road one evening last week, and talked about what he wanted me to focus on for my sketches and work at Indigo this week."

"So you'll go?"

"It's my job, Burke. There were some happenings at Indigo in the past that made me not want to go back, but I know I need to deal with those things. Now I'll also need to deal with Edward with his anger, confusion, and problems. And possibly with Clarice, who is not one of my favorite people. I'm not sure I look forward to any of that."

Burke smiled. "I found a quote in the old keeper's log at the top of the lighthouse I've read so many times I've memorized it. It's been a help to me. I don't know who wrote the words, but it says: *'God made all the stars, the galaxies, the universe, the waves and the seas. Surely, he can help you, no matter how difficult your problem is.'*"

"That's wise advice. Thank you. I'm going to write those words down so I can reread them again."

Burke stood. "I'd better go check on Drew now. I'll see you tomorrow. You don't need to get up to let me out."

She left and Lila pulled out a small bound book she put favorite quotes in and wrote Burke's words in it.

"Lord, I thought I wouldn't have good spiritual help and advice here as at the Community, but I see You are always full of surprises, sending others to give me the advice, help, and encouragement I need exactly when I need it most. Thank you."

With the day still fair and warm, Lila decided to take a walk down the beach before she needed to go to the inn for dinner. She knew tonight's dinner, after a big lunch, would be simple, a ham and vegetable soup using the ham and vegetables from lunch, plus the remaining fruit salad, French bread, and cake.

She slipped on tennis shoes and a light windbreaker. The breeze off the sea, in the late afternoon this time of year, was still chilly.

Letting herself out the back door of her cottage, she cut through the garden to find the pathway behind the lighthouse, that led from the pavilion down to the sea's edge. The beach was quiet today, although Lila knew, as spring moved toward summer, it would grow busier.

Today, however, she had the beach to herself as she walked, heading toward the island's end where the Townsend River had formed a new wide pathway between Watch Island and Edisto Island. Her dad had told her often how he remembered walking directly across the inlet as a boy before Hurricane Gracie swept in from the sea in the 1950s, wreaking havoc. The sea and the coastline could change so quickly with a big storm. She'd seen old pictures, too, of Edingsville Beach, a prosperous old beach community, obliterated in another hurricane in the 1800s.

Finding an old bench further down the beach, Lila sat down to think for a few moments. She knew she wasn't being honest with herself or anyone else to act like she'd been indifferent to Edward Calhoun. She closed her eyes remembering how handsome he'd looked, in his sharp, tailored Sunday suit, more muscled than she recalled, more mature and stronger in his looks, his dark hair cut short, his deep brown eyes so familiar. Even the remembered scent of him—that rich Armani cologne he'd always favored—almost made her dizzy when she'd moved closer to him. No, she was not past her feelings for Edward Calhoun, although they had drifted apart after that last summer. So much happened then.

Lila knew some of the things Edward and his father argued about so harshly that summer, some of the things Edward was so upset about. He'd been angry at his mother, too, over them. The problem had something to do with Isaac Jessup and his fiancé Tanya, serious enough to anger Isaac so much it sent him and Tanya away. Everyone at Indigo had been upset for a time, too, filled with unrest, hurt, and anger. She experienced her own bad time then, too, making her not want to return to Indigo again. Threats were given to her no one knew about. Is that why she'd become restless, couldn't find her peace at the Community? Because these old issues had been left unresolved? If she could find her way through them now, should she return to St. Mary's again?

Picking up a handful of sand and letting it sift through her fingers, Lila felt the answer to that question was no. The Community had been her place for a time, but she'd found a new purpose and identity here since coming home. She painted pictures that showed the beauty of God's world. She knew God helped her with them and it was His talent He'd given her that she used when she worked. No, that change in her life she felt good and centered about. She had become a recognized artist rather than simply a girl who liked to draw pictures now and then. God had developed her gift into her work and a vocation.

She looked out to sea, thinking back. "Lord, when I saw all the changes to come for my sisters and me, I thought moving fully into my artistic gifts and purpose was my intended change. Now I have all this stormy and upsetting mess to work through with Edward and Indigo. Please help me know what to do."

Lila hated the unrest this situation had brought, disturbing her usual peace. Perhaps Edward would visit Edisto for only a short time and then leave again. He always said he'd never come back to stay. That would make things easier.

She got up to walk back. Despite how Edward acted today, surprised to see her, maybe even a little interested, he had not shown himself in past to be a constant person in his affections. And that hurt had gone deep into her soul.

CHAPTER 4

On Monday morning, Edward sat with the Jessup men, Levi, the oldest of the four, his son Earl, and Earl's two sons, Isaac and Tommy Lee, on the porch of Levi and Annamae Jessup's home. It was a rambling, spacious two-story farmhouse with chimneys on both sides and a big screened porch across its front. Most all the farm homes on the Indigo Plantation property were white with gray roofs, even the barns, all built in a gracious style similar to the main house of the plantation where the Calhoun descendants had always lived.

"It's good to see you home again," Levi's wife Annamae said, bustling out to the porch to bring a plate of freshly baked fried apple pies and a refill of coffee in a large thermos. She set the plate and coffee on an old wooden table. "I'm going over to the big house to help Della clean," she said. "You men be kind to one another, you hear?"

"You know we will," Levi said, pushing his battered straw hat back on his head and reaching for a fried pie.

The Jessup families were African Americans and had lived on the plantation, like the Calhouns, for generations. However, the Jessups had never been slaves at Indigo. Some of their earlier ancestors had been enslaved people at plantations in the Lowcountry but not at Indigo or on Edisto. The Jessups had come here to the island, after the Civil War and its destructions and after the boll weevil ended the island's lucrative cotton production, seeking work in farming, a skill they all knew well.

Edward's great grandfather, Malcolm Edward Calhoun, realized he needed to diversify to survive the times, and he saw farming as a new route for the plantation to be more productive. He made an alliance with the Jessups, hiring them as salaried farm managers, and moving them into farm homes on Indigo's grounds, adding more homes for them on the land as the family grew. A strong respect had always existed between the two families, both wanting to build new lives, after hard times, and to use their best skills wisely.

All the Calhoun men, including Edward's great grandfather, his grandfather Malcolm, his father Sam, and now himself, had always been attorneys as well, another way to enrich the family finances in the uncertain times agricultural life always brought. Edward's grandfather Malcolm and an attorney friend William Maybank, who also owned a plantation on Edisto, established their own law practice on the island as their lives prospered. They named it the Maybank-Calhoun Law Firm and it was still a well-known law practice in the Lowcountry area.

The Jessups prospered, too, with promotions and pay increases as time moved on, sending their children to college, helping to see them established in productive lives. Levi, of his three brothers, chose to remain at Indigo, loving the land and farming. His son Earl had stayed, too, and now two of Earl's sons worked at the plantation. Tommy Lee, the oldest, lived in another of the homes on Indigo, and he and his wife Gladys also managed the Indigo Plantation Market at the end of Point of Pines Road on the main Highway. In busy seasons, Indigo hired outside workers as needed.

Isaac had only recently returned to Indigo, with his wife Tanya and two children, and Edward was glad to be reunited with him. Friends since childhood, Edward had kept in touch with Isaac over the years, and he knew Isaac would never have returned to Indigo at all if Edward's father Sam hadn't died. However, knowing Isaac's education and skills, and knowing Isaac's family wanted him to come back to help run the plantation, Edward reached out to him shortly after his father's death, asking him to return. He made the offer worth Isaac's consideration, too, and felt happy when Isaac accepted.

"How long will you be here?" Levi asked Edward after Annamae left them.

He sighed. "I'm not sure. I need to give thought and prayer to my direction." He grinned. "Besides, I'm not really needed here at Indigo full time with all of you running the plantation so well."

Levi shook his head. "That isn't true. We each have our needed parts here. Despite all our problems with your father, Big Sam, he had business and legal strengths we needed. He had ties all over the Lowcountry and beyond, strings he could pull, deals he could make, contacts he could tap to help us find sales contracts and markets we needed, the best prices for equipment and supplies. Big Sam had a good sense for business and we all know the Calhoun name helped open doors for us. It's the way of things. We need you here, too, Edward, despite your reluctance to want to stay."

Isaac grinned at him. "You talked me into coming back, Edward, made me an offer I'd have been foolish to refuse. I admit Tanya and I are glad to be back home now, near our families again. We have more autonomy and respect here than we did at the plantation near Georgetown where I helped to take care of things. The old manager there reminded me of an overseer in how he ran things. Sometimes, he was mean as an old snake when he got his back up. He called me uppity when I had good ideas for improvements but then he used my ideas and took the credit."

"Your years in Georgetown grew you in new experiences though," his father added.

"Maybe," Isaac replied.

"Well, I'm glad you invited him back," Isaac's grandfather Levi put in. "I also appreciate you seeing to it that the Caretakers House was fixed up nice for them to live in. It had gotten a little shabby."

"Isaac deserved to be recompensed," Edward said with a frown.

"We appreciate your goodness and generosity, Edward, but always keep in mind it was your father who did us harm, not you,"

Earl replied. "Don't be taking Sam Calhoun's sins on yourself or carrying around the guilt that man should have felt himself for things he did."

Edward looked out from the porch across the land and the rich fields, plowed and already green with early vegetables springing up. He'd seen the old trees in the pecan grove leafing out, too, on his walk over from the main house. They'd soon have early crops to harvest and to sell through their commercial and local markets. Plus, fresh produce to sell at the Indigo Market on the highway, popular with the tourists as well as the locals. The herb gardens behind the main house, and in the greenhouse buildings, were leafing out, too. Days would be busy now with spring arriving.

"I enjoyed walking around to see how everything is greening up," Edward said, changing the subject. "I'd forgotten the pleasure of spring on the land."

Earl chuckled. "One thing your father did right was see to it you learned every aspect of the work involved here at Indigo. You always had chores, spring and summer work. You learned to plow the land, plant the crops, weed and worry over freezes, frosts, and pests, put in long hours during the harvest."

Edward frowned. "My father worried about me not being tough enough, being too soft, too kind."

"You were exactly like his own father Malcolm, a fine good man. Malcolm Calhoun did his best to see to it Sam became a good man, too, but Sam always had other ideas about the way to live. A pridefulness sprang up in him no one seemed able to eradicate. He developed a sarcastic tongue, too, and a disrespect for others he saw not as tough or wealthy as he was. He also preyed on those weaker."

Edward winced. "I remember."

Levi leaned over to put a hand on Edward's shoulder. "You let the past, and its bad memories, go. They'll only keep festering and hurting you if you keep holding on to them. There's a long life left ahead for you to enjoy and to find happiness and good work in. Don't be keeping any old millstones from the past hanging around your neck, weighing you down."

"I hear you, Levi, but it's hard with everything here reminding me of the past," he argued.

"Well, here's the thing to remember instead, son. There are as many good and fine memories of the past, and as many good things to remember as the bad," Levi replied. "Like the Good Book says, *'Think on those things.'* It's just a matter of how you set your focus."

Isaac laughed. "I got the same lecture myself, Edward, but Grandad is right. We need to move on and let the past be the past."

"We also need to go over a few farm matters before the day gets away," Earl put in. "We've got a busy day ahead."

Tommy Lee looked at his watch. "I need to head up the road to open the store, too. We've got shipments coming in today and Gladys will need help with the boxes. With April here, the tourist traffic will begin to pick up."

"Will you have enough help at the store?" Edward asked. "We can hire additional employees to work there."

"I'll keep that in mind, but outside help brings their own kind of trouble sometimes. My own boy, Sawyer, and my girls Ruby and Lorraine, help out after school and on the weekends. Mostly we've managed." He hesitated. "I've had this kid, Ambrose Fleenor, working a little for us. Felt sorry for him. Lives nearby and has a hard family situation. He's pretty good to do what I ask but not very good with the public."

"Well, hire additional help later if you need to," Edward repeated. "You'd know better than me who would make a good employee for the store."

"Thank you for that confidence. You come up to the store one day and let Gladys and me show you some of the changes we've made that have been good for business." He paused. "I also have a few legal things to ask you about, things you'd know about that I don't."

"Sure, I'll come up this week," Edward replied.

Tommy Lee grabbed an extra fried pie to take with him and then left for the store. His old truck backfired as he pulled out of the driveway.

Levi shook his head. "We need to do something about replacing that old truck."

"It sounds and looks like it needs replacing." Edward grinned. "Is Tommy Lee just overly fond of that old truck?"

Levi looked away. "No. A lot of replacements and updates got put on the back burner of budgeted expenses."

Edward glanced after the truck. "Meaning my father didn't want to put a new truck in the budget any more than he wanted to put money into keeping some of the houses around the property in the best repair."

Levi didn't respond but Isaac did. "Yes. Like the Caretaker's House we moved into. I told you it needed work before I came back. The roof leaked. The place needed painting inside and outside and some of the appliances needed replacing. Thanks for budgeting in those updates and getting the work done before I brought Tanya and the kids back. The house looks good now."

Edward sighed. "We need to sit down and look at more things like that soon. Put together a list of things we need to talk about."

"We'll work on that," Levi answered. Changing the subject, he added, "We also need to talk about watering well around the property while it's dry and checking out all our fire alarms and equipment. There's been a fire on the island this week."

"Another one?" Isaac asked.

"A shed over near Sunnyside Plantation across the highway burned. They caught the fire early and got it out before it made its way to the house or fields, but it was a scare." Levi shook his head.

"That's the third little fire around here," Isaac put in, "Always starting with a structure, too. That isn't natural. Seems more likely someone is setting fires to cause trouble or something."

"Well, it's worrisome." Earl looked to Edward. "Do you think it might be criminal, arson or something? You know more about these legal things than we do."

Edward considered it. "Arson is more common than we think. Sometimes it's professional, someone paid to burn a place so the owners can get insurance money."

"I hardly think that's been the case here, with mostly small barns and sheds affected," Isaac said.

Earl stood up to leave, reminding Edward he was a tall man, fit and strong. "We need to get out in the field now," he said, glancing toward the sun, reading the time by its height in the sky.

Levi pushed his old straw hat back before standing, too, and then he picked up the remains of the coffee and Annamae's empty plate to carry back into the house to put away.

As he came back out, he turned to Isaac. "Walk Edward around to see things around the place he needs to know about. Be sure to tell him, too, about that man you've been talking to who's working on a book about Edisto's old plantation homes and sites. Edward will need an update on that."

Earl shook his head. "Clarice left that to us to handle, not wanting to bother with it, but, Edward, I think you need to give your input about that now and be the one to approve what the man writes later. He said he'd take out any wrong information, or words we didn't want included, in his account."

Levi grinned. "If the man's going to write about us, we don't want him writing things that might hurt our business here or be slanderous. He said he'd put things in a good light."

"He did, but I made him put it in writing that we get to approve any written content about the plantation," Isaac added. "The man hoped to talk with Clarice, of course, but she fobbed him off on us instead."

As the two older men left, Isaac stood, too.

"Let's go walk around the place a little," he said. "We can talk while we walk. I'll take you to see how nice our place looks now, maybe by the stables. I do hope you plan to do some riding while here. You know our horses work on the plantation, help in the fields, pull the carriages now and then when we have events, but they need to be ridden, too, for fitness and so they won't get wild and not as used to the saddle. You remember how they get a little full of themselves if you don't keep the discipline of riding up."

"I do remember that." Edward smiled as they walked off the porch and started up the dirt road.

After a minute he added, "I saw Lila at church yesterday with all the Deveaux family. I was really surprised to see her back. I thought she was still at that religious community in Sewanee for Episcopal sisters."

Isaac glanced toward him. "I didn't know she'd come back either until recently. I assumed you already knew so I didn't mention it." He grinned. "How did she look?"

Edward laughed. "Not like a nun."

"She always was a pretty girl. Sweet girl, too." He reached down to pick up a stick in the road and threw it into the brush. "That man who is working on the history book said Lila was doing illustrations for his book. He asked if she could come to draw and paint in different spots around the plantation. I think she's supposed to come today after lunch. Is that still all right with you? If not, I can call her, postpone it."

"Why would it be a problem if she comes?"

Isaac shrugged. "Well, it seemed like you drifted away from being interested in her over time so I wasn't sure what you'd think about it. Lila knows the plantation, of course, but it seems like it ought to be you who should show her around when she comes. Clarice took off to Charleston again. I hoped she might be social and welcoming to Lila on her visits. I have a lot of work to do, like Dad and Grandad."

"Don't worry, I'll talk to Lila, show her around as needed. I suggested we might go riding, too, since you mentioned before the horses needed more exercise."

"Well, it's a tough job escorting a pretty girl around the plantation but I guess somebody has to do it." Isaac laughed. "Are you going to try to get something going with Lila Deveaux again?"

Edward looked away. "I probably got something going with Lila before I should have when younger. We were both only kids then. Neither of us had seen much of the world outside of Edisto. You know even then I had so many problems with my dad and my mother. You're blessed you have such a good family."

"My family were like family to you, too, with the two of us growing up like brothers. You know you talked me into coming back, Edward. I'd like to see you do the same. The reason we both left, and the reason we swore we'd never come back, is gone now."

Edward walked along quietly for a minute. "I became a very different person at Vanderbilt, Isaac. I came into myself, got away from being constantly criticized or ignored. I met a lot of good people in Nashville, at the college and in the law school, who encouraged me and helped me find my way and become a better man. I always lived a little in fear that I might become like my father, you know."

Isaac snorted. "I never worried that would happen. Dad and Grandad said you were exactly like your Grandfather Malcolm, even in looks, and he was a fine, good man. I heard my dad say to my mother once he believed one reason your father, Sam, was so hard on you was because you served as a constant reminder of the kind of good man he should have become—that his father wanted him to become. Big Sam didn't like all those good character traits in you, so unlike his less-than sterling attributes."

The idea took Edward by surprise. "I never thought of that."

"Dark hates light, you know. Light convicts the dark." Isaac glanced Edward's way. "You came to know the Lord when younger. It shone out. It always does. Your daddy was an old reprobate if he ever got any religion at all earlier in his life." He frowned. "I could never see much evidence in him of knowing God well or trying to live for the Lord, could you?"

"I never really thought about it much in a spiritual way like this, but no, I didn't."

"My folks talked about it a lot, especially after Big Sam came after Tanya the way he did, nearly raping her. I fought him over that, caught him trying to disrespect her. You know it's why I left, me and Tanya both. I learned then it was a bad habit of your father's, preying on young innocent girls. Thinking it fun in some perverse way."

He kicked at a pinecone in the road. "After that happened, Mother and Daddy heard a few other stories and they sent my sister Maisie off the plantation to live with some of our family up the road near Hutchinson House. Before then, they'd always assumed if Sam Calhoun wanted to cat around he'd be decent enough, at least, to do his carousing away from the plantation. However, after what almost happened with Tanya right here on our own land, they didn't want to risk him catching Maisie off by herself one day. So they moved her to keep her safe."

"I didn't know that. I'm so sorry to hear it."

"Your father, Sam Calhoun, wasn't exactly a morally righteous role model, even if he was a brilliant, strong man with excellent leadership and business skills. There's nothing pretty about trying to seduce or rape young girls. I could never figure out how he thought it okay for himself to do so. But I heard some twisted logic come out of him about it all. As though him being Sam Calhoun of Indigo Plantation, important and rich, made it all right."

"I hated that kind of attitude he showed so often. I was often ashamed to be his son."

The morning turned into a day of honest revelations. Edward and Isaac talked out a lot of old issues, walking around the plantation. It helped Edward, getting out painful feelings, long buried, talking honestly about the past, about his father, his strengths and his sorrowful weaknesses. It helped him, seeing how other people had come to terms with his father's problems, how others had been impacted and hurt as much as he had. Maybe even more so. It eased his mind to begin to put old memories into a new perspective.

Back at the house later, Edward heated up the lunch Annamae left him in the kitchen. He didn't carry it into the formal dining room but sat at the old wooden kitchen table instead to eat it. He liked the memories here better, of Annamae and Della's happy talk, their warm laughter and singing. He marveled again that those women, and all the Jessups, could be so kind and loving, so good to him from his earliest memories, hugging and kissing him, praising the things he did well, big or small, giving him the affection and attention that his parents seldom did. He owed all the Jessups so much for their caring.

Lost in thought, Edward almost missed the sound of the front doorbell ringing. He sprinted from the kitchen down the long hallway to the door. Glancing out the doorway's glass side panels, he saw Lila standing on the porch, her back to him, looking out across the circular driveway that led from the gate posts into the landscaped grounds around the main house.

CHAPTER 5

Lila felt swamped with old memories, a mix of sweet and bitter, as she drove past the "No Trespassing" sign at the start of the private road into Indigo Plantation. With permission to come, she soon followed the hard-packed dirt road, first through a mix of pines and hardwoods, then under the shaded alley of ancient oak trees lining the quiet drive. The gnarled oak limbs, dripping with Spanish moss, reached across the road, as if in loving friendship, to touch each other as she drew closer to the old plantation house.

Through the trees, she could see familiar sights along her way, winding farm roads and dirt driveways reaching back into the property to fields, barns, sheds, and houses that were a part of the big plantation. It was a beautiful historic property, and Lila was glad it was one of the old places at Edisto that had survived the years. As a girl she had walked and ridden the entire acreage so many times with Edward that she knew the plantation and its grounds almost as well as Watch Island around the lighthouse where she lived.

Knowing she planned to explore and walk the property today, and to ride with Edward as well, she'd worn her old black riding boots her mother kept from the past, along with a pair of worn jeans, a white knit shirt and a long maroon sweater, to ward off the chill of the early spring day.

She drove her black Audi today, a practical little car for getting around the backroads of the island and city highways, that she'd bought used last summer after a few of her large paintings sold. The back seats folded down to give her extra room for carrying paintings and art supplies or for stuffing in an easel and chair when she wanted to paint outdoors.

As the drive narrowed, Lila turned her car through the tall ivy-covered gate posts, flanked by a line of crisp white fencing, and into the circular drive leading to the front porch of Indigo Plantation. She'd forgotten how beautiful the house was, a tall, white Antebellum home, two-storied with double porches on front and back. Neat, symmetrical black-shuttered windows marched across the upper and lower levels of the house, with gracious grounds, tasteful statuary, and early flowers enhancing the property.

Lila pulled her car over to the side of the drive and then got out to walk up the rise of steps to the front porch. All the old homes on Edisto, like Indigo Plantation, were built off the ground to protect them in case of flooding from the rivers, ocean, and marshes nearby. She knew the North Edisto River lay not far behind the old plantation home with a private dock and wide beaches on the riverfront. She and Edward had often ridden their horses along the river's sandy banks, paddled their canoes and kayaks in the river and its tributaries, picnicked or fished on the long dock that reached out into the river, laughing and splashing their feet in the water—life so sweet and carefree then.

When no one answered the door, Lila turned to look out across the sweep of landscaped property leading to the house. If Clarice or Edward weren't here, she could probably find one of the Jessups to give her an okay to start her drawings.

At a noise behind her, she turned to see Edward opening the door. "Hi. Sorry I didn't hear you knock sooner. I was in the kitchen in the back of the house eating a bite of lunch." He held the door open. "Come in. I'm glad to see you again."

"Thank you." She started toward the door.

"I see you wore your riding boots." He glanced at her feet with a grin. "I'm glad you came ready to ride. Both sets of our horses, the whites, Lex and Maddie, and the two bays, Butler and Narita, need riding. Isaac and I stopped by the barn earlier today, and both were acting a little spunky."

"Well, I'm somewhat out of practice being on horseback," she replied, following him into the living room to sit down in a side chair. "But I know it's like riding a bicycle; the skills will come back quickly."

The living area, like much of the interior of the house, was painted in soft greens with deeper greens in the curtains and furnishings, a lovely backdrop to the antique furniture pieces. She glanced around, taking in the gleaming hardwood floors and vintage carpets, gilded mirrors, ornate chandeliers, and tastefully placed decorative items displayed around the room.

Lila had spent little time as a girl in Indigo's formal rooms. She and Edward usually talked or played on one of the house's porches, in the family's informal den upstairs, in the kitchen eating a snack or a quick lunch, or outdoors in one of the barns or sheds.

"It feels funny to be here like company," she offered, with a small smile, making the moment less awkward.

Edward grinned. "Yes, I keep expecting Della to pop in and say, 'You children get outside and get out of this room. I just finished cleaning here and I don't want to start in all over again.'"

Lila laughed at Edward's almost perfect imitation of Della's voice.

"How are all the Jessups?" she asked, relaxing a little.

"Fit and well. Haven't you seen them since you've been back?"

"At the market and here and there. You may remember Novaleigh's son Gavin married the Jessup's daughter Maisie. That brings them to the island often to visit with Novaleigh and Clifford with their little girl Junie. Sometimes others in the Jessup family tag along."

He ran a hand through his hair and sighed. "You've been like me, avoiding the old place because of bad memories."

She bit her lip. "I suppose I have."

"I'm sorry we got caught up in all that mess our last summer together. Isaac and I were talking about it today. You know he came back recently with Tanya and the children." He paused. "I contacted him and asked him to come back after my father died. He would never have come before."

She looked down at the rug. "Yes, I imagine he wouldn't have wanted to, Tanya either. Are they happy?"

"Yes. They've been happy and still are. Isaac said they were glad to be back at Indigo near family again though. I had the old Caretakers House renovated for them."

She smiled. "Oh, that's a fine old house, near the event barn and that outdoor picnic area under the trees, and it's not too far from the stable." Another memory popped into her mind. "Isn't that the house where Levi's parents lived in the past?"

"Yes, it is, and it had run down badly, but Isaac and I had it updated and repaired to make it a comfortable family home for him and Tanya and the kids." He paused. "Tanya said she'd love for you to come by to see her. The four of us were close once—Isaac, Tanya, you and me."

"Yes, we were," she said softly, not adding more.

He looked at her with a question. "You wouldn't feel differently toward Tanya now because of what happened would you?"

She raised her eyes to his in shock. "Edward, how could you ask that? Tanya was an innocent girl and we've always been friends."

Edward frowned. "I guess I'm simply remembering how Mother spoke about her a few times, not kindly."

Lila tensed, clasping her hands in her lap. "I hate remembering a lot of the ways your mother acted, overlooking wrongs to save face. Blaming the innocent rather than putting the blame where it belonged."

He let out a long, deep breath. "Do you think we can ever get past those bad times and memories, Lila? I want to. Levi said today I needed to begin to focus on all the good times, the good memories, to let the bad memories go. He said it wasn't healthy to keep carrying them."

"He's right, you know. As hard as it is, we need to forgive and forget all those wrongs, to give them to the Lord, to ask Him for healing in heart and mind."

He smiled. "That sounds like the Lila I remember. You always lived close to God. I did, too, somewhat, but I grew closer to God while at Vanderbilt. You remember my dad hooked me up with his old college friend's son, Ryan Markman, and put us in a condo he decided to buy as an investment near the law school. He selected and bought the place himself, made all the arrangements without even asking me about it."

"I remember you resented that. You said it was typical of how your father ran your life, never giving you a choice."

"It was typical. He also made it crystal clear he'd only pay for my college if I studied law, kept my grades up and my life straight, so I could come back and take my place in the family law firm later."

She shook her head. "He was such a hard man."

"Yes, he was, but my roommate Ryan Markman turned out to be a blessing in my life."

Lila saw Edward smile at the memory.

"Ryan, curly-headed and seemingly always grinning, was easy-going, funny, warm-hearted and a strong Christian from a good family," he added. "I got lucky, or blessed you might say. Ryan got me into Young Life on campus with him, made it easier for me to make good friends, helped me to 'Lighten Up' as he often put it, to enjoy life more, to see the good in my life and my blessings."

"You wrote me some about Ryan that first year."

"Yes, before that bad summer when Dad went after Tanya, fought with Isaac, ran them both away. The summer when all sorts of ugliness about my father came out, totally disgusting and disillusioning me, making me hate my father for a time."

He closed his eyes and leaned his head back. "I said I never wanted to come back here after that. I really lost all respect for my father at that time, for my mother, too, in how she handled the situation, the callous and unkind things she said. I was so angry. I'm sorry you had to see me like that, listen to my tirades. I know I pushed you away."

"Is that what you remember?" she asked.

"I remember you pulled away from me as the summer moved along, wouldn't see me for a time and when you did see me at the island later, you were different. You acted different. You wouldn't come over to Indigo at all any more either. Not that I can blame you for that. But a rift formed of some kind."

She looked away, not meeting his eyes. "I remember you went back to school early that summer and soon stopped writing to me, except for an awkward note every now and then."

"Well, you went off to school at Sewanee, too, and you started your own new life. You kept writing me for a while, about your art, your classes, the volunteer work you started doing over at St. Mary's, and about your roommate."

Lila smiled. "Her name was Ginger Murphy, a freckle-faced happy red-head. I was lucky, or blessed like you, to also get a fun, joyous, exuberant roommate at Sewanee. Ginger was from New Orleans. I needed fun and laughter then. We still keep in touch."

"Then you quit writing to me at all."

"You quit before I did, Edward." She shook her head. "In fact, you seldom wrote at all after that difficult summer and when you did your notes were brief and stilted. I came home the following summer after my first year at Sewanee, hoping to see you, hoping things might be better, but you didn't come home at all."

He ran a hand through his hair. "I worked at the college over the summer, took some extra classes. I went home with Ryan to Asheville for a visit with his family. I didn't come home much during the whole time while getting my undergrad degree at Vanderbilt, even for a holiday like Christmas. When I did, I only stayed a short time, maybe a weekend, trying not to get into an angry dispute with my father. Later, while in law school, I started volunteering and working at the clinic part time around classes and in the summer more."

A little quiet space descended in the room.

Edward sighed. "Lila, I'd like to say I'm sorry I wasn't a better friend. I should have been no matter what happened in my family. I should have stayed in touch, too. I regret that now. We had a long, good friendship growing up. Do you think we could choose to remember those good times and not the bad and be friends again?"

"Yes, I'd like that, Edward." Lila reached out a hand to take his across the small table between them. "I wish we'd worked harder to stay in touch. There is something special about old friends you've known since you were small. We need to cherish that."

He smiled, looking relieved at this turn in their conversation. "We share a great legacy of memories, Lila, mostly good and happy ones. I want to remember those more."

"Then we will," she answered. "But right now, we need to talk about the drawings and paintings I need to do at Indigo today and over the next week or so. Have you met Morgan Richards who is writing a book about Edisto's plantations and historic sites?"

"No, but Isaac told me a little about him today."

"Morgan is doing personal interviews to add to the history he's researched, extensively, about the sites and plantations he plans to include in the book. He's including only the homes, churches, and sites that have survived through the years. Part of his interest is in how they survived when others didn't."

She crossed her legs, relaxing a little with this new turn in the conversation. "Morgan has already done interviews for several of the old plantations and I've created many of the illustrations for them. We've also completed work on a couple of the churches he wants to feature. Morgan gives me ideas of different places he wants me to sketch and do watercolors of after his visits and interviews."

"Sounds interesting," Edward commented.

"It is." She paused. "That's what I did for Myron Andric's book about coastal birds, too." She pulled a copy of the book out of the satchel she'd brought into the house with her and handed the book to Edward. "Morgan asked me to do similar illustrations for his book, like these I did for Myron's book. Morgan likes the unique idea of paintings used for illustrations, rather than photos, to make the book unique from others done in past."

Edward opened the book and began to look through it. "These watercolor paintings are beautiful, Lila. I had no idea your art talent had grown like this. The color and detail are incredible."

"Thank you. I grew greatly in my art skills in my four years of college at Sewanee. I was fortunate they encouraged me in developing the type of art I do best, a more detailed, illustrative style like this."

She hesitated. "At the Community of St. Mary, I did more art, too, creating paintings and gift cards to sell in the gift shop, sometimes doing commissioned works for churches, often creating graphic arts pieces for the groups who came to retreats at the Ayres Center next to us. We worked often with the retreat center, with the college, and with different groups around the area near the college. St. Mary's was very involved and interested in organizations and businesses that furthered conservation and helped to develop protective and educational aspects related to nature. They were deeply concerned with care for the body, the soul, and the earth."

Edward studied her quietly after that, looking down at the art in the book in his lap in between. "I have a hard time imagining you in that role at St. Mary's, Lila. I read about the Community online, looked at pictures, watched services at the chapel. There was so much silence, so much ritual. I tried imagining myself there, in a similar role, and I simply couldn't."

"Spending so much time there as a volunteer while at Sewanee for four years, I grew into my understanding of the sisters' way of life. I gradually came to know each sister as an individual, working with them in the gardens and the gift shop, coming to know the oblates and other volunteers, the people at the retreat center, the professors and teachers at the college who taught in Sewanee's seminary, and the priests." She paused, trying to think how to explain it. "As the time for my college graduation drew closer, I found myself not wanting to leave, feeling drawn to stay. I really thought it the vocation I was called to."

"What was your sister's name there? I know you get one after the first six months, after a sort of a trial period ..."

She interrupted. "It's called a postulancy. After that six months you do get a new name when you start your two years as a novitiate. I was Anne Marie after that, a simple name I helped to choose. It is believed the Virgin Mary's mother's name was Anne and there have been many sisters, schools, and churches named after her. I admired several sisters named Marie from the past, too. For example, Marie Morin, who became St. Marie, was an early Canadian sister and historian, a brilliant woman who worked to educate women and left a great legacy."

He looked at her for a few long moments. "Why did you leave the Community when you did? Was it because your father died that fall?"

"No, I don't think so, but after going back to the Community after Daddy's funeral, I suddenly felt different, restless, not at peace." She leaned back, closing her eyes. "The sisters soon picked up on it. In time, after much prayer and many talks, they helped me to see I wasn't ready to move on and take renewed vows as my two-year novitiate period was ending."

She looked down at her lap, avoiding his eyes. "It was really kind of embarrassing, like failing or getting fired or something."

Edward laughed. "No, I don't think that's true. God just had another route for you in mind."

"But why then?" she asked.

"I don't know. Perhaps you'll find that answer in time. It would seem to me that much of your reason for leaving can be seen right here." He pointed to the book. "Perhaps God wanted to take you onward in your art. Could you have done work like this there?"

"No, there was too much duty, prayer, and work for the time I spend in art now. I couldn't have personally marketed or profited from my art in the Community either."

"Perhaps that's the reason you were meant to leave when you did, Lila." He reached over to lay a hand on her knee. "Life has different purposes for us at different times, different turnings, different people and experiences for us to meet in order to take us to the places we need to go. God always knows the way better than we do."

Lila put a hand to her heart. "That's very sweet and kind of you to say, Edward. Thank you for those words."

He grinned. "Surely you didn't think I'd say you should have stayed, that I thought that place and vocation was the life meant for you."

She shrugged.

Edward laughed out loud then. "Please remember, dear friend, I am also the young man who knows very well how sweetly you kiss. It would seem a waste to me with that knowledge, that you could never use that lovely skill again."

Lila knew she flushed and that her mouth flew open. "Edward!" she said in shock.

He put his hands out apologetically. "Just being honest."

She tried to regain her composure, sitting up primly. "Well, I need to redirect this conversation and ask if it would be all right now for me to do some sketches around the main house and in the gardens today. If I remember correctly, there is a greenhouse in back, several sheds and out buildings, and a guesthouse. I thought I'd begin my work near the main house first and then gradually branch out, following the suggestions Morgan Richards gave me."

"You are welcome to draw and paint anywhere you like, Lila," he answered, trying, also, to help her change the subject. However, she saw the smirk he hid after his words.

She stood, picking up her satchel.

"Here's your book, too," he said, standing to see her out.

"You keep it," she offered. "It's my gift to you for being kind enough to let me work here. It will take me some time to do all the drawings Morgan asked for. I also want to paint some days when I'm here, too."

"Come as often as you want and stay for as long as you'd like, Lila, and thank you for the book. I'll cherish it." He laid it on a side table before starting to the door with her. "Also, know the house here is open to you. Feel free to let yourself in whenever you'd like to use the bathroom, to get water from the refrigerator, or to make yourself a snack in the kitchen. You know the house well. I'll be in my father's office today, going through files and papers, a needed job I don't especially look forward to. But one that has to be done." He pointed down the hallway. "You know where that office is. Come find me if you need to."

"Thank you." Lila suddenly felt fidgety in Edward's presence and turned to go.

"What time will you get through so we can ride?" he asked.

She'd almost forgotten that promise. "It's about one-thirty now," she said, glancing at her watch. "Let me work for about two hours or so. I'll come to find you later. Will that time work well for you? I drove my own car over from the ferry, and I took one of the skiffs from the island so I wouldn't need to worry about catching the four o'clock ferry back."

"That time to ride will work fine for me," he assured her. "The days are getting longer now. We'll have plenty of time to take a ride."

Lila felt relieved to slip back outdoors into the fresh air and to head to her car to get her art supplies. The talk she and Edward had was a needed one. She felt glad they'd cleared the path for a return to being friends again. However, that last bit of conversation had rattled her, stirring up the air between herself and Edward in a different way. She wasn't ready for that or for a return to more than friendship with Edward yet, if ever.

She hoped, by redirecting the conversation, that he'd gotten that message. She had a lot of work to do here this week and probably into next, and no time for senseless flirtations. Despite their talk, Edward's life was still very unsettled. And Lila did not want to return to a romantic relationship with him that might confuse her even more about the direction God wanted for her life right now.

CHAPTER 6

After Lila left, Edward walked back to the kitchen to clean up from his lunch and then made his way to his father's office. He stood at the door with reluctance, remembering it was here his father always made him come for his stern lectures, his no-option directives, or to deal out punishment for his infractions. It was no wonder Edward dreaded the room, full of so many harsh memories.

With the echo of punishment particularly strong in his remembrance, Edward glanced toward the closet in the room, where his father had kept the worn, shortened belt strap he used on Edward when he crossed a rule or order or got into some trouble.

It wasn't that Edward didn't believe in the concept of discipline for wrong-doing. The Jessup children had received spankings for wrongs, usually administered with a strong, firm hand or a switch. He remembered a few times when he and Isaac both got a switching for one of their childish pranks they'd tried around the plantation.

He smiled as an old recollection came to mind, when he and Isaac were sent to clean out the weeds along a garden fence line. Knowing goats would eat almost any weeds or vegetation, they decided to let the goats out, kept in a fenced field nearby, to do the job for them so they could slip down to the river to fish. The goats ate not only the weeds around the garden, but pushed through the garden gate, not secured, and ate a neat portion of the family vegetables before Isaac's father spotted them. He and Isaac got a needed lecture, a well-earned switching, and had to do penance chores for a week after.

As he stood at the office door, hesitant to go in, Isaac's mother Della walked down the hallway to stand in the doorway beside him.

Edward turned. "I didn't hear you come in."

"No doubt you were lost in thought."

"I was." His eyes moved to her warm gaze, taking comfort from it, and from the tall Black woman's presence, her graying hair cut short around her face, her eyes dark and warm as they looked at him.

She put an arm around his waist. "Your father was too tough on you. I know this room holds some harsh memories for you."

"It does, that," he admitted. "However, I need to go through papers here, sort through everything, decide what needs to be kept and tossed."

She nodded. "Well, let's start by tossing out that old belt." She walked into the room, opened the closet door and reached in to get the worn leather strap from the hook by the door. "I've always had a hankering to burn this thing and I've got some trash to incinerate later today. I'll just toss this old belt right in the fire unless you're wanting to keep it."

Edward couldn't help laughing. "No, I don't want to keep it."

She gave him a hug. "Earl and Levi said they counseled you that you need to let all the bad memories go. Those are wise words. This is a new day, son. The past doesn't rule you any longer. You can make anything of your future you like, and I hope you'll make it all good."

She laid the belt on a table outside the door. "If you find anything else in this room, while you're sorting through things, that needs to be added to the fire, you just pile it all in a box and bring it to me. The Good Book talks often about burning up the chaff with fire, burning the worthless, the wicked, and the dregs no longer of value. I've always liked that idea. Sometimes, we burn up crop residue as a management tool here on the plantation after harvesting. Burning can help prepare fields for the next growing season, get rid of pests and diseases you don't want to affect the next crop."

Della gave him a smile. "I've cleaned this old room a lot, Edward, prayed in it a lot for your father, hoping he'd let his old reprobate ways go, worried for his soul. But here's what I know. The man who used this room had issues for sure, but it isn't the room's fault. Annamae and Levi can tell you lots of good memories of laughing with your good Grandfather Malcolm here, talking business and sharing as friends, even praying here. When you start looking around and looking through things, you'll find pictures of your grandfather and grandmother, and old photos and paintings of this beautiful plantation God has so faithfully preserved."

She walked across the room and swept the curtains at the window open, turning on lights and lamps as she went. "Look what a fine distinguished room this is. Pretty dark green walls, rich old rugs, comfortable leather sofas and chairs, bookcases to the ceilings filled with great literature and helpful books on law, farming, and business, a big fireplace for cozy winter nights."

Della moved to smooth her hand over Edward's father's big desk that dominated one part of the room. "Did you know this old desk has been here since the house's earliest days? It was hand-built up north in the 1800s by a freed African American who worked for a fine furniture maker named Robert Walker. There's paperwork here somewhere about it. So don't you be looking at that desk, or anything else here, and only thinking of your father and any dark memories about him you still hold." She paused. "You be the one to make new memories here, good fine ones, creditable ones. You live a clean, good life and you'll leave a clean, good legacy." She smiled at him. "Doesn't this old place deserve that? You think about that as you look around in every room."

Edward couldn't think of anything to say in answer, her strong words wise ones.

Della turned to leave. "I've got to get back to work in the house now, but you come over to our place to see us one evening." She paused. "Actually, with the weather turning nice again, we've started getting together on Friday evenings at the old pavilion by the event barn between our house and Isaac and Tanya's place. We all bring food to share, and Levi, Earl, and Tommy Lee like to play a little banjo, guitar, and fiddle. You probably remember those times. You're welcome anytime you want to come, Edward."

"Thank you," he said and then added, "You may see Lila around the plantation doing sketches for a book. She'll probably be here now and then for a week or so. I told her she was welcome to come in the house for anything she needed."

Della turned back to look at him. "I heard she would be here and was glad to hear it. I know that sweet girl is haunted with some old memories, too. You be good to her and help her burn up any of her hurtful trash while she's here, too."

"I'll try," he answered.

As Della left, Edward moved into the office, trying to think of the room as Della suggested, filled with good rich memories reaching far back before the time his father worked here so often. He spotted an old painting of the house in its early years over the fireplace and, as he walked around, he saw other photos and paintings of earlier times and of earlier Calhouns.

Taking a deep breath, Edward went to sit down in the leather chair in front of his father's desk, opening the drawers to begin going through papers and files. He knew he'd need to set an appointment and go over to the Maybank-Calhoun Law Firm soon, as well, to talk to his father's old partner, Raymond Maybank. They'd communicated often by phone and email since his father died, and he'd told Raymond he was coming home for a time, the visit overdue.

"I know we need to talk," he told Raymond before he left Nashville, "but let me go through my father's papers at the house, speak to the Jessups, and get caught up about the plantation and everything else that I can before I come to meet with you."

"That sounds wise," Raymond said, not pushing, such a different man from Edward's father.

A few hours later, after getting a lot done, Edward noticed the time and decided to walk outdoors to see if Lila had finished the sketches she wanted to do today. He sprinted upstairs first to pull on his riding boots and then walked from the front of the house outside to the back before spotting Lila sitting on an old bench sketching.

He slowed to watch her for a moment. She held a notebook open on her lap and was absorbed in her work. From the time she'd been a girl, Edward had watched Lila sit and draw pictures like this. She'd always carried some sort of journal or notebook around, sketching flowers, trees, insects, birds, or little scenes she saw that took her fancy, sometimes coloring them in with colored pencils later. He thought about that early talent now, that neither he, her family, or most who knew Lila ever took seriously as a career option for her. Even when she was in high school, and some of her paintings in art classes began to draw attention and win awards in shows, he couldn't recall anyone really thinking of Lila as an artist. Yet, someone at school, probably her art teacher, must have encouraged her to consider majoring in art in college. And now look.

He walked closer and, hearing his steps on the walkway, she turned. "Hi, Edward. Is it time to go riding already?" She glanced at her watch. "I forget the time sometimes when I'm working."

She took a drink from a water bottle that sat beside her box of art supplies.

"Let me see what you've done today." He sat down on the bench beside her.

"I did a lot of sketches of the house and some of the side buildings." She flipped through her big sketch pad to show him pictures, all in pencil, most rough drawings, but others detailed, shaded, and more complete. "Annamae came to work in the vegetable garden and I loved getting some sketches of her there. I snagged another of Levi driving by on the tractor, wearing one of his old straw hats, and a quick sketch of the dog running along after him. What is that white dog's name?"

"That's Percy, a white lab, really smart. He has a great sense of smell, is a good dog to alert anyone of danger. He senses problem situations and problem people, too. If you saw a little rat terrier running along behind him that would be Tippy."

She looked at her picture, smiling. "Animals are a big part of a plantation. I remember Percy as a pup but not the terrier."

Edward crossed his leg. "Tippy showed up one day and took a fancy to Levi. He follows him around everywhere. Energetic little thing. Rat terriers are good farm dogs; they help to keep rodents down."

"Do you still have the Manx cats? I remember when Pandora had her litter. Neither you, Isaac, or me could figure out why the kittens didn't have tails, but Annamae knew they were Manx and had a Manx daddy."

"Manx cats are a good breed to keep rats and vermin down, also smart, loyal, and affectionate cats, so we kept all three of the kittens."

She grinned. "I remember we helped to name them." She stopped to think. "Jemimah, Marmalade, and …" She paused. "What did we call the black and white one?"

"Saxton." He looked at her happy face, her beautiful blue-gray eyes shining in the sunshine, her dark wavy hair, with loose strands drifting around her neck and face. Her thick hair had always come out of whatever barrettes, bands, or ribbons she tied it back with.

Without thinking, he put a hand to her face. "You're wearing a little makeup," he said. "I imagine you didn't get to do that as Sister Anne."

She pulled back a little. "No, but if you remember I never wore much makeup or was drawn to fancy nail polish, bright lipstick colors, or hair-do fads like Celeste and Gwen."

"You've always been beautiful just as you are," he said, his voice softening.

She shifted on the bench and gave him a stern look. "Edward, I don't want to start a little flirtation with you while you're visiting here. Be aware of that."

He spread his hands again in an apology. "All right, but we were developing a sweet relationship before all the trouble here. It's hard not to remember how good that was. We agreed to try focusing on the good times of the past, letting the bad memories go."

"Well, you can remember without acting or without voicing your thoughts," she said in a schoolmarmish voice that made Edward laugh.

Shifting the subject, he glanced at the sketch she'd been working on. "If you're finished drawing that wisteria, blooming and hanging over the archway, maybe we can go ride now."

She looked toward the wisteria with a sigh. "Isn't it beautiful, with those lush violet cascades draping down from the archway?" She laughed then. "This isn't one of the drawings that Morgan wanted me to do, but I couldn't resist it. I think I'll do a painting of it later. I took some photos, as well."

He looked to see her iPhone lying amid her art materials.

"I do a lot of my paintings from photos I take." She began to pack her supplies away. "Let me put everything in my car and zip inside to the bathroom and then we'll head for the stable."

She turned bright eyes to his. "Which horses are we going to ride today?"

"The whites," he answered. "Isaac said they need exercise the most. Earl used the bays to help plow earlier this week, and he and Isaac rode them to the field and back. But the whites need to get out."

"They're pretty things," Lila remembered, "both with a bit of Roan in their bloodline that gives them that speckled gray look in their coat. How old are they now?"

"I remember Earl bought them, with Father's okay, when I was starting high school," he answered. "They were about four then, still young. I'd say they're about twelve now."

"That's still young when horses live to be twenty-five to thirty."

He laughed. "Young enough to be full of themselves today."

"We'll let them gallop then," she said as they headed back to the house.

A little later, they took the familiar dirt-packed road from the house to the big plantation barn. The elaborate white barn, with its gray roof, decorative cupolas, and crisp white fencing, plus a similar barn, now an event center, had once housed many horses and carriages, the early means of transportation for all the plantation owners around the island. Now Indigo Plantation only kept four horses, two matched sets for work, pulling carriages, and riding, plus one strong, and occasionally stubborn, gray mule named Jasper.

Other buildings, barns, and sheds around the plantation held the equipment and needed machinery for the farming they did at Indigo, plus an assortment of trucks and wagons. Nearer the house a smaller, but no less elaborate, garage held the family cars. And all of it required upkeep, Edward knew, having just spent much of the afternoon looking through the farm records.

Inside the horse barn, they took Lex and Maddie out of their stalls after giving each half of the apple Edward had tucked in his pocket. They saddled and bridled the horses, talking with them, and chatting with each other, remembering riding memories of the past as they led the horses into the sunshine, mounted, and started down the dirt road.

As Lila had said, it didn't take long for both of them to get comfortable in the saddle again, letting their horses move into a trot, posting in the familiar rise and fall with the horses' gaits, as easily as if they'd ridden every day since last here.

At a turn, where a wide stretch of road turned through the field, Edward asked. "Ready to gallop?"

"Yes." She grinned and nodded, giving Maddie her head. Lex soon pounded along beside Maddie, both horses glad for a romp.

"I'd forgotten how much horses love to run," Lila said after a time as they slowed down to a walk again.

"Yes, and I love the feeling of the horse's power underneath when they run. It gives you a rush, doesn't it?"

"It does," she agreed. "It's exhilarating."

They followed familiar trails and old roadways that threaded around the plantation, easily remembering the way, even at narrow turns and intersections.

Neither talked too much at first, intent on the ride, enjoying seeing all the old familiar places along their way.

"It seems like only yesterday we last rode, rather than so long ago," Edward commented as they started down a road on the back side of the plantation, not too far from the river now.

"I'm so glad you asked me to come riding," she said, sending him a happy smile. "I hope we can ride often while you're here."

"You can count on it," he said, glad she wanted more time with him. "Do you want to ride down to the folly?" he asked.

"No," she blurted out, a distressed look crossing her face. "And I probably need to get back now. Mother will expect me for dinner at the inn. I'm not always prompt when I'm out working, but she worries if I'm late coming back."

Edward turned the horses into a shady lane leading back to the barn now. He didn't make a reply to Lila's quick negative response about going to the folly, but it hurt a little that she seemed so eager to avoid it. The folly, an elaborate ornamental building, somewhat like a round gazebo, had been built long ago beside the plantation's dock strictly for decorative purposes. A picturesque brick structure, with windows all around, the old folly had always been like a playhouse to Edward and Lila.

The folly had also been their sweetheart spot, where they'd first kissed and discovered the flush of young love blossoming between them. He hated to think Lila wanted to avoid even going to the folly with him. Did she think he would push his attentions on her there? Had her feelings toward him changed so much that she wanted to avoid any closeness or intimacy with him at all? Edward knew, with honesty, his old feelings toward Lila were aroused now, spending time with her again. Did she hold no old feelings for him or had their problems and her time away at St. Mary's changed how she felt about him entirely? Or perhaps about all men?

CHAPTER 7

Lila knew Edward wondered at her reluctance to ride down to the folly, but she didn't know how to talk with him about her feelings about that yet or even if she ever would. She knew he'd grown quiet after her reaction, turning the horses back toward the barn, but he didn't question her. She felt glad for that.

Back at the stable, Isaac was there, lightening the moment, helping them both to laugh and chatter again as before.

"Mother said you were here today," Isaac said, sweeping Lila into a big hug. "And, goodness me, you've grown even more beautiful than I remember. It's so good to see you."

"And you," Lila said with sincerity, happy to see her old friend. He looked tall, fit, and more mature now, but still had the same warm smile.

"It looks like you gave these two horses a good workout," Isaac commented, turning toward Edward, who'd unsaddled Lex and was wiping and brushing him down now. "Did you enjoy riding again?"

"We did," Edward answered, "and Lila says she'll come back often to ride with me."

"Well, that's good news." Isaac grinned before moving to help Lila unsaddle Maddie.

He walked amiably with Edward and her around the corral to cool down their horses, chattering away, asking her questions. "Can you come by to see Tanya before you leave?"

"I'm sorry, Isaac, but I was just telling Edward I need to start home," Lila answered. "I drove my car over from the Jenkins Landing, and I left one of our skiffs there to pilot back to the island. Mother worries if I'm too late for dinner."

He laughed. "Novaleigh doesn't like anyone to be late for dinner at the Deveaux Inn either. I remember that about her."

Lila smiled.

"Listen, I'll finish wiping down the horses and putting them back in their stalls. You two go on to the house. I know Edward will want to see you off."

"Thanks, Isaac." Edward slapped him congenially on the back.

Before they left Isaac added, "Edward, I know Mom told you we're starting our Friday night get-togethers again at the pavilion by the event barn, with the weather warming. I hope you'll come." He grinned at Lila. "You're also welcome to come, Lila. I'm sure Edward could pick you up at the island in his boat and take you back later. I know your mother wouldn't want you out on the river alone at night."

Edward's eyes met hers. "I hope you'll come, Lila. You know all the Jessups will be there and they'd love to see you."

She glanced away, thinking. "I'll see how my week goes and what the family's plans are. I know it would be fun to enjoy a Friday night at Indigo again."

She and Edward walked back along the well-worn roadway from the stable then.

After a time, Edward asked, "What plantation does Morgan Richards want you to visit next for his book?"

Relieved at the change of topic, she smiled. "He is actually doing interviews and visiting this week at Crawford Plantation on Oyster Factory Road, talking to Jane and Colby Broadwater who live there now. It's a lovely old place, the home built in 1834, with ancient live oaks and scenic grounds. It has a stable and picturesque outbuildings like Indigo, although it is not nearly as large."

"It is a beautiful old place, about 250 acres. I've been there often in the past."

"Morgan Richards says the lake is especially pretty with a covered outdoor room for pleasant times and gatherings by the water." She paused, thinking. "I don't think I've ever been there, but I'm sure Mother has at one time or other." She tried to think what else to say to keep the conversation moving along. "I think Della said you were running errands and visiting at Gladys and Tommy Lee's store this morning."

"Tommy Lee and Gladys have added a lot to the store since I left, brought in a lot of color and artistry," he added. "The store was busy today, even on a weekday morning, and I smiled seeing the blue-painted indigo-blue chicken on the store sign."

Edward glanced toward her with a grin. "Do you remember the blue pet chicken Tommy Lee used to keep at the store? He spotted it originally at a farmer's market around Easter when someone was selling little dyed chicks. A blue one caught his attention and he picked it up for Gladys as an Easter surprise. The little chick turned quickly into a pet. Gladys kept it in the store or on the porch in a big wire pen."

"Doesn't the dye wear off of a hen or chick after a time?"

"It does, but Gladys kept dying the hen's feathers." He laughed. "Remember, we still grow indigo shrubs at the plantation. Annamae, Della, and Gladys make indigo dye from them, and they package and sell it at the store. They also make pretty dyed craft items, fabrics, aprons, quilts, and skirts to sell."

"So, they kept re-dying the little hen indigo blue?"

"Yes, with care you can use the dye we create to color chickens, painting it on their feathers," he answered. "The feathers will hold the color for quite a time. Gladys named her hen BlueGirl. She and Tommy Lee even sold blue baby chicks a few Easters. A lot of people came by the store just to see those blue chicks and to see Gladys's hen. Tommy Lee later had a sign made for the store with a painting of BlueGirl on it after the old hen died."

Lila thought back. "You know, I do think I remember that blue hen. Tommy Lee had just gotten married then, and we were only kids."

"Probably about eleven or twelve," he said.

"Does dye hurt chickens?" she asked.

"It can. There are ways that some people dye birds or chicks that are harmful to them, and for that reason dying birds or chicks is illegal in some states. But natural dyes like Gladys uses are safe."

She smiled at him. "Indigo Plantation got its name from the indigo the plantation once produced., didn't it?"

"Yes, most early plantations tried rice, cotton, and sometimes indigo, before they found the unique long staple, Sea Island cotton that brought such marketable wealth to the Lowcountry of South Carolina." He slowed to pick up a branch, that had fallen off a tree, tossing it into the field out of the road, before continuing.

"The early indigo, at one time, brought great wealth to the plantations as an import to England before the Revolutionary War and other changes. The indigo was harvested, processed, and packed into cakes before being shipped abroad. It was called 'blue gold' for the profit it brought, but it is difficult to produce indigo to any large extent because the process is so labor intensive. It took almost two-hundred pounds of indigo leaves to produce one pound of indigo dye."

Lila slowed. "It also took slave labor for that kind of production."

"Sadly, it did. That was a part of the way of life in plantations here, and in the Caribbean islands, Barbados, Haiti, Jamaica, Brazil, in the French and Spanish colonies, in Cuba, and in many other parts of the world—even in Africa. Many nations were involved in profiting from it, even if they didn't all heavily utilize slave labor. People were often considered merchandise or units of labor in those early times, not just here in America. Actually, only six percent of all Africans shipped across the Atlantic were taken to America. Not just blacks became slaves, either, but often whole families ended up in debt bondage to landowners or worked, often cruelly, as indentured servants."

She shook her head. "Slavery and the sale and exploitation of people isn't new. In Biblical times in Egypt, Athens, Rome, and in early European countries slavery was rampant, too."

"Yes, and unfortunately, slavery isn't gone either. Over fifty million people are entrapped in types of slavery today in factories, mines, farm fields, brothels—many even children. I learned a lot about that in classes I took at Vanderbilt. Issues of human trafficking, forced labor, and child slavery are issues that lawyers often have to work with, trying to help the exploited and defenseless. I especially saw this in the legal clinic where I worked so much."

"Is that one reason you liked working there?"

He nodded. "Yes, it is. We often helped the defenseless, the poor, who couldn't afford other legal help or advice."

She took a breath before asking, "Will you go back to that work?"

"The clinic and those I worked with at Vanderbilt knew my situation and that I needed to leave my position and come home for a time." He hesitated. "However, they do have a full-time position opening at the clinic in the fall that I have been tentatively offered. They aren't interviewing for it yet, but I know it will be opening and I know I have preference. I would do a lot of supervision with the law students, handle cases, do some teaching, speak and help with fundraising. It would be a place to make a real difference."

"Do you not think you could make a difference here?" she asked as they reached the house.

"I didn't think so all the years I was away." He paused, sitting down on an old bench and gesturing to her to join him. "My father held little respect for me or for any of my opinions and ideas. I came to hold little respect for him either. I couldn't imagine being effective in any way with my life always under his thumb."

Lila thought about his words. "I can understand that. I remember how he was." She hesitated, but then added, "He is gone now though, Edward. You might be able to do much good here."

"There is a lot to think about and consider," he replied. "I did help Tommy Lee today with some legal concerns he had. When you're working with people in law you forget how much other people do not know about it, about their legal rights, legal options, ways to get needed understandings."

She waited, hoping he would add more.

"Tommy Lee has had some shoplifting at the store. The other day he asked my advice about it. Knowing that shoplifting is often more internal than external in retail, I suggested he first talk with anyone who works at the store, delivers to the store, that sort of thing. His other employees are only family. It's a small business."

He stopped to pick up a pine cone by the road before continuing. "Today, Tommy Lee said Ambrose, the boy who works with him part-time, totally overreacted, got defensive and angry when Tommy Lee only casually asked him if he'd seen anything suspicious."

"Do you think the boy might be the problem?"

"Maybe. Tommy Lee says he and Gladys feel a lot of compassion towards Ambrose because they think he might be getting abused at home by his grandfather Vale Fleenor, maybe even by his grandmother Marta, since both have hot tempers. The boy lives in a rundown trailer behind their house with his mother, Carmen, who is Vale and Marta's daughter. She evidently has a host of health problems. She's on welfare, doesn't work, isn't emotionally stable."

"It makes you feel sorry for him."

"It does," Edward agreed. "Also, Carmen's brother Butcher Fleenor lives in the main house with Vale and Marta, along with his wife Wyleen and daughter Damara. Butcher and Vale own a little pest control business on the highway not far past the store. Marta runs the office."

"Are you talking about Fleenor's Pest Control? In that run-down old building?"

"The same. I hear they do fairly good work but Vale and Butcher are difficult men. They've had a lot of run-ins with the law." He hesitated. "I know the police were called in at least once for a domestic abuse altercation with Butcher, who claimed his wife was running around on him and needed to be dealt with." Edward shook his head. "Anyway, that's the sort of family life Ambrose has."

"Do you think he's doing the shoplifting?" she asked again.

"I don't know. He might be. Not much loss is really involved. I'm more concerned about Tommy Lee and Gladys believing the boy is being abused. They've seen some bruises, found the boy hiding out, sleeping on the back porch of their store once. They also witnessed Vale coming in the store, looking for Ambrose, hollering and acting ugly, blaming him for something at home, jerking him out of the store by the arm, pushing him in the truck and cuffing him. Hearing a lot of angry words spoken."

"Is there anything legal you can do to help?"

"Not over just that alone, Lila, and maybe not at all. Someone has to report something and it's hard to get any action to check into things with a situation like this. Sometimes it can make things worse, escalate the problems." He rubbed his neck. "I did ask Tommy Lee to watch the situation though."

"Do you think the boy might confide in them?"

He shook his head. "I doubt it. Both Vale and Marta Fleenor, and their son Butcher, have intolerant, bigoted views as well. They don't even like Ambrose working for Tommy Lee. With their tempers, Tommy Lee could be in danger if he tried to put his oar into the situation."

"What will you do?" she asked.

He frowned and stood, restless. "I don't know, but I don't like the idea of the boy being abused. Also, Ambrose is an odd, no-fit kid with that Fleenor clan, not tough, a sensitive, bookish kid. About all I can do is watch things, maybe talk to Raymond Maybank about it when I meet with him at the firm this week. See what he knows." He shrugged, giving her a hand as she got up from the bench. "I didn't mean to dump all this on you. I know you need to get home."

"Edward, I asked you about it and you answered. I can see you're concerned about it, too." She paused. "I do think I know who that boy is, after hearing you talk about him. I've seen him riding his bicycle around. He must not drive yet or have access to a car. You're right. He doesn't look like Vale or Butcher Fleenor in any way—or act like them. Mother had those Fleenor men out to do some pest control spraying at the Inn and she said she'd never have them back again. They were rude and uncouth, acted offensive to her, and made sarcastic comments about 'women running things.' That didn't sit well with Mother."

Edward laughed. "I imagine not."

"Who is that boy's father?"

"I don't know. Neither does Tommy Lee. There was always some glib, flippant talk that some big shot business man and plantation owner around Bluffton got Carmen pregnant. Tommy Lee told me that Carmen worked at a restaurant down in Bluffton for a time, probably hoping to get away from her family. But she had to come home after she got pregnant. She moved into that old trailer behind her parents' house, and Tommy Lee said she was never the same after. He told me Carmen had been nicer than most of the Fleenors, real pretty once as a girl, but now she doesn't care about her appearance, is obese, a borderline hypochondriac, and acts the victim about everything."

"Perhaps she was a victim," Lila said.

"I thought of that," he replied. "She might have been. I doubt Carmen knew legally what to do as a young girl, away from home on her own, no matter what happened."

"Some of this makes you think of your father," she said.

He winced, his eyes traveling to the house and then up the driveway. "Lila, so many things here make me think of my father. It's one of the reasons I didn't want to come home."

She put a hand on his arm. "Keep in mind he's gone now."

"Perhaps, but his memory lives strong and it still impacts me more than I like." He put his hand over hers. "I can't tell you how much happier I was away from this place, away from my father and from my mother."

"Where is Clarice?" Lila asked.

"At her sister Eula's in Charleston. She had clubs and luncheons she wanted to attend, said I didn't need her here. She told me to decide what I wanted to do with this place and she made it clear she doesn't want to stay here, that she wants to move in with my Aunt Eula in Charleston, who is widowed, too. Eula lives in the Alston family home where both sisters were raised." He ran a hand through his hair. "My mother was never really happy here. If you remember, she stayed with Eula in Charleston often. Annamae and Della, Levi and Earl, raised me more than she or my father ever did."

Lila couldn't help laughing a little then. "That's probably a blessing, looking back on all we know now, Edward. The Jessups are such wonderful people and they always loved you like another son."

"Yes, it's hard to know what to do about everything, Lila. Thanks for talking with me, for spending time with me. You were my heart and soul growing up, my solace and best friend."

She glanced at her watch. "I need to start home. I don't want to boat in the dark on the river. But I'll pray for you as I find my way home. I'll pray for you to find your direction, to find the best answers for your life. I hate seeing you in so much unrest, so troubled in your soul. Reach out to God and let Him give you His peace and His direction. He'll be there for you if you reach out to Him."

He smiled at her. "That's the other thing I so loved about you, Lila, how close you always were to God, how you relied on Him, trusted in Him. It helped me more than you know in those hard years."

"Always remember you're God's child first, Edward. He loves you, calls you the apple of His eye. If you need wisdom, He'll give it to you. If you ask Him for peace, you'll feel it fall over you sweetly like a soft blanket, giving you comfort. He has a purpose and plan for your life and He wants you to walk right into the center of it."

"I know you're right but I love hearing you say the words to me, reminding me I need to trust more in His wisdom than my own muddled thoughts and mixed emotions."

"You'll find your way, Edward. I'll be praying for that." She paused and then smiled. "I'm going to pray John 16:13 for you, that the Spirit of Truth will come and guide you and that He will show you things to come so clearly and well that you'll know the way you should walk."

He leaned toward her. "Did your close walk with God ever run off boyfriends from you, Sister Anne?"

She felt her eyes fly open, embarrassed at his words, and remembering some of the times when it did just that.

His voice softened. "Well, let me tell you that your sweet and Godly counsel, your prayers and the bits of knowledge and revelation God so often gives you, never chased me off. They always just made me cherish and love you more. You take those words home as a comfort yourself and know they're true."

He leaned in, while she was caught off guard, and kissed her, tucking his hand behind her neck. And, oh, Lila remembered the sweetness of moments like these so well. She sighed and yielded more than she should have.

Edward pulled away after a moment to look in her eyes. "This type of loving God created, too, Lila. He saw that man was lonely and needed a helpmeet suitable for him, and out of man's rib he created woman to share life with him. I've learned over time, being around other happy and healthy couples, if not from my own parents, how good life can be when the right two people are knitted together in love. We've always had that sweet harmony. I think we still do. You think about that in your prayers, too."

He winked at her then and strolled off to take the porch steps to his house two at a time. She stood, shocked for a few minutes, and then went to get in her car to head to the landing and home.

CHAPTER 8

The next morning, Edward wondered if Lila would come again to work. It had rained last night, but now the sun was out, the day warming up. She would have nice weather to continue making her sketches around the plantation or to set up her easel and supplies.

For himself, he had an appointment this morning with Raymond Maybank at the Maybank-Calhoun Law Firm. They planned to have lunch together afterward and he knew there was a lot to talk about and that there would be questions.

For his visit, Edward wore a crisp white shirt, a brown suit vest and pants, and he tossed the matching suit jacket into the back seat of his car in case he needed it. After letting Isaac know where he'd be for much of the day today, Edward drove out Point of Pines Road from the plantation, angled left on the highway, crossed Store Creek, and then turned right into the law firm's shady parking area not far from Peters Point Road.

As he sat in the car for a minute, looking at the old law building, another car pulled in beside him. Raymond Maybank got out, waving as he did.

"Good to see you, Edward," Raymond said as Edward opened his car door to climb out. "It's good to see you again, too," Edward replied, as Raymond shook his hand and then impulsively leaned in to give him a hug. "It's been far too long."

Edward noticed Raymond's neat navy suit and wondered if he should retrieve his jacket.

As if picking up on his question, Raymond pulled off his coat and loosened his tie. "I had to go over to the Magistrate Court this morning to represent a client in a dispute, an assault and battery case."

"A domestic issue?" Edward asked.

Raymond nodded. "A willful attempt to inflict injury with a weapon. There were several witnesses. The trial didn't take long."

Edward glanced toward the two-storied Maybank-Calhoun building with a smile. "I've always loved this old plantation house the offices are in. I was trying to remember just now how the firm ended up with this place."

"It's a good story. My father Jarrett Maybank and your grandfather Malcolm Calhoun grew up together, with the Maybank and Indigo plantations not far from each other. They both ended up as attorneys for a big firm in Charleston, but in the 1960s, development at Edisto here began to kick up and they started to see an opportunity to provide legal counsel here on the island."

As Raymond paused, Edward added. "By the 1960s the state park had been built, World War II finished, and a good highway developed to the beach, also. The island was changing."

"Yes, the timing was good and property was cheap then. This Greek Revival house, with its double porches and pretty decorative touches, was once part of the McRaven plantation. The house was empty then, run down, and hadn't been lived in since the death of the two spinster McRaven sisters. It took a considerable chunk of money to clean the place up and renovate it for a business office, but the location on the main highway was perfect."

Raymond turned and smiled at Edward. "My father Jarrett and your grandfather Malcolm went in together to buy the place and formed their partnership. It was a wise move. They were honorable men, had a good legal reputation, worked hard, treated people honorably and honestly. What you see here today is to their credit and faithful efforts."

"Thanks for reminding me of that," he said.

"Let's go on inside," Raymond said, turning up the brick walkway toward the door. "I set up a meeting so you can say your hellos to everyone before we go to lunch. I'll introduce you around in case you've forgotten who everyone is and what they do."

"Thanks for that," Edward replied. "It's been a long time."

Although once a stately old residence, the Maybank-Calhoun Law Firm had now taken on the look of a prosperous island business, the house painted a muted yellow with white trim and crisp black doors and shutters. In addition to the law firm's sign out front, there was also a marker near the door, denoting the home as on the National Register of Historic Places.

Inside the entry area and hallway, and throughout many of the business's rooms the same muted yellow tone continued, creating a feeling more like a plantation home than a modern law office. However, Edward knew the carefully created look of class and elegance was perfect for the Lowcountry business and the clientele the practice catered to.

The firm's receptionist was talking on the phone to someone as they walked in. Raymond waved to her with a smile and then said to Edward. "Let me walk you around briefly before we meet in the conference room. When our receptionist gets off the phone, she'll let everyone know we're here."

Edward was glad for a brief reminder tour as he'd barely set foot in the law firm since high school. However, he found things generally much the same.

They walked across the entry first and then past the stairs into a richly furnished waiting area, more like an Antebellum parlor in looks.

Raymond said, "As you see, our waiting room with its two long couches, facing each other, also serves well as an informal place to meet with new clients in a comfortable home-like setting."

He glanced back toward the entry. "That was Barbara Ruth Maxcy at the front desk, smart young woman with the rich Southern grace to lure in new clients and make anyone who calls, or comes by the firm, to feel warmly welcome. I'm sure you know how important first impressions are, especially in the deep south."

He led Edward down the hallway next. "Three partner offices, our conference room, two baths and a small kitchen lie off this downstairs hallway which then leads outside to double porches on the back. That was the architectural style then in the early 1800s to allow air to flow freely through these old homes before air-conditioning."

"We have the wide hallways like this, too, at Indigo."

Raymond gestured to several of the doors along the hallway. "The offices of the three partners, myself, my brother Hudson, and your father are off this hallway."

He stopped walking to turn to Edward. "Your father was, and I still am, a criminal defense attorney. You know that basically we defend individuals who have been accused of committing a crime and protect the rights of defendants. Hudson is a civil litigation attorney, and he handles non-criminal cases and legal disputes, where no criminal laws have been broken. It adds an advantage to our firm to have attorneys who can handle both criminal and civil cases, and as you well know the cases often overlap."

Raymond paused by the doorway to Hudson's office, which was closed now. "Do you remember Hudson's son Stanford Maybank? He was older than you but went to the same school."

"I do, and I think I remember he went into the Navy after college and is serving as a JAG attorney right now. Is that still correct?"

"Yes, that is right. He handles military and civil law, but fortunately he plans to retire and come back to work with us here at the island later on."

"That's good news. Isn't one of your other sons studying law now, also?"

Raymond smiled. "Yes, as you probably remember, my oldest son, Zach, lived and breathed football and is a coach at Appalachian State in North Carolina now, but Paxton decided to become an attorney. He's in school right now at the University of South Carolina in Columbia. He comes home now and then, so you'll probably see him at some point if you hang around. Zach was closer to your age, Paxton younger, but you knew both."

"Yes, Zach and I were friends at school, but I remember both your boys well and also Hudson's son Stanford and his two daughters."

"This is my office," Raymond continued, gesturing to an open door, "and the office on the back right, of course, was your father's. You can check it out later on your own, go through anything you want to." He grinned. "We've been saving that job for you after getting out any needed papers required for ongoing cases and business."

Edward grinned back at his words, glad Raymond was taking a light tone with him today and aware of some of his discomfort.

Turning, Raymond added, "Let's walk upstairs quickly and then we'll head back down for the meeting planned."

Edward trailed Raymond to the entry again, tasteful with its sunny walls and antiques, and then followed him up the beautiful old staircase to the building's second floor.

"You may not remember, but we have a paralegal and a legal assistant on staff, both needed and both such a help."

"Is Graham Murray still your paralegal? I always liked him."

"Yes, and that's Graham's office on the left there." Raymond pointed down the hallway. "He does all our legal research for us, investigates cases, drafts legal documents, summarizes interrogations, depositions, and testimonies, and usually goes into court with us. He's better than a good golf caddy to keep me in line and on target with proceedings. He's an important cog behind the machine of our firm, a fine young man, with excellent communication and computer skills, too."

"Who is the legal assistant?"

"Marlana Russell, who has been with us five years now. She provides administrative and clerical support, schedules appointments, communicates with clients and other parties. Like Graham, she often does legal research needed and drafts documents. She has great communications and computer skills, too, and she and Graham work well together, their jobs often overlapping."

He turned to smile at Edward. "These days, with all the new

technology out in the world, clients like to be communicated with in the way of their preference, via phone, emails, texting, or in other ways. Marlana is good with all of that, and she handles people with an exceptional diplomatic art." He paused. "We've got fine people on staff, Edward. We all work together well and get along easily."

Edward wondered if that had been so when his father was with the firm but wisely decided not to voice his thoughts.

"Our library is here on this floor, too, with work and conference space in it." Raymond opened the door to the richly paneled old room lined with the multitude of law books firms always needed.

He gestured across the hall. "That big room, as you probably remember, is the work room with all the duplication machines, printers, supplies, extra computers, work tables, files and other equipment we need for the day-to-day operation of the business."

Glancing down the hall, he added, "Another bathroom and two more offices sit further down the hall, waiting for future employees." He smiled. "I admit, both Hudson and myself are pleased our sons Stanford and Paxton hope to join the firm one day."

Edward knew well his father had held the same hopes for him but without the amiability expressed by Raymond. He well remembered, too, that Raymond hadn't pressured his older son Zachary to pursue law when his heart was set on athletics and coaching. For himself, any options other than his father's plans for him were never considered.

Downstairs everyone gathered in the conference room, an elegant old room with a long table and eight leather upholstered chairs, with a dark rug under the table and a chandelier overhead. It was a good place, with its old south elegance, to meet around a table for staff meetings or with clients.

As everyone trailed into the room, Edward was introduced or reintroduced, and he felt more comfortable with everyone after the update and tour Raymond had given him. The meeting was brief, a catch-up session on firm business with a chance for Edward to sit in. A little sociable talk was mixed in with the discussions but none probing. Obviously, Edward wasn't meant to be quizzed here about his intentions related to the firm.

He studied the two Maybank men, the partners his father had worked with for so many years, while they talked business. Raymond sat at the head of the table, obviously assuming the more in-charge role. Hudson sat to his right. The men had a similar appearance as brothers, Raymond a little taller with a longer face, Hudson sturdier in his physique, his face squarer, his smile and laugh flashing out more often.

Graham Murray, the paralegal, was a somewhat serious young man, as Edward remembered, with a short beard around his chin.

Marlana, the legal assistant, had that erect poise, confidence, and bearing that indicated a woman sure of herself and her place in the world, while Barbara Ruth was easy-going with a million-dollar smile, gracious manners and an obvious warmth that made him comfortable with her right away. Raymond had been right they all made a congenial work group.

Watching them, Edward couldn't help but frown, trying to picture his father here among them, so harsh, dictatorial, and over-bearing with him at home. His mother always told him his father was different at work than at home, a strong leader, competent, respected, resourceful, and with a decided strength, charisma, and persuasive manner that made him a force to be reckoned with in the courtroom. The two pictures never seemed to mesh or combine in Edward's mind.

As they finished their meeting, Hudson stayed back for a moment to speak to Edward. "Son, I'm sorry but I'm going to be unable to go to lunch with you and Raymond. I have a dispute between a landlord and tenant to sit in on and help to resolve. I don't want their relationship to grow any more volatile. I think I can show them both their legal rights and help them find a congenial resolution."

"Is that who you were tied up with earlier on the phone with your door closed?" Raymond asked.

"Yes." He shook his head. "I'll fill you in later about everything."

Hudson turned again to Edward. "It's good to see you again. I hope we'll get another chance to talk soon. Come by any day to chat with me about anything you'd like, okay?"

"I will," Edward promised.

After more small talk with others Edward followed Raymond out to his car. "I think I'll take you up to the Roxbury Mercantile on the highway past the causeway for lunch," he said. "Have you been there since it opened?"

"No, I haven't," he admitted.

"Well, they have good food and it's a little less busy and touristy for lunch. I think you'll like it."

They talked comfortably on the way up the highway, Raymond catching him up on more family and island news.

At the restaurant, he asked Edward if he would mind sitting outside at one of the patio tables under an umbrella. No one else was eating outside, making the area quieter, and the day was pleasant.

"That will be fine," Edward agreed.

They ordered lunch, Raymond choosing pulled pork, that he raved about, with slaw and red beans. Edward decided on shrimp and oysters, with grits and slaw. Both ordered sweet tea to drink, a southern staple.

"Well, I guess we need to talk a little business now," Raymond said after their waitress brought their tea. "I first wanted you to get a sense of where the business is now, meet all the staff, see the firm again before quizzing you about your plans. I know you've been indecisive about what you want to do. Do you mind if I remind you of your legal options? You probably already know them, but I'd like to put them out there in front of us to look at."

"That would be fine," Edward agreed.

Raymond leaned back in his chair and crossed an ankle over one knee. "The Maybank-Calhoun Law Firm is a small family firm owned by the Maybank and Calhoun heirs, who are also attorneys in the firm. There is a contractual understanding, in writing, that all owners in the firm must be credentialed, practicing attorneys in the firm. As you probably know, your father, Hudson and myself, as heirs of our fathers, could only retain ownership in the firm and share in its profits as attorneys working within the firm. Our ownership will pass hands to any of our sons, or daughters, who want to help continue the firm as practicing attorneys in the Maybank-Calhoun Law Firm."

He paused. "If an owner-attorney in the firm dies, a member of the other family has the option to buy out the family's ownership if there is no son or daughter in process of becoming an attorney or already working as an attorney, either in the firm or wanting to join the firm." He hesitated again. "Some legal clauses are built in to give space and time if an owner-partner in the firm is ill and can't practice for a time, dies unexpectedly, needs to take leave. As we both know, estates do take time to be resolved and unexpected problems happen more often than we anticipate."

He smiled at Edward. "We were all shocked your father died so young. Both our families, in general, tend to live to ripe old ages. As you are the only son, the only child of your parents, their heir and also your father's heir in the law firm, you have some decisions to make about that. Do you understand what those choices are?"

"I think so," Edward replied. "Unless you and Hudson, as the Maybank owners and partners, find me objectionable or unqualified, I can take my father's place in the firm. If I felt another life called to me and I didn't want to step into my father's role in the firm, the Maybank family could negotiate with me for a buyout. That was always the way the ownership of the firm was set up and those legal options still stand, as far as I know."

"That's accurate."

Edward fidgeted in his seat then.

"Talk to me about your concerns, Edward," Raymond said. "I know you've taken longer than expected in coming to terms with your father's death and with the obligations and choices left to you as his heir. Let's talk about any concerns you have."

Edward thought what to say. "I kept wondering as you took me through the firm today and as I sat and congenially visited with all the staff, how you all could stand working with my father."

Raymond shook his head. "Keep in mind, Edward, that Hudson and I grew up with Sam. We saw early, as boys, how different he was in character from his father Malcolm. Your grandfather kept Sam in check until he died—not always an easy task."

He stopped to take a drink of his tea. "However, Sam wanted his father's position as owner of Indigo and as an owner and partner in the law firm. He also knew there were clauses in the partner and ownership contractual agreements of the firm that could allow the other partners to ask a partner to leave. The points were serious ones, linked to behavior and ethics within the firm. Sam never stepped over those points within the firm, no matter what he thought about them or if he agreed with them. He knew they were designed for a strong profitable business and for maintaining a sterling reputation in the community."

He hesitated. "On many occasions, after Sam joined the firm after college, your grandfather and my father held some strong talks with Sam with rather stern ultimatums. Sam learned that in the firm he had to comply or leave."

"I didn't know that."

"Later on," Raymond continued, "Hudson and I had to hold some similar sessions with your father. We were often grateful for our two-against-one advantage, if you'll pardon me saying so."

Edward smiled. "Thank you for your candor."

"Now, let me add this additional information on a positive note. Your father, Sam Calhoun, was a brilliant businessman and an excellent attorney. No one liked to face him in the courtroom. He could read people, and he had a formidable strength and an almost enviable charisma in all his business and legal relations. People knew if they wanted anything done, Sam was probably the man that could get it done. He was highly respected all around the Lowcountry and abroad for his knowledge and gift in wielding power. It was hard to cross him and most people didn't try."

"I knew that latter aspect of him well."

Their lunch arrived and they stopped to speak to the waitress for a few minutes and to dig into their food, both quiet for a time.

As they finished their lunch, Raymond sighed and said, "Edward, I want you to know our father, and my brother Hudson and myself, did not respect the way Sam ran his home, related to his wife or to you. We saw he was often dictatorial and cruel, and these characteristics emerged more after his father Malcolm died. I often think Sam took out some of his frustrations over his restrictions at the firm in his personal life and household. He made it clear, on the few times Hudson or myself tried to talk to him on these matters, that his personal life outside the firm, and at his own plantation, were none of our business."

Edward thought about his words. "I can imagine those conversations were not pleasant ones."

"No, they never were. In your father's eyes, his ways and methods were always justified. He held a very high opinion of himself."

Edward snorted. "That's a kind way to put it."

"I know the way your father treated you has made you reluctant to come home and to consider working in the firm and picking up the ownership role at Indigo." He rubbed his neck as if reluctant to speak the next words. "Your relationship with your mother Clarice doesn't act as a further inducement to make you want to return home either. My wife Dora once said Clarice lacked the natural nurturing gene most women possess."

Edward laughed. "I never thought of it that way."

Raymond looked out toward the highway. "Clarice has made it clear to us at the firm that she does not want to stay at Indigo and that she is leaving it in your hands totally as to whether you want to come home to run the plantation or to sell it off. I hope I'm not stepping out of line to say that."

"My mother has told me the same. You've breached no confidence. She spent a large portion of her married life at my Aunt Eula Heyward's home, their family home, in Charleston, and she told me emphatically she wants to move there and wants nothing to do with Indigo, despite wording my father put in his will that she could stay there as long as she wished. Frankly, Mother has been annoyed that I haven't come home sooner so she could leave sooner, and she told me, with no apparent regret or thought to the lives of others on the plantation, to do whatever I wanted about everything. That she didn't care what I did at all."

Raymond winced.

"My mother and I have not had a good relationship since I was small, and it deteriorated more when some of my father's less than stellar behavior surfaced in past."

Raymond shook his head. "I remember some of that. Edisto is a small place. Talk gets around."

A thought came to Edward. "Did you and Hudson have a talk with my father then about that, how his behavior might affect the reputation of the firm?"

"We did and it was a heated and unpleasant discussion." Raymond hesitated again. "Your father had a canny way of justifying his actions, even when they were objectionable. And although it is unkind to say so, Sam could be an artful liar if it served him."

Edward streaked a hand through his hair. "You and Hudson knew my father far better than I imagined. I greatly appreciate your honesty with me today."

Raymond put a hand out and placed it on Edward's arm on the table. "I'm sure you wondered, at times, if we condoned your father's actions. I want you to know we did not. Ever. However, Hudson and I are proud of what a fine man you have become, a good attorney, too." He waited for a moment and then added, "I've talked with many of the people you've been working with at the clinic at Vanderbilt and they have only the highest praise for you, for your work and for your character. Your grandfather would have been very proud of you."

He smiled at Raymond. "Don't feel bad for checking me out. I would have done so, too."

"Edward, we have no objections to you coming into the firm with us and we would be pleased if you would consider it."

He looked away.

"You still have some reservations?" Raymond asked.

"The old memories are hard to get past. Levi and Earl Jessup, and Della and Annamae—and even Isaac—keep telling me I need to put the past in the past, focus on the future, remember the good, but it's hard."

"In kindness toward the Jessups, if you don't stay at Indigo and you sell it, there is no legal assurance any of them will be kept on. You can't put that kind of control on a sale. You know that, don't you? Even if a buyer agreed to the idea at the sale, he could turn around later and ask the Jessups to vacate. The entire plantation could also be broken up and sold in pieces."

Edward leaned forward. "I could stay an absentee owner. Come back now and then to the plantation."

Raymond smiled. "You know there would be problems with that. I don't think I need to enumerate them."

He closed his eyes. "For as long as I can remember, I've felt that I never had any choices about the life I would live. I was always told who and what I should be. My life was always planned and laid out for me with no options in practically every detail."

"I'm sure that felt confining."

"It was. Did you never feel that way growing up, knowing your father Jarret expected you to come into the firm that he and my grandfather established, that you would be expected to take care of his estate and property, keep Maybank Plantation up, protect it and any employees on it?"

Edward could see Raymond considering his words. "Looking back, I can remember some moments when I entertained a few feelings like that, but I was always counseled to see both the firm and the Maybank Plantation as blessings built up and left to me. Blessings I hadn't earned but should value and care for and pass on. I was often reminded that many would envy my fortune in having such blessings handed to me."

He chuckled. "My family was strong in faith and the Prodigal Son story was told to me often, of how the son asked for his portion, went away and left his home to live life his own way, selfishly, and then regretted it, returning home later in humility. Surely, you've seen how many young people on the island here haven't valued their heritage, the land, the businesses their parents worked so hard to build and leave to them, and simply sold the land and the businesses off, and left."

"Do you think all of them are unhappy over doing that?"

"I doubt all were unhappy in doing so but I know many who were and are. You do, too."

"So, you're saying I'd be like the Prodigal Son, ungrateful, if I decided to be an attorney at Vanderbilt and handle the plantation from there or sell it."

"I can't say that, but let me ask you this, what is so objectionable to the idea of running Indigo Plantation, coming home again to do so, and possibly working at the Maybank-Calhoun Firm? Is the work you could do in Nashville so much better and more valuable than work you could do here? Is God calling you to leave? Do you feel like He doesn't want you to stay and make your life here?"

Raymond hesitated again. "I don't mean to get overly spiritual with you, but I do believe God has a best design for our lives that He wants for us to follow."

Edward couldn't help smiling. "You sound like Lila."

"Lila Deveaux?" he asked. "I seem to recall she left and came back. Perhaps you should consider that, too." He looked thoughtful then. "It seems like you and Lila Deveaux were once quite sweet on each other. I always liked that girl. Still do. Kind, good, thoughtful, talented, smart."

"Are you matchmaking?" Edward asked. "My father wouldn't approve. He always thought Lila too spiritual, too influential on my character. He said she was making me soft and not tough. He also said religion got in the way of good business."

A pained look crossed Raymond's face. "I hope you've gotten past your father's teaching and views in that area."

Edward nodded. "I have. Especially at Vanderbilt, I found new ways to think, people to admire and emulate of good character. I became a better and stronger man there—and a more spiritual one."

"I can see why the good influences there might draw you back."

They sat quietly for a few minutes.

"Edward, let me make a suggestion for you to think about. Give this opportunity and legacy here what I'd like to call a trial. Think about coming to work in the firm, for a time as a part-time intern, to see how you like being associated with us. Begin picking up the management of the overall plantation at Indigo in the same way. Wade in, work in both capacities part-time at your own pace. See how this life fits you now as a different man, as you say you are, with your father gone, and with your mother obviously planning to move to Charleston, too."

He smiled at Edward. "See how the role fits. Hudson and I already discussed the idea of you working your way into the firm in a trial, to see if you like being a part of the Maybank-Calhoun Law Firm. I know you did internships and part-time work at the clinic at Vanderbilt before deciding to accept a job there. You can do the same here and you don't need to begin this work role right away."

He leaned back in his chair. "I know you have many responsibilities to catch up on at Indigo right now, adjustments to make. I remember you said you planned to stay for several months before returning to Nashville. In the next month, see if you can get the leading you need to make your decision about working with us. Pop in and out of the firm as you wish. Sort through your father's office, hang out and talk with us. I know you need some time here to know clearly the way you should go."

Edward sat for a moment, considering Raymond's words. "I guess I expected an ultimatum today versus an option." He grinned. "I'm not used to being given options, and I well know I've dragged my feet a long time in coming home to face my choices, undoubtedly leaving you short-handed in the firm."

Raymond laughed. "I have spent a little more time in the courtroom than I'd like with Sam gone. My wife Dora has grumbled. We have a new grandbaby in Boone she is eager to see more often than we do, but it's hard to find time for a few extra days right now."

"I'm sorry," Edward offered with sincerity. "I've been more self-concerned in this time than is justified."

Raymond put a hand on his arm again. "You've had cause, son. Keep in mind, however, that this is a new day, and with a new day come new opportunities and a chance for new beginnings. The old philosopher Seneca once wrote, *"Every new beginning comes from some other beginning's end."*

"You've been kinder to me than I expected today and given me good counsel, wisdom, and a fair opportunity to consider." Edward paused. "I will think over your offer in the next few weeks, as you suggested, and get back with you as soon as I can."

"Take your time, son, and remember to pray about the situation. God is wiser than either of us in knowing the way you should go."

CHAPTER 9

On Tuesday, Lila stood on the porch of the Indigo Plantation house, trying to get up her nerve to ring the doorbell. She hadn't slept well last night, after Edward impulsively kissed her, and she'd experienced problems regaining her usual peace, despite her prayers.

She'd actually considered calling to cancel today, but Morgan Richards was eager for her to finish her assigned sketches and paintings here. It would be totally unprofessional and ethically wrong not to follow through on her commitments to him.

Ringing the front bell at last, Lila admitted she felt relief when Della Jessup answered the door instead of Edward.

"Good morning, sweet girl," Della said, catching her up in a hug. "It is a blessing to see you again. Come on in."

Lila followed her into the old house's wide entry.

"Edward's not here today," Della said, shutting the door behind her. "He had meetings over at the law firm and a lunch to attend. He has a lot to see to and a lot of responsibility to take on for one so young."

She smiled. "I told him you were planning to do sketches today of Annamae and me working in the Indigo Shed. That professor, Morgan Richards, got real fascinated learning how we still harvest and process indigo here and create indigo dyed products to sell at the plantation's market on the highway."

Lila trailed Della down the hallway, listening.

"We had the quilt frame up one day last week when he came by, too, and I told him you could do some sketches of us working here today if you wanted. He seemed eager for us to do that. We're finishing a real pretty quilt and we'll be happy to enjoy your company today while we work. Is that plan still good for you?"

"Yes, I'd love that," she replied, glad for work to keep her busy today and grateful she'd have another day to calm her jangled emotions before seeing Edward Calhoun again.

"I saw some of those sketches you did yesterday of the house, garden, and sheds out back. You surely do have a fine gift, Lila."

"Thank you, Della."

"I left Annamae working in the shed to come answer the door," Della continued, as she opened the door at the end of the long hallway to head across another broad porch toward the back yard. "There's a bell rigged up out there and in several other places around the plantation to let us know when someone comes."

"I'm sure that's helpful. This is a big place."

"That it is. A buzzer sounds, too, when someone crosses the property line into the plantation road," she added, leading Lila across the back property to a long shed near the indigo fields. "The plantation is private property with no trespassing signs, but some folks don't pay any mind at all to that sign and come driving out here, usually harmless or just curious, but sometimes with no good intent."

"We have that problem at the island, too, with trespassers. They're fascinated at seeing the lighthouse high above the beach and walk into the island overlooking all the no trespassing signs."

"Well, folks are what they are."

The Indigo Shed was a long barn-like shed with an over-hanging roof on the front, back, and sides for work outdoors, but with a large interior for work inside.

"If you remember, a lot of the indigo dyeing is done outdoors in these vats." Della pointed toward them. "Cooking down the indigo leaves, letting the fermentation process begin, adding what's needed, and then separating out the plant material from the dye.

The work is a right intense process that needs to be done outside in the open air. It's a long messy process, too, and takes a lot more skill than most know. The men come in to help with getting the crop in and getting the dyeing process started."

Della paused near several big vats, trays, and racks around the shed area. "Once we finally get the dye down to a paste, it's spread out in the drying shed out of the sunlight. It gets turned a few times a day and then when the paste is really dry and hard, we cut it into squares. Then those squares get more turning as they cure."

Lila looked around at the big work area, the barns and sheds. "I imagine this was an intensive effort when the plantation used to process large quantities of indigo."

"Those were harsh times for those who worked the indigo." Della held out her hands to show bits of blue on her finger tips. "We still get a little dye on our hands now and then, even working small batches of indigo. Back in those old days, slaves and workers arms and hands often got dyed a lasting blue. Of course, we wear long gloves now, which helps, and we know more ways to get stain off."

She turned to Lila. "You know we don't have to grow and harvest indigo anymore here, but we chose to still keep the art going. We're one of the few plantations around here that still produce indigo and our indigo products sell well in the store."

Lila's eyes moved to the field nearby. "When is the indigo crop planted and harvested, Della?"

"Planting is done in the late spring. After a time, you can see the leaves drying out and turning a dark blue, showing it's about time to harvest. We usually do a harvest in August and another in early fall. A lot of folks are growing a little indigo themselves now and doing their own small harvests to make their own dye. Having true dye for fabrics, art work, and crafts is making a comeback. Indigo makes a pretty color." She walked Lila over to a clothesline where a row of assorted blue fabrics hung on a long clothesline, blowing in the breeze.

"There are so many different shades of blue and so many diverse patterns in these fabrics," Lila said, studying them.

Della pointed to an old basket under the shed filled with blue lumps that looked like coal. "After you put the dye cakes in a hot water vat and add fabric to it, the length of time you leave the fabric in determines the shade of indigo blue you get. It can range from these faint light shades to deep, richer hues. The different patterns can be made with tie-dying techniques, with tying, binding, or wax to areas of the fabric to keep the dye off, making patterns like these starbursts, flowers, and stripes. In Japan they call some of the dyeing techniques we use *Shibori*."

She fingered one of the fabrics. "The girls, Isaac's wife Tanya, my daughter Maisie, who's married to Novaleigh's boy Gavin George, and Tommy Lee's wife Gladys, especially like to create artistic pieces like these. They're all good crafters and seamstresses, too. They make pillows, aprons, tea towels, potholders, skirts, and other pretty items to sell in the store. I'm sure you've seen them there."

"I have and they do gifted work."

"Annamae and I do most of the quilt work with dyed fabrics, like the quilt we're working on now. Hand quilting is time consuming and we don't have little children underfoot or jobs off the plantation as Tanya, Maisie, and Gladys do. We've been teaching the girls to quilt, though. They can do it now if they need to."

She led Lila into the shed where Annamae sat at a big quilting frame working.

Annamae waved at them. "Lila, it's a blessing to see you again. You come over here and hug me so I don't have to get up."

Where Della was tall, fit and slim with close-cut graying hair, her mother-in-law, Earl's mother Annamae, was shorter and fuller of figure with a warm beaming smile and bright eyes.

Lila walked over to hug her where the older woman sat seated at the quilting frame.

"Mama, tell Lila about the quilting frame while I go in the side kitchen and get us all some iced tea."

Annamae gestured to a chair near her own for Lila to sit down in.

"This is an old quilting frame, Lila. As you can see, it's four big boards, or long pieces of wood, crossed over each other to create a square frame to stretch the pieced quilt on. The boards are propped over the backs of four old chairs, the old-timey way, and clamps hold the corners together to keep the quilt taut to work on."

Annamae spread her hand out over the stretched quilt, pieced in an assortment of indigo blue squares in different shades. "I'm sitting on this end of the frame to sew and quilt; Della sits on the other side." She pointed to a chair across from her. "This is a big quilt, so two could sit on either side to work on the quilt at once. Other women could sit on the sides here to work, too, like women of the past did when they held a quilting bee and all worked on the same quilt together. The more hands quilting, the quicker a quilt is finished."

Della came back, bringing glasses of tea in old colorful tin glasses, probably valuable antiques now. After handing them around, she set her own glass on an upturned wooden carton beside her chair and sat down to work across from Annamae.

"This is a simple quilt," Annamae said, after drinking some of her tea and setting it on a battered crate beside her own chair. "It's just a quilt of squares and rectangles, placed in rows in a pleasing, repeating pattern. We handstitched the pieces together and now we're finishing the quilt by hand, stitching it to the backing we chose with a soft layer of cotton batting between."

"I read that a handmade, hand-finished quilt is more valuable than one done on a sewing machine," Lila put in.

Annamae smiled. "Most folks don't know all the work and time that goes into creating a quilt, and, of course, our quilts are made with hand-dyed fabrics, adding to the value. We're putting little rows of dark blue, bird-shaped embroidery stitching across the rows of this one, too, adding another unique touch. The price won't be cheap, Lila, but there are those that know the value of work like this who will snatch it up quick enough."

"We often have a waiting list for our quilts," Della added. "We do a lot of custom quilts, too." She pointed to a folded-up quilt on the table nearby. "That quilt with the pattern of dark and light rows of color is a custom quilt. Pretty thing, isn't it?"

"It's gorgeous," Lila said, getting up to walk closer to study it.

The women talked to her then about the stitches they used in quilting and how they could roll up the quilt as they finished each section, resecuring the corners with the clamps.

Lila pulled out her sketch pad to work then, making sketches of the women working from different angles.

"Honey, it sure is nice to see you here at the plantation again," Annamae said after a time. "I remember when you first came over here to play with Edward. Of course, we watched after you, as we did Edward, since Ms. Clarice had usually taken herself off somewhere knowing Edward was well entertained with a playmate."

Della nodded. "I remember, too, how Lila took to the horses right off. Earl and Levi worked with her and soon had her riding as good as Edward, both of them galloping those horses all over the plantation exploring and making happy times."

Lila smiled as she drew. "I enjoyed riding again yesterday."

"We're all glad for you and Edward to be back exercising the horses more," Della added. "We're all too busy to be keeping it up much, and you two always liked it."

Annamae paused in her work, laughing. "Do you remember that time those two were riding along the beach and ran into an old alligator sunning himself on the river bank? Those horses tossed those two kids in the sand and ran off back to the barn. Edward and Lila came running back to the house soon, too, crying and scared."

Della snorted. "Gators are nothing to mess with. I was just glad to see those two back safe and well."

The women chattered away, entertaining Lila with old remembrances of times when she and Edward were younger, some stories Lila had forgotten, others she remembered and laughed over.

She pulled her chair a little closer to the quilting frame after a time to sketch some close-up pictures of the quilt and of the women's hands stitching.

Della sent her a fond look. "I also remember when you and Edward got sweet on each other later on, trying so hard to be careful Big Sam and Ms. Clarice didn't see anything of your feelings."

Lila knew her eyes widened.

"Oh, honey, we saw your affections blooming, but we acted like we didn't see a thing and never said anything. We all knew how Big Sam had every little aspect of Edward's life planned out and that he and Clarice wouldn't have been pleased to see Edward getting overly interested in any one girl with his future charted out in detail as it was." Della hesitated. "We also knew Sam's way of keeping Edward in line with his wishes was a harsh one, too."

Annamae snorted. "I'm glad you burned that old whipping belt he used on the boy."

Lila winced, remembering some of the times when Edward was too sore to ride horseback after a particularly harsh beating, and usually over something not worthy of physical discipline of any kind.

"Why was he so cruel?" she asked. "And why did Edward's mother, Clarice, never intervene on his behalf? I never understood that or why they neither one showed him more genuine love and affection."

Annamae shook her head. "They were a couple with their own problems. They neither one married for the right reasons, either, and then Clarice had trouble bearing babies. She lost three after Edward. Did you know that?"

"No," Lila said.

"You'll find their little graves in the family cemetery. Two other sons and a daughter. I felt for her then," Annamae said, pausing in her sewing. "Big Sam only saw it as a weakness. He wasn't kind to her when she lost the babies, often when Clarice was right far along carrying them, but with it too early to save them."

"What caused her problem?" Lila asked.

"At first, they just called her high risk for bearing, suggested it might be nerves and stress. That angered Sam who wanted more heirs." She hesitated, thinking back. "In time the doctors said they thought she lost her babies because she had a weak cervix, that would open before it should and caused the babies to come too early. They said the risk would grow greater with future babies, including the risk to Clarice's health, miscarrying so often. I recall Sam and Clarice fought over that."

"That's sad," Lila commented.

"Clarice would get depressed with each loss, go into a decline, while Sam just got angry." Annamae stopped to drink a little more of her tea.

Della sighed. "I always wondered why Clarice didn't cling to Edward, love and nurture him more in those times, after she lost those other babies. But oddly she pulled away from him after her losses, left caring for him more and more to me and Annamae, took off to Charleston to stay with her sister for longer and longer visits."

"Her sister was widowed by then," Annamae added. "When her husband died young, she moved back into the Alston family home in downtown Charleston where she and Clarice were raised. The sisters' parents passed early so the two women had the old home to themselves. Eula comforted Clarice in those hard times, took her home with her, loved on her and tended to her, and Eula formed a hatred for Sam then. It was rare Eula ever came here when Sam was around, and I heard Eula tell Sam he wasn't welcome in her home even for a visit."

"I don't remember Edward going to Eula's often," Lila said, pausing in the sketch she was working on.

"No, Eula and the family home in Charleston were Clarice's escape world. Especially when Sam started catting around more. That was an embarrassment to her. Edisto is a little place. Things get around."

Della shook her head. "The worst time was when Sam went after Tanya that summer Edward came home from college after his first year away. Tanya and Isaac were engaged by then, spending a lot of time together and Tanya came over to Indigo often, knowing she'd soon be moving here."

Annamae closed her eyes. "I'll never forget that awful day. Big Sam found Tanya out in the stable alone, looking for Isaac who was supposed to meet her there. He tried to force himself on her, had her down on the hay in an empty stall trying to separate her from her clothes." She shook her head at the bad memory. "Blessedly, Isaac came in and caught him. They had words, came to blows, but Isaac wouldn't stay at the plantation after that. He left that very day, went to stay with a friend, found a job in Georgetown and took Tanya there after they married. I suppose if Sam hadn't died, they'd still be there."

"It was Edward who called and asked Isaac to come back." Della tied off a thread. "Lordy, Lordy. Big Sam was sure full of the old devil back then. That was a hard time," she remembered. "He'd even been giving our girl Maisie some looks that Earl and I worried over, so we sent her off the plantation to live with my sister. I just didn't want to take a chance on anything happening with her, too, the way he'd taken to preying on young girls."

Upset, Lila felt herself tense.

"You knew about all this, didn't you, Lila?" Della asked, noticing her discomfort.

Lila couldn't find words to answer.

"Honey, you've gone as pale as a ghost," Della added. "I know Isaac told me that you knew about all this."

Lila found tears trying to well up now.

"Ahh, sweet girl," Annamae said in a soft voice, reaching a hand out toward her. "You're remembering the time Big Sam came after you in the folly that same summer, not long before Edward went back to college, upset over Isaac and Tanya leaving and angry with his father."

Della put a hand to her heart, interrupting her. "Oh, Lila, I'm so sorry to remind you of that time. Please forgive me."

Lila couldn't find words and in shock, she let her sketch pad drop off her lap.

"Honey, that was a very hurtful moment for you," Annamae

said in a soothing voice. "We all knew how Sam was acting back then, even on his own plantation with those he knew and should have respected and loved. My Levi had even started following you around when you came to ride, although we never expected he would harm you."

"It's a good thing Levi was following her around," Della put in.

"It was," Annamae continued, her voice kind. "Levi saw you'd gone to the folly that summer day, Lila, and he hung around, keeping an eye on you while working to repair some fence line. He saw Big Sam ride down the path toward the folly. Sam obviously spotted the horse you'd been riding tied up there, and he got off and went in the folly. Of course, Sam could have just been checking to see if you were all right, but Levi crept up closer to the folly to look and be sure."

Lila hung her head, weeping now.

"Honey, it's good to remember this and put it in the past," Annamae said. "We all know Sam pushed himself on you and that you were scared and crying at his attentions. However, you need to remember and take comfort in the fact that he didn't rape you, girl, and he didn't take his actions any further than some forced kissing and groping because Levi hollered out and interrupted him."

Della leaned forward to add, "It was smart of Levi to call out to Sam that there was an urgent problem on the plantation he needed to come see about, telling him one of the mares was about ready to foal."

"Yes, Big Sam knew that mare could drop any time and he was counting on top dollar from her foal," Annamae continued. "Sam knew, too, that if the mare dropped too early the foal might have a low birth weight, be weak, have incomplete bone development, maybe even get sepsis. Hearing that mare might be in trouble, he took off with Levi for the stable."

Lila covered her face, weeping harder now.

Annamae got up from the quilting frame to come over to squat down and put her arms around her. "Honey, look at me. Levi said he told you later he'd called Sam away so he wouldn't harm you, and he said he warned you it might be good for you not to come to ride without letting someone on the plantation know you were here. Why are you so upset and crying about this?"

She leaned against Annamae sobbing. "It was so awful and embarrassing. It was Edward's father. His very own father, grabbing at me, pushing me down on the bench, saying all those awful things to me, telling me I wasn't a good influence on Edward, that he was going to fix it so Edward would never want me."

"That awful man," Della said, coming to hug on Lila, too.

Annamae lifted Lila's chin to look at her after a minute. "Who did you talk to about all this after it happened, Lila? Did you tell your mother and your sisters to let them comfort you?"

She shook her head, still crying.

"Did you talk to Edward and tell him?"

Lila covered her face and wept more.

Annamae got up and pulled her chair next to Lila's. "Sweet girl, I'm guessing now that you never told anyone, that you locked this up and kept it all inside, ashamed and afraid no one would understand. Maybe even believing people might blame you, think you encouraged Big Sam to come after you."

Lila began to cry again.

"Did you think we didn't know?" Della asked her.

"I wasn't sure," she said on a sob. "I didn't know what Levi had seen or if he told you anything. No one ever said anything to me afterward. And I was so ashamed."

Lila looked at them in anguish. "Edward's father said before he left the folly that he'd be watching for me and would finish what he started if I didn't stay away from his son. He threatened me, even slapped me before he left. He cursed and called me some awful names." Her voice broke. "I was always so afraid to come here later for any reason."

She saw the two women look at each other and shake their heads, upset at her revelations. Della took her hands. "Lila, we loved on Tanya after Big Sam tried to rape her," Della said then. "We let her know it wasn't her fault what happened. We cleaned her up and comforted her. We made sure she knew none of Sam's ugly words to her held any truth and that his words and actions were just the ugliness of the old devil coming out of him. I want you to know those same things. All that happened then wasn't your fault. No one who learned of it would think so. You need to know that, Lila, and you need to let the guilt and shame of that time go, honey."

Annamae wiped Lila's face with a scrap of fabric. "Sweet girl, you need to find a time to share this with your mother and your sisters. It will be healing for you, and it will explain a lot. You need to share it with Edward, too. He was confused at why you wouldn't come to the plantation again that summer, why you pulled away from him. You hid part of your life from the person who wanted to be a part of your life back then, from the person who loved you and still does. It's easy to feel the love is still there between you and Edward, but that love and trust is broken from all the hurt you've both been through. From the betrayals and pain and shame."

"Life is too short for shame, Lila," Della added. "We've all had our times of hurt, but we need to free ourselves from it by not hiding it away, by thinking we wouldn't be loved if anyone knew of our humiliations and sorrows. It's time to free yourself. You've hidden this away for far too long. You may be grieving and crying right now but you'll be glad later all this came out to the light."

"Della's right, Lila, and you'll find that scripture about 'joy coming in the morning' to be true once you think on it," Annamae counseled. "I'm not sorry we helped this matter come to the light for you today. It was needed and I'd say God orchestrated it to set you free of this."

The two Jessup women talked more to her then, sharing instances in their own lives that had been hard to get past. They shared hurts and wrongs they'd experienced, helping her to see that others had walked through pain, fear, and suffering but in time had put it all in the past and found new happiness and new joy. They prayed with her, and their words comforted her and helped to dispel her embarrassment.

As Lila headed home later, her mind was filled with mixed

emotions and unanswered questions. Had God brought her home to help get her free from the embarrassment and shame locked inside her all this time? Had He brought her back for this time of healing? To help free her from her hurtful memories? The words of a Psalm came to her as she prayed softly in the quiet of her living room later: *"In thee, O Lord, do I put my trust; let me never be ashamed: deliver me in thy righteousness."* Maybe God had graciously done just that, delivered her in His righteousness, knowing she needed it.

CHAPTER 10

The morning after Edward had met with Raymond Maybank at the law firm, his phone rang early as he sat having coffee in the kitchen.

Seeing it was Waylon Jenkins, he picked up the call. "Good morning, Waylon. How are you?"

"Good," Waylon answered, "but I was wondering if you could come down to the lodge right now. Do you still have your boat or one you can borrow? If not, I can come to get you."

"You sound upset," Edward replied. "Is anything wrong?"

"Lonnie Culler with the Edisto Police Department is here. There was another fire on the island yesterday afternoon. He wants to talk to several of us who live on the northeast end of the island as several of the fires have occurred near us. You remember the last one was at Sunnyside."

"I do. Where was the fire last night?"

"At Cassina Point, much too close for comfort," he answered. "Again, it was started in a shed but spread to a barn this time and threatened one of the guest houses and even the plantation house before it was contained. It's concerning. I've called Hal Jenkins to come meet with us, too. Lonnie has talked with others already. He'll explain when you get here, if you can come."

"I can be there in about fifteen or twenty minutes. We have two boats for the plantation's use in the boathouse and another that was my father's. The Jessups maintain and use them all and tell me they are in good condition. I'll be there soon."

"Good. Thank you."

Edward called Isaac to check with him about the boats.

"All are in good shape to run down to Waylon's place at the island," Isaac assured him. "I'll meet you at the boathouse to help you get launched."

Grabbing his jacket hanging by the back door, Edward set off from the house, down the pathway through the gardens, and toward the family's dock and boathouse on the river.

Isaac met him there and gestured to one of the boats. "Your father just bought this new Pursuit before he died. You might as well take it. The boat has a deep vee hull, two Yamaha outboards, plus a hardtop and a tempered windshield. Nice for a cool morning. It's a fine boat." He grinned. "Your father always did like nice boats and cars."

"You want to come with me for this meeting?" Edward asked.

"Not unless you need me to. My current "To Do" list is long today with spring planting ongoing." He untied the boat. "Come give us an update when you get back though."

"I will."

Isaac hesitated. "Lila called to say she had work to do in the gift shop today and wouldn't be over to sketch at the plantation. You might want to stop by to see her. Mom said she got a little upset yesterday reminiscing with them about that bad time with Tanya and Maisie. It seems like all of us carry bad memories and problems we need to work out related to your father and his way of doing things."

Edward frowned as he climbed down into the boat. "I'll check on Lila after my meeting."

Isaac laughed then. "My boy Lawson said the other day that if Big Sam got into heaven, he'd probably have to do a lot of remedial classes for a long time."

"Yeah, I'd say that's true." Edward grinned as he settled in at the helm of the big boat. "I'll see you later."

The Pursuit was a beautiful luxury boat and a dream to drive. Edward enjoyed his run down the river, having almost forgotten the joy of being out on the water. He pulled in at the island's new dock, tied up his boat and made his way up the ramp and pathway to the lodge.

Waylon met him at the door and led him inside to where Burke and a group of men sat around a big captain's table in the lodge's main room. He gestured to Edward as the two of them got to the table.

"This is Edward Calhoun of Indigo," he said, introducing him. "And, Edward, you know my wife Burke and Henry Bouls, our caretaker, and I'm sure you remember Hal Jenkins from up at the Jenkins Landing." He gestured to the other man. "This is Lonnie Culler with the Edisto police department."

Lonnie stood to shake his hand. "Thanks for coming down, Edward. With the incidences of fires escalating, I've been trying to talk to all the plantation owners this morning. All the fires on Edisto so far have occurred at different plantations around the island—none at other sites, showing a pattern in the arsons occurring."

Edward sat down at the table after shaking Lonnie's hand. "Do you have evidence at this time that these fires are arson?"

"We weren't sure at first, but some specialists came after the last two fires and found evidence showing the fires were set deliberately."

Edward nodded. "I know fire and arson investigators can thoroughly examine a scene and determine if the cause of a fire was accidental or deliberate."

Lonnie grinned, sipping on a cup of coffee. "I remember now Waylon said you're an attorney. The team that came out is with the Charleston Fire Investigation Team. They found evidence that an accelerant had been used in the last two fires—the one at Sunnyside and this one at Cassina Point. Those two fires, and the two previous ones, all started at old sheds or outbuildings on the properties, but this time the investigators found a line of accelerate from the shed to one of Cassina's guest houses. The house sustained some damage but it didn't burn to the ground, with the fire caught early. The shed burned to the ground, though, and a nearby barn. You can imagine we're concerned about this matter with these plantation homes occupied and historic sites, too."

Edward got up to pour himself a cup of coffee from the sideboard by the table.

"Four fires aren't a good thing," Burke put in. "It seems like this arsonist, or arsonists if it's a team, seem to be enjoying setting these fires around the island at old plantation homes. Why would they do that, Edward? Have you ever been involved legally in situations like this as an attorney?"

"A few times," he said, thinking back. "Generally, the arson cases I got involved with were criminal acts where properties were torched to collect insurance. Most arsons occur for that reason. But we all learned about the firebugs or pyromaniacs who deliberately set fires, too."

"The investigators think we have a firebug, or a group of fire setters, going here, probably with some kind of impulse control disorder that causes them to want to set fires for fun or for revenge of some sort," Lonnie added. "To me the main point is that these people are not mentally healthy. They get a kick out of intentionally and repeatedly setting fires."

"So, you believe they will set more fires?" Hal asked.

"The investigators think so," he answered.

"Do you think this is a gang of some kind?" Henry leaned forward to ask. "Do you think these people will cause other types of damage? Steal things, carry weapons, and threaten people?"

"I'm not sure," Lonnie replied. He turned to Edward. "Do these arsonists move on to other types of crime?"

"Generally, an arsonist who sets fires deliberately works alone, not in a group. Many are social isolates, troubled with other behavioral problems, and most are adolescents under eighteen."

Burke looked shocked. "You mean most of the people who set fires deliberately are basically children themselves?"

"Sadly, that's statistically true. They also tend to have a 'burn pattern' as you're seeing here," Edward explained. "From what

Lonnie told us, all the fires on Edisto so far have been of structures, mostly vacant sheds or barns, but threatening other buildings nearby. Some arsonists target vehicles while others target specific kinds of buildings or structures."

"Do you think this might be a racial issue with the target buildings all at old plantations?" Waylon asked. "Perhaps a young black person?"

"I wondered about that, too," Lonnie admitted.

Edward shook his head. "Probably not. Statistically ninety percent of arsonists are white adolescent boys or white young men, rarely ever black and rarely ever women."

"What else can you tell me about arsonists?" Lonnie asked. "I've never encountered this since I've worked in the police department."

Edward searched his memory. "Most arsonists have other mental issues and they often set fires for revenge, anger, or spite. They are not rational in what they do. They seem to have little remorse for their actions, and they often have been in trouble in other areas, like in school or in their community."

"The investigators told us an arsonist will set a fire as a way to relieve built-up tension, anxiety or arousal," Lonnie told them. "They get some kind of weird satisfaction or emotional relief in setting a fire."

Burke sighed. "That sounds all too much like the sick individual we dealt with last year who killed with no natural remorse."

"Most criminals, of all types, justify their actions, Burke, even when their ways are heinous." Edward smiled. "It's probably to mitigate their guilt in doing wrong."

"Well, with all this psychology aside, we've got ourselves a real problem here at Edisto until this arsonist is caught."

"Do you have any suspects?" Edward asked.

Lonnie frowned. "One, but unfortunately no proof. We caught a young man at the fire site yesterday, going through the ruins, snooping around, his footprints all over the place. His name is George Souder. He lives up at Adams Run, but he swears he knows nothing about how the fire started. He admitted he came to look around, probably hoping to find something to thieve. George has a record of trouble with fights, shoplifting, and past school problems. We'll be keeping an eye on him, but we can't arrest him with no more evidence than suspicion."

Lonnie pulled out a couple of photo copies to pass around. "This is George, twenty years old now. If you see him around your property anywhere, you give me a call. In fact, let me know if you see anyone suspicious around your property and keep a more careful watch than you usually do at your sheds, barns, side buildings, and at your homes. This arsonist tends to target vacant properties, but like most criminals, repeated crimes often escalate to worse. That's what we're worried most about."

"We'll be watchful," Hal Jenkins said. "Cassina Point, the plantation where this guy hit this time, is not far from Edward's and my places. Sunnyside, the last plantation where a fire was set, isn't far from us either. I don't like the idea of these places being centralized around our part of the island."

"It's worrisome," Henry agreed, standing. "If we're through meeting though, I need to head to the back dock. I'm taking a few of the Inn's guests, who have some experience on the water, kayaking for an hour or two before lunch."

"I need to leave, too," Lonnie said. "I want to stop to chat with a few other plantation owners around here, like Raymond Maybank at the law firm that I haven't contacted yet. Each of you spread the word, too, if you will. I don't want anyone getting hurt before we find this firebug, and I sure don't want to see any of our old historic properties torched. We're getting enough media notice already. I don't want more."

Hal, Lonnie, and Henry all left, and Burke went to check on Drew, who was starting to wake up from his nap.

Edward smiled at Waylon then. "I like your place here, Waylon, and I'm still getting used to the idea of you and Burke being married."

"I always had a thing for Burke from the time she was about twelve. I just never acted on it. Lloyd warned me off, picking up on it." He drank the last of his coffee. "When I came home last spring, I found my feelings even stronger than before. In a little confrontation, I learned Burke had carried feelings for me, too. Isn't life a funny thing? The two of us holding all that inside?"

"People can do that." He looked away from Waylon.

"Seems to me you showed a little interest in Lila Deveaux at church on Sunday. Do you wanna talk about it? You might remember I knew the two of you were getting sweet on each other before you went away to college. When I was home on leave once, you talked to me about it, worrying what your father would think or do if he found out. You asked me to keep it to myself. I did, Edward, but I wondered what happened. The two of you seemed like a good match to me, always happy together and well-suited. Even as toddlers you hit it off."

Edward sighed. "You were off in the Navy that summer when everything blew up with my father. He'd always been controlling, overly strict and harsh, and you know there was no love lost between the two of us or with my own mother. That last summer he tried to rape Isaac's fiancé, caught her alone in the stable. Isaac fortunately interrupted the scene. But it ran Isaac and Tanya off from Indigo, caused a lot of hurt and sorrow for the Jessups."

He stood to pace to the window to look outside. "Word got around about what happened, too. My mother made excuses for my father, tried to put the blame on Tanya. I lost so much respect for them both then, and as you know I had little to begin with. It was an awful time of disillusion and disappointment for me and others. It impacted my relationship with Lila, too. She acted different, avoided even coming over to the plantation again. I left, heading back for college, not wanting to ever come back to the island."

Waylon came over to stand beside him. "I know from a few of our talks over the years that getting away to college was good for you, that you made strong ties and new healthy friendships there. You know you were like a little brother to me growing up. I'm proud of the man you've become. You had some hardships to overcome."

Edward turned to him. "I appreciate the genuine affection and wisdom you always shared with me, the good counsel when I needed it. If I never said thank you before, I want to say it now."

"You're welcome." Waylon smiled. "Times change. You have the opportunity now to make a new life here at Edisto if you want, maybe to see if Lila is still holding some of those old feelings for you locked up inside, like I believe you still hold for her."

He grinned. "I'm checking that out, Waylon. I can't deny to you I still carry love for Lila Deveaux. It didn't take me long to see that, but a lot of trust has been lost between us over the years. And, mercy, Lila has been away in a religious community much of the time. I'm not sure how that's impacted her."

"You ran away. She ran away. Maybe there are some links in that. You're wise to explore it. Will you stay here, manage the plantation, go to work at the law firm?"

"The day I first came back home, I would have said emphatically no. Now I'm more torn, but still not sure of my way, of what I should do. I'm thinking about it, praying about it."

"That's good. The right answers will come to you."

"Thanks for that confidence in me, Waylon."

Waylon walked back to settle into a chair. "Do you think Lila would go with you back to Nashville if that is the choice you make?"

Edward lifted his hands, coming back to sit down, too. "I have no idea. I haven't gotten far enough with Lila to know what she wants."

"Well, she's working up at the lighthouse gift shop today. She told Burke she needed a day to catch up there, so I imagine if you walked up to the gift shop before heading back home, you might find her there. Look at some of her art work while you're there, see what she's done with the gift shop, ask her to show you her studio at the cottage. Learn more about her work. It's astonishing, Edward. Highly detailed, realistic and illustrative, with a softness to it and a combination of colors and depth that make you want to stop and look at it several times again."

"I saw some of her sketches she did at Indigo and she gave me a copy of the book she illustrated for Myron Andric."

"Those detailed drawings and paintings of birds are only one dimension of her work, but they don't show the depth and diversity of what she can do." Waylon shook his head. "I had no idea when she was a little girl doodling in notebooks of the artist she would become."

"I thought about that, too," Edward agreed. "I felt a little guilty I hadn't fully appreciated her gift." He smiled as he stood to leave. "I'll walk up to see her and ask to see more of her paintings. I'm sure we've both grown and changed over these years while we've both been away. I know I have."

Waylon stood and winked at him as they started toward the door. "A good and beautiful woman is always worth checking out, Edward."

He laughed. "You're right, and you can be sure I'm going to explore the possibilities of that."

CHAPTER 11

Lila sat on a stool at the gift store's checkout counter sorting through a new order of silver seashell bracelets and necklaces she'd ordered for the shop. They sold for a higher price than some of the cute, colorful, less expensive jewelry she carried, but many of the guests at the inn bought these nicer pieces.

Busy at her tasks, she was surprised to look up suddenly to see Edward standing at the door of the gift shop.

She gathered her composure and smiled at him. "What a pleasure to see you. What are you doing here on the island?"

"I came for a meeting with Waylon, Burke, Henry, Hal, and Lonnie Culler with the Edisto police department. There was another fire yesterday and it's raising concern."

She leaned forward. "Where was it? Was anyone hurt?"

"It was at Cassina Point Plantation, not far from Hal's and my place. No one was hurt, and only a shed and barn burned, along with some damage to a guest cottage. If the fire hadn't been caught early, it would have spread, possibly even to the main house."

"Here, come sit down." She pointed to another stool near the counter. "I'm so sorry to hear about this. Tell me what you know."

"Well, this is the fourth fire. The first two started at sheds or outbuildings at Brookland and Middleton plantations across the highway, the third at Sunnyside nearer to us, and now this last one at Cassina Point, coming even closer. Arson investigators came in after the last two fires, confirming they had been deliberately set."

"Who would do this?" she asked.

"Someone with problems." Edward filled her in on the conversation held at the lodge earlier and the understandings about arsonists they'd shared.

"Do they need any help at Cassina?" Lila asked. "I know they hold a lot of weddings and events there."

"I think they're good," he replied. "Probably very grateful, too, that someone spotted the fire at the shed early."

"Are there any suspects?"

He told her about George Souder, found foraging around the ruins, his footprints everywhere, but with no other evidence. "Lonnie asked all of us to be watchful for anyone suspicious around our properties and to take extra precautions."

She glanced out the window. "It's been dry at Edisto this month, too, and breezy. That makes any fire more dangerous."

"The Jessup men mentioned that point the other day. I'll fill them in on this when I get back, and I want to check to be sure we have fire-fighting equipment in good order and easy to get to if needed."

Lila felt her mouth drop open. "Oh, my goodness. My mind hadn't moved ahead to consider Indigo might be targeted, but of course it could."

"We won't believe for that," he replied, getting up to walk around, looking at things in the gift shop. "I heard you'd fixed up the gift shop to be more attractive. It looks really nice, Lila. I can see your artistic touch and creativity everywhere."

"Thank you," she said, not sure what else to add.

He stopped to look at different things as he walked around.

She slid off her stool to go walk with him. "I painted most all the old shelves, racks, and furniture pieces white to brighten the décor and to make them stand out more crisply against the wood floors and brick chimney. I put in track lighting, too." She pointed up at the ceiling. "This is an old building, small and charming, but it had poor lighting."

"You arranged everything in an attractive way, making it more organized than before…jewelry all in one place, postcards and gift cards on racks on the wall, gift items like these cute collectible lighthouses all in a lit shelf, coasters and mugs tucked around colorful plates and signs on the table here. I see you moved the T-shirts, hats, and other clothing items off to a corner."

She laughed. "People will find those shirts and hats wherever I put them. They're big sellers with paintings of the Deveaux Lighthouse screen printed on the front."

"Are they your paintings?" he asked, going to look closer at one of the shirts.

"Yes, and they're certainly better than the old paintings I created long ago."

"Show me some more of your work," he said. "Are the paintings in that alcove all yours?"

"Yes." She followed him closer. "I put mostly sea coast related paintings here, along with gift cards picturing the lighthouse, inn, guest cottages, trails around the island, the lodge, and marina. People like souvenirs." She picked up a packet of mixed greeting cards. "This is a favorite seller, with a variety of paintings to take home as a souvenir."

He walked closer to the paintings on the wall. "These paintings are so beautiful and appealing, many whispering of stories untold, like this one of the young girl looking out to sea or this with a cat asleep on a sunny porch. I like this painting, too, of the moon over the night sea and this of colorful umbrellas dotting the beach behind the sea oats."

"I'm glad you like my work," Lila said in a quiet voice, hating to let him know how touched she was at his comments.

He turned and kissed her on the forehead, surprising her. "I am humbled by your gift and to realize how little I saw it developing when we were younger. Forgive me for that and for not encouraging you more, for not having any vision of where your talent could take you." He put a hand to her cheek. "You shouldn't wonder anymore why God brought you back home, Lila. Surely, He wanted this gift to grow and develop like this, to give so much joy and pleasure to others."

She stepped back from his touch, afraid she might cry. Her emotions were still stirred and unsettled after her day at Indigo with the Jessup women yesterday.

Edward smiled. "Will you take me to see your studio at your cottage and show me your work there? I want to see more of what you can do."

"If you like," she answered, not sure how to refuse him without sounding rude and ungrateful at his interest. "Let me put the jewelry away I was sorting first if you don't mind."

"I'll look around more while you do."

From the counter, she watched him stop and look at the bookshelf where she kept a few local books, including some about lighthouses. He spent time looking at the wooden carvings of birds, too. She remembered he'd always loved the birds around the island.

As she finished cleaning up and getting her purse from under the counter, Edward suddenly laughed, pointing to a colorful sign with a lighthouse and quote on it. "I love this saying," he said, reading it out loud. "*In high tide or low tide, I'll be by your side.* Maybe we should adopt that as our new motto." His voice softened. "I don't ever want to lose our friendship again, Lila."

She smiled. "Come, and I'll take you over to my studio." Letting him out the door, she locked it behind him.

He started down the road to her cottage with that familiar, easy gait of his. Like herself today, he wore jeans and a pull-over sweater on this cool April morning, a rich brown one that matched his eyes. It felt so familiar and dear to have Edward around and near her again, as if she'd regained an old part of herself that she'd lost.

At the door to her little house, she let him in, conscious he'd never been here before, and aware she was alone here with him. To break the spell of that thought, she said, "I have strawberry punch in the refrigerator I made yesterday and shortbread cookies with a touch of cinnamon and vanilla in them. I remember you like both."

"I do." He turned to grin at her. "Can I look around downstairs while you fix it?"

"Sure," she said, a little embarrassed but glad she'd made her bed and cleaned up earlier before going to the gift shop. "My cottage is small, you know, so it won't take you long to see everything."

He joined her in the little kitchen after a short time. "It's a great place and it feels like you in every corner, especially with all the red in the decor. You always loved red. I remember that."

She turned away so he wouldn't see her blush at that remark, remembering what Celeste had said about people who loved red having a passionate nature. Hers was certainly nipping at her consciousness right now and she was more aware of Edward's every movement than she should be. Whatever was wrong with her?

They carried their iced drinks and a plate of shortbread cookies back into the small living area. Lila carefully chose her favorite easy chair, giving Edward the sofa, not wanting to put herself too close to him right now.

Gratefully, instead of asking her about her visit to Indigo yesterday, Edward told her about his visit to the law firm. "I learned so much I didn't know from Raymond Maybank," he said after a time. "Many things he shared explained my father and his ways a little more. Not that the knowledge excuses him for so many of his attitudes and actions, but it helped me to learn that others saw my father's problems clearly and had their challenges, too, in working with him."

Lila nibbled on a cookie, listening.

"It's sad that a man, who was as brilliant and accomplished as my father, had so many problems, and was too arrogant to see them and too egoistic to change. In everything he always thought his ways were right, his opinions best, his plans superior to others. And he was so unkind, Lila. I'm learning that more and more, and I'm so grateful others have shared with me how much like my grandfather I am, rather than anything like my father."

"That's true, Edward. Don't let the enemy torture you and make you think you'll ever become like your father."

"That idea has scared me a few times in the past, when people said things like 'The apple doesn't fall far from the tree.'"

She shook her head. "People often don't think about the things they say. And their words can be hurtful."

"Yes, like that scripture about picking out the darts of harsh words. I can't remember where it is exactly. But words can feel like darts and wounds, don't you think?"

"I do, and we need to pick those darts out, to let God heal our wounds and hearts and move on."

He grinned then. "Let's move on upstairs so I can see your studio, and then I want to take a walk down the beach before I need to head back to Indigo. I haven't walked on the beach here for a long time. Will you go with me?"

"Sure," she said, glad to be heading outdoors soon and away from the intimacy of the two of them in her little cottage alone.

As she led Edward upstairs to her studio, she remembered the vows of chastity she'd made at St. Mary's, committing herself to a life of consecrated celibacy, giving her love to God above all. She almost laughed at the remembrance. Her flesh was certainly getting the upper hand now. She hoped that fact was all right with the Lord.

In the studio, Lila shifted her mind toward the questions Edward was asking her about her work.

"You've just started this painting." He pointed to a large sheet of watercolor paper taped to one of her work tables. "I see the sketch of the scene you plan to paint, and you've laid in some of the background color of the sky and trees. Do you always begin a work like this? I see photos and little side sketches scattered around. I assume those help you know where you want to go in the painting."

"That's a good way to describe it, Edward. I do a lot of planning before I paint, then I lightly sketch the picture with an art pencil whose lines will disappear later when I paint. I've seen and envisioned ahead the scene I want to create, so my sketch provides a skeleton for the painting I'll begin to layer over the paper little by little. In a way, I feel like I tell stories in paint." She smiled. "I also enjoy music in the background as I work, lyrical music with no voice to it, often piano music that feels like the scene I'm working on."

"I want to come and watch a painting happen one day," he said, beginning to walk around the studio, picking up her paintings stacked around the room or stopping to see different ones on the wall. "Would it hinder your work for me to watch?"

She thought about it. "I don't know, but we could try it some time." She paused. "Perhaps outside. I do a lot of plein air paintings outside. I'll probably do one or two at Indigo next week."

He moved a little closer, smoothing a hand over her cheek. "That might be safer," he said in a husky voice. "This small creative space gives me too many creative ideas."

Lila knew her eyes widened, and she gasped faintly.

He winked at her then. "We'd better go walking, Sister Anne. I think we could both use a little crisp fresh air."

Edward chased her down the bank to the beach a few minutes later and the two laughed and walked along the sand, reminiscing about their years growing up and about their times playing here at the island with her sisters, and with Waylon and his sister Sally Ann.

Lila was soon comfortable again with Edward, and she commented, "Isn't it interesting how easy it has been to slip back into our old friendship when it's been over six years since we walked along the beach together?"

"I think old friends always know us better than anyone else," Edward replied. "Old friends have known you at your worst and at your best. They know your past already so you don't have to try so hard to explain it or hide it."

They'd taken off their shoes and left them on a bench earlier. Now, they walked along barefooted in the soft sand, enjoying the day that had warmed quickly after a chilly night, the sun a bright blaze in the sky overhead.

Lila smiled at Edward. "Maybe old friends simply know us inside-out where others only know what we show them on the outside but don't really know us inside at all."

"That's true somewhat, but we grow into different people, too, as time moves along. I once thought I'd hate being an attorney, and I only studied law because it was the only college major my father would pay for. I planned in my heart that when I graduated later, I'd go off in another direction entirely, choose another vocation. But as I studied law, I loved it. I really found myself in it." Edward frowned. "It kind of vexed me that I ended up loving what my father pushed on me."

"Well, remember your grandfather and great grandfather had been attorneys, too. Careers often run in families, teachers begetting teachers, musicians begetting musicians."

He raised his eyebrows. "Who was an artist before you?"

She laughed. "I don't know. I guess I'm a black sheep. My parents were certainly shocked when I decided to enter the Community of St. Mary."

Edward took her hand. "Well, I'm glad you came home. That we reconnected."

"Oh, look, Edward." Lila pulled her hand free to reach down to pick up a small clam shell still connected at the hinge. "We're like this butterfly coquina shell. Life pulled us apart and the waves of life beat us up and tossed us around, but here we are still connected anyway after all this time."

"That shell is a pretty purplish color." He studied it. "The color reminds me of that purple velvet prom dress you wore to senior prom. Do you remember that dress? I certainly do, and I remember how it felt under my hands when we danced and how you felt, close to me when we were dancing in that old gym with the lights low."

"Edward," she chided him, but smiled as she did. "I wore that dress to your senior prom, if you remember, and not to mine. You weren't home from college in time the next year for my prom, and I went with a sweet boy I worked with on the school annual staff."

"Should I be jealous? Did you wear the same dress?"

"No to both questions. But Thomas Ravenel was a nice boy, and very shy. I was probably the only girl he had the nerve to ask out."

He laughed. "I doubt that."

"It's true. I wasn't fast like most of the girls. I wouldn't have been a fun date for many of the boys either, who wanted to go out drinking and partying after the prom."

"You always had that moral streak, even as a girl."

"Was that wrong? Is it wrong to hold strong principles?" She sighed. "I troubled over that as a girl, being different, being close to God, knowing He talked to me sometimes. I always loved my times with Him but no one really understood that. So, I mostly kept it to myself. Even my own sisters rolled their eyes over my thoughts and comments many times."

"I was different, too, Lila, with such a harsh father. And my mother Clarice had no warmth, no welcoming nature to offer to any of my friends I invited over. Most didn't want to come back after a few visits." He kicked at a shell. "I knew my friends sort of felt sorry for me in a way, even though my family was well to do."

Edward waded into the edge of a wave washing up on the shore, but then stepped back quickly with the water still cold in April. Walking on, he added, "Even talking with Raymond the other day, I remembered how comfortable it was to visit in their home where there was so much easy love and affection, so much laughter."

"I like the Maybanks. They go to Trinity Church. Raymond's wife Dora is a truly sweet, good woman."

She slowed to look at him. "Will you stay at Edisto now, Edward, to work with Raymond and Hudson Maybank at the firm? They are good people. And you know the Jessups want you to stay. If you sell, they might lose their places at the plantation, lose their homes. I'd hate to see that. They are such fine people and I would miss them."

Edward stopped, rubbing his neck and looking out to sea. "It's hard when you feel pressured to follow a life course without feeling you have any choice in the matter."

"Is it so objectionable?" she asked after a few moments. "The idea of continuing the legacy of the Indigo Plantation your family has owned for so many years? To have good people like the Jessups to work for you? To help in a fine law firm like the Maybank-Calhoun Firm in that gorgeous old building, with its sterling reputation?" She couldn't help laughing a little. "It's not like someone is suggesting you go to work in a dark mine with cruel and heartless people, where you would only know harsh days, sorrows, and unhappiness."

He sent her an annoying glance. "I also have other fine options to consider, Lila. Other honorable people at Vanderbilt who want me to come back to the clinic to work, who want me to teach at the college. Is it so wrong I should wonder if that isn't a better life direction for me?"

She stayed quiet, not answering.

Edward turned and put his hands on her arms, looking down at her. "If we grew more serious, would you go with me to Nashville? Would you share that life with me? You could do your art there, too."

She stepped back from him. "Until you find your own direction and get peace in your heart, I couldn't consider any of those questions. God has a best plan for each of us, Edward. You need to seek and search to know the way God wants you to go. Only when you can know that way with clarity and surety would it be time for you to think of joining your life to anyone else's."

He turned to walk back up the beach then, quiet for a little while, and Lila could tell he was irritated, too.

As they stopped to sit on the old bench to put their shoes back on, he turned to look at her. "The truth is annoying sometimes, Lila."

"Yes, I know it is."

"You've always been honest with me though," he added and then grinned. "Maybe I'll thank you for that later, if not right now."

She pushed at his arm. "You know I'm fond of you and want only the best for you, Edward Calhoun."

He grinned at her again as they stood to walk up the path back to her cottage. "Did you know that 'to be fond of' means to have an affectionate liking for, to be sweet on, even crazy about. I like those synonyms better."

Choosing not to reply, she looked at her watch and said, "Do you want to eat lunch at the inn? It's nearly time for the buffet to start."

"No, I need to get back to talk with the Jessups about all I learned at the meeting earlier, but thank you. Will you ride with me tomorrow if you come to sketch at Indigo? I'm going to the law firm in the morning to start going through my father's office, but I'll be back by lunch. If you sketch early, we could pack a picnic in our saddle bags and take our lunch to the river to eat or ride to the old Grimball ruins, whichever you'd like."

"I could bring the lunch," she suggested.

"You could, but you know Della and Annamae enjoy fussing over us. It's one of their ways of loving. Why don't you let them fix something for us and you just bring yourself?"

"All right," she said as they reached the turn to either her house or to the marina and Edward's boat. She leaned forward impulsively to kiss him on the cheek. "Thank you for coming to see me and for encouraging me in my art work."

He pulled her closer and kissed her back on the mouth, a sweet, quick kiss, smiling at her afterward. "I want more than this, Lila, but I'll wait. Just spending time with you has been pleasure enough for today."

CHAPTER 12

Edward spent the next morning at the law firm, beginning to sort through his father's office. Raymond, Hudson, and others in the firm stopped by every now and then to chat for a minute, to bring him a cup of coffee or a donut, making him feel welcome.

He came back to the plantation at about noon to find Della puttering in the kitchen. "I saw your note that you and Lila wanted to take a picnic lunch with you as you rode the horses today. Do you still plan to do that?"

"Yes, if it's no trouble. I can make up a few sandwiches myself if you'd prefer."

She gave him a considering look. "You know I don't like folks messing around in my kitchen. Besides, it will be my pleasure to pack you both a lunch. I've already started working on some nice egg salad sandwiches with leftover bacon from breakfast added in. I remember you and Isaac always liked those. I'm making some for him, and for Earl and Levi, too. They're plowing and planting out in the south fields with the month of April moving along now. It's harder work with the weather still so dry and the ground like a brick."

Edward saw Della open a big tin canister.

"Ummm. You've got homemade potato chips, too. I haven't had those in a long time."

She smiled at him. "I'm adding in a bag of my dried fruit mix for both of you, too, with a combination of raisins, dried cherries and apricots, sunflower seeds, peanuts and almonds."

"What about dessert?" He grinned.

"Some of my peanut butter brownies." She turned to continue loading lunch items into two plastic lunch bags.

"Tanya gave me a whole bunch of these insulated lunch bags in different colors to pack the men's and our lunches in when we're working outside. Aren't they fine? They keep things nicer than just putting them a brown sack. You can tuck these in your saddle bags, too, but bring them back to me so I can reuse them, you hear?"

"I will, Della," Edward said sitting on a stool to watch her finish making their lunch.

"Isaac said for you to take the white horses again today. He and Tanya had the bays out yesterday for Lawson and Kinsey to ride. Those two children didn't learn to ride up at Georgetown. Not too many folks keep horses anymore today."

Edward decided not to mention that horses were expensive to keep. He remembered the plantation had kept more when he was small and his grandfather was still alive.

"Where are you going to have lunch today?'

"I told Lila she could choose. I thought the folly would be a good spot, out of the cool air and with its views out across the river, but earlier this week when I suggested stopping by there, Lila seemed to get upset over the idea. I guess it's because it used to be a special place for us."

Della stopped packing their lunches to look directly at him. "That girl has some bad memories associated with that spot, but it's got nothing to do with her feelings about you. It actually might be good if you pushed on her to go there. Sometimes we need to face what's hurt us to get past it, like you got past the bad memories in your father's office in the house this week. You know, too, that when you get thrown off a horse, you should get right back on that horse again, not avoiding it and fearing it. It's the same principle."

"You're right, and like you reminded me, it isn't a place's fault bad things happened there."

She smiled, closing off the lunch bags and passing them to him.

"Well, you tell her that and you push on her. It ain't the folly's fault if anything bad happened at that pretty spot."

Della turned back to start packing up the other lunches. "You get yourself a couple of bottles of water from out of the closet, too. You'll find Lila down near the barn drawing pictures of the horses and such."

Edward started to ask her what they'd talked about with Lila the other day that upset her, but he decided not to. Isaac had told him Lila left a little upset, but he'd prefer Lila to talk to him about it, whatever the problem was. They both needed to quit keeping things from each other. In past they never had, one reason he treasured their relationship so much, his own parents always living such lives of pretense, distanced from each other with their buried secrets.

Leaving the kitchen, he stuffed the two lunches and water bottles into an old backpack to carry to the stable. He'd changed after coming back from the law firm into jeans, riding boots, and a clean T-shirt, with a long-sleeved flannel shirt unbuttoned over it. The weather outside today was warming, heading into the upper sixties if the predictions were correct. He could pull off the flannel shirt if he got warm and stuff it in one of his saddle bags.

Whistling as he set off walking toward the stable, Edward wasn't surprised to soon find Lila sitting at a rough table with one of her drawing tablets in front of her. She was sketching the scene nearby of Indigo's stable with the two bay horses and old Juniper, the mule, grazing in the corral in front of it.

"Nice work," he said, leaning over her shoulder.

She studied it. "A hallmark of many old Lowcountry plantations were fine stables like this, each architecturally beautiful. Look at the cupolas on the stable here. You don't see that often."

"I suppose not." He looked toward the long building with the decorative domes on the top. "I'll go get the horses saddled while you pack up. Okay?"

"Yes." She smiled at him. "I'm at a good stopping point, and this old table folds up easily. I found it in the barn and might use it again if it's all right."

"Any time," he said, heading to get the horses ready for a ride.

Lila had parked her little Audi near the stables today, so it didn't take her long to pack up her art supplies and put away the small table. She came into the barn afterward to help him finish getting Lex and Maddie ready for a ride.

"I'll put this lightweight saddle bag behind my saddle and then stuff our lunch bags and a water bottle into each side. They won't add much weight." He grinned at her as he tightened the cinch on his saddle. "Della packed us a great lunch."

"Where do you want to ride today?" she asked.

"I thought we'd head west following the trails that lead to the far end of the property at Indigo Creek and then ride down the river bank. It's been dry so we won't have a wet trail to navigate anywhere. We'll find a spot along the river to eat."

"Good plan," she agreed. They soon climbed into the saddle and headed out. "How did your day at the firm go this morning?"

"Better than I expected. I didn't have a huge sweep of memories to contend with at my father's law office, like at his office at home. I found everything neat and well organized. It didn't take me long to go through the remaining papers there that Raymond and Hudson hadn't already cleared out. We sat down over coffee about midmorning for any questions I had and to confer about what to toss or keep."

"I'm glad the day went well. I know it's been hard coming back to a lot of your bad memories here."

He looked across at her. "Well, as Della has reminded me on several occasions, it isn't a place's fault bad memories happened there. She reminded me of happy times and of so many better remembrances, associated with my father's office at the house, and she has since added more good memories and stories for me about other rooms in the house, too. It's helped. As she's said so often, it isn't the house's fault my father had serious failings."

He glanced across to see her wince and grow a little quiet.

"Come on, let's have a good gallop down the main road until our turn." He clicked at Lex and gave him a nudge with his knees and that's all he took for the big horse to stretch out his legs and run.

Lila's horse Maddie soon followed and he glanced over with pleasure to see Lila laughing and smiling, her dark hair blowing in the wind behind her.

A tenderness hit him for this beautiful, sensitive, creative girl, so long his friend. As they slowed the horses later, moving into a narrower trail, he said, "My mind was just filled with a sweep of memories from our childhood."

She grinned at him. "Like what?"

"Like talking you into going deeper into the waves one day when you were seven. You promptly got caught in the edge of an undertow and then spit out by a wave on the beach. You were so mad at me, crying and scared. I kissed you on the beach that day for the first time, trying to get you to quit crying."

"I don't remember that." She tossed her head. "But I do remember you were a daredevil and always trying to get me to try some stunt or other when you were at the island."

He laughed. "Well, I couldn't try anything very adventurous at the plantation. If I got caught, or something happened, I'd pay for it from my father. At the island, Waylon or your mom might fuss at us, or give us a little lecture, but that was usually all."

"Mother rarely even switched or spanked us, and if she did, she made us go sit in our rooms first and think about what we'd done. I think that was worse than the little spanking we got later."

"You had such great parents," he added. "They taught us to play so many games—board games, card games, outdoor games like croquet, badminton, and horseshoes. Your mom knew great jump rope rhymes and so many songs. She had a good voice, too; so did your dad. I guess that's where Celeste got her gift."

She smiled across at him. "My sisters and I were blessed to know such a happy childhood, to live with parents who loved each other well and loved us."

"I want that when I marry and have a family one day, Lila. I want a happy home full of love, caring, laughter, and sharing, with no hidden secrets. Don't you?"

"I do," she said.

He turned Lex down a side trail leading along an inlet, called Indigo Creek, that emptied into the river. "We used to come put our kayaks in here. There's the old shed by the water where we kept them. I'll have to ask Earl or Levi if some of the old kayaks are still there and whether they're in good shape. If they are, we can go boating one day."

"I also remember kayaks were kept at the other boundary of Indigo's property at Grimball Creek, too. We used to kayak from there and take that narrow channel across to Ocella Creek and into South Creek to the lighthouse island."

"I'd forgotten that." He laughed then. "Do you remember the stormy day our kayaks got tangled in some submerged tree branches on that narrow channel and flipped over? The water was up from the rain, the current higher than usual. We were both scared, trying to right our kayaks and get them to shore so we could climb back in them and paddle home."

Lila leaned her head over to avoid a tree branch overhead. "You remind me that I was a lot more adventurous and daring in those days than I am now."

"I remember your dad was really mad at us, too. He was supposed to come and get you later at the plantation, but we decided to kayak back without asking anyone. I don't know how we slipped away from the Jessups, but when your dad took me back to the plantation, he told them no harm had been done and suggested they didn't need to mention the episode to my mother or father at all."

Edward grew quiet. "Everyone knew my father whipped me more than he should have. Looking back, I can remember a lot of times when people shielded me so he wouldn't know about some of my minor childhood escapades."

Lila sighed. "You were only a little boy, Edward, and everyone's heart went out to you that your parents weren't as loving and kind as they should have been."

"I appreciate those kindnesses more now, looking back."

They followed along the wide sandy bank of the North Edisto River now, the river that had once been the main transportation route for all the early plantation owners. Here, riding along the bank, they enjoyed pointing out sea birds, dolphins, familiar sites across the river on Wadmalaw and Johns Island, and remembering more happy times.

"I always loved going to St Christopher's Camp in the summer, didn't you?" Lila asked, pointing to the camp's buildings they could see across the river.

"I did, and it's done my heart good to remember so many fun times of the past today, Lila. I want to think on those things more and more, and not the hard times, the painful things."

As the dock and boathouse came into sight later, Edward could see the brick, octagonal shaped folly, with its decorative roof and tall spire ahead. The folly stood on a slightly elevated point by the bank, with a long dock of its own reaching out into the river. Glancing across at Lila, he could see her tense as they drew nearer.

"Let's eat our lunch in the folly," he suggested, smiling at her. "We'll get away from the river breeze there. That old ornate metal table and chairs still sits in front of the windows closest to the river. We can eat there and enjoy the views."

Lila slowed her horse as they reached the dock and boathouse, and he could see her hands had grown taut on the reins. "We could sit out on the dock here and eat, too." She gestured toward it.

"The wind has kicked up, Lila, coming in off the ocean. It will blow us and our lunch away on the dock."

She stopped her horse and Edward could see her struggling with her thoughts.

He moved Lex closer to her and reached across to put a hand over hers. "Lila," he said softly. "It's obvious you hold a bad memory of some kind associated with the folly. Don't you think you should face it and put it behind you? I'll share the hurt of it with you. I hate to see you hesitate to enjoy the old folly that was one of our favorite places. Couldn't we try revisiting it together today? It might not be as bad as you're envisioning."

She closed her eyes, trying not to cry. "And it might be worse. You might change in how you feel about me."

He shook his head. "Lila, with all the crap you know about me and all I've shared with you, I refuse to even consider that possibility. You're my best friend of all time, the love of my heart." He started toward the folly. "Come on. Be brave. A scripture you taught me is that *'God has not given us a spirit of fear but of love and power and a sound mind.'* Don't you believe that?"

"I want to," she whispered.

"Then let God show you it's true. Kick fear in the face, Lila. You know the origin of it. Don't let the old devil win even one round with you. I remember you told me the same thing once in the past when I was scared."

"All right," she said in a quiet voice.

They rode closer to the folly, tying their horses to an old hitching post. Edward got their lunches out of his saddle bag and walked to open the old door leading into the folly. A few stairs led to the familiar room, with long windows on all sides looking out over the river. He could hear Lila following him, but when he dropped their lunches on the table and turned back, he saw her still standing just inside the door, weeping with her eyes closed.

He went and picked her up in his arms, carrying her to the long bench along one side of the folly, keeping her on his lap with his arms around her after he sat down. Holding her head against his heart, he said, "Tell me about it. Whatever it is. Tell me, Lila."

She cried for a little while, and then said, "I came here one day riding. You were home from college and I stopped by impulsively after going into Charleston on some errands for Mother. I hoped to ride with you, but learned you'd gone into the city. Levi said it was to get some needed school clothes or something. I can't remember. He thought you might not be long, so I decided to ride some myself until you got back. I rode down here. You know I've always liked it."

Edward waited while she cried a little more before continuing.

"Your father was out riding that day, too. He saw my horse and walked up to the folly. I was sketching inside, sitting on that bench right there." She pointed at it across from them.

A fear welled up in him now, at what his father had said or done. He knew his father had disapproved of his strong friendship with Lila.

"Your father came over and sat by me, talking casually at first, but then he changed suddenly," she said, her voice choking up. "He grabbed my arm and told me he didn't want me seeing you anymore. He said you had big plans ahead for your life and that I was just a little interlude, fun for when you came home from college."

She wept some more. "He started saying awful things, Edward, suggesting the folly was our little love nest and calling me names I don't even want to repeat." She raced on with her story, her voice occasionally breaking. "He started grabbing at me then, pushing me down on the bench and kissing on me. I was so shocked. It was your own father, but I began to push and fight back. He hit me then and began to grope me, trying to pull off my clothes."

She lifted frightened eyes to him. "He was a big man and strong, Edward. I was so scared. He laughed at me and said he was going to fix it so you'd never want to be with me again."

"Oh, Lila." He hugged her close. "I'm so sorry. I'm so sorry."

"I don't know what would have happened if Levi hadn't called out to him. 'Big Sam, are you in the folly?' he hollered. 'I think that mare's about to foal and it's too soon. You need to come quick to help us decide what to do and if we need to get the vet in. I know you've counted on this foal being a strong healthy one with the breeding fee you paid, but there might be real problems if she foals now.'"

She closed her eyes. "I don't remember the exact words, but it interrupted your father's mood and intent. He stood and hooked his pants back to leave, but before he did he looked at me and said, 'If you come around here again I'll finish what I started. You keep that in mind and it would be smart if you discourage your relationship with my son, do you hear?'"

Anger laced through Edward at her words. "How could he do that?" he asked out loud. "Such an evil thing and to you, a family friend, just a young and innocent girl."

Edward lifted Lila's chin to look at her. "Those words he said were all the lies of a man with an evil heart. Please believe me when I tell you that. You know he tried to rape Tanya, too, that his ugly act on that day ran her and Isaac away, causing all sorts of hurt and problems that same summer. I don't know how my father justified those things he did like that. So crude and despicable. I learned that summer he'd tried to force other young girls around the island, too. It gave me such a disgust for him, made me so ashamed I had a father who would do such things, and a mother who turned a blind eye and even suggested the girls led him on. It made me sick that summer."

She looked at him with tears in her eyes. "Oh, Edward, you don't hate me that your father tried to get intimate with me, do you?"

"No, no, Lila. I am just so deeply remorseful that my own father shamed you like that, frightened you and hurt you. That he was the kind of man who would do such a thing. Forgive me that he was my father. I wish I'd known he might try to hurt you so I could have protected you from it."

She sucked in a breath, wiping away tears. "I will be forever grateful Levi came when he did. He told me later he thought Big Sam might have been trying to hurt me and he knew telling him the mare might be dropping her foal early would get him away from me. He said he thought it a better plan than trying to fight him, for my sake and his. The ploy worked, and the mare was close to foaling early, so it just seemed as if the concern had been arrested when they got to the barn and called the vet in."

"What did you do after he was gone?"

She shook her head. "I sat in shock and wept for a few minutes. Then fear hit me that he might come back. I sneaked away to my car as soon as I could quit shaking and crying, leaving the horse tied near the house. I was so scared he might come back to the folly looking for me." She sniffed. "It's why I didn't come back to the plantation after that."

He stroked her hair. "I can understand that now and why you wouldn't ride with me. Also, why every time I mentioned my father you turned pale. I thought you were disgusted with me and my whole family over what my father had done to Tanya. I knew the talk had gotten around and that stories about other women had come out, too. Some even uglier. I thought you were starting to hate me. You wouldn't even let me kiss you after that."

She covered her face. "I felt so dirty, Edward."

"What did your mother and father think about this? I'm surprised your father didn't come to the plantation with a police officer or carrying a gun. I know how protective he always was toward all of you girls. Your mother was, too."

She climbed out of his lap. "I never told anyone, Edward. I wasn't even sure how much Levi knew until yesterday when the Jessup women began to talk about that time."

CHAPTER 13

Lila looked at the pain on Edward's face and she knew she'd done the right thing in talking to him. He didn't hate her for learning what his father had done. He didn't despise her or hold her in disgust that his own father had handled her, felt of her body, and tried to rape her. All the ugly things Edward's father told her, that had lingered in her mind all this time, were untruths, too.

She sat down beside him and took his hand. "I told you it was bad. Are you sorry now that I told you everything?"

"No, a million times no. It helps to explain the rift between us I never understood."

"I was always afraid to tell anyone, Edward. I thought people might think I encouraged your father in some way and I was so humiliated. I was afraid to talk to anyone about what happened, scared of what your father might say or do in retaliation. I kept remembering he said you would have a disgust for me, too, and never want to see me again or spend your life with me, as I'd dreamed." She couldn't help crying again as she voiced the words.

"Don't believe any of that anymore." He turned to put his hands on either side of her face, "I love you, Lila Deveaux. I did then. I do now. I want you to know that nothing in what you have shared with me has changed those feelings. And I am so grateful to Levi for stopping the evil my father intended."

"Did he never tell you anything about that time?"

No." He shook his head. "Nothing. I knew about Tanya, and I

only learned this week that Earl and Della decided to send Maisie to live with Della's sister that summer after I left, because they worried my father might come after her. Isaac told me they saw my father watching her in a way that troubled them."

She thought about his words. "I bet that's why Levi began to trail me whenever I came to Indigo to visit or to ride when you weren't here. Della and Annamae said it seemed as if an evil spirit or something had gotten a hold of your father then. She said they knew he wasn't being faithful to Clarice and they had heard of him going after young girls, but they didn't think he'd ever bother anyone at the plantation."

"It's disgusting to think he would prey on any young woman, Lila, no matter who it was."

"I know. I've prayed a lot for him, felt sorry for him that he allowed himself to walk away from being a good decent man to becoming such a despicable one."

Edward sat back and closed his eyes. "From what others have shared with me, my father began to pull away in his character as a boy and then as a teenager more. It makes you wonder, doesn't it, what causes a person to begin to step away more and more from a right and true way of living." He sighed. "I've seen it a lot in the legal field, how criminals justify to themselves and to others some of the most heinous and abominable crimes, saying a person deserved in some way to be knifed, killed, abused, or thieved from. It's so twisted."

She took his hand in comfort. "I think we often forget we have an enemy in this earth who hates us and wants to destroy us, who wants to separate us from a right and abundant way of living and from a rich relationship with a good and loving God. Remember the Bible says *'the enemy comes but to kill, steal, and destroy.'* We've certainly seen that to be true in our lives, and I know you see it often defending criminal cases as an attorney."

"I'd like to say it stops being shocking after a time, but it never does, the ugly and evil things one man or woman can do to another."

Lila felt weary from her emotions, and leaned her head back

against the folly's brick wall for a moment, closing her eyes. When she opened her eyes after a few moments, she saw Edward watching her.

"One thing I know of a surety now, Lila Deveaux, is how deeply I love, cherish, and honor you. I hope you believe me when I say that, and I am so sorry for the pain my family has caused you. I wish there was something I could do to make that right, to change the memory of that ugliness for you."

Lila could feel his sincerity and see the guilty pain on his face. How it must hurt him to learn his own father could do such ugly things.

She turned and leaned toward him. "You could kiss me and make it better." She gave him a little smile. "This was where you first kissed me when you were sixteen and I was only fifteen. That was the sweetest moment. I never came here after that without remembering that day. And, of course, we kept adding to that memory, which means there are more good memories here in this old folly of love and sweetness than of hurt and harm. Della was right in saying it isn't a particular place's fault if bad things happened there."

A sweep of relief touched his face just before he gathered her into his arms to kiss her and this time not with only a gentle, soft kiss but with a passionate, heartfelt one. Regardless of any other feelings Lila had about Edward, this moment felt totally right. They both needed it, too, like a purging and a cleansing.

Edward took their kissing deeper than in the past, wrapping her against him, and she could feel their hearts beating between them, feel their breathing escalate. She smiled to herself. Celeste would be pleased to learn she was discovering how wonderfully exciting and satisfying passion could be. She'd been a little fearful of intimacy in relationships in the past, each reminding her of the time with Edward's father. She supposed keeping that incident locked deep within had only made those old fears and hurts fester.

She found herself laughing with a new joy now, running her hands with gratitude down Edward's back and through his hair, kissing him back with abandon. "I feel like you're bathing me in joy to cover up old pain, Edward," she whispered against his ear.

He pulled back, to relish her words and then moved in to kiss her again.

"You've learned more about kissing than I remember, too," she said, giggling. "You put me at a disadvantage."

"It's a glorious disadvantage. I'm overwhelmed with my love and hunger for you, Lila. I'm so happy we're together again. My heart always missed you, but there were so many mixed-up feelings and old pains and hurts keeping us apart. Isn't it sweet to have them erased?"

She leaned in to kiss him again. "It is, and to think I might have missed this if I hadn't come home from the Community of St. Mary."

"I think this is another of the reasons God brought you back home, knowing in His infinite wisdom I would be brought back after my father died and that I would need you and your love." He took her face in his hands again. "You do love me, don't you Lila? I'd love to hear the words if you do."

"Of course, I love you, Edward. No matter where you go or what you do with your life, that will always be true. And thank you for still loving me after learning what happened with your father."

"How could you wonder about that?" he asked, nuzzling her neck with his lips, before leaning back to look at her with a question in his eyes. "Do you think this is another of the reasons God brought you back home, Lila, made you restless in your heart at St. Mary's so you would come? Made the good sisters give you a little shove out the door?"

She couldn't help laughing. "Perhaps. I certainly see I would have missed a lot if I hadn't come back."

"Amen. I would have missed a lot, too."

He taught her a little more about kissing before he pulled back again. "We have much more to explore about loving and passion, Lila, but this is not the time. I would never take advantage of your innocence. My morals are strong ones, perhaps because of what

I've seen in my family growing up." He let his eyes move over her. "Not that I don't hunger for more, Sister Anne, but I am wise enough to know we've shared enough kissing and passion for one day."

She leaned her head back against the wall again. "This started out to be the worst day ever, but now has turned into such a sweet, blessed one." She felt a blush steal up her neck. "I didn't know men and women could have such pleasure together."

Edward stood and walked across the room. "No more tempting words like that, Lila. Be kind and help me with restraint here."

"Well, perhaps we could eat that lunch you brought." She teased. "Appease another natural appetite instead."

He laughed. "That might be good. You put out the lunch on the table while I go out and check on the horses and get a needed breath of fresh air."

They shared lunch in the folly a little later, a lighter and happier mood in the air. Lila couldn't believe, in some ways, she'd finally put the memory of that awful time with Edward's father behind her, truly believing deep inside that others might not love and respect her anymore if they knew what had happened.

As she and Edward rode back to the plantation, Edward said, "Lila, you know we believe in being honest with each other. I think you need to talk with your mother about this and perhaps with your sisters. I know you fear they might disrespect you for what happened, but believe me, they won't."

She considered it. "Perhaps in time I will."

He frowned. "There are some things we should postpone and think about, times we shouldn't react quickly, but I believe there are other times when things have been postponed for far too long and need to be acted on." He reached across to pat her leg. "I think this is one of those times, Lila. In this instance, the quote that comes to my mind is: *Don't put off until tomorrow what you can do today.* Haven't we both done enough of that already?"

"I'll pray about it," she said, feeling testy at his words.

"You pushed me to deal with a lot of matters I wanted to avoid.

I'd feel false not to do the same for you." He grinned at her. "Are you chicken?"

She had to laugh. "I probably am. I'll see if God will open a time for this."

"Or maybe make one?"

She shook her head. "Or maybe make one."

Later, back at the island, Lila found it was only her mother and her for supper that night.

"Drew is sick," her mother told her when she came up to the inn at dinnertime. "Burke says he has one of those little intestinal bugs, so they're both staying to cuddle him and see him through it. Waylon came up to get some dinner for them." She smiled at Lila. "I remember those times when little ones are sick. Burke and Waylon are probably in for a somewhat sleepless night."

"I'm so sorry to hear that," Lila said. "We'll pray for comfort, healing, and a quick recovery."

Lila's mother, Etta Deveaux, had been visiting around with their guests in the dining room, talking to them before Lila came in.

"Do you want to eat in here and mingle with our guests or take our dinner into the family apartment tonight?" she asked. "You know there's a nice small table there we could use."

"Let's eat in the apartment," Lila said, seeing easily how a time to possibly talk with her mother alone had opened up.

They checked with Novaleigh in the kitchen to see if she needed any further help, and then fixed themselves a plate to carry through to the family wing.

"I love this little apartment," Etta said as she and Lila settled in at the small table near the kitchen with its blue painted chairs and jute placemats arranged on a blue and white striped runner. "It's where Lloyd and I first lived after we married. His parents had the big main bedroom downstairs in the inn where I stay now, but I remember how happy and cozy we were here in our own little world after Lloyd's parents decided to add on the apartment wing for us. I'm thinking of moving back over here."

She looked around. "Lloyd and I wanted a nautical look with a lot of blue. We dug out old pieces from the storage area, repainting many, having others reupholstered. One of Novaleigh's brothers over on Edisto did most of the upholstery work. Novaleigh's mother helped me make a lot of the pillows. I'd never been taught to sew, but now I can sew a little when needed." She glanced at the sea pictures, many with boats. "You can tell your father picked a lot of the art and nautical items around the room, like that old globe, the ship in a bottle." She sighed. "I still miss him so much and I guess I always will."

Lila cut into more of her meatloaf, listening. The dish was what Novaleigh called Sicilian Meatloaf, stuffed with ham and cheese. Lila had always liked it, and Novaleigh had made a baked potato dish to go with it, peas with little mushrooms, and a grape salad Lila liked.

"Dad was a special man," she said after a moment. "Edward was just saying today how blessed we were to have such a good father."

Her mother finished up more of her dinner before adding, "Novaleigh said Della told her Edward is settling in some now, a little happier. They hope he'll stay, of course."

She stopped to drink some of her iced tea, "You've been spending time with Edward riding horses again. I'm glad you're being kind to him. He knew a hard childhood, an only child and with a mother lacking in natural affection and a somewhat unbending father. Sam Calhoun was an admirable man in many ways, highly respected as an attorney and businessman, but his personal life was abysmal. I know Clarice grew very unhappy with him."

Lila made a face. "Mother, Sam Calhoun preyed on young girls. He tried to rape Isaac's fiancé, Tanya, and he forced himself on several young girls around the island. Surely you know that."

"Well, I hesitated to say too much about it to you girls at the time when the rumors were circulating at their worst. Also, Clarice was my friend, as well, and I didn't want to make the gossip worse for her."

Lila grew quiet. This conversation was not going the way she had hoped.

"What did you think about Sam Calhoun's behavior, Mother?" she finally asked directly. "What did you and Daddy think about it?"

Etta gave her an odd look and then said, "You know your father was friends with Sam through business, but he pulled away from that friendship when Novaleigh came to tell us all that happened with Tanya, how awful it was for the family and how the Jessups decided not long afterward to send Maisie off the plantation to stay with Della's sister Vergie Meggett and her husband Fisher. I can't imagine how hard it would be to send your own child away from your home like that and to know you worked for a man who might abuse your child and who had tried to rape your own son's fiancé."

Etta crossed her arms, leaning forward, her expression intense now. "I kept a lot of this to myself, Lila, rather than talking about it to you and your sisters at the time because you went to school with Edward and because you, in particular, spent a lot of time with Edward. I didn't want to carry gossip."

She waved a finger at Lila. "But I will tell you this now. Your father said if Sam Calhoun ever laid a hand on either of his girls, he'd go after him and beat him to a pulp. We wondered why no one had done it before, no matter how rich or powerful the man was. Evil is evil, Lila, and since you pushed this issue, that's what we thought of it." She took a breath. "It broke my heart when your father died, but I thought a sort of justice occurred when Sam Calhoun had a stroke and died two months later. You may think it unkind of me to say that, but I thought it."

She lifted her chin as she finished, and Lila burst into tears.

Her mother's mouth dropped open then. "Lila, whatever is the matter? Did you find my words unchristian? Too harsh and unkind? If so I'm sorry, but I felt you were pushing me to share what I really thought. And I don't regret my thoughts or your father's. Or any of our words in past about that situation. I'm sorry if you find that upsetting."

Lila looked across at her mother through tears. "Mother, I was one of those girls Sam Calhoun attacked. If it hadn't been for Levi Jessup, I would have been raped, too."

Her mother put a hand to her heart. "Oh, Lila. Why have you never told me this?" She got up to come around the table to pull Lila to her feet to hold her tight, the last of their dinner forgotten. "Bless your heart. When did this happen? Why didn't you come to me? Surely you knew we wouldn't fault you, a young girl as you were."

She stepped back. "That awful man. How dare he attack you. He was a friend of our family, a close neighbor. And Lord have mercy, did he not remember how often we entertained his son here, fed him, cared for him, parented that little boy when his wife Clarice was off sashaying around Charleston with her sister, going to all sorts of social events? It makes me so mad I could spit nails."

Lila sat back down in her chair, her knees feeling a little weak over bringing all this situation out.

Her mother pulled her own chair closer to Lila's and said, "Tell me all about this, Lila. Surely you know I have no condemnation for you in this, only love and compassion. I assume this happened before you left home. You didn't come home much after you left to go away to school. The reason for that is suddenly all too clear."

Lila began her story again. "It was the summer after my senior year at high school, the summer after Edward had been away at college for the first time."

Her mother's face hardened. "That was the same summer when Sam tried to rape Tanya, when Isaac and Tanya left the plantation and went to Georgetown, wasn't it?"

"Yes," she admitted. "I had gone to Charleston on errands that day and stopped by Indigo on my way home, hoping to ride horses with Edward. Levi said he might be back later so I decided to ride down to the folly in the meantime. I didn't know it at the time, but Levi followed me, worked near the folly to keep an eye on me. I sat inside the folly for a while to sketch that afternoon, and Edward's father came by. He'd been out riding, too. I thought he stopped in to be congenial."

She wept then and shared the rest, no matter how hard it was to tell it again. Her mother was only loving and kind. Tender and sweet, offering comfort. Like Della and Annamae had been. Like Edward had been. Why had she kept this hidden away for so long? Why had she thought people would judge her and disrespect her for what had happened?

Her mother asked her the same questions.

"I think I was afraid to tell anyone because it was Edward's father, because it was someone we all knew. That seemed to make it so much worse, Mother. I knew Sam and Daddy were friends. I knew you and Clarice were friends. I knew Sam could easily lie, too, about what happened. He said he did what he did to break Edward and me up, to give Edward a disgust of me, to make him never want to have anything else to do with me. How did I know that might not happen and that everyone I loved would be disgusted and disappointed in me? I was only a girl, barely eighteen. I'd known only a loved and sheltered life. I'd never dealt with anything like that before."

She and her mother had some long sweet talks after that, and it was a healing time for Lila. Knowing she was loved despite what had happened. Knowing her mother felt angry for what happened to her.

Lila shared with her mother, too, about talking with Della and Annamae Jessup, and about talking with Edward today at the folly.

"He encouraged me to talk with you, Mother. Pushed me to do so." She smiled over the words. "He was convinced you would understand and not condemn me."

Etta smiled. "Well, then I owe Edward my thanks and a big hug for that. And I love hearing how kind and understanding he was with you." She paused. "Is there more going on between you two? Your father and I always felt a relationship was starting between you and Edward that last year or two before he went away to college and even that summer before you went to Sewanee."

Lila sighed. "There had always been affection between us since childhood and it bloomed into more in those high school years, but all the problems that last summer ended everything between us." She hesitated. "I think more might be blossoming between us again now, but I don't know whether it will move past only a loving friendship. Edward is still so unsettled about his life, what he wants to do. He has a lot to resolve in himself before he's ready to think about more."

"And what about you, Lila?" she asked. "If Edward gets all his problems worked out, will you want to see your relationship move into a lasting one with him?"

She smiled. "My heart says yes, but my head isn't sure yet. And I need more time to pray over all this. I've gone in one direction I thought was God's best will for me already and then found it wasn't the right direction after all. I don't want to do that again."

Her mother leaned over to kiss her cheek. "You'll find your right way, and God will help you."

Before she left, Etta asked, "Will you tell your sisters about this?"

She sighed. "I think I need to, and I'd like to tell them all at the same time."

"Well, you'll figure out just the way to do that, I'm sure." Her mother stood to give her one more hug. "Sleep well, Lila, and know you are loved by all who know you."

CHAPTER 14

Getting dressed on Friday morning, Edward looked back with amazement to realize he'd only been back at Indigo a week. So much had happened in the week since, it seemed like he'd been here longer.

He found his way downstairs to the kitchen, following good smells in the air, where he found Della taking hot biscuits out of the oven.

Edward smiled at her. "You don't have to cook breakfast for me every morning, Della. I learned to cook in Nashville."

She raised her chin. "It's my job, son—and Annamae's—cooking and cleaning for Indigo Plantation. I'm working on food for everyone for lunch and dinner at this time anyway. It's no problem to scramble or fry you an egg, cook you a piece of bacon or two, and pop toast or some biscuits in the oven. I've been doing it since you were knee high to a grasshopper and for both your mama and daddy, too." She turned to frown at him. "Why do you want to be taking that pleasure away from me? Are you not enjoying my cooking anymore?"

He laughed. "No. Your cooking is fabulous. Surely you know that. I just feel pampered and indulged being waited on when I also know you have so much to do. I don't want to be taking advantage of you."

She poured him a cup of coffee and put it on the kitchen table. "You said you were going into the law office for a little while this morning. When someone pays you to handle a legal case for them, do you feel guilty about it, like they're taking advantage of you?"

"No, of course not." He frowned.

"Well, it's the same thing for me. This is my job. I've been well-trained for it and I'm am well-qualified to do it. I don't like the idea of someone taking it over from me."

Edward laughed. "I guess I never looked at it that way."

She put a hand on one hip. "I suppose I could cook and clean for other folks. Novaleigh cooks over at the Deveaux Inn, but I've always liked it here. This big house and me are old familiar friends after all this time. I like looking after this house and the people who live here. You'd do well to respect that, like you'd want your legal clients to respect you, to honor what you know and what you do."

Della turned to crack two eggs into a skillet on the stove. "We've all got our jobs and roles in this life. If we're blessed, we like our work and are grateful for it. All of our family like working and living here at Indigo. It's home for us in a way that's hard to explain, and it was home to Jessups before us. We know we could all pack up and leave any time, but we like it here."

She plated the two fried eggs for him, put two pieces of bacon beside it, and added two biscuits on a side plate. "I seem to remember you used to like Annamae's homemade strawberry preserves, so I brought a jar over for you today to go on your biscuits."

He dug into his breakfast. "Thank you, Della. I feel like a king."

She wiped her hands on her apron. "I admit I'd like you to stay king around here and not sell out this place. Maybe settle down with a sweet girl and raise some babies for me to bounce on my knee. I can't figure out why you wouldn't want to keep this old place going. It's endured for so long. Don't you have a love and value for its history, for all the sacrifice and caring that's gone into keeping and preserving a beautiful old place like this?"

"Are you trying to make me feel guilty for following in the way I think I should go with my life, if it's not to stay here?" he asked, spreading butter and preserves on his biscuit.

She shook her head. "No, just wondering on it. Two of Levi's brothers went off and chose to do other things, made other lives. Isaac left, too, for a time for different reasons. I admit I'm happy now I've got all my sons here, working at the plantation, and Maisie not far away, teaching at the middle school with her husband Gavin George."

"Didn't Maisie and Gavin build a house not far from here, up Point of Pines Road?"

"Yes, they did. Nice place, too, on a piece of land my sister Vergie and her husband sold to them for a song. Vergie and Fisher only had one son, and he was killed in the military. You remember Maisie lived with them all through high school and they sort of unofficially adopted her, like second parents." She turned to grin at him. "However, even my girl doesn't live far up the road, and I have six grandchildren now with Maisie and Gavin expecting another before Christmas. I just found out yesterday."

"Well, congratulations."

"What are you going to be doing at the firm today?" she asked.

"I think Raymond wants me to tag along with him to Charleston for a Preliminary Hearing being held at the court there."

Isaac wandered in the kitchen then to ask, "Is that the court case about that woman who left her baby in the hot car all day?"

Della interrupted. "Lord, have mercy, that little baby died from heat and dehydration left in that hot car all day without even a window cracked. It happened right in Maisie and Gavin's school parking lot. They knew the woman really well, too. She worked in the cafeteria. Maisie said she dropped her other three kids off at the elementary school on her way in to work, ran by the bank, and said later she simply forgot she hadn't dropped her baby off at the Day Care. She was running late to work, raced into the school after she pulled into the parking lot, and had her mind on all sorts of things."

Isaac snagged a couple of biscuits from the stove, put them on a plate, got himself a cup of coffee and settled down at the table with Edward. "Maisie and Gavin told me the hearing for that case was coming up and that Raymond Maybank was handling it."

Della crossed her arms. "Well, I'd hate to go to court and try to defend a woman who'd leave her baby in a car all day and not even remember she'd left it there. What kind of mother is that?"

"A sorrowful, broken-hearted one from what I hear," Edward said. "And someone has to help her with her defense. There are still three other children at her home, needing a mother, and before this she's never had a criminal offense charge against her, not even a speeding ticket. She's gone through a rough time, too, since her husband ran off and left her last year before this last baby was born."

Isaac ate part of a biscuit before adding, "That baby was in the car in the heat for eight hours. She came out after school ended, opened the back door to put some stuff in the car, saw the baby in there and screamed. They took the baby to the hospital but it was too late for it to be saved."

"It was a sad thing." Della turned from the kitchen counter where she was working to Isaac. "Do you want some eggs, too?"

"Sure." His eyes brightened.

She frowned at him. "Didn't you eat this morning before you left the house?"

"I grabbed a bowl of cereal. Tanya took Lawson and Kinsey to school and then went to work at the store with Gladys, helping her with some decorations or something today."

"Those girls are working on getting the store ready for summer when the tourists all start swarming in. With April moving along, things are already getting busy at the Market." Della broke two more eggs in the skillet for Isaac.

Sipping on his coffee, Isaac studied Edward. "You look sharp, all dressed up like an attorney."

Edward laughed. "I am an attorney."

"Is it hard sometimes representing someone as a client when they've done something really bad, like that woman leaving her baby in the car all day, not giving it a thought until she came out to leave for home?"

"The Sixth Amendment guarantees that every person accused of a crime has the right of Counsel for his or her defense. I think, no matter what people have done, they all deserve that."

Della brought Isaac's eggs over to the table, adding a couple of pieces of bacon to his plate. "Maisie said that baby's death was an awful sorrow and tragedy. Counselors had to come in and talk to the children and staff, and they closed down school for a day after it happened. People even came and piled flowers and baby toys in the parking space where that little child died." She shook her head. "That mother and all that family had a grievous time. Maisie said they were afraid for a time Bethany would kill herself with guilt and remorse. That was the mother's name, Bethany."

She glanced at the clock then. "I need to get on upstairs to clean and to get some laundry started. You boys clean up in here after you finish your breakfast. You know how a sink works and there's a bottle of dish soap beside it."

"We'll clean up, Mama." Isaac winked at her. "And thanks for fixing me some breakfast."

She left and Isaac and Edward ate in silence for a few minutes.

After a time, Isaac turned to Edward again. "Is it tough defending a case like for that young mother? What will happen to her at this hearing today?"

"Hopefully the judge will accept the negotiated plea the prosecuting attorney and Raymond, as the defense attorney, are presenting. At that point, the judge will either accept or reject it. If he accepts the plea, the case won't be carried over for a jury trial."

"Will she get off?" he asked.

"Raymond hasn't told me the details of the plea they're presenting." He hesitated, thinking. "It seems unlikely, however, that the case will simply be dismissed."

He drummed his fingers on the table, thinking about it more. "If the woman had discovered she'd left the baby in the car earlier and if the baby had been taken to the hospital and hadn't died, it might have gone differently. But this was eight hours. Legally, it's child endangerment and maybe criminal neglect. Law enforcement could bring criminal charges. Even though the actions of the perpetrator, or young mother, weren't intentional, it could still go as a misdemeanor or negligent homicide, with possible jail time or maybe house arrest and probation."

"What would you try for?" Isaac asked.

"I might push for a lenient sentence since the woman was otherwise a good citizen, working, known as a good mother, well-respected and liked at the school. There are also three other children who need her. Unless she has a pattern of negligence or other problems, the court might see it, like the media is playing it, as just a tragic accident."

Isaac made a face. "Can you imagine trying to live with something like that if you'd left your child in the car all day and it died? While we were talking earlier, I was remembering a friend of mine whose little boy was killed in a car wreck, with him driving. Another driver plowed directly into them. It wasn't his fault in any way, but he kept looking back, trying to think what he might have done differently. He tortured himself with it. And his wife left him, unable to forgive him that he was the one driving the car when their boy was killed."

"Life is filled with some hard things to get through, whether you cause them or they simply happen to you," Edward said.

"That's true." Isaac rubbed his neck. "Will you let me know later how this turns out? To me it would be a tough case to defend and handle."

"Raymond had me do some legal research on it yesterday. This type of case happens more often than you'd think. I read that more than thirty-three children have died in hot cars in the U.S. in the last five and a half years. There are hundreds of cases, too, of intentional negligence, kids being left in cars while parents run into a store to shop or stop off at a bar."

"Not everybody is cut out to be a good parent."

Edward snorted. "As we well know, not everybody chooses to be a good parent or even a good person."

"Do you have time for another coffee before you head to the firm?" Isaac asked. "I actually came looking for you to tell you some of the precautions we're taking around the plantation to be more prepared for the possibility of fire. It's still been dry, and even lightning and brush fires can get whipped up. I'm sure hoping we'll get rain soon. It's needed for the crops getting started. We're having to use the sprinklers and irrigate some in the fields."

"I saw that when I was walking around yesterday."

"Dad said you took time to help in the fields."

"I did, and I have some sore muscles today. The fields are looking good though."

Isaac nodded in agreement. "We'll have strawberries and asparagus and other early Lowcountry vegetables soon with more to follow as the summer moves in—beets, beans, squash, onions, peppers, corn, cabbage, tomatoes. We'll have blueberries later, cantaloupes and watermelons, pumpkins in the fall. We run a good variety of produce, and we sell a lot of corn, sweet potatoes, and soy beans to big suppliers. We'll have pecans later, too."

Edward smiled. "I've been relearning things, but the old knowledge comes back quickly. I was particularly impressed with how well the market does in selling produce, not only to the tourists and locals at the store, but to restaurants around the area."

"We have your father to thank for most of those restaurant contacts, and all of us for the good store profits. People don't want to cook when they come to the beach, and anything we can make up—casseroles, slaw, chicken salad, pies, cookies, cakes, jellies, fudge—they'll buy at the store. They like to get fresh produce, too, tomatoes, corn, okra, beans, strawberries and blueberries. As the island keeps growing in tourism, the store sales grow, too." He got up to get a little more coffee. "Gladys said you stopped by to look at all the craft items the women make and sell. The indigo crafts sell particularly well, being unique and unusual."

"They're doing a great job with the market." Edward hesitated. "Are you still doing any of those carriage tours out to the plantation from the store? I remember during the summer those used to bring in some extra money. I drove some of those tours a few summers, with two of the horses pulling that big covered carriage with all the seats in it. We could take about ten people down Point of Pines Road, stop to see the old Hutchinson House being restored, detour off to Swallow Bluff Plantation and the old Grimball Ruins, then back to the main road and on to our plantation, letting the tourists get out to walk around in the gardens and enjoy a little snack before heading back again. I remember I'd make several hundred dollars profit every day I did a tour. Nice side money."

"We haven't done any of those carriage tours or events at the house since your father died. People have asked about both, but your mother didn't want to mess with it."

"That doesn't surprise me much." Edward glanced at his watch. "I'd better clean up here and head to the law firm. I'm hanging around over there today and going into Charleston to court with Raymond."

"Is Lila coming over today?"

"No, she runs the gift shop on Fridays when Burke does the lighthouse tours."

"Is she coming for our Friday night dinner at the pavilion?"

"No, but I'll be there." He grinned.

Isaac rubbed his neck, looking thoughtful. "I knew Lila was here, riding with you on Wednesday and that you both rode to the folly. Grandad saw your horses there for a time. Lila hasn't come back since. Is everything all right?"

He smiled at Isaac. "Everything is more than all right, friend. We shared some very good talks and some sweet times, too, for which I'm grateful. I didn't realize Lila had been through her own hurtful time with my father. Della said you knew a little of it."

"Only that he tried to mess with her. I hated hearing that. It's another reason Mama and Dad sent Maisie away. Your father just really went to the dark side during that time." He paused. "Are you sure Lila doesn't want to come tonight? Everybody would love to see her."

"She said she was having dinner with Burke and Waylon tonight, and then going into Charleston Saturday after the lighthouse tour to spend the night at her sister Celeste's. She told me Gwen planned to drive up, too. Lila's been trying to have some honest talks with her family about her past. We'll probably see her at Indigo again next week, if she isn't finished with her sketches here."

"Well, we all like Lila, and Tanya and I are personally rooting for you two to get back together," Isaac said, getting up to start gathering up their plates. "Let me wash these dishes so you won't get anything on those pretty attorney clothes of yours. It won't take but a few minutes. You head on over to the firm."

"I will, and I'll see you tonight."

In the car on the way to the law firm, a few minutes later, Edward called Lila on his cell phone. His dad's car, that he was driving most of the time now, had one of those hands-free devices to not interfere with your driving. Several states were passing laws to demand them in cars now for safer driving.

His dad had always favored Cadillacs, and this was a nice one, black and sleek with all the luxury bells and whistles. At first, he'd been reluctant to drive it, but then he decided, like his dad's office, that it wasn't the car's fault his dad wasn't what he should have been. And his dad had always bought fine cars and boats. Top-notch computers, phones, and tech toys, too.

"Am I interrupting your work time in the gift shop?" he asked Lila when she rang him back.

"No. I would have answered right off when your call came in a minute ago, but I was on a ladder hanging a new painting to replace one that sold this morning. We turn over guests at the Inn on Fridays, if you remember, and I open the store before they leave so they can get a few souvenirs or keepsakes to take home with them." She paused. "Are you on your way to the firm? I remember you said you'd be there most of the day?"

"I will. I wish we were spending the evening together tonight. I'm already missing you."

"Well, those are sweet words." Her voice softened. "However, you know I'm going to have dinner with Burke and Waylon tonight and then heading to Charleston on Saturday after the tour. I'm meeting with Morgan Richards at the college first, on Saturday afternoon, and then spending the night on King Street in Celeste's old apartment above her store CeeCee's Place. Gwen is coming to stay over with us, too, and she, Celeste, and I are having a girls' night."

"No boys?" he teased her.

"No, not even Celeste's husband Reid." He heard her sigh. "You know I talked to Mother yesterday, and tonight I plan to talk to Burke and Waylon. It's hard, but needed. I'll talk to Celeste and Gwen Saturday night. Burke couldn't leave Drew to go to one of our sisters' nights right now, so I had to split these talk times up. It's really hard, Edward. Pray for me."

"I will," he said softly. "And I'm proud of you for this. I hope you see from talking with Annamae, Della, your mother. and me, that everyone will understand that what you went through was a hard and painful situation but in no way your fault."

"I'm seeing that more and more, Edward, but thanks for that encouragement, and for being so sweet to me through this."

"You've always been kind to me through all I went through. You keep me in your prayers, too. I still have a lot of decisions to deal with and an inevitable encounter with my mother coming up eventually."

"Has she still not come back to the plantation since you came?"

"No. She called once to check in with me and to let me know she thought it better that I dealt with all this without her around to muddy up my decisions. She made it clear again to me that she planned to move in with Eula in Charleston soon, and she told me to not be expecting her to come back and handle things if I decided to go back to Nashville. She said, and I quote, 'That place is yours now, Edward, and good riddance of it to you.' Those were her exact words."

"Oh, my, she's carrying a lot of bitterness. That's not healthy, Edward."

He chuckled. "Well, I'll let you be the one to try to tell her that."

"I'll need to work up my nerve to do so and pray a lot before I do. But I feel sorry for your mother in many ways." Her voice softened. "Have you seen the graves of the three babies she lost in the family cemetery?"

"Yes. I often felt resentful to them for not living. They might have taken some of the pressure off me, some of the heavy expectations. I used to wonder if they had lived if Father might have been less hard on me and if my parents might have been happier, our homelife better."

"Somehow, I doubt more children would have changed the problems your parents had."

"You're probably right." He stopped at the intersection to the highway. "I'm nearly at the firm now, so I'd better go. Will you call me when you get back on Sunday afternoon?"

"Yes, I will, and I plan to come to Indigo on Monday to finish up any further drawings Morgan wants me to make. I've been doing most of the follow-up paintings he wants back in my studio, so I should be ready to start going to Crawford Plantation sometime next week."

"I was just realizing this morning how much has happened in our lives in only a week. It's been a really full and revelational time, hasn't it?"

She laughed. "Yes, and I'm ordinarily a somewhat quiet, introverted, sort of person. Usually always calm and peaceful, too."

"Well, I'm not sorry for anything we've had to cope with, if it's brought us back together again."

"We have enjoyed a sweet reunion," she said, almost in a whisper, then adding. "I'm glad we're friends again. But I do need to go now. You have a good day."

Edward scowled. Her last words reminded him that she still wasn't totally committed to him yet, despite them reuniting. He remembered her past words that he needed to decide clearly the best direction for his future before he could ask anyone to share in it, and Edward well knew he was still conflicted.

CHAPTER 15

Lila enjoyed greeting the visitors for the lighthouse tour a short time later. She liked watching what attracted their attention at the gift shop, as they visited with her before and after Burke's scheduled tours. Inside the old lighthouse were several levels, connected by rising staircases, and on the early, broader levels were lovely old museum rooms, filled with artifacts and bits of history about the Deveaux Lighthouse. Everyone enjoyed the tours that Burke, and sometimes Waylon, gave and it always thrilled their guests to look out across the ocean from the high upper levels of the lighthouse and across the broad expanse of sea.

"Are you still coming to dinner with Waylon and me tonight?" Burke asked as the tour ended and the visiting tourists and guests at the inn mingled in the gift shop.

"Yes, I'll be there at six, as you suggested, but not earlier. I have a watercolor painting to finish to show Morgan Richards at our meeting in Charleston tomorrow. I think we might be nearly done at Indigo, but I'm not sure." She laughed. "As Morgan works on his write-ups, he often uncovers new bits of history he wants sketches or paintings of."

"Does he write and lay out the book text as he goes?"

"I'm not sure," Lila answered. "I'll have to ask him that."

Checking the time, Burke signaled to her tour group to let them know they needed to head back to the Deveaux Inn or the ferry waiting at the marina. Lila shut the gift shop behind them and began to put things away to close. She looked around with a smile at the familiar little shop. She'd been surprised at how much she'd enjoyed fixing it up since she got home, repainting and rearranging everything to make it more appealing.

With surprise, she found she now held a better marketing sense than before. Good marketing in the gift shop was mainly just watching and discovering what items people liked and bought the most, and then stocking and carrying more of those items. The same was true with her paintings. People didn't always recognize the best art when they saw it, but they knew what appealed to them and what they liked, and that's what they bought.

She'd begun making prints of her paintings that the tourists and visitors to the Deveaux Inn and Lighthouse liked the best, of the inn and lighthouse, the beach and sea, of sea birds, ships and shrimp boats, coastal flowers, and lyrical works that seemed to tell a story, often including people, animals, and cute little sea cottages.

"I simply love your shop. There are so many beautiful things here," a woman said today, stacking a lighthouse painting, a colorful paperweight, gift cards, and several other items by the register for Lila to ring up. "I wish I knew more cute shops like this to visit."

"If you go to Charleston, be sure to stop at my sister, Celeste Deveaux's, store on King Street called CeeCee's Place," Lila suggested.

The woman's eyes brightened. "Oh, I'd forgotten your sister opened a shop there. We will definitely look for it."

"I'll add a brochure with your purchases to remind you exactly where the store is," Lila said as she popped one into the woman's bag.

She always kept brochures by the cash register for Celeste's store in Charleston and for Gwen and Alex's restaurant in Beaufort. She knew they promoted the Deveaux Inn and Lighthouse, too.

Back at her cottage, Lila enjoyed some quiet moments and needed time in prayer while she finished working on the new watercolor she wanted to take to her meeting with Morgan Richards tomorrow. She'd pack it in her briefcase with her other new paintings and sketches for him to look at. He'd scheduled their meeting at the college for four-thirty in the afternoon after his last class.

At nearly six after finishing all her work, Lila walked down the winding drive to Burke and Waylon's home at the lodge. Burke had fixed a new dish that turned out good, baked Chicken Chimichangas, served with yellow rice, beans, and a tomato and avocado salad. They talked and laughed over dinner, mostly about recent tourist happenings and fun with Drew.

Thankfully, Lila's more candid talk after dinner with Burke and Waylon ended up being a sweet one. They lovingly listened to her story with only kindness and compassion, hurt and upset for her and for all the problems Edward's father had caused.

"I feel bad I didn't sense all the difficulties Sam Calhoun was creating," Waylon said.

"Waylon, you were away in the Navy by the time the worst of it started with Sam," Burke added. "We girls were still young, somewhat isolated at the island, and very naïve about such things. Also, think about it. The Calhouns were our neighbors and friends. You don't expect that sort of thing from people you know who are close to your family." She paused. "I think, because of that, we even tended to discount the troublesome stories we began to hear about Sam."

"Well, he caused a lot of pain and harm." Waylon reached out a hand to stroke Lila's cheek. "I'm so sorry he tried to hurt you as he did. It was evil and disgusting of him. Don't you ever tell yourself anything less. There is no excuse for a man to do anything like that ever, especially to a young innocent girl."

"Do you still need counseling or outside help?" Burke asked. "Are you all right now? Did the sisters at St. Mary's counsel and help you with this issue?"

Lila shook her head. "No. I never told anyone, Burke. Not until now. Not a single person. I didn't even know how much Levi saw before he lured Sam away from me that day. We never talked about it again."

"Well, I'm going to personally thank Levi for watching after you and intervening," Waylon said. "I'm confident that if his diversional tactic hadn't worked, he would have physically intervened, as Isaac did for Tanya. Levi is tough and strong. And a good moral man."

"Yes, and I've been praying God's blessings on him," Lila said.

Walking home later she thought of Edward as she often did. Was he beginning to find his way? When she prayed for him, she still felt he harbored resentment in his heart toward his family home and toward many who had hurt him there. She knew he needed to let those old painful memories and resentments go as she was finally doing herself."

The next day after the lighthouse tour ended, Lila headed to Charleston to meet with Morgan Richards. She parked at the garage across from Marion Square Park, draped her satchel over her shoulder and headed down the sidewalk toward Calhoun Street and on to St Phillips Street.

Maybank Hall, where the college's History Department could be found, stood on the corner of Calhoun and St Phillips. It was a tall, stately two storied, somewhat pinkish building with old Southern pillars, palm trees and green space around it. Inside, Lila followed Morgan's directions to his office, and he gestured her in with a smile when he saw her at the door.

"Hello, Lila. It's good to see you." He stood for a moment to shake her hand. "There is coffee on the table behind you, some bottles of water, and brownies one of my staff members brought me earlier. Help yourself."

"Thanks," she said, getting a bottle of water and snagging one of the brownies and a napkin.

"I've been so pleased with all the sketches and watercolors you've been creating for the book. It's going to lure anyone who sees it to want to buy the book for the art alone."

"Thank you," she said, smiling.

He sipped on the coffee he'd poured himself. "I like all the Indigo sketches you've sent me so far, and I'm eager to see the new drawings and paintings you've brought me today."

Lila began to take out the new work from her satchel to pass across Morgan's desk. She enjoyed listening to his comments about them all.

At one point, she asked him, "Do you lay out the book text and pictures as you go, Morgan?"

No." He grinned. "I don't have the kind of graphics skills to do either, but one of our professors who teaches Graphic Design at the college does. He did Myron Andric's book, and he has started laying out the text and illustrations for my book now. Would you like to see how it's shaping up?"

"Yes, I would."

On his desktop computer, Morgan pulled up the Adobe InDesign book text, in process, and let Lila look over his shoulder to see how the book was coming along.

"You can see he's using many of your watercolors in different places and tucking in a few black-and-white sketches around the text, too. Do you like it?"

"I do," she said. "He has a gift for layout, using the art and text very creatively."

"His name is Allen Greenspan and he said to tell you he especially loves putting color illustrations wherever possible." Morgan grinned. "He says they have much more spazazz."

"He's right," she agreed. "Tell him it would be easy to add color to any of the black-and-white sketches he'd like to update."

"I will." He shut down the book program and then they talked about any sketches and paintings needed to finish the work at Indigo. As usual, Morgan had read some history bits that made him want her to add a few new related sketches. Then they began to make plans for the work at Crawford Plantation.

"Jane Broadwater is eager for you to work at her place. She has several cottages and she says she would be happy for you to call one of them home for a few weeks, rather than driving and boating back and forth to the island every day."

"That's sweet of her but I'm used to commuting, and it isn't far from their plantation to Jenkins Landing and then only ten minutes to the island by boat."

"Well, let her know if you change your mind." He handed Lila a file folder. "I've printed out a rough draft of my Crawford Plantation text so far, and I penciled notes around the sides of it or circled things I'd like you to consider doing drawings and paintings of. I think you're used to my roughshod ways of doing things now."

"I am and it's no problem. I enjoy reading the text, too. It helps my focus as I'm working."

"Well, keep doing those random sketches that stand out to you, too. As you saw from the layouts, Allen incorporated a lot of those."

They finished their discussions and Lila returned to her car, walking through a portion of Marion Square on her way, a handsome city park of over six and a half acres. It was nice to relax and enjoy the warmth of the afternoon and to stop at one of the park's big fountains, splashing away cheerfully. She strolled by an ongoing art fair and market, and spotted early flowers in bloom. The park, originally established as a parade ground by the Citadel, was a favorite place for students of the nearby Citadel and College of Charleston to gather.

After returning to the garage, it wasn't far down King Street to CeeCee's Place. Lila parked behind the store, retrieved the parking pass Celeste had given her from her glove compartment, and hung it on the mirror by the driver's seat. Then she took a deep breath and said a short prayer under her breath before getting out of her car. Somehow, she knew talking with her two sisters tonight would be harder than sharing with Burke and her mother. Gwen and Celeste were more reactive, emotional, and often outspoken.

She popped into Celeste's store first, where she was greeted with affection by Celeste's store manager, Imogene Hathaway, and then wrapped in hugs, first by her sister and then by Novaleigh and Clifford George's daughter, Vanessa, who'd worked at the store since Celeste bought it.

"Your beautiful artwork is certainly selling well in the store," Vanessa said, patting Lila's arm and pointing to one of the walls where they'd hung several of her paintings..

"I hope you're working on more pictures we can put in the store, too," Celeste added. "I'm totally out of back stock when these sell."

"I have more at the house and copies of the ones you already carry if you want duplicates of any of them." She smiled at Celeste. "I'm so glad the paintings are selling well."

"Never diminish your work. It's fabulous and I wish you could hear all the complimentary comments about it."

"Thank you."

Celeste grinned at her. "If it's okay I'd like for you, me, and Gwen to go to Thurman's tonight for dinner. It helps business for me to drop in at the restaurant, even if I don't sing. And sometimes I sing a song or two and play the piano on nights when Marcus is not there."

"Will Reid join us?"

"No, he and Ben are going to a baseball tournament their old high school is playing in. They're all stoked about it." She laughed. "Besides, this is our sisters' night. Reid respects that."

Celeste took Lila upstairs to settle in at her old apartment over the store. She'd kept the apartment for a guest space after marrying and moving in with Reid this winter. A short time later Gwen joined them, after driving up from Port Royal.

"What are Alex and the kids doing tonight?" Celeste asked her, after they'd greeted and hugged, glad to see each other again.

She laughed. "Alex is taking the kids and Dallas, the little boy from across the street, to this Glowcountry Mini Golf place in Beaufort where they play miniature golf under black lights in the dark."

"That sounds interesting, I guess." Celeste grinned. "How does that work in the dark?"

Gwen shrugged. "Supposedly the balls glow in the dark and there are brightly lit obstacles and holes throughout. It's a popular new trend around the U.S. and the kids are excited about going."

"Well, I hope they have fun."

Celeste glanced at her watch. "Let's get dressed for Thurman's. I made our reservation for six before they get too busy."

Knowing Celeste usually picked a fancy restaurant for any girls' night in Charleston, Lila had brought a nice dress with her, and it didn't take long for the three of them to get ready, around laughing and giggling about one thing or another.

At Thurman's, they ordered fried green tomatoes for an appetizer, and the evening's flounder special with ground grits and apple fennel slaw for their main course. For dessert, Celeste talked their waiter, Tony, into bringing them mini red velvet cakes the restaurant often served guests for birthdays.

Back at the apartment, they changed into satin pajama sets Celeste had gifted to them. The pajamas were lush to the touch, with long sleeves and silky pants.

"They're called Lounging Pajamas," Celeste told them, "And lounging and relaxing is exactly what we're going to do tonight."

"Ooooh, I love them," Gwen said, stripping off to slide into her emerald green pajamas. Celeste's were crimson red, and Lila's were a rich, sapphire blue.

Lila ran her hand over the silky fabric, enjoying the feel of it.

Celeste smiled at her. "Even when you were a little girl, Lila, you loved the feel of silky slips, dresses, and fabrics. I remember we visited some of Mother's relatives once at Hilton Head and you fell in love with the satin sheets on the bed."

Lila blushed. "Well, some fabrics are really lovely to the touch."

"I'm sure Alex Trescott will agree when I wear these at home tomorrow night!" Gwen giggled.

Celeste laughed, too. "I did have other pleasures in mind with these, Gwen, but we married women need to mind our talk around Lila, our young innocent tonight."

Somehow their banter wasn't making Lila feel more comfortable about talking to them about her past. She grew quiet while they laughed and visited in the living room, trying to watch for a time when she could share what she needed to.

"I'm sorry Burke couldn't be with us but I know Drew is too

young to leave alone easily," Gwen put in, then adding a new thought. "Burke told me Mother asked them if they wanted to move back to the family's apartment in the inn since none of us are staying there now. Did you know that, Lila?"

"Burke mentioned it," Lila replied. "She and Waylon love having their own place though and living at the lodge. I think they will stay there for now. It's easier with the baby. Babies can be a little noisy and messy, too."

Gwen shrugged. "So were we, but we all lived in the apartment."

"Actually, I think Mother has decided to move into the apartment and live there herself," Lila added. "You know it was built for her and Daddy when they married, when our grandparents lived in the room Mother is in now. She's actually very sentimental about that apartment and wants to move there so she'll have more privacy, a little kitchen, and her own sitting area."

"She'd be able to rent the big downstairs bedroom, too, if she wants to. It's larger and more private. Some people would gladly pay more for it," Celeste put in. "I know Reid and I would love to stay in it when we come for a night."

"Our favorite place to stay is at Seaside Cottage," Gwen said. She hesitated and then added, "You know, Mother moving back to the apartment is really a good idea now that I think about it."

"Well, we'll all tell her that," Celeste finished. "Not that she needs our approval. The Inn is hers, after all."

Gwen leaned forward, taking a sip from one of the chilled bottles of Perrier Celeste had brought to the table. "Do you think Mother is interested in Dean Anderson, the chaplain at the camp, who lives in our family's condo at the Bohicket Marina?"

"I don't know, but he is obviously interested in Mother. He has been for some time. You know he finds every excuse to come over to the Inn for one thing or the other," Celeste said, thinking about it. "What do you think, Lila?"

"I think Mother sees him as a dear friend, knowing he and Daddy were good friends," she answered. "I agree, too, that Dean might wish for more than friendship with Mother, but I don't think her heart is ready to consider it yet. So often I hear her talk about Daddy in a way that shows how close he still is in her heart."

"It hurts me Daddy died so young," Gwen said after a space of quiet.

"Sam Calhoun died young, too, and only two months after Daddy, but I doubt Clarice is grieving his memory much," Celeste remarked, propping her long legs on one of the big ottomans in the room. "She and her husband were never close from what I saw, and I heard lots of rumors about Sam cheating on her."

"I remember Burke told me Sam Calhoun tried to rape Tanya Jessup, Isaac's fiancé, who's now his wife," Gwen recalled. "It caused a big stink. Burke said that Isaac apparently caught him at it. They had a fight, and that's what caused Isaac to leave the island. He and Tanya lived in Georgetown until Sam died this fall. Burke said he wouldn't have come back to Indigo at all if Sam hadn't died."

"Burke told me that, too," Celeste added. "She also said that's why Earl and Della sent Maisie off the plantation to live with Della's sister, Vergie. Evidently, Sam Calhoun was preying on other young girls and it worried them."

"Were all the girls Sam tried to attack African American?" Gwen asked.

"No," said Lila in a strong voice. "Not all were Black."

Arrested by the tone of her voice, Celeste and Gwen turned to look at Lila in question.

"Sam Calhoun tried to rape me, too," she said into the silence.

"What?" Celeste almost screeched. "Are you serious?"

"Lila, this is nothing to make jokes about," Gwen added in a stern voice. "If this is true you need to talk to us about it."

"It is true," she replied, feeling the tears gather in her eyes. "It's one of the reasons I encouraged having a sisters' night right now. With Edward back and me spending time at the plantation again, working on drawings and paintings for Morgan Richard's book, this knowledge surfaced once again. I see now it's a healthy thing that it did, but it's been hard to face and talk about."

Both of her sisters looked shocked.

She sighed. "I've talked to Mother, Burke, the Jessup women, and Edward, and I wanted to also talk to both of you. It was an awful thing. I was young and scared when it happened and Sam Calhoun threatened me, as well. I never told anyone. I was too ashamed such a thing could happen and that it could happen to me. I was also afraid of what people would think, scared they would change toward me."

"Oh, Lila, honey, bless your heart," Gwen said at last, starting to cry herself.

Celeste got up and went over to sit down on the couch to pull Lila close. "Sister, surely you know I understand your hurt and pain in this after all I went through with Dillon Barlow. He raped me many times, beat me up as well. He made me feel like the lowest of the low."

Lila wept now. "It was Edward's father, though, Celeste. That made it so much worse and more confusing. I couldn't believe Edward's own father would try to hurt me like that, talk to me the way he did, be so cruel to me. It was shocking."

She told them everything then, letting it all rush out once more, telling them the whole story.

"And you didn't tell anyone afterward?" Gwen marveled.

Celeste snorted. "If she'd told Daddy, he would have gone after Sam full throttle, friend or not, and believe me Sam would have regretted his actions by the time Dad finished with him. Daddy was a strong man, working at the lighthouse so much and on the grounds, taking boats out, living a very physical life. I watched him intimidate bigger, stronger men than Sam Calhoun many times when he went with me to sing at clubs and shows. He watched all of us girls like a hawk, if you remember. He would have been so angry over this, Lila. I wish you'd told him and Mother."

She shook her head. "All I thought of at the time was that Sam was Daddy's friend. Clarice was Mother's friend. Sam handled all the Inn and Lighthouse's legal matters and problems. Who would have believed me? And what if Sam had lied?" She put a hand over her mouth. "He told me Edward would never want anything to do with me again if he learned of it."

Gwen and Celeste gave each other raised-eye looks then.

"You and Edward did carry feelings for each other back then, didn't you?" Gwen crossed her arms. "Otherwise, you wouldn't have cared about that."

Lila sighed again.

Celeste grinned. "Lila, you might as well come clean about everything, about your relationship with Edward both then and now. We have plenty of time here."

She got up to get some snacks and drinks, and then she and Gwen began to quiz Lila until all was confessed.

"I admit I'm somewhat delighted you and Edward are getting together. I always did like him," Gwen acknowledged.

Celeste laughed at her words. "And isn't it fun our little Sister Anne may now possibly become the grand lady of Indigo Plantation?"

Despite Lila's denials that she and Edward weren't that serious yet or more than friends, her sisters waved her words aside.

"I remember you saw changes coming for all of us last year," Celeste said after a time. "Did you ever think this might be part of the change for you, Lila, reuniting with Edward?"

"It's certainly obvious, too, with all that happened why you didn't come home before," Gwen put in. "Like with Isaac Jessup and Tanya leaving, I don't think you would have come home to stay if Sam hadn't died."

Celeste agreed. "Yes, somehow you knew in your spirit, Lila, the way you always know and sense things, it was time to come back. That's why you were restless. God knew all that would happen, even if you didn't. He knew Sam Calhoun's days were numbered and He knew Edward would come home if Sam weren't there anymore, just as Isaac would."

Gwen put a hand on one hip. "Do you think the reason you went into the Community of St. Mary was to avoid coming home to the island?"

"She does have a point," Celeste agreed. "Graduation was coming up at Sewanee then. You would naturally need to come back home, and you were scared. Sam Calhoun had told you he'd finish what he started one day if you did."

Unsettled by their words, Lila started crying again. "Please know I really felt called to enter the Community of St. Mary's. I didn't just choose that life because it was a way to escape. I could have gone other places if I simply hadn't wanted to return home."

"We didn't mean to upset you," Celeste said softly. "But it could have been an unconscious motivation behind your choices. It's not sinful to recognize that, Lila. You'd held all this in, almost blocked it out of your life, told no one. At the Community you knew you'd be safe and protected from men and from the hurts they can bring. Give prayer to that understanding, not to make you feel ashamed, but to answer some of your own questions as to why you felt restless and why you left when you did. We've all had our upsetting things to deal with in this last season. This is yours to work through."

They talked longer, and in time moved to other topics but Lila still felt upset when she finally went to bed. She slept in the second bedroom alone, while Gwen slept with Celeste in the other room. Lila felt glad for the privacy after being grilled by her sisters all evening. She needed privacy for prayer and for crying quietly. Perhaps she had joined the Community in part to hide, even if unconsciously, and perhaps that was why her spirit grew restless about taking further vows. It was a hard understanding to come to, but Lila also knew how much she'd gained while at St. Mary's, how that time had shaped and grown her, strengthened her faith. She couldn't regret it.

CHAPTER 16

As the weeks of April slipped by and May began, Edward found himself happier than he'd expected to be back at Indigo. He knew in part it was because of his days with Lila. She'd finished her sketches and paintings at Indigo for Morgan Richards' book, and now she'd started spending time at Crawford Plantation not far away.

The two had fallen into a comfortable routine of riding and spending time together most afternoons after they finished work. Edward, trying to give life at Edisto a fair trial, like Raymond Maybank had suggested, worked early in the day either at the law firm or on the plantation. Lila would usually stop by Indigo after finishing her sketches and paintings for the day, and they would ride together or take one of the kayaks out on the creeks that bordered the plantation property. Sometimes they simply strolled along the river, stopping to sit on one the old docks or in the folly, or they took one of Indigo's boats out for a ride. Edward also sometimes drove his boat to the island in the mornings to pick up Lila and then took her home in the evening, so they didn't need to worry about enjoying a longer day if they wanted to.

In their times together, they'd caught up on their years apart, with Edward sharing about his work at the clinic and his time at the college. Lila, in turn, had painted for him a more accurate picture of her time at St. Mary's and at Sewanee.

As he sat in his home office going over the accounts one morning, his cell phone rang, interrupting him. Seeing it was Ryan Markman, his old college roommate, Edward snatched up the phone eagerly.

"Ryan. Hey, man, how are you?"

"Good. I'm on a break and haven't talked to you since you headed to Edisto to take care of business at the plantation last month. How are things going there?"

Edward leaned back in his desk chair. "You know I really dreaded coming home but things are going better than I expected. The long shadow of my father doesn't seem as ominously dark and overshadowing now."

Ryan chuckled. "I'm glad to hear that. I know he was tough on you and not a very admirable man from all you told me."

"That's the truth," Edward replied. "Are you still enjoying being in practice with your dad's law firm in Asheville?"

"I am and things are going well. It's kind of a family deal with my Uncle Benny and one of my cousins in the firm, too. Fortunately, my family are all easy people to work with. We're a sociable, agreeable lot. Have you been spending some time at your Dad's firm? How's that going?"

"Better than I expected," he admitted. "Evidently, my father acted more honorably in the firm than he did at home. However, Raymond and Hudson Maybank seemed aware of my father's dual nature and regretted the problems I'd known at home, too. I've been spending a little time at the firm most days, getting my feet wet to see if it might be a fit for me."

"When your dad died, I told you things would be different at home for you," Ryan added. "How are you getting along with your mother?"

Edward gave a disgusted snort. "She's basically been absentee at her sister Eula's in Charleston since I got home. She's let me know, in no uncertain terms, she wants to move there permanently, doesn't want to stay at Indigo, and doesn't care what I do about the place."

"Ouch," Ryan said. "However, maybe that's a good thing. If she'd stayed at the plantation, you'd probably be packing up by now. She sure was a cool, frigid number most of the times she came to Vanderbilt to visit with your dad."

"I hear you," he agreed. "It always kind of scared me that I might start becoming like one of them one day, but since I've been back, everyone has candidly told me I'm just like my Grandfather Malcolm, my dad's father, in looks and personality." Edward paused. "I remember my grandad with warmth, a good man with a strong character, a hearty laugh and lots of smiles. He was admired and loved by everyone. The comparisons really have made me feel better and more comfortable around here."

"It's funny how character traits often skip a generation. Do you remember all those Bible stories where the kings had sons that did evil, not living right before the Lord; then oftentimes their sons did good, turning back to a right way? It's not a new concept. God gave us all free will, but we each have to choose to live right. You can choose to be like your grandad, you know. It's never a given we become like our parents. We have free will to choose our own way."

"Thanks for that, counselor. You sound like Lila."

"Isn't that the girl you used to date that became a sister? Are you hearing from her again?"

"She's back home again. She left the religious community not long after my dad died. There's a story there. Apparently, Dad threatened and scared her, wanting to break us up." Edward decided not to say more. "I never knew about it until now."

Ryan laughed. "Does that mean romance is in the air, friend? I remember you talked about that girl a lot. Got in a real funk when you heard she went into that religious community in Sewanee."

"Well, I'll be honest and admit I never quit caring for Lila, and we've gotten back together since I've been home. It's a perk; I can honestly say that. I hope more will come of it."

"You know I love Vandy and Nashville," Ryan said, "but I'll be honest and tell you I was wowed at that gorgeous plantation on Edisto, where you grew up, the time I visited with you. If you stay, I'm going to come down often for vacations and long weekends. Edisto is only about five hours from Asheville. We can hang out at the beach, take your boat out and fish, do a little kayaking. You've got a nice deal there if it works out for you."

Edward grinned. "Well, you can come any time, Ryan."

"Thanks. You come to the mountains whenever you want, too. I've still got my condo in downtown Asheville, not far from the Blue Ridge Parkway and the mountains."

"Any new women in your life?"

Ryan chuckled. "I'm seeing someone, a girl named Megan Bowman. It feels like she might be the one. We'll see. The family likes her; that's a good sign. And they know and like her family. I'm texting you a photo now of the two of us when we were up at Mount Mitchell. You'll see she's better looking than I am."

"Well, bring her with you when you come down if you want."

"Maybe I will," he answered. "Listen, I need to get back to work now. I have a new client coming in."

"It was good to hear from you," Edward replied.

They hung up, and hearing the ping on his phone, Edward popped over to his text messages to see the photo of Ryan and his new girlfriend Megan. They were standing smiling on the observation tower at the summit of Mount Mitchell State Park, a spot Ryan had taken him to once on one of his visits to Asheville in the past.

He texted back. "She is better looking than you. You better hang on to this one." Smiling, he added, "Good to hear from you."

Edward glanced at his watch after putting his phone down. He had an appointment coming up. One of the men who'd reached out to his mother about buying the plantation had tracked him down and wanted to drop by to meet with him. Trying to keep his options open, Edward agreed to talk with him.

A short time later the man called, as Edward had asked him to, before heading past the private property sign at the entrance road to the plantation. Edward went out to the porch to watch for him.

The man parked and headed up the steps, sending a smile Edward's way. He was older, polished, a little stocky, but dressed in a sharp suit, shirt and tie, and what Edward called "monied shoes."

"Good to meet you, Edward," he said, coming up the porch

steps to reach out a hand to take Edward's in a firm, practiced handshake. "I'm Harold Woodrow with Lowcountry Premier Properties. I appreciate your very charming, gracious mother connecting us to meet at last. Perhaps she told you I have a client very interested in your property. She said she doubted you'd want to stay at the plantation with your father gone, and she let me know she had no objections to selling it."

Edward gestured to a chair on the porch. "Why don't we sit here on the porch? It's a fine day."

The man glanced toward the front door, obviously disappointed not to be ushered inside.

Edward tried to keep a congenial expression on his face as the man settled into one of the wicker porch chairs, crossing a leg to get comfortable. He glanced around as he did, casing out the property. Edward disliked him immediately. The man felt smarmy and phony, calling his mother "charming" and assuming he wanted to sell the plantation before even talking with him about it at all.

"As I said, I have a client very interested in this fine property," Harold continued, grinning at him again. "They have been looking for a place on the water like this, with a dock and quick access to the ocean. They want a big place where they can entertain. They like that you have a guest house in back. Your mother took me around to see things the time I called on her before you got back."

Harold opened the briefcase he'd tucked under his arm to pull out some papers, glancing at them. "My client might want to convert some of the other homes on the property into rentals. A lot of people would love to come and stay here. My client thinks it might be a nice historic home for hosting events, too. I think your mother said your family in past had opened the place for a few events."

Edward's annoyance grew. His mother hadn't mentioned she showed this man around.

"I've run some figures, Edward, and I think you and your mother can get a fine property sale and an excellent return with a place this big. I have some figures here I think you will really like."

Edward cleared his throat and interrupted. "Mr. Woodrow, this is a working farm and plantation. Ideally, I'd like to see it kept that way."

A little confusion flashed in Harold's expression. "Your mother did say you had some help living on the plantation." He hesitated. "My client might be able to find a place for some of them in the house, keeping up the grounds, and such. However, I don't think my client has in mind continuing the plantation as a producing farm."

Edward stood, fed up now. "Mr. Woodrow, I appreciate you taking the time to stop by today. However, I believe my mother didn't give you a clear understanding of the type of property owner we might be looking for, if we decide to sell Indigo. The plantation is a highly productive farm and we have a strong team that manage the farm and live on it as well. Additionally, the plantation is not my mother's and mine to sell. It is mine to sell. As you have seen, my mother is living in Charleston and intends to reside there. She's never had much interest in the plantation, and I regret she gave you the wrong impression about what sort of client we might be interested in talking with."

A flash of irritation touched Harold Woodrow's face. "I could certainly discuss alternate possibilities with my client, and, of course, we might locate other potential clients through our company more interested in maintaining Indigo as a working plantation. From my research into the plantation's profit line, I saw it is a very lucrative enterprise." He grinned at Edward again, trying to recover the situation.

However, Edward didn't sit back down. "I am not sure at this point whether I will sell Indigo Plantation or not yet, Mr. Woodrow. So, actually, it's too soon to be discussing any potential offers yet. However, if you'll leave me your card, I can get back in touch with you if I determine later that selling is a route I might like to pursue." He glanced at his watch, indicating closure. "I'll give my mother your regards and let her know I met with you."

Finding it difficult to hide a frown, Howard tucked his papers back into his briefcase and stood. "Son, it is important to look at all serious offers with an open mind when you're considering selling a property of this size and at the price it will command. It isn't every day you will get a viable offer to consider."

Recognizing the sales push, Edward took a few steps toward the porch steps. "I'll see you to your car. Thank you again for your time."

After listening to a few more patronizing bits of knowledge from Harold Woodrow, Edward finally watched him drive out of the circular driveway toward the entry gate. He stood there for a few minutes to see that the man headed out of the property.

"Is he gone?" a voice asked.

Glancing to his left, Edward saw Levi Jessup standing beside one of the big shrubs by the porch, dressed in his usual work clothes, his old straw hat on his head.

Edward grinned at the older man. "Have you been listening?"

Unashamed, Levi said, "It was thoughtful of you to meet with the man out on the porch near where I was working in the side yard. Sound carries well."

Edward couldn't help laughing. "Wasn't he a smarmy, pompous man? I couldn't wait to get rid of him as soon as I shook his hand."

"I'm glad you didn't sell Indigo to him. Earl and I met him when he came out to cozy up to your mother before you came home."

"I didn't know that," Edward said, gesturing to Levi to follow him back up to the porch. "Did you think I might sell the plantation to him?"

Levi followed him, dropping into the chair where Harold had sat before. "You're young. Money can be very persuasive to the young."

Edward sat down, too, rubbing his neck as he did.

Levi gave him a straight look then. "This old place is yours now, son. You have the right and choice to do with it as you want. If you sell it off to someone like Mr. Woodrow or anyone else, none of us will have any say about what happens with this place after that. As an attorney, you know that as well as I do. We know that, too. We can move on, find other jobs. We won't starve or come to harm, but I admit we'll miss the old place."

"I haven't even decided if I'll sell Indigo yet, Levi."

"No, but I haven't heard you commit to stay, either, so I was just letting you know how it is with us. I'm asking, too, that you'd let us know if you ever decide to sell and write into those sales contracts a little time for us all to make new plans and move if need be. You can do that as an attorney, and I'm asking it as a kindness."

Tears pricked Edward's eyes. He couldn't help them and he reached out to take Levi's hand. "You and your family have been like my family, Levi, more family to me than my own parents ever were. How could you imagine I wouldn't do everything I could to see that nothing wrong would happen to you?"

Levi shook his head. "I hear you. And yet you're still undecided as to whether you will stay or sell this old place, steeped in our joint family histories as it is. I have to tell you I don't understand that, boy. It's not like Big Sam or Clarice are still here making problems for you. Makes me think sometimes of that other Edward, that king of England, who abdicated the throne back in the 1930s. It made all the news. I never could figure how come he would do that."

Edward couldn't help grinning. "Edward VIII is hardly a parallel to me, Levi. That Edward was running around with a married American woman, a socialite type, who had been divorced another time before, and he abdicated, against government objections, to run off with her and marry her when she got divorced again."

"So, it was all for a woman," Levi commented. "You got some woman in Nashville wanting you to come back to her?"

He shook his head. "No, but I've got one here I'm interested in now. And while we're sitting here, I want to thank you for following Lila that day and keeping my father from hurting her. It shamed me to learn he would do a thing like that."

"I don't know what got into your father in those years after you went off to college in Nashville. He and Ms. Clarice got more and more estranged, fought a lot, had arguments of all sorts. She spent less and less time at the plantation after you left and Eula wouldn't even let Big Sam in the house at Charleston. Maybe he was unhappy. I don't know. Your father was admired, but not many people loved him."

"That was his own fault, Levi."

"Maybe, but even the sorrows we bring on ourselves hurt us. I watched Sam grow up, saw his strengths, his intelligence, that charisma he had in doing business and working as an attorney. Did you ever see him in the courtroom, fighting for someone? He was powerful and he did a lot to prosper and grow this old plantation, despite all his faults. I suppose I kept hoping for a turnaround in his heart and life, imagining if he pursued goodness how fine a man he could be."

Edward studied the older man. "I'm amazed you could hold any admiration for him after what he tried to do to Tanya, how he disrespected your family. You saw, too, other ways he acted that were so wrong. How cruel he often was to me as a child. How harsh with many others, how he tried to hurt Lila, only a sweet young girl."

"Well, my mama always taught me to look for the good, to see the potential in others. You never know when life, and the good Lord, might turn someone around. It's what you try to envision, what you pray for in those not living right." He nodded. "Think of all Paul in the Bible did after he got changed, all the good the man did after doing such evil. It's never a good idea to hold hate toward anyone. It just hurts you to do so. As an attorney, you often have to create a defense for people who do some really wrong things."

Edward sat thinking over all Levi said.

"I need to get back to work." Levi stood to leave then. "Look around over the days to come, son. See the beauty of this old plantation, its possibilities and potential. Imagine yourself here, maybe raising your own family, sharing this beauty with them. Watching the sunsets. Feeling the sea breezes. Enjoying seeing the green fields ripen with crops. Hearing the sounds of the gulls and egrets, birds, and animals. Savoring the pleasures of this unique and special Lowcountry."

The old man glanced toward the house, and then continued the poetry of his words. "You listen with your heart to the creak of the old staircase rising up to the second floor of the plantation house. Look out from its balconies and porches over the land, knowing its yours. Know that you are loved and can love others well. That you can leave a good legacy like your grandad did that will be remembered."

He tipped his hat then, heading off the porch.

Edward sat for a long time after Levi left, thinking over his words. Lila found him there later, after parking her car and walking up on the porch toward him.

"You look pensive," she said.

"It's been that sort of day," he answered. "How did your work at Crawford's go?"

"Very good. With the day fair and sunny, I painted a nice watercolor of the big plantation house. It's a beautiful old home, like Indigo." She sat down beside him. "Are you still planning to take me out to eat at the Edingsville Grocery Restaurant tonight?"

"I am and I'm looking forward to it."

"Me, too, and I had fun last Friday night with the Jessups at the plantation, didn't you? I enjoyed spending time with Isaac, Tanya, and all the family again. I loved hearing Levi, Earl, and Tommy Lee play and sing, too. Aren't the Jessups good people?"

"Yes. Yes, they are," he agreed.

Edward glanced at his watch. "We have time to ride before we go to eat. Did you bring your riding boots?"

"I did and some clean clothes to change into before we go out." She smiled. "It was nice of you to come pick me up at the island this morning early and to offer to boat me home after dark so I could stay out later."

"It's my pleasure any time," he said. "Let's go put on our riding boots. I told Isaac we'd be riding the bays, Butler and Narita, today."

As Lila turned toward the house, she paused, looking back behind her. "The beauty and charm of this old place never fails to touch my heart. I'm so glad we've put our old painful memories to rest so we can fully enjoy it now, aren't you?"

Edward glanced behind him, out across the circular driveway and the neatly clipped hedges, the flowers a colorful riot now that May had arrived. As he studied the scene the dogs Percy and Tippy ran by barking, hearing Levi whistling for them in the distance.

Catching his glance, Lila said, "Novaleigh says 'It's the sweet, simple things of life that are the best.' I think she's right, don't you?"

CHAPTER 17

After their ride around the familiar trails and farm roads, Edward and Lila returned to the barn, unsaddled their mounts, walked the horses, and then made their way back to the plantation house.

Lila chatted with pleasure about her day at Crawford Plantation as they walked back to the house. "Jane took me on a nice tour inside the house this morning before I began painting outside."

"Who took care of the gift shop today?" Edward asked. "Burke?"

"No. Mother did so I could spend the day working on my drawings. Morgan is eager to move on to another site soon. He's been visiting at Trinity Episcopal Church, already. I was able to tell him some of its history and I shared a few of my own memories to add to his research."

She paused to lean over to sniff one of the pink roses on a sprawling shrub near the house.

"That's a Carolina Rose," Edward offered. "They're pretty, just starting to bloom now, but watch out for the long thorns on the stems."

"A lot of roses are blooming around the plantation now."

"Yes, Della and Annamae know all the names and can tell you about them. This one is a wild rose, tough and hardy; the bees love it."

"There are so many more flowers here on the plantation than on the island. The windswept land and salty soil in many places aren't very hospitable to flowers, but Clifford works hard to grow what he can, especially around the inn."

He smiled at her. "Do you ever see yourself as the lady of the manor here, possibly in a long hoop skirt to greet tourists on island tour days? In my grandfather's time, I remember my grandmother dressing like that. Indigo used to participate in island tours."

Lila looked away, not sure how to answer, not really wanting to pursue this subject either. With the porch in sight, she skipped forward to start up the steps. "Let's change and go out to eat. The ride made me hungry, and I haven't been to the Edingsville Grocery Restaurant yet. It's new."

Edward let the subject go without more comment, and it didn't take them long to change and drive the short distance from the plantation to the restaurant on the main highway. They'd arrived early on purpose, knowing the restaurant often got busy on Friday evenings, and they were soon seated at a small table inside.

"Have you been here before?" Lila asked, studying the menu.

"For lunch one day with Raymond and Hudson."

"What did you eat?"

Edward grinned. "Burgers, Po Boys, and Quesadillas—all good— but I think we might want to try one of the dinner specialties tonight." He glanced at his menu. "I think I might like the pan-seared scallops in a special sauce with spaghetti noodles. It also has bits of country ham in it. Most everything on the menu comes with great homemade hush puppies, too."

"I think I'll try the shrimp and deviled crab with lima beans and stoneground grits. We can share a little. "

"I like that idea. Do you want to get some appetizers?"

"No, but we can split a piece of that fabulous carrot-hummingbird cake I saw on the counter after dinner."

"We'll do that," he said, giving the waitress their orders.

A man spotted Edward then, waved, and came over to say hello. "Good to see you again, Edward," he began, glancing at Lila.

"Lila Deveaux, this is Russell Hughes, one of the owners of the restaurant," Edward said, introducing them. "Lila's family owns the Deveaux Inn."

"I'm pleased to meet you, Lila. I remember visiting the lighthouse at Watch Island where you live when I was a boy." He smiled. "It's a pretty place, and Novaleigh George's cooking at the Inn is legendary around Edisto."

"We're blessed to have Novaleigh, and it's nice to meet you as well, Russell."

"I'll send my brother Robert, also our chef, out to say hello to you when he can get a break," Russell added. "What did you order tonight?"

They chatted about food and the restaurant for a few minutes before Russell moved on, seeing another couple come in that he knew.

"It's nice the owners visit around in their restaurant," Lila said.

"Yes, it is," Edward agreed. "Russell and his twin brother Robert grew up in Conway near Myrtle Beach but the family had a vacation home here and always loved the island. Their dad was a surgeon in Conway until he retired, but he lives not far from the restaurant now in a place on Fishing Creek. The brothers bought this place, a former country store, and renovated it into a restaurant not long ago."

She smiled. "Edisto has a way of calling you back."

Deciding not to comment, he asked instead, "You haven't talked much about how the visit with your sisters went in Charleston. Did they upset you about something?"

"A little," she admitted. "They suggested that I only joined the Community of St. Mary after graduation to keep from returning to the island, because of my fears and your father's threats and everything."

"What if it was a factor?" he asked. "Would that be so bad?"

"Yes." She crossed her arms. "You don't understand. I felt led by God to give my life into the work at St. Mary's. Could I have missed that leading so much? That's what troubles me."

He considered it. "Maybe it was the right decision and the right leading at the time, Lila. As you've shared with me, you changed in many positive ways while at St. Mary's."

"I know that." She heaved a sigh. "I'm just uncomfortable with the idea that I didn't hear well from God."

"Why don't you go talk to our rector, Wey Camp, about this?" he suggested. "Or with Dean Anderson. He's been a rector in past, too, and he's the chaplain at the camp now. One of them might have some comforting advice for you."

She frowned. "I could, but it's a little embarrassing to discuss all that happened in my past with another man. You know."

He chuckled. "Then find another Sister to talk to. There's an Episcopal community in North Augusta."

"That's almost three hours from here, Edward, and most Sisters are innocents and haven't had encounters like I did with men. Talking to them might even be worse."

"I think you're forgetting these women also live close to God. You don't need to have the same painful experience as another person to be able to counsel and help them." He snapped a finger, leaning forward. "Why don't you go to see that counselor you told me Celeste went to see in Charleston? He wouldn't be someone you know, and you said he was a good help to Celeste with all she went through with Dillon."

She looked at him thoughtfully. "That actually might be a good idea. I'll pray about it."

Their dinner came and they talked about other things then, for which Lila was grateful. The idea she had totally missed God's leading and entered The Community of St. Mary only to escape and hide from coming back to Edisto troubled her.

After dinner, they took a walk along the river before loading into Edward's boat to head back to the island and the inn. It was a beautiful night with the moon full in the sky above them. As Edward pulled his boat into the marina and turned off the motor, he turned to her. "I keep thinking about what you said at the restaurant, that it worried you what your sisters said about why you went to St. Mary's. Why does it trouble you so much you might not have heard God right?"

Lila sighed. "Because it's how I know my way."

"And?" he queried further.

She looked toward the light from the lighthouse flashing its light in the dark sky in its familiar pattern. "It's like the light from the lighthouse," she tried to explain. "The sailors far out at sea watch for it to know the way, to know and find the safe route for their boats. Seeing the light of the lighthouse clearly is essential to keep them from making a wrong turn, running into the rocks, missing their way. Even in a storm, when they see the light they feel comforted. They know the way to go then. The light shines to help them find their way out of the dark. Over time as you come to know God better, you hear from Him about the way to go, too. You ask and seek from Him before large and small decisions in your life to help you know the right way to take." She hesitated. "Like looking for the lighthouse, you begin to look for and to expect to hear from God to keep you from making mistakes, from going off in a wrong direction, not following in His best will."

She could see Edward thinking about her words for a minute, watching the light from the lighthouse as he did.

After a moment he said, "I've been trying to hear from God about what He wants me to do right now in my life, too, so I can understand that." He paused. "I wish I could tell you I've heard a big 'thus saith the Lord' about exactly what God wants me to do right now but I'm trying to listen. It is somewhat like driving my boat along in the dark, looking for the light, the right direction, the answer to know what to do."

"What if you thought you heard and then realized later you missed it?"

Edward shook his head. "I'm on the train of faith, Lila, but I haven't arrived. There are times I miss it. We all do. I missed a lot of things in that time heading off to college, after the issues with Tanya, angry, confused, embarrassed." He reached out and took her hand. "Can't you look back and see you missed doing everything in a perfect way then, too? It was a hard time."

"I suppose," she admitted.

"And how do you know, when you graduated from Sewanee, that

you weren't supposed to go to The Community of St. Mary at that time? Perhaps God had things for you to learn there, like we've talked about before." He grinned. "Remember that old children's song *He's Still Working On Me*? I know He's still working on me. I'm a person in progress, on a journey of growth every day. Aren't you?"

She smiled. "Those are wise words, Edward."

He leaned over to kiss her on the forehead. "What else did Celeste say to you that keeps bothering you?"

"She suggested that entering the Community might have been my way to stay safe and protected from men and from the hurts they can bring. She said it might have been an unconscious motivation behind my choice and that it wouldn't be sinful to recognize that since I'd held everything in the way I did."

Lila watched Edward think about those words. "So, what if there was an unconscious motivation behind what you did? We all work with the best information and knowledge we have when we make any decision in our lives, and you know hindsight is always better when we look back at a situation and analyze it later. You shouldn't beat yourself up over stuff like this. You were doing your best, trying to follow God in the best way you could. How do you know He didn't lead you at that time to the Community to grow and learn there?"

"I always felt He did. But now when I'm praying and seeking His counsel about issues and decisions in my life again, I don't feel as confident as I used to." She gave him an anguished look. "I don't want to mess up and miss God."

He grinned at her. "I hope those decisions about the direction for your life revolve around whether you should say yes to aligning your life with mine. I've been praying God would show you that we're meant to be together, Lila. I believe He has reconnected us. I feel a deep peace and certainty in my heart about that."

"Well, I thought I knew my direction before and look what happened." She bit her lip over the words.

He tilted her chin up to look into her eyes. "How do you know your right direction isn't right into my arms and my life, Lila Deveaux? No matter what decisions we made before or why, no matter what problems we had or bad memories we're still working through, I believe we're meant to be together. Can't you feel that deep down in your soul? I can tell you this is the one thing I'm totally sure of, and I'm praying God will make it totally clear if I'm meant to stay at Indigo now or leave and come back later. I'm not totally sure of that answer yet, but I'm beginning to feel strongly I'm not supposed to sell the plantation."

Not waiting for her answers this time, Edward gathered her in his arms to kiss her long and well. "How can you doubt?" he whispered in her ear. "How can you doubt when everything within feels right when we're together? You're my other half, my love, my soul."

Lila pulled away to smile at him. "I think you've made me feel better tonight and I think I may not need a counselor now. As you've helped me to see, I simply need to remember I'm always growing and learning in the Lord, and in my faith, and I need to always keep pursuing in that direction with all my heart. Following the Light the best that I can, even if I miss it a little bit sometimes."

"Wise words," he said, hugging her close.

She heaved a big sigh. "You know, I'd almost pulled away from God a little, feeling I might have missed Him or failed Him in some way. That was wrong of me. We're all built to hear His voice. Sometimes in a storm we can't see the Light clearly for some reason, but it's always there, continuing. We need to persist in God faithfully, too, always looking for and seeking more of His light."

"Spoken like a girl who grew up by a lighthouse," he said, giving her a quick kiss again before giving her a hand to help her out of the boat. "I'd better walk you to your cottage and head home now."

As they started up the road, he asked, "I know tomorrow is Saturday, and you'll need to work at the gift shop, but can I come over later in the evening to take a walk on the beach with you?"

"Of course." She smiled at him. "And you know Novaleigh would be delighted if you'd come for dinner, too."

"Thanks. I'll plan to do that," he said.

As Lila waved goodbye to Edward a short time later, her heart felt lighter. One thing she was learning now was how much others could be a comfort and counsel to her, as she often was to them.

CHAPTER 18

At two a.m. in the morning, Edward's phone rang, startling him awake. Seeing the call was from Isaac, he answered quickly. "Is anything wrong, Isaac?"

"We've got a fire on the island."

Edward sat up, fully awake now. "At the plantation?"

"No, but close, and it's spreading. The fire started in a couple of out buildings near Swallow Bluff and it spread to the house. We got a call from Della's sister Virgie and her husband Fisher. They can see the smoke billowing from their place on Point of Pines Road and they heard fire trucks roaring by."

"I'm getting dressed," Edward said, already out of bed and reaching for the jeans he'd draped over a chair last night. "Come pick me up in your truck and we'll head down the road to see what we can find out."

"I doubt they'll let us get too close."

"We just need to get close enough to see the situation and maybe talk to someone. Before you leave, call Earl and Levi and tell them to start loading our firefighting equipment in another of our trucks. If the fire is near our property line, we'll want to dig some firebreaks or fire lines to keep it from spreading our way. We'll need to start wetting down any outlying structures and removing any flammables on the property, too, that might be in the fire's potential path."

Pulling on his boots, Edward added, "I'll try to find a news

station or make a few calls for any other information we can get
while you're on your way."

"I'm on it," Isaac said. "Anything else?"

"No. I'll see you out front in a few minutes."

A short time later, Edward and Isaac headed out of the plantation
and down Point of Pines Road, soon running into a road block.
Lonnie Culler, with the sheriff's department, saw them and walked
over to their truck. "I can't let anyone down Swallow Bluff Road
because of the fire. It's bad, and unless you have an emergency
somewhere, I'm blocking through traffic on the road here."

He pointed to the heavy smoke and flames decorating the night
sky. "This is a really bad blaze. The fire has burned two sheds and
the old plantation house is engulfed. As dry as it's been, the flames
spread quickly. You know the Swallow Bluff plantation house is
empty right now with no one living on the property. By the time
anyone saw the fire and reported it, we had a real inferno going."

Lonnie gestured again toward the smoke and flames. "We've
got firefighters from St. Paul's Fire Department and from another
station at Adams Run, already working to contain the fire, and
more firefighters are coming from other nearby departments to
help out. This is a concern to all, if it keeps spreading."

"It's been so dry. That makes it worse," Isaac said.

"Yes, and the wind has picked up, coming from the land and
pushing the sparks. That doesn't help." Lonnie glanced up the road
as they heard more firetrucks heading in.

Edward glanced toward the incoming vehicles. "Ask to see what
we can do to help, if you would."

"I'll go see what I can find out." Lonnie ran to remove the
barriers to let the trucks into Swallow Bluff Road and spoke briefly
to one of the men before walking back to them. A fireman, who
had been following the engines in a truck, followed him.

The man, in full fire gear, nodded at Edward as he drew closer.
"I'm Romney Berle, one of the Deputy Chiefs with the St. Paul's
Fire Department. Lonnie says you live down the road at Indigo."

"Yes, I'm Edward Calhoun. I own Indigo Plantation. This is

Isaac Jessup, one of my managers. What can we do to help with this fire?"

"Protect your farm and property. We have several additional fire departments coming in to help get this thing under control, but one of our main concerns is that the fire doesn't spread and jump Grimball Creek, threatening homes and property on the other side."

"My land borders the creek as you probably know."

He nodded. "I do, and we have bulldozers already developing a fire line to the east of the creek, across from your property. The creek itself is a natural fire line, but we'd like to see any fuel near that creek on your side reduced as well. Do you have people to help you work to create a fire line on your side of the creek, to wet down structures and outbuildings and remove any flammable materials, like burnable vegetation, around the fire line area?"

"There are four of us that can start work right away, others I can call to come in."

"Good. Let me drive in to Swallow Bluff to talk to our fire chief and I'll see if we can send a few of our men to help later, as well." He glanced toward the flames and smoke in the sky. "We want to try to arrest this thing as soon as possible and keep it from causing more damage."

As Romney headed back to his truck, they could hear the sirens of more fire engines coming in.

Lonnie glanced up the road toward the incoming trucks. "I'll try to send you some help at Indigo as we get more help in here. In the meantime, get on the phone and call anyone you know that might come to help you, like Hal and Dewey Jenkins, or any of Isaac's family who aren't working to secure their own places right now."

"Have you called Waylon at the island?" Edward asked.

"I have and I suggested they secure the island and evacuate all the guests staying with them as morning comes. The smoke everywhere is already bad, as you can see." He hesitated. "The wind from the land has sent fire sparks and embers across Ocella Creek and into the back regions of Botany Bay, starting up fires there, too. The South Carolina Forestry Commission firefighters are coming in to help with that. They don't want that fire spreading further into Botany Bay and toward historic structures. Believe me, we're glad for their help, too."

As Isaac drove back to Indigo, Edward called Hal and Dewey Jenkins and other friends Isaac suggested. They would all need to work hard and fast to do all they could to protect the plantation.

"I hope the wind doesn't turn," Isaac offered, frowning. "We're lucky, I guess, that it isn't coming off the ocean. Winds from the sea might blow the head of that fire and the embers in our direction. Tanya and I saw on the weather last night that rain and storms were predicted around Walterboro and Summerville. I'm sure those storms are what's been sending the wind from the land and blowing those sparks across Ocella Creek into the Botany Bay property."

Isaac shook his head. "Dad was just bemoaning yesterday that rain and storms were predicted in the area but not here to give us any relief from the drought. It sure would be a blessing if some of that rain headed our way about now."

"It would." Edward rolled up the window as they drove down the private road back into Indigo. "The smoke is already getting bad. We'd probably be wise to tie bandanas over our faces while we work, and we'll all need to get into some of those fire-retardant overalls, jackets, boots, gloves, and such that we have on hand from times in the past working as volunteers with the fire station. I want us to all work safe."

The next hours until daylight were grueling ones. Edward, Isaac, Levi, Earl, and Tommy Lee secured the interior of the plantation as much as possible and then loaded their equipment into trucks to head through the fields and woods to Indigo's property line bordering Grimball Creek. There they began to clear out excess vegetation, leaf litter, overhanging tree limbs, vines, and other fuels a spreading fire might feed on if the fire moved closer and tried to jump the creek.

Hal and Dewey came to help as the night hours moved along,

as did others who lived nearby including Sally Ann's husband Don Nagel, Earl's son-in-law Gavin George and others. The women at Indigo, along with volunteer helpers, too, did their part, helping to water down structures around the property, clearing out brush and dead vegetation near buildings, and helping to trim back vines.

Indigo had always kept fire pumps they could set up for small unexpected fires, and they incorporated these now, hooking the pumps into wells, ponds, the river, and directly into Grimball Creek for a water source. With the fire raging more to the east end of their property, they worked hardest there to keep it from crossing the creek and getting into their fields or spreading to the barns and sheds there.

Edward followed Levi's instruction now in setting up one of the pumps near the east end of the property. "This is a good place to wet things down closer to where the fire is burning across Grimball Creek," Levi said. "We've got a power source in the barn here and we can use the water from the creek. Since we've already cleared this area, we can wet everything down good now. To stop fire, you have to take away its fuel, its heat, or its oxygen. We can't do much about the oxygen part for a big fire like this, but we can try to pull fuel away from the areas where we don't want the fire to burn and we can soak things down to take away its heat source if it tries to move our way."

The older man pointed to the heavy smoke they could see now more clearly with daylight coming, sparks flicking up in the sky above it. "I'm still seeing a lot of smoke and flame to the east of us. I've seen some fires as a boy, but this one is sure bad."

"Those firefighters that came to help for a while said the fire totally destroyed the Swallow Bluff plantation house."

Levi shook his head at Edward's words. "That's a real shame. Beautiful old home. It once belonged to the Mitchells back in the 1800s. Julian Mitchell practiced law, like you do, and he was a South Carolina legislator. He once owned a lot of land around here. His mother was a Grimball. That old plantation had the prettiest dovecotes, too, fine little decorative buildings with spires, kind of like our folly. The old place had a guesthouse and a pretty barn and sheds. I guess it's all gone now. What a sorrow." Levi shook his head. "I figure it was that arsonist again, causing this trouble, don't you?"

A slice of anger streaked through Edward's mind at the thought. "You're probably right, Levi. I hope they catch him."

"And I hope nobody gets hurt. There are a few little homes tucked around the place where that old plantation stands. I imagine the folks that live there had to evacuate."

A little later, they had a scare as the blaze moved closer to the creek on the east side. They could see the fire fighters working to contain this new section of the fire, trying to keep it from spreading by soaking it with water and retardants from the firetruck hoses. The sight of flames kicking up nearer their property had brought a rush of men to their area, trying to further soak the ground closest to the blaze that had ignited across the creek.

Just as the fire was almost contained and moving away from them, toward the Swallow Bluff area again, a shout from one of the firefighters across the creek alerted them to some embers that had blown over the Grimball Creek to settle beyond the fire line they'd created, kicking up a new blaze there.

Edward's heart leaped to see fire on his own land. Would this nightmare ever end?

"Let's get after this," Levi called out and Edward ran to join Levi, along with Earl, Isaac, and several other of the men to turn water on the ignited area until they finally got the flames totally out.

Blessedly, in the next hour the fire across the creek from them seemed to be fully contained, and many of the workers moved on to other areas more impacted where the fire was still spreading over the surface of the ground in the forestland there.

"We missed a bullet here," Isaac said, watching the last firetruck across the creek pull away, one of the men turning to wave at them.

"Yes, we did, for now," Levi agreed. "We'll have to keep watch on this area, though, and continue to do all we can further down the creek nearer our homes and barns. Wind can carry embers a long distance."

The idea of that sent a thread of fear into Edward that he quickly squelched, praying under his breath instead as he went back to work and walked to examine the scorched ground where they'd put out the fire to be sure no smoldering remnants of the blaze remained.

To Edward's surprise, shortly after the sun rose, Raymond and Hudson Maybank showed up in a big van with a bunch of men to help with the ongoing efforts to keep the fire from spreading into Indigo. Wey Camp and several men from Trinity Episcopal Church followed in another van. They'd brought coffee, donuts, and breakfast food their wives and members at Trinity Church had prepared.

Edward sat down by one of the old barns for a few minutes to eat a bite and gulp down some coffee.

"Tell me what you know about the ongoing fire now," Edward said to Raymond Maybank as the man walked over to sit down on the rough bench beside him.

"The fire completely took Swallow Bluff," he said. "It's nothing but charred ruins now. It's heartbreaking."

"I'm really sorry to hear that. Was anyone hurt?"

"I heard there were a few minor injuries with the volunteers and firefighters working to contain the blaze, but nothing serious, thank the Lord. A property closer to Ocella Creek burned to the ground though. It sat near the point where the fire jumped over the creek and began to move into Botany Bay. A couple of other families were evacuated that live nearer Point of Pines Road, too, but I think their places were spared." He paused. "With the fire moving mostly back through maritime forest and marshland, it hasn't impacted many homes or businesses on the main highway."

Edward finished off a donut and then drank more of his coffee while Raymond talked. He was worn out and tired after working all night and knew everyone else was, too.

Raymond continued. "The news said a lot of acreage has burned at Botany Bay and firefighters are still working there to get that fire out." He paused to sip the hot coffee in his hand. "They've closed access to Botany Bay for tourists, as you would expect. Many people have packed up and left the beach and the island, too, because of the smoke and because they're scared. Some businesses have closed. I heard the Deveaux family is sending all their guests off the island. They've been working to secure their place as much as possible, with the fire still spreading around the back end of Botany Bay and toward Fig Island. Hopefully, with all the firefighting ongoing, it won't spread more." He paused. "But fire is unpredictable."

"It is."

Raymond smiled at him. "You look rough, son. I hear you and the others have put in a hard night of work."

"You'd do the same to save your place." Edward answered, pulling a cloth out of his back pocket to wipe soot off his face. "Thanks for coming to help out and for bringing food. Tell Wey Camp that, too."

"What else can we do that would be a help?"

"One of the Deputy Chiefs with the St. Paul's Fire Department, Romney Berle, has been here since dawn, helping to organize our efforts. I'm sure he'll put you to work doing something, if there's still work to be done." Edward looked toward the sky, where he could still see thick smoke in the distance and an occasional flare-up of flames flashing into view.

Raymond glanced toward the sky, too. "I hear with the day coming now that they're getting things more under control, but there is still fire burning in many spots and a lot of smoldering areas the firefighters are keeping an eye on." He stood. "Let me go see if I can relieve anyone so they can take a rest or if Romney has anything else Hudson and I can do to help here."

"Thanks again, Raymond." Edward stood to head back to the ongoing work, too.

Raymond glanced down the road toward the plantation where he knew the big Antebellum house stood. "I'm glad the fire didn't spread this way more. I'd hate to see your fine old home harmed.

It's endured here a long time."

"I'd hate to see that, too," said Edward, and he knew he meant those words with all his heart.

CHAPTER 19

Lila had enjoyed her Friday afternoon and evening with Edward, riding horses and eating dinner at the Edingsville restaurant. She'd loved their quiet trip back to the island, too, in Edward's boat, skimming down the North Edisto River, talking in the dark at the marina and watching the beams of the lighthouse streak across the sky. She'd slipped into bed afterward with a happy heart, but in the middle of the night Lila woke with a sense of foreboding. She got up to get a glass of water and glanced at the clock in the kitchen. It was only four in the morning. What had wakened her and how should she pray?

Before she could get an answer, she heard a knock on her door. Going to look out the window, she saw Clifford George, their caretaker.

"I saw your light on," he said. "I hope I didn't startle you, knocking on your door in the middle of the night like this, but there's a fire burning on Edisto. We learned about it a little earlier from a call Waylon got from Lonnie Culler. He said it's a bad one. It started at a shed at Swallow Bluff Plantation and spread. No one is living at the old plantation house right now, so the fire wasn't spotted early by anyone."

Lila's heart stirred in alarm. "Swallow Bluff is near Edward's place at Indigo, isn't it?"

"Yes, it is. Lonnie told Waylon, in a later call, that Edward, the Jessups, and many others around the area are already working hard

to secure things as best they can in case the fire spreads their way."
She put a hand to her heart. "We should go and help them," she
said in a rush.

"Multiple firefighter teams are working at Edisto to contain
and stop the fire, Lila." Clifford smiled at her. "We'll have enough
of our own cares to contend with here. Lonnie said the fire had
jumped Ocella Creek on the backside of Botany Bay. It's still
spreading there now. That's not too far from the back border of
our property. Lonnie advised us to do all we can to secure things
here and to evacuate our guests."

"Are we in danger?"

"Waylon's contacts on the island say it's unlikely the fire will spread
too far our way before it's contained, but the smoke is already thick
and that will make the air unpleasant. Rather than take any risk the
fire might move here, it is safer to move the guests. Your mother
thinks we should wake them early to pack, eat, and evacuate. She'll
explain everything when you go to the inn."

"I'll get dressed right now and go learn what I can do to help."

"I planned to suggest that, seeing your light on." Clifford tipped
his old hat before turning away to leave. "I'll get on my way, too.
I'm working with Henry and Waylon to get any combustibles put
away securely and to do all we can to be as safe as possible here.
We're trying to get any flammable machines, any accelerants, and
debris out of the potential path of fire if it should come here. I
think your mother and Novaleigh are working now in the kitchen
to get an early breakfast prepared."

After pulling on her clothes, Lila snagged a flashlight from the
drawer and made her way in the dark to the back door of the inn
to let herself into the kitchen.

Her mother looked up as she came in and smiled at her. "Lila, I
was just getting ready to come get you."

"Something woke me earlier. Clifford saw my light on and he
came and knocked on my door to tell me about the fire." She
leaned against the counter. "Tell me what I can do to help."

"Novaleigh and I have started breakfast casseroles to feed the guests. I'm sure there will be a number of things you can do to help."

"What about the fire?" she asked. "How bad is it?"

"Right now, we're all in a waiting game about that. Aileen Jenkins is keeping me in touch about the fire situation at Indigo, since Hal, Dewey, and Don have been there since three this morning working to help Edward and the Jessups. Waylon's friend Lonnie Culler, with the police department, is keeping Waylon in touch with any broader updates about the fire as much as he can and about the island's progress with containing and stopping it."

"Is Indigo safe?"

"Right now it is, but the fire is close to the plantation. It's a serious threat, but so far it hasn't spread into their property to cause damage."

Lila sighed. "I'm glad to hear that." She turned to Novaleigh. "I know your parents and some of your family live near Point of Pines Road, not far from Indigo. Are they safe and well?"

"They are. Thank you. They live further up the road toward the highway. But this fire is a serious concern to everyone, for sure."

"I hope they get the fire put out soon."

"We all do," her mother agreed.

"Are you still going to evacuate our guests?"

Etta nodded, while stirring canned orange juice into a pitcher of water. "Yes. I strongly believe in taking the 'better-safe-than-sorry' viewpoint in a situation like this. That fire jumped Ocella Creek and moved into the back of Botany Bay. It seems likely they'll be able to contain it, so it doesn't spread our way, but fires are very unpredictable. If fire did spread through the marshes and maritime forests closer to us, embers could be blown by the wind onto our island."

Continuing, Etta said, "Aileen tells me the wind is blowing from the land toward the coast, which has pushed the head of the fire toward the ocean rather than west toward Indigo and Jenkins Landing where she and Hal live. However, if the fire keeps moving closer to the coast, the sea breeze may start to impact it. Those breezes could pick up embers and toss them around more than we're seeing now. I don't want to take the chance that fire could ignite and start here on Watch Island and endanger our guests."

Novaleigh frowned. "We are all praying and believing the fire will be contained soon with little to no damage here," she added. "But it's best to get these guests out to safety, just in case. We can get more done around here ourselves without needing to worry over them, too."

"So, what is the plan?" Lila asked, sitting down on a kitchen stool.

"Right now, our guests are sleeping, unaware of any problems going on. However, when they wake, they'll begin to pick up on the fire news on their cellphones and they will start to see and smell the smoke on the air."

"Then the panic will set in." Novaleigh grinned. "They'll start to hear tales of folks leaving the beach and the rentals, and they'll hear about the Edisto State Park evacuating people and closing the park, and they'll get scared."

"Yes, I imagine they will," Etta agreed. "So rather than deal with that situation, I want to wake them early. We'll do that gently and kindly, of course, telling them we're evacuating the inn for safety purposes." Etta wiped her hands on a kitchen towel and sat down on the other stool beside Lila.

"Perhaps you don't remember we have a clause in our guest contract about this. If we feel the need to evacuate guests for their safety at any time, we give them one of two options. They can return home and receive a rain check to make a reservation and come another time or, if we perceive the danger might be only temporary, we offer to take them to stay at one of the inns off the island we have emergency plans set up with. For many guests, who come to us from quite a distance, they like this second alternative plan best."

She picked up a cup of coffee to sip on it. "I've contacted the Andell Inn across the river near Freshfields at Kiawah. It's a big Marriott inn with a buffet breakfast included and it's close to

Freshfields Village for other meals and shopping. As you know, the Inn is very nice. Madeleine has plenty of vacant rooms right now and she was able to offer to accommodate the five couples staying with us. Only five of our six rooms are in use right now and, as you remember, the two men who were staying in one of our cottages went home yesterday."

Novaleigh finished putting together the big breakfast casseroles she'd been preparing and popped them into the oven.

"Do you think all the guests will want to go to the Andell Inn?" Lila asked.

Her mother looked thoughtful. "My guess is the two couples staying for the weekend only will simply take the rain check option and head home. However, the other three couples, who expected to stay all week with us until next Friday, may want to go to the Andell and come back tomorrow or on Monday if things are better."

"Where is Burke?" Lila asked.

"She'll be over as soon as Drew wakes to help as much she can." Etta smiled. "Babies change your life."

"I could keep Drew," Lila offered.

Her mother patted her hand. "I have better use for you here to help me wake our guests, staying calm and peaceful as we do so. Many of them might become anxious and upset at the news while a few might get annoyed or irritated, as though we should be able to control the weather in some way."

Novaleigh laughed. "I'll bet that Mr. Hardison, who is staying with us in the Sunrise Room, will bluster and argue and want to stay right here."

Etta chuckled. "You're probably right about him, but that will not be an option." She paused, glancing around. "I want to feed everyone breakfast by seven instead of starting at nine, as we usually do, and then Waylon will take them in the ferry to the landing and to their cars. From there they can drive home or on to the Andell Inn if they chose that option. Burke created a nice directional sheet to the inn and I already printed some copies out."

Lila glanced at her watch. "It's about five in the morning now."

"Yes, so let's begin setting up the buffet and the tables in the dining room. Novaleigh will finish here, and then we'll start waking our guests."

As Lila worked with her mother to get the dining room set up, she considered calling Edward, but she knew he'd be busy working with the men to protect Indigo. She hated not knowing how he was, if he was safe. She prayed softly while she worked.

As if picking up on her quiet and unrest, her mother said, "I admit I am worried about Indigo and about Edward and the Jessups. I'm sure you are, too. Hal and all those helping have been working in the dark trying to dig out fire lines, clear brush, and do anything they can think of to keep that old plantation safe if the fire moves their way. Aileen said she thought Swallow Bluff was already a total loss. Doesn't that break your heart to think about? I remember what a beautiful place it was."

She hesitated, looking Lila's way. "Wasn't Swallow Bluff one of the plantations Morgan Richards wanted to include in his book?"

"Yes, it was." She shook her head. "I guess we won't be able to include it now. How sad."

By seven their guests had all come downstairs to eat their breakfast in the dining room. Most had been gracious about the unexpected fire, disrupting their vacations and stay at the inn, but only a few had acted testy.

Mr. Hardison got up at one point to look out the window. "I see a lot of smoke in the sky but no sign of any fire. Are you sure you women aren't over-reacting?"

Lila's mother turned to him with a smile. "No, Mr. Hardison, and be assured our local police office instructed us to evacuate the island for everyone's safety. Our men here at the island, Waylon, Henry, and Clifford, have been working on our 500 acres since early in the night. They've been clearing out combustibles, moving boats and kayaks to safer places, securing and hosing vulnerable spots, and running sprinklers over many areas of the island to deter the possibility of embers falling on outlying docks and buildings to start any blazes."

He frowned at her. "Well, some of us men could help with that."

"It's kind of you to offer," Etta replied, "but it would pose a problem with our insurance if anyone was hurt, Mr. Hardison."

Betty Dorsey, one of their guests heaved a sigh. "Aren't you all scared about this?" she asked. "Isn't it dangerous for you to stay here?"

"I'm sure the day will be a somewhat anxious one for us, but I'm sure we will all be fine. We have places to go for safety if needed." Etta glanced toward the window, where the smoke seemed to be growing thicker. "We're all very concerned, of course, because we have neighbors and friends around the island in vulnerable areas, far more threatened by the fire than we are. We want to be able to help them if needed and to be ready to evacuate quickly if fire should spread here. I'm sure you can see how all these efforts will be easier for us, not having guests with us, as well."

Betty Dorsey's husband shook his head. "I agree, and I sure hope they get this fire out. I saw a news report earlier that said the fire had already burned a lot of acreage."

"Oh, my. That's such a shame," Betty added. "I feel so sorry for all the people whose homes might be harmed."

Etta sent her a kind glance. "Our chef, Novaleigh, has been making extra food this morning to send to one of the plantations where we have friends. The men and women have been working there most all night to protect their homes and properties."

Mr. Hardison huffed back to his table, still cross at having to leave.

Etta walked closer to him and to his wife Faye at their table. "I think you'll both be very pleased with the Andell. It's a lovely inn, and you'll enjoy visiting the shops at the Freshfields Village at Kiawah nearby." She patted Mr. Hardison's shoulder. "Hopefully, by tomorrow or Monday we'll be able to bring you back to the island."

Waylon and Henry came in a little later to begin loading everyone's bags and belongings into the Deveaux Inn's big tram as the guests finished breakfast. Not long after, Etta and Lila walked to the front porch with Burke to wave their guests off with smiles.

"Whew. I'm glad to see them all gone," Burke said as they came back into the inn.

She'd arrived with Drew while the guests were finishing breakfast. He now lay tucked in a playpen in the kitchen under Novaleigh's watchful eye.

Burke turned to her mother as they walked back into the kitchen. "Mother, why don't you and Novaleigh go take a nap now? I know you've both been up since three or four. Lila and I will clean up the dining room and the kitchen."

At her mother's anxious look out the window, Burke added, "Be assured, I'll come and wake you if there's any more news. Please try to get some rest. Waylon says he thinks all the firefighters are beginning to get the fire under control now to some degree. He is hopeful that the worst is past."

"All right," Etta agreed at last.

Novaleigh spooned breakfast casserole into several takeout boxes. "I'm taking breakfast to the men as I head toward the house," she said. "They're hosing down the Bouls' house and yard near the back dock of the island. Clifford said Rita Jean has about freaked out about the fire. The smoke is bad their way. I think Henry may run her over to spend the day at Calvin and Maggie's home across the river." She paused. "I'll come back later to help you change bed sheets and such upstairs. I'd say Rita won't be any help today."

"Lila and I can take care of that," Burke assured her. "With no guests around, I can take Drew with us as we work. We'll be fine."

Novaleigh stacked her takeout boxes, utensils, and a thermos of coffee into a big sack. "Well then, I'll come back to fix a small dinner for everyone later. And when I talk to my family at the island, if I learn anything, I'll call you, Burke."

"Thank you. I'd appreciate that," she said, shooing both the older women out the kitchen door.

"That was good of you," Lila said as they left.

"How about you? You've been up since early morning, too," Burke commented as they headed back to the dining room to clean up from breakfast.

"I'm sure you have, as well," Lila said to her sister. "I'll be okay." She looked toward the dining room windows at the white smoke blocking out most of the day's early sunshine. "I wouldn't be able to sleep anyway, thinking about everyone working to combat the fire."

Burke came and gave her a hug. "You mean thinking about Edward. I'm sure it's been a frightening and stressful night for him."

Lila sighed. "Yes, and only last night we were making plans to take a walk on the beach tonight, and Edward expected to come to the inn for dinner. How quickly life can alter our plans in only a moment."

Burke smiled at her. "Well, sometimes those moments make you realize how much you care for someone. I still remember how I felt last year after Waylon and I managed to escape from that crazy man over at Otter Island. He could easily have killed both of us without an ounce of regret or remorse."

"I remember that time," Lila said, starting to stack dirty dishes on the dining room tables to carry into the kitchen to wash. She glanced toward Burke. "I really hope Edward is all right."

"Waylon talked to him once, not too long ago, while speaking with Lonnie. He said to tell you he was fine."

Burke began to help her clean up the dining room. "I'm sure Edward is worn out and exhausted from the stress and all the physical work they've been doing at Indigo. I heard they had a few close calls, too. Lonnie told Waylon the fire was really awful at Swallow Bluff, spreading into the fields and pine forests around it, and toward many places along Grimball Creek. I'd say they've had their hands full fighting that fire today, as have all the firefighters at Botany Bay, getting that inferno contained after it roared out of control like it did."

She gave Lila's arm an affectionate squeeze. "I'm sure Edward will call you as soon as he can. He'll know you're worried." She smiled at her as she followed Lila toward the kitchen with a stack of plates. "He'll know you're praying, too."

At Burke's words, Lila felt immediately guilty. She'd worried far more than casting her cares upon the Lord, praying and believing for everyone's safety. To remedy that, she began to pray softly as she cleaned up the dining room and as she worked upstairs afterward to change beds and clean the now empty guest rooms.

Toward the afternoon, they had a small scare at the island. Some embers caught in the breeze and blew across Ocella Creek at the back end of Botany Bay. This brought a new branch of the fire into the maritime forest and marsh areas closer to the Townsend River that separated Botany Bay from Watch Island and the Deveaux Light Station.

The men, who had paused for a break at lunch, got back into their boots and gear to head to the back of the island. There they began to remove any flammables and excess vegetation along the back river banks to remove any possible fuel that could encourage the fire to spread. Traveling sparks or embers from the new blaze could easily get in the air and be blown in their direction. Even Lila and Burke went to the back of the island to help spray water from their pumps onto the bank by the river and over the docks and vulnerable outbuildings to provide any protection they could.

Waylon, filthy from the day and with mud-soaked boots, paused in his work when his cell phone rang.

"It's Lonnie," he called to Burke and Lila, working near him, as he listened to Lonnie on the cell phone. "He says, blessedly, we have no fire risk here anymore. The fire, or at least that new piece that was a threat earlier, is contained and won't spread more now."

He listened for a few minutes longer. "They'll work to check for smoldering areas for a time, but it's no longer moving or spreading."

"Praise God," Lila said, sitting down with relief on the dock where they'd been spraying down the boards with water.

"I agree." Burke joined her. "I haven't put in this much physical work in one day in a long time. I imagine I'll sleep like a brick tonight."

"Until little Drew wakes you up." Waylon grinned at her and sat down beside them. "This has been a rough day though. Lonnie says Indigo is out of danger, too, they think. The firefighters are still watching smoldering areas near the Grimball Creek area, and firefighters at Botany Bay are still getting many areas contained. Lonnie said about sixty acres burned in Botany Bay and more acreage around Swallow Bluff, especially between the old plantation and the back of Botany Bay across the creek."

Waylon called Henry and Clifford on his cell phone to let them know the immediate danger was past and then he leaned back against a post. "You know what allowed that fire to jump the creek so easily into the back of Botany Bay? An old rickety wooden bridge over the creek. That fire just skipped and burned its way right over that bridge into the back end of Botany Bay. The bridge nullified the creek as a natural fire line to stop the blaze."

Burke grinned. "Well, I guess even fires aren't stupid. They can't burn through water so the fire just crossed the bridge, like anyone else would."

"Isn't there a little wooden bridge across Grimball Creek, between Indigo and the old Grimball tabby ruins on the other side?" Lila asked. "I seem to remember riding horses across that bridge with Edward in past or needing to climb out of the creek to take our kayaks around it."

Waylon glanced her way. "Lonnie said Levi and Edward burned that bridge to the ground last night, not wanting to risk it interfering with the creek and the cleared areas they'd dug as natural fire lines."

"Sounds like they were thinking smart." Burke looked at her watch. "I need to go get Drew from Novaleigh and feed him. Then I think I'll head home and enjoy a good bath after I put him down for a nap."

She looked at Waylon. "I'll probably make you hose off and drop your clothes outside on the porch before coming into the lodge. You're a muddy, dirty sight."

He grinned at her. "You wait on that bath of yours and I'll join you. We have a large shower in that master bedroom."

"Waylon, we're not alone here." Burke glanced toward Lila,

blushing.

"I think all of us will be ready for a hot bath and an early bedtime tonight," Lila said, overlooking Waylon's remark.

"I left Drew with Novaleigh at the kitchen at the inn," Burke added. "She was making a big pot of homemade soup, thinking it would be just the thing for a bunch of tired, worn-out people tonight."

"That sounds great," Waylon said. "I hope you won't mind, but I don't think any of us will be getting up for Sunday services in the morning."

Burke nodded in agreement. "I think God will understand if we rest and have our own home services tomorrow."

As Lila and Burke walked back toward the inn, leaving Waylon to finish putting equipment away with Henry and Clifford, Burke said, "I think it would be all right if you call Edward now. I know you're worried about him."

Lila thought about it. "I'm sure he's exhausted, like we are, and probably still working." She glanced back toward the smoke in the sky behind them, glad she could no longer see red or yellow embers flashing in the sky like fireworks as they'd seen earlier today.

"I'm sure Edward will call me when he can. I'm just so grateful and thankful right now that God protected us through all this. We have been truly blessed."

"What's that Psalm that says God will deliver us from the noisome pestilence?" Burke asked her. "I kept hearing pieces of it in my mind."

"That's Psalm 91, that those in the Lord will *'dwell under the shadow of the Almighty and be safe from the snare of the fowler, the noisome pestilence, the terrors by night, the destruction at noonday.'*"

"That's the one." Burke smiled. 'I'm going to read it later and thank God big time. My heart was a little fearful today, thinking of our home being threatened by fire. Our old inn and lighthouse have weathered hundreds of years through hurricanes and storms, but I think this is the first time we've been threatened by fire."

Later after enjoying a bowl of Novaleigh's hot soup at the inn and a hot bath at her cottage, Lila, too, read those comforting words in her Bible and then she prayed.

"Thank you, Lord, for being with us in trouble, for delivering and honoring us, for giving your angels charge over us and keeping us in all our ways. How good You are." She closed her eyes. "I offer You my loving thanks tonight for protecting us here and for protecting Edward, the Jessups, and Indigo Plantation. Give them your sweet sleep tonight after all they've been through."

CHAPTER 20

Last night and today at Indigo had proved one of the most difficult, trying times Edward could ever remember. As darkness began to fall, word came at last that the fires on Edisto, that threatened Indigo, had finally been contained. Edward spread the word to the Jessups and others still working at the plantation, thanking them for all their dedication and hard work, so grateful to be able to send them home at last. He'd already thanked others who left earlier after the worst threats to the plantation abated. Now, after policing the area a final time and putting away gear and supplies, Edward finally headed back to the main house.

Della met him at the back door. "Son, don't you even be thinking about walking into my clean house like that. Lordy, Lordy, I've never seen so much mud, soot, and dirt."

She looked him over, shaking her head. "You strip out of all those clothes right here on this back porch. I put an old robe here for you over the chair and a few towels if you need them."

Edward nodded in agreement, slumping into a metal porch chair to start taking off his boots.

"After you get out of those filthy clothes, make your way upstairs and get yourself a hot shower. Then dress and come down to the kitchen. Clifford George came by an hour ago to bring us dinner from Novaleigh. Wasn't that good of her? I sent part of the food to Annamae and Levi, some to Isaac and Tanya and the kids, and kept the rest for you, me, and Earl. Gladys's family already brought food to her, Tommy Lee, and the kids. Everybody has been so kind."

She turned to head back indoors. "I'll give you some privacy and head to the kitchen to set out some food for you."

"Thank you, Della," he managed to say.

"You're more than welcome. God's been good to us. After you eat a little, you need to climb into your bed and get some rest."

Mindlessly, Edward stripped out of his clothes, wiping off what mud, soot, and filth he could, before heading to the shower.

In the kitchen afterward, he ate a wedge of some sort of casserole with eggs, ham, and cheese in it, along with biscuits and hot cinnamon apples. Della talked less than usual while he ate, tired herself.

"Go home now, Della," he said as he finished. "We've all had a rough day. Go tend to Earl, get some rest, and sleep in tomorrow. We all could use a day off. I can heat up what's left of this casserole in the morning and make a little coffee."

She studied him. "Well, I admit I could use some extra rest." She walked over to kiss him on the cheek. "We're all so proud of you, Edward, of the hard work you put in with all the men. Levi said your strong leadership and quick thinking through this made him think of your grandfather. He said you're a credit to the Calhoun legacy."

"Those are kind words, but I did no more than anyone else," he answered, getting to his feet. "Actually, I am the one indebted to everyone who worked so hard to save this place, to keep it safe."

She patted his cheek before leaving. "Well, you remember to thank the Good Lord for His help, too."

"I will," he said, heading upstairs.

In his room, he shed his clothes and fell into bed, exhaustion hitting him now. Before he dropped off to sleep though, he sent Lila a text: "Thinking of you, Sister Anne. Indigo safe. I'm crashing now. See you tomorrow."

"Sleep well," she texted back." My prayers cover you."

Edward meant to answer something sweet, but he fell asleep

before he could, his phone dropping into the covers.

Surprisingly, it was Isaac who woke him the next morning, tapping on his bedroom door before leaning in to grin at him. "Good morning my friend. Levi wants us to ride along Grimball Creek and then over to Swallow Bluff with him and Dad to check everything out now that day is here. He said he thought you'd want to go with us. He wants to go early because there's still a lot to clean up and put away when we get back. Tommy Lee is coming later to help with that."

Edward rolled over, nearly every muscle in his body screaming at him when he did.

Isaac grinned again, hearing him wince. "Grandad said the best answer to sore muscles from a hard day's work is to get up and get going again. I thought I'd spare you the lecture in case you came downstairs grumbling."

Edward pulled himself up to the side of the bed. "How can he go on and on like he does? He's over two times our age."

"Yeah, I hear you. I was hoping for a little sugar-time with Tanya when he showed up at my door." Isaac laughed. "Get up and take a couple of aspirin and come down to the kitchen. Della made coffee and put some fresh biscuits in the oven to go with the rest of that breakfast casserole from last night. She said she wasn't about to let us take off without putting some good food in us."

Isaac hesitated before leaving. "Of course, you do own this whole place, Edward. I suppose you could pull rank and sleep in."

Edward snorted. "As if I'd ever hear the end of that or live it down." He headed to the bathroom. "Tell Levi I'll be there in a few minutes."

An hour later, they'd saddled the horses at the barn and started down a side path to the North Edisto River. In pecking order, Levi led the way riding Butler, with Earl on Narita, and Isaac and Edward following on Lex and Maddie.

"I want us to ride from the river along Grimball Creek following our east property line," Levi said as they started out. "We can cut through the field later, past where the fire was the worst, and ride down Swallow Bluff Road to where the old plantation used to be."

He whistled to Percy, their white lab, to follow them.

"Why are you taking the dog?" Isaac asked.

"That dog has a good nose. That's why. I heard Lonnie Culler say those arson investigators from Charleston are coming in this morning to examine everything. Percy might pick up on something. I can't tell you how many times around here he's alerted us to a little gas leak or some other kind of problem. He might be a help."

"Can he follow us that far?" Edward asked. "It's a couple of miles to the old plantation site."

Levi laughed. "A working Labrador like Percy can cover a lot of miles every day, even through rough undergrowth and across water. I'd say he'll have less problems than you boys today, wincing as you did climbing into the saddle."

As if in answer, Percy took off at a run ahead of Levi, leading the way to the river.

With the path widening, Edward soon nudged his horse Lex to move up to walk alongside Levi, astride Butler. "Tell me what else you heard Lonnie say last night," he asked the older man.

"I heard them talking about how they were going to go check out some suspect they thought might be responsible for these fires before the investigators came in."

"That might be George Souder," Edward said, remembering what Lonnie had told them about the young man after the last fire.

"Well, I didn't catch a name. The rest the men talked about was the damage and extent of the fire. They were talking about all the work the state folks would have to do to repair damages at Botany Bay, planting trees and grasses, putting up new fences, hauling out burned timber, and such. About sixty acres burned there."

"Did Botany Bay get the worst of the damage?"

"Probably. There wasn't much damage to the state park at all, just smoke, so they won't have much to do there at all. Other properties around Swallow Bluff, along Ocella Creek and back in the woods and marshes, like our own place will need work, though. For us, most of the work will be along Grimball Creek where the fire came closest to us. That's what I want to check out today, and why I brought you and Isaac along. You two are Indigo's future, and you boys need to look at this sort of thing and think it out."

Listening in, Earl said, "Those firefighters came in with bulldozers and cleared a big swath of brush, vegetation, even trees along the other side of the creek from Indigo. It looks like a barren dirt road over there now. We did a little of that clearing along the creek on our side, too, mostly by hand and especially at the southern end of our property where the fire raged the worst and where we had the scares."

"With that machinery they used, they could really bulldoze down brush and trees fast," Levi added.

"All that bulldozed area will be a mess with the first big rains we get around here, too." Isaac glanced across the creek they'd begun riding along now. "If they don't get to this area soon to start restoration, we might want to do some work over there ourselves. Otherwise, it might wash out the creek banks, make problems with our crops in the fields."

"That's good thinking, boy. What else would you suggest we do?" Levi asked.

"Find out what the plans are for work over there and if it isn't scheduled soon, see if they'll let us do some work ourselves," Isaac answered. "We can put in some shrubs and grass, maybe a few new trees and big rocks, whatever we think might restore the area partially, especially in spots adjacent to our fields."

Levi nodded. "Maybe you can ask a few questions of the folks from the fire department at Swallow Bluff while we're down there this morning. See what you can find out."

"I can find out legally what they're obligated to do," Edward offered. "If we offer to do some of the labor they should compensate us and pay for any materials."

"That's good thinking." Levi grinned at him. "Talk that up while you're down there this morning, that you plan to look into it. Folks always seem to jump to it more to get things done when they start hearing legal talk. Your father was good at that, too."

Edward frowned at those last words.

Levi leaned toward him. "Your father might not have loved people wisely or well, but he loved this plantation. That's a good thought you can hold on to. Most people have some good in them if you look hard enough for it."

As they rode the narrowing trail that wound along Grimball Creek through the woods and by the fields, they talked about areas, on both sides of the creek, that would need the most work. Percy trotted along beside them or ran ahead of them, exploring.

"I want to restore this old bridge we took out," Edward said as they came to the point where it had crossed the creek before. "It was our only access to the old Grimball Tabby Ruins and across the creek without riding through the water."

"It will take some work to replace it, but we can rebuild it," Earl replied. "I often used the bridge myself to get back to some good fishing spots on Ocella Creek. That old creek, more like a river, is broader than Grimball and the fishing is better there."

"After we get other things done, we'll get to it," Levi added, whistling to the dog as they moved on. "Tommy Lee is good with tools and building. We'll get him to help."

As they got to the end of the property along the creek, they could see more clearly now all the damage the fire had done, the ground scorched and black in places in the pine woods and fields to the east of their property, many trees singed or burned entirely.

"This sure isn't a pretty sight," Earl said, taking it all in as they rode by. Percy whined, picking up on the scents of some of the firefighting fuels and repellants used and going to nose them out.

Levi pointed now toward the scorched and burned area on their side of the creek where the embers had leaped over. The area was close to one of their barns and not far from one of their big fields with green corn stalks already shooting up in straight green rows.

"No matter what damage we've got to contend with, it could have been worse," Earl said. "It's fortunate we were working nearby when those embers found their way over here. We got to them quick."

Isaac grinned. "Maybe we ought to put a little marker here on this spot in remembrance."

Earl laughed. "What do you want it to say, 'Almost Got Us.'"

They were all glad for a little humor, looking at all the burned land so close to their own.

Cutting across the fields next, they turned their horses down Point of Pines Road and then into Swallow Bluff Road. Two road blocks to traffic stood across the entrance of the road for cars, but it was easy to ride around them on horseback.

"Do you think it's all right for us to ride back to the old plantation with the road blocks still here?" Isaac asked.

Levi turned to him. "Actually, I got an okay yesterday to ride over here from Lonnie Culler. He'll be here today, too, checking into all of this further along with the arson investigators. He thought, like I did, it might be a good idea to have an attorney on hand if there were any legal questions to think on. I told him about Percy, too, and how good the dog was to sniff things out. He didn't think the arson investigators had a dog, and he thought, like I did, they might appreciate a little canine help."

Isaac laughed. "Grandad, you didn't tell us any of that."

"Well, I'm telling you now," he said.

As they rode down the road to Swallow Bluff, Edward asked, "Tell us what you know about this old place."

"It's had a few owners since the earliest days," Levi answered. "The house, probably built back in the early 1800s, was a grand old place. Still was a fine place, too, until yesterday. You've seen it. They built the plantation house at the end of this long lane we're riding down on a bluff overlooking Ocella Creek. The house originally had landscaped gardens and ponds, outbuildings, and pretty decorative dovecotes. I always liked those; you don't see architecture like that much anymore. Anyway, throughout most of its latter years, the plantation belonged to the Mitchell-Simons family. I seem to recall not many years ago there was another small fire here, not as bad, and the family spent a lot of money restoring the place."

"Well, this time they won't be doing that," Earl added as the charred ruins of the house came into view.

Edward's heart caught. All that remained were blackened chimneys and a few walls here and there. Piles of rubble that hadn't completely burned and skeletons of trees and shrubs gave the scene a ghastly look, along with a little smoke still filtering around in the air.

"Looking at this, I'd say every ache and pain, every blister and sore muscle, we have today was worth it to keep Indigo Plantation from coming to this sad fate," Earl said, shaking his head.

Percy was whining and wanting to run ahead of them, seeing men walking around in the ruins, digging into walls and debris.

"There's Lonnie." Edward pointed to him leaning against a police car to one side, talking to another man. "Let's head over there, see what he knows today about the fire."

"You and Isaac go," Levi said. "Earl and I need to go talk to those guys from the arson department." He pointed toward their truck. "I want them to know why we've got the dog here before they start trying to scare him off or something."

In talking to Lonnie a few minutes later, Edward found there was little new knowledge about how the fire started. "We know it was arson again," Lonnie said. "There are ways these investigators can tell by examining the site. Bright yellow-orange flames, like we saw yesterday, were clues an accelerant was used to start the fire. Firefighters also saw rainbow sheens on metal they hosed down around the house that showed an accelerant was applied. A lot of the rest of that evidence they talk about is over my head, but they know what to look for at a site afterward."

"Most arsonists use kerosene or gasoline as accelerants," Edward put in. "Have they found any ignition devices around—lighters, matches, or any fuel cans on site? If so, there might be fingerprints."

Lonnie shook his head. "No, but they found flammable evidence forming a trail between structures, and this fire has similar patterns to the ones before, first starting in a small shed. They think it likely the same arsonist is behind all the fires we've had."

"Did you check out that suspect, George Souder, to see where he was late Friday night and into Saturday morning?"

"A couple of our officers went there immediately in the middle of the night to see if we could catch George with any evidence. He was over at a party at his girlfriend's place, still there at around four in the morning when we tracked him down. A little drunk but he'd been there since the evening before. It looks like George might be a dead-end suspect. Which leaves us with nothing. No one saw anyone around this place in the night on Friday. No one lives near enough to the house to have seen anyone that time of night. We're at a stalemate."

Lonnie glanced around, gesturing to a group of people across the charred lawn of the plantation. "Like always, we've got some local folks that have walked in, wanting to see what's been going on here. Curious. Some live not far away. We've questioned everyone. No one saw anything, heard anything, spotted a car coming down the road. It's discouraging, I tell you."

Following Lonnie's glance, Edward saw Percy run up to a teenage boy in the crowd, jumping on him and running around him.

"Percy!" Levi called from across the road.

Seeing the dog at the group of people, Levi hollered at Edward. "Go get that dog. He doesn't need to be nosing around people there."

Leaving Isaac with Lonnie, Edward sprinted over to the group.

The boy had squatted down to pet Percy now, scratching the dog's head and smiling. "Is this your dog?" he asked.

"Yes, it is," Edward answered. "Sorry he ran over here and jumped on you. I hope he didn't scare you."

"No." He stood. "I like dogs."

Edward recognized him then as the boy who worked part-time with Tommy Lee at the store and he knew the boy's family didn't live far away.

He spoke to Percy again to come and was surprised when the dog began to sniff around Ambrose's shoes. Ambrose reached a hand down to pet the dog again and Edward noticed the stained spots on the boy's shirt and shoes and the small burns on the side of his hand and fingers.

Schooled as an attorney not to react in an unexpected situation, Edward reached down to grip the dog's collar and then walked him over to where Isaac and Lonnie stood.

"Isaac, take this dog over to Levi and don't let him loose again," he said to him in a quiet voice. "Trust me in this. Act normal and natural, and go get the horses to leave. I need to talk to Lonnie for a minute, and then we need to head home."

Isaac nodded at him, no questions asked. Then he leaned over to get a good grip on Percy's collar and started across the lawn with him.

Edward moved then so Lonnie's back was to Ambrose and the little crowd watching the arson team at the plantation ruins. "Don't turn around, Lonnie, but listen to me carefully. Percy ran to Ambrose in that crowd because I think he has accelerant on his clothes. As the boy was reaching down to pet the dog, I saw some burn marks on his hands and I think stains on his shoes and shirt, which might be gasoline or kerosene."

He saw Lonnie tense. "Isn't that the Fleenor kid?"

"Yes, it is, but try not to let him realize we're talking about him, Lonnie," Edward said, keeping his voice calm and even. "Evidence is everything in an arson case. See if you can find a quiet way to get one of your men to go to the Fleenor's house to look around their sheds, on the grounds, behind the garage, and around Ambrose's mother's trailer to see if you can find some accelerant, matches, fuel, anything that could be incriminating. You have cause to suspect him and to search and ask questions."

"One of my officers, Ben Sutherland, is here with me," Lonnie said. "I can send him. He's seasoned and reliable."

"Good," Edward smiled, noticing that Isaac, Levi, and Earl had headed to the back side of the property now where they had left their horses, taking Percy with them. "Lonnie, after you get someone heading toward the Fleenor's place, you might want to get one of the arson investigators to check Ambrose out. They have equipment that might give you more evidence that he has accelerant on his clothes. You may need help with some restraint at that point if Ambrose tries to bolt. He'll probably panic."

Edward patted Lonnie on the back. "I'm going to head home and get out of the way in this. This is your job, and I know you'll realize the best way to handle it. You won't need us around if Ambrose turns out to be a possible suspect for you. We're going to take the dog and head back to Indigo. You let me know if anything comes of this."

Lonnie wisely kept his back to the little crowd gathered and to the boy. "Thanks. We know that boy has a troubled home life. This might be his way of getting out some of his anger, frustration, and tensions, even if in a sick way."

"If that's so, there will be people who can help him."

Edward walked casually across Swallow Bluff's charred yard then, not sure if he felt good or bad for fingering Ambrose Fleenor as a possible arson suspect. The boy carried his share of life problems already, but if he also had the sort of mental problems causing him to love and enjoy setting fires, and to achieve a revved-up satisfaction from it, he needed to be stopped.

And Edward knew well from the studies and cases he'd been involved in with arsonists in past, that they loved to hang around the scenes of their crimes, to watch the fires, and to watch the aftermath.

CHAPTER 21

Lila loved getting the short text from Edward last night, letting her know he was thinking about her. She went to bed relieved, knowing he was safe and well, back at the house. He'd sent her a text this morning, too, saying he was heading to the island to see her after finishing work at the plantation today. "I can't wait," he added.

"Me, neither," she texted back. "Come eat with us like we planned before if you want to."

"Excellent plan," he shot back. "See you later."

Lila stared at her phone for a moment as she disconnected. Texting was not as satisfying as seeing someone in person, texts always so brief and impersonal, when you wanted to look into someone's face and eyes, to touch and be with them. In truth, there was so much more she wanted to say to Edward than a few brief text words. So many feelings swimming inside, her heart hungry to see him. She knew she hated to even wait until the day's end.

"You're being silly," she told herself, not quite sure what to do with the sweep of emotions that had overwhelmed her mind and heart since yesterday. There was little sense in telling herself any longer that she wasn't madly in love with Edward Calhoun. As foolish as it sounded, it was true.

Fortunately, with extensive clean-up effort still going on at the island, and with everyone tired from the events of yesterday related to the fire, Lila's mother opted to leave her guests at the Andell Inn until Monday morning.

"Even if we brought the three couples back this afternoon, we'd still have to pay for their stay at the Andell for today," she said, "We couldn't get to them before the 11:00 am checkout this morning, but we can easily make plans to be there before that time tomorrow. The Andell Inn will feed them breakfast in the morning before they leave and we'll only need to provide lunch and dinner on Monday."

She heaved a sigh. "With all the stress we've been through, I think we could use a break. What do you think?" Etta looked around the table in the main dining room where they all sat this Sunday morning, having a late breakfast.

"I'm with you," Waylon agreed. "Henry, Clifford, and I are wasted from all we did yesterday, and we still have clean-up to do this afternoon. I won't miss needing to pick up and bring guests back."

Burke grinned at her mother. "Additionally, with Rita Jean still at Calvin and Maggie's house, we don't have Maggie to cook for us today. I told Novaleigh to take the day off, as well. We cooked our own breakfast this morning and we'll need to do the same for lunch and probably dinner."

Waylon grinned. "I'll take care of dinner at our place at the lodge. I can cook fresh shrimp outside on the grill. Henry brought shrimp to me yesterday after he took Rita Jean to Calvin's place across the river. Calvin caught them from his shrimp boat, the Della Belle, yesterday. Believe me, I have plenty of shrimp."

"Do you mind if Edward joins us?" Lila asked. "He said he wanted to come over this afternoon, and since he didn't get to eat with us the other night as planned, I thought he could join us tonight."

"You know we'll be pleased to have Edward," her mother replied.

"Yes, and Burke and I will be happy for him to join us. I look forward to seeing him again, too," Waylon added. "We'll have plenty of food. Burke and I will figure out some easy sides to add to the shrimp."

"I can make a big dish of slaw, cheesy scalloped potatoes, and some garlic bread," Burke suggested.

Etta smiled. "That sounds wonderful. I'll come to watch the baby later on while you get everything ready. I think I'll make a chocolate cake for dessert, too. I want to contribute something to the meal."

"I won't say no to that." Waylon laughed.

Etta glanced around. "After we clean up here, I plan to go and put my feet up and finish that mystery novel I've been reading. With all these problems we've had, I'm going to enjoy a little rest today."

"I could use a good rest, too," Burke said. "Let's just fix a quick sandwich or something at our own places for lunch today, too."

"I like that idea," Lila said, eager for time alone.

"Great," Waylon said, getting up to leave. "I'm going to head out and get some work done. I'll see everyone around six at our place." He glanced at Drew, playing contently in the playpen they'd pulled into the dining room. "Burke, do you and Drew want to head back to the lodge with me?"

She glanced around at the breakfast dishes and frowned.

"Go on back with Waylon," Lila put in. "Mother and I can clean up these few dishes easily."

"Well, okay," Burke said, going to get Drew's diaper bag while Waylon scooped their son out of the playpen.

As they left, Etta smiled after them. "I bless the day Waylon Jenkins came back to this island, Lila. He's been a wonderful help to us as well as a good and loving husband to Burke."

"Yes, and a fine father." She grinned at her mother as they began to clean the table.

In the kitchen, as they finished putting the food away and loading the dishwasher, Lila's mother turned to her. "I do look forward to seeing Edward again. Please know it would be a joy to have him in our family. You know how much time he spent here as a child. I've always loved him."

Lila blushed and looked away.

Her mother walked closer to her. "I've been so happy to have you home with us, Lila, but if your heart calls you to leave, you know we will be all right."

Lila tried to think what to say. "I'm truly glad I came back home when I did. I know it was the right thing for me."

She patted Lila's cheek. "Well, go and enjoy some free time of your own until dinner at the lodge. I'll see you later."

After a final check around the kitchen, Lila walked through the inn and out the front door toward her little cottage. At her own place, she had a quiet devotional time, long overdue with all that had been going on. She had drifted away from the regular, scheduled rhythm of prayer times she'd grown so accustomed to at The Community of St. Mary, but in many ways, she loved choosing her own times to pray and worship in her own way now.

For lunch, she heated up a can of vegetable soup, eating it with crackers on the back porch where she could hear the sea breeze, the occasional chattering of the sea gulls, and the sounds of the waves gently washing up on the beach not far away.

After her lunch, Lila puttered around in the garden behind her cottage for a time, praying and enjoying more private time, gathering her peace around her. Time alone with God always brought her peace.

The lush azaleas around Clifford's well-tended garden had already peaked in April, but iris grew tall by the garden pathways now and yellow jasmine covered one of the trellises. Lila found several early roses blooming, too—one a soft pink that Clifford called a Marie Pavie and another, a hardy, violet pink named Ebb Tide, with a rich, sweet scent that drifted out across the air on the breeze. It wasn't easy growing roses this near the ocean, but Clifford had a knack for it and he worked hard to nurture them.

Lila walked over to sit down on a garden bench. Big clumps of orange butterfly weed grew next to the old bench, thick with blooms, and she enjoyed watching the butterflies flicker around them. The scene called to her with its beauty, and she slipped into the house to bring out her sketch pad, and her colored pencils as well, sitting to sketch what she saw.

When she glanced up after a time, she saw Edward coming down the path toward her. She put a hand to her heart, so glad to see him. He wore tan slacks and a dark green golf shirt, and an old pair of leather boat shoes on his feet without socks. She soaked up every detail, so relieved to see him safe and well.

"You're early," she managed to say.

He stopped, just standing and looking at her. "I always forget how beautiful you are, how my heart feels like it has come home every time I see you."

Lila put a hand to her mouth, feeling like she might cry at the sweet words, echoing the thoughts of her own heart.

Edward came closer, moving to sit on the bench beside her, laying her sketch pad aside, and pulling her close to kiss her. "You are truly my heart and joy, Lila Deveaux. It was brought home to my soul more yesterday than ever before how much I love you, how much I need you in my life. I know you told me to wait until I was more certain about my life direction to ask you to share my life, to marry me, to be my own love for all our days, through good and bad, but my heart is so certain we belong together. Can you not commit to me, say you love me in the same way, that you want to be with me forever?"

She felt the tears now. "I do want that, Edward. Even if you want to go away, I will go with you, wherever your heart leads."

"Then we will get married and be one." He wiped her tears away, and kissed her again, long and well this time. "I will make you happy, Lila," he said softly, wrapping her in his arms, tucking her head against his heart.

Lila felt a new peace and rightness as he did, leaning her head against his chest, feeling his heart beat so close to hers.

"I love you richly, Lila," he whispered against her hair. "Tell me you love me, too, that you are sure we're meant to be."

"I'm sure, Edward, and I love you with all that I am." She leaned back to look into his eyes. "This is the right path for me, to be with you. Perhaps God in his wisdom knew that, bringing me back to the island when He did."

"And bringing you back to me." He kissed her again. "I will be ever grateful to God for that and to those sisters at St. Mary's who pushed you out of their nest when they did."

She giggled at his words. "Is all well at Indigo now, Edward?"

"Yes, and we will live there and raise our children there. That strong knowing that I belonged to Indigo Plantation, to the land, to this life here at Edisto, came to me fully yesterday through all that happened. I will be taking you to live with me at Indigo when we marry. Will you be happy there? Is that choice one that feels right to your heart, too?"

She put her hands to his face and kissed him. "Yes. It feels right to me although I'm not used to being a grand lady of a big plantation. Do you think I will be a credit to you there?"

He shook his head. "How can you ask that when everyone at Indigo loves you almost as much as I do?"

"Do you really know that to be true?"

"Yes, I do, and I admit I told Della before I came to offer for you—and I told Earl, Levi, Annamae, and Isaac. They have been like my family. They are happy for us, Lila. In fact, thrilled."

She felt like crying again. "I do love them all. Those are such sweet words to hear."

He smiled at her. "Well, I have some more of my well-planned proposal to finish." He got down on one knee before her and pulled a small, old felt box from his pocket. "This is the engagement ring my grandfather Malcolm Calhoun gave to my grandmother Regina Leigh Edings. I have only the most beautiful memories of my grandmother from my childhood years, and I know she and my grandfather shared a deep and abiding love."

He paused. "From what I have been told, everyone loved and admired my grandmother for her loving heart, her grace, and her kindness. Seeing you in the garden here reminded me of how much my grandmother loved the gardens at Indigo. Della and Annamae can tell you more of her."

Edward took out the ring to show it to her. "This ring is called a Halo Ring, a round carat diamond surrounded with a halo of smaller diamonds." He grinned at her. "A halo ring seemed a perfect choice for Sister Anne."

Lila put a hand to her heart seeing it, realizing the ring's age and beauty and imagining the years and love it had known. "Where did you get this ring, Edward?"

"Della knew where my mother had put it away. She said Mother never wanted it, preferring a new and striking engagement ring when she became engaged to my father. My father wanted to buy my mother a more stunning ring, also, that others would admire as representative of his wealth and importance. I doubt he realized the true value of this lovely old ring."

He turned it in his fingers, looking at it. "Mother had Della put the ring away, along with its matching wedding band, and the gold wedding ring my grandfather wore," he told her. "When I told the Jessups I planned to stay on at Indigo and planned to ask you to marry me, Della suggested I might want to offer you this ring."

He paused, holding it out to her. "What do you think, Lila? It's a lovely ring, but if is it too old to suit you, we can go shop for something more to your heart's desire."

Lila shook her head. 'How can you ask me if I like it? To me it is filled with love and stories and rich legacy." She smiled at him. "Let's see if it fits."

He slipped it on her finger and the fit was close to perfect. "Oh, it's really glorious, isn't it?" She held her hand up to let the sun flash on the gem stones. "I'll feel like I'm wearing beauty and history every day, Edward, and sharing in their love."

"It does fit well." He smiled. "Grandmother was about your height and with a similar build. There are even dresses of hers put away in old trunks and wardrobes somewhere in the house or attic. You are welcome to look through them some day."

"I will have fun doing that." She looked at her ring again and then asked him, "Have you told your mother about this?"

"If you mean about asking you to marry me, no I haven't." A frown crossed his face. "I've hardly spoken to her since I came home. She's been at Eula's. The fires at Edisto were well reported on the news, even in Charleston, but she never even called to see how things were with the plantation or with me."

"Perhaps she didn't know of it, Edward."

He gave her a small smile. "Perhaps she didn't."

"We will need to go and talk with her about this. We will want her at the wedding. She is your mother."

He leaned back against the bench to stretch his legs out in the sunshine. "When should we plan this wedding, Mrs. Calhoun-To-Be?"

She giggled. "I don't know. What do you think?"

He leaned forward to kiss her again, pulling her closer for more passion than before. "The sooner the better," he whispered.

She sat back to think about it. "Will you join the firm full-time now?"

"Yes, after a space, I will. I took the UBE Bar Exam in past, specifying South Carolina in taking it. My father insisted on that, and he was paying the bills for it and the licensing fees. However, that exam also gave me reciprocity to practice in Tennessee, too. I was utilizing conditions with that to practice at the Legal Clinic at Vanderbilt in a limited capacity, teaching and advising there."

She listened.

"My South Carolina fees have been kept up, too," he continued. "I can begin to practice here without any problem. Raymond and Hudson allowed me time to work with them part-time, giving me a chance to catch up with business at the plantation and to think things through. They've been very gracious, Lila. I plan to talk with them this week to give them my decision."

"I do like the Maybanks and the firm has a good reputation."

"It does. I think I can do some good things here."

"I know you will."

"Where do you want to get married?" he asked her, returning to the wedding discussion.

"In church, and at our church at Trinity Episcopal if it is all right with you." She stopped, thinking. "I believe Wey Camp would be happy to marry us."

"Trinity Church is small," Edward said. "Would a small wedding there with a big reception after at Indigo be all right with you? I want to begin our life together the way I want to go on, opening our home to others, being welcoming as my grandparents were."

He hesitated before continuing. "So many of our friends and neighbors came and worked long hours to help me when the fire threatened Indigo. Many brought food, prayed, supported me, and stood beside me even though I had been away so long. I want to give back, Lila. Our wedding will be a perfect time for that. I am blessed financially and we can have something really lovely with good food, beautiful flowers, and joyous entertainment. We can create a really memorable day everyone will enjoy."

Lila smiled. "That's certainly different from the quiet life I'm used to, but it sounds like fun. It's also very generous of you to be thinking of others and to want our wedding to be a blessing and a happy memory for them."

He looked relieved. "I was hoping you would be okay with the idea."

She wrinkled her nose at him. "You'll find I'm very easy to get along with, Edward, especially with warm and loving requests."

He sent her a smirk at those words that made her blush.

"Edward, you know that wasn't what I meant."

"Well, I like the thought. Don't spoil my imaginings."

She studied a butterfly lighting on the shrub near them. "Do you have a date for the wedding in mind?"

He stopped to consider her question. "May is nearly over now. I'd like to plan something soon, this summer before I get more involved in the firm full time. Right now, I have flexibility with my schedule to organize a wedding, for us to spend time together planning everything, and to take time deciding on any changes you might want to make in the house."

She knew her eyes flew wide at his last words. "I suppose I hadn't really thought about a move yet."

He grinned at her. "I think you'll need to move in with me instead of me moving in here with you."

She glanced toward her little cottage, thinking of her studio.

As if reading her mind, Edward said, "We'll find a special place for you to have a fine studio at Indigo with lots of light and space. You could convert part of one of the guest houses behind the main house into a studio or create a studio in one of the less used rooms in the house. You'll know the right spot when you see it."

Lila remembered the old carriage house as he spoke, a two-storied structure with long windows on the upper floor that let in streams of light. It was little used now, except for storage below, and she'd always thought that a little sad. "I think I have the perfect spot in mind, the old living area in the upstairs of the pink carriage house." She paused. "Thank you for realizing my art is important to me."

He looked surprised at her last comment. "I hope you will always paint and use the gifts God has given you and work as He directs you." Edward took her hand, studying the engagement ring on it. "I know, too, when I marry you, Lila, that more of the Lord and His heart and ways will move into my home and life. Believe me when I say I look forward to that. I want to honor the Lord above all, as I know you do."

His words relieved her.

After a moment she asked, "How much time do we need to plan this wedding and all the transitions you envision?"

He looked out across the garden. "I think we could get everything planned by the middle to end of July. Especially since Indigo has its own event barn. It's hosted many weddings and events in the past and will only need a little face lift to be perfect for a wedding reception for us. It holds well over a hundred people for an event. What do you think about having the reception there?"

"I love the event barn. I remember attending a few events there as a girl. It's almost a twin to the horse barn, a gracious white building with a gray roof and pretty cupolas on top, with a covered pavilion beside it. Indigo created fine barns when built long ago."

"I love that barn, too, and it holds many happy memories for me of events held there over the years. I used to sneak over there when Grandad and Dad rented it out to watch the guests arrive for weddings, parties, fancy luncheons or suppers. I want Indigo to return to being a place others can enjoy, too."

She smiled. "Then it will."

Edward pulled out his cell phone to look at his calendar on it. "Mid-July is about two months from now. That should provide plenty of time for any planning that needs to be done, don't you think?"

I think so." A sweet warmth filled her heart just thinking about it all. "I love the idea of a summer wedding at Indigo."

He winked at her. "Maybe that date is not as soon as I'd like, but I know weddings take time to plan and arrange. Are you really happy with this idea? I don't want to push any plans on you that don't feel good to your heart, also."

"I think your ideas are all very good ones, Edward. Burke's and Celeste's weddings were rather a quick surprise for Mother and for everyone else. I think Mother will like the idea of this one giving her a little more preparational time."

He laughed. "Well, let's go talk to them about it." He glanced at his watch and at the sky, beginning to darken a little. "It's after five, and you texted earlier we're going to Waylon and Burke's for dinner tonight instead of the inn. We'd better head that way, don't you think?"

"Yes, but let me go inside and put my art materials away and tidy up a bit. Burke said not to dress up, but I want to brush my hair at least." She glanced down at her shorts, deciding she'd change them for a clean pair of capris, too.

He pulled her to his feet and into his arms. "I'm so happy, Lila. Thank you for loving me. We're going to have a wonderful life." His eyes lit suddenly. "Maybe we can honeymoon at my place in Nashville and drive to Sewanee one day so I can thank your Sister friends for sending you my way. I'd like to see where you went to college, see where you lived and stayed at the Community. I could take you to places in Nashville I know you'd love, too."

Edward hesitated. "I actually have a really nice condo in Nashville, very close to the college. I'll probably need to put it on the market and sell it soon but we could enjoy it one more time before I do."

She smiled at the idea. "I've never been to Nashville, Edward. There are some beautiful art museums there and gorgeous gardens I've read about. I think that's an excellent idea."

"I've always wanted to see the Community where you stayed, too, but I'd much prefer visiting there after we're married. They can't have you back now, Sister Anne."

She laughed with him as they headed into the house. "Actually, I think I've breached too many of my vows to return now, but I'm sure they'll all be happy for us."

CHAPTER 22

Edward was pleased Lila's family expressed so much joy they planned to marry. He had expected Waylon to be pleased, but he was glad to see Burke and Etta felt the same when they shared their news over dinner.

"How could I not be pleased, Edward?" Etta asked him, seeing the concern on his face. "I've known you since you were a little boy. You've been like a son to me."

"Thank you, Etta. I'm glad you're happy for us, and keep in mind Lila won't be far from you at Indigo."

"Yes, I know, and Lila has always loved it there." She paused. "What does your mother think about all this, Edward?"

They'd finished dinner now and were sitting outside on the screened porch, relaxing. Drew was beginning to nod in his baby swing and would probably be ready for bed soon.

"We haven't told Mother yet," Edward admitted. "But Lila and I plan to go to Charleston soon to share the news with her."

"Will she feel usurped at the plantation with you taking a wife?" Burke asked candidly.

He shook his head. "No. Mother hasn't been to the plantation since Easter Sunday last month. She's been at my Aunt Eula's ever since I came. She made it clear to me that she wants to move there and doesn't want anything to do with the plantation anymore."

"Well, I'm sure she felt concerned about you during the fire though," Etta added.

Catching his expression, Waylon grinned. "My guess is you haven't heard from your mother through all this."

"I regret to say I haven't."

Burke looked annoyed. "Honestly. Both radio and television covered the fire, and it was all over the internet. I'd say her lack of contact and concern through this settles any doubts you might hold about her interest in the plantation."

"Frankly, she was never very interested in Edward either," Waylon added. "So, I'm thinking it's a blessing for Edward and Lila that Clarice will be staying in Charleston. I seldom dislike people, but Clarice Calhoun was never on my favorites list."

Etta shook her head. "I imagine once Clarice learns you're staying at Indigo and marrying Lila, she'll soften a little. Her life wasn't easy with Sam. I think she was eager to leave as soon as Sam died."

Edward couldn't help laughing. "That's the truth, Etta, and Mother felt annoyed I didn't come back sooner to 'pick up the reins' as she put it. The fact that I dragged my feet in returning left her with a lot of problems she didn't want to handle. We'll give her credit for staying at Indigo until I came home though, but in all honesty, it would have been difficult for me to decide to stay if I'd known I'd be sharing my home with my mother."

Burke grinned at him. "Well, fortunately, you'll be sharing your home with Lila instead. I know Celeste and Gwen are going to be thrilled about this. Have you started making wedding plans yet?"

"We have started making a few plans," Edward replied. He and Lila shared their tentative plans then and everyone was soon excited, offering ideas, and asking questions.

"Who will walk Lila down the aisle?" Burke asked, and Edward hated to see Etta look away at the words, her face touched with sadness.

Lila leaned toward Waylon. "You're my brother, now, Waylon. With Daddy gone, would you consider standing in for him?"

Waylon reached across to take her hands. "I would be truly honored to do that, Lila. I am touched you would ask me."

Lila looked at Burke. "I'd like you to be my matron of honor if you would and I hope Celeste and Gwen will want to be bridesmaids. I also want to ask Tanya. We've been friends a long time, and we spent a lot of time catching up while I painted and sketched at the plantation."

She paused, turning toward him. "In that small church, I think four attendants will be enough. Did you have more than four people in mind to ask, Edward?"

"No. I want to ask Isaac to be my best man. He's been like my brother. So has Tommy Lee. I'd like to ask him to be a groomsman plus Celeste's husband Reid and Gwen's husband Alex. I really don't have a wealth of friends around the island anymore I'm close to, so I think having mostly family and close friends at the wedding would be best. However, I do intend to ask many people on the island to the big reception at Indigo."

He looked toward Etta. "Do you know anyone on the island or nearby who is a good wedding planner? Lila and I need to get started with plans about that soon."

She smiled at him. "Actually, I do know someone who lives on John's Island nearby who is very good with weddings. Her name is Angela Weston with Weston's Wedding Designs. She's held many weddings at the lighthouse island with us over the years and works with a very good florist and photographer that would do a beautiful job with everything. I think you can count on her to make the event run smoothly and well and to sparkle and delight everyone. I'll give you her contact information so you can call and talk with her."

"I remember Angela," Burke added. "She is so organized and capable. She will make everything easy for both of you. It will be a coup for her, too, doing a big wedding reception at Indigo."

"We will definitely contact her and see what we think," Lila said. "Will that be all right, Edward?"

"Yes. I like the idea that all the wedding planning, the set-up, food preparation, decorations, flowers, and work will be on seasoned and capable shoulders. I want all our family and the Jessups to enjoy the day and not worry over anything."

He and Lila shared about their honeymoon idea then, bringing some laughs that he thought The Community of St. Mary might try to lure Lila back.

"We are definitely keeping her," Burke affirmed. "They can't have her back."

Hearing Drew beginning to fret, she added, "I need to go feed Drew and put him down for bed. Afterward, I'll cut Mother's cake and we'll have it with some coffee."

"I'll make the coffee," Waylon suggested, following her.

After they left, Edward propped his feet on a small table. "I want you to know, Etta, that I love Lila and will take good care of her. You won't need to worry that I won't be good to her or faithful to her. I'm not like my father."

"Edward, we know that, dear," she answered. "But I'm glad you know that for yourself now, too. We each get to chart our own course in life and make our own way. You're a very good man, and I know Lila will be a kind, good, and loving wife to you."

Lila leaned toward her mother. "Thank you for those kind words, Mother, and I hope I can continue working at the lighthouse gift shop on Fridays and Saturdays to help you and Burke, if it's all right."

"If you have time for it, you are more than welcome to continue. Any time you can't come to help, you know I can open and close the lighthouse gift shop and ring up sales. I may not carry your artistry and organizational gifts with the shop, but I took care of it during all the years after Lloyd and I married. I'm sure I can manage again, and you know Waylon and Burke will help, too."

"I'm happy for Lila to work at the gift shop and to enjoy it for as long as she wants," Edward added.

"Well, I hope Lila will continue to bring us paintings and gift cards to sell." Etta frowned. "Where will you paint at Indigo, Lila? If you need to, you can keep your studio at Inland Cottage."

"Actually, Edward gave me a marvelous idea earlier." Lila leaned forward, her eyes lighting in that way Edward always loved. "Do you remember the old carriage house behind the main house?"

"Do you mean that old place painted a salmon pink color?"

Etta asked. "I recall it being in a little disrepair when I last visited Clarice, but it has a distinctive charm."

"It does." Lila smiled. "Edward said I could have the upstairs rooms for my studio. It's much bigger than my studio at the cottage and the area has huge long windows to let in the light."

"That old place has a rich history, too," Edward added. "The lower garage floor held carriages and still has some stored there. The apartment above in times past belonged to the stablemaster. I remember when I was a boy, my parents used the apartment as a guest house when they held parties, but we can easily convert it to an art studio. I'm going to call an architect friend of mine to start work on it right away. I want him to fix up the entire carriage house, too."

"Why is that building painted pink?" Etta asked. "None of the other structures at Indigo are."

Edward chuckled at her question. "I think my Grandmother Regina Leigh got charmed with pink houses of that color in the Caribbean when she and my grandfather made a trip there once. Because the carriage house was no longer being used for carriages and servants any longer, she had it painted Caribbean pink to host guests they entertained."

"Well, I want to leave it that dusty salmon pink with its white trim and gray roofs," Lila said, smiling. "It makes me think of some of my favorite houses in Charleston. It's such a southern thing having a pink house. Where else do you see them as often as you do here?"

"We have some old furniture pieces in the storage attic above the garage at the Inn," Etta offered. "You are welcome to any you need for your new studio. Please take any furniture from your current studio you like, too. I'll probably convert that upstairs area back into a second bedroom when you move out. Inland Cottage is small but really charming. I like to keep it available for friends who visit to give them a little privacy."

"Well, I admit I've drizzled paint on several of the cabinets and chests in my studio at the cottage." Lila laughed. "It will be no loss to you if I carry those pieces off with me."

Etta laughed, too.

Burke and Waylon came back to join them at that point, bringing chocolate cake and coffee. Edward felt comfortable and happy with this family he'd always loved, and he felt a new contentment about his life to come. It would be a new beginning starting his life with Lila, and he wanted to leave all the old painful memories behind now.

As they all sat watching the sun beginning to go down, spreading its rich colors over the river, they heard a boat approaching the marina.

Waylon stood to see if he could recognize the boat pulling in to the dock. "It's Lonnie Culler. I hope nothing else is wrong on the island."

Lonnie waved in greeting as he made his way up from the marina, after tying off his police boat.

"I hope you haven't come with bad news," Waylon said to him as he reached their back door, noting Lonnie still in uniform.

"It's been a long day," he said.

"Have you eaten dinner?" Burke asked. "I still have extra grilled shrimp, slaw, fresh sliced tomatoes, and scalloped potatoes in the kitchen, plus garlic toast. Do you want me to make you a plate?"

"I'd love that, Burke. Thank you. I admit a perk of bringing news to you any time is that I often get blessed with one of your good meals."

Burke grinned at him and headed back into the kitchen to fix him a tray, pulling a small table in front of him when she returned to put his food on. She went back to get him a glass of tea and then settled down to eat her own slice of cake.

Lonnie ate most of his supper with pleasure, talking casually, and then finally turned to Edward. "I actually came looking for you, Edward. I went to the plantation and Della said you'd come here. I hope you don't mind that I came to find you, but I thought you'd want to know the news about the arson situation."

"I do," he said.

"We did find conclusive evidence that Ambrose Fleenor had set the fire at Swallow Bluff. Young and upset, at getting caught, Ambrose gave further incriminating evidence to indicate he'd been behind the other fires as well."

"Was he read his rights?" Edward asked.

"Yes, but he was angry and he panicked at being arrested. Somehow, he had justified everything in his mind and didn't feel he deserved arrest or punishment."

"Did Ambrose offer any reason for why he'd set the fires or why he always started them on old plantations?" Lila asked.

Lonnie frowned. "He kept suggesting they were only fancy properties rich people owned, and that wealthy plantation owners took advantage of and hurt people all the time. He kept saying they deserved to get some of their own back."

"Arsonists seldom have remorse for their actions," Edward said.

"Someone could have been seriously hurt with any of those fires though. Didn't Ambrose realize that?" Burke asked.

"Again, arsonists appear to lack normal feelings and concern for others. Many, like Ambrose, have so much hurt and dysfunction in their home life it impairs their thinking." Edward sighed. "A factor with Ambrose could be anger, as well, over the knowledge it was a plantation owner in Bluffton who took advantage of his mother, causing her to get pregnant, and refusing to help her in any way after. Tommy Lee told me some of the stories he'd heard about that, but we don't know for a fact what truth is in them. Perhaps more of that story will come out when Ambrose gets some mental health counseling."

Lonnie considered his words. "I'll be sure to pass that knowledge about his background along."

"Does he have legal help?" Edward asked.

"His family wasn't very sympathetic to his predicament. I'd rather not repeat some of the harsh words they had to say. His grandfather, Vale Fleenor, didn't indicate he had any interest in reaching out to an attorney to help his grandson. Ambrose's mother is too much of a mess herself for the boy to hope for much help from her." Lonnie rubbed his chin, thinking. "We might be able to get him some representation from one of the Legal Aid Offices."

"I'll talk to Raymond Maybank tomorrow at the firm," Edward said. "I'll pay the boy's fees for good counsel to represent him. He's a minor and it's his first offense. Property was damaged but no deaths occurred, so that will help his defense. His reasoning for arson was mentally and psychologically based, and his home life is riddled with abuse, neglect, and poor parenting. He didn't commit the arsons with intent to hurt someone. He just has a pathological desire to burn things."

"He could have hurt someone though," Lonnie argued, frowning. "All of the fires resulted in property damage, plus anxiety and expenses for the owners. A lot of good taxpayer money, law enforcement and firefighter time got involved here, too, following up on all these arsons. Personally, I'm greatly relieved we caught this boy before any of this situation grew worse. The next time somebody might have gotten killed."

"I'm not justifying the boy's actions, Lonnie, only saying he deserves a good defense attorney to represent him and to hopefully see he gets some good counseling and help."

"He'll need it. Arson is a felony," Lonnie put in, still frowning.

"You're right about that. Arson is a felony, but we know that young people, whose cases are prosecuted in adult criminal court, and who serve time, have higher rates to return to crime again. I'd like to see Ambrose not start down that road, if possible. He hasn't been involved in other criminal activities before this."

"I see your point," Lonnie finally agreed. "I'm glad you're going to try and get some help for him."

"I'll get in touch with you after I talk to Raymond tomorrow."

"That will be fine. Let me know what I can do. I also came to thank you for your part in apprehending the boy." Lonnie grinned. "And to thank you for Percy's part in helping. We owe that dog a lot. The arson investigators were impressed."

Burke, who had taken Lonnie's empty plate away, brought him a piece of Etta's chocolate cake now and a cup of coffee. "We just learned Edward and Lila have become engaged," she announced.

"Well, that's fine news," Lonnie replied with a grin.

The subject changed then as Lonnie offered his congratulations, the former discussion of Ambrose and his future shelved for a time.

The next day, however, Edward called to set a time to talk to Raymond Maybank and later headed into the law firm. He first visited with Raymond and Hudson to talk about his decision to accept their offer to join the firm and to stay at Indigo.

"This is good news today," Raymond said, walking to shake Edward's hand with a big smile.

Hudson added his own warm welcome. "Congratulations on joining the Maybank-Calhoun Law Firm, Edward. I look forward to seeing your name on your father and grandfather's office door."

They spent time discussing how Edward would begin integrating into the firm, Edward pleased to learn Raymond and Hudson were still open to him continuing part-time for another month or two. This would allow him time to contact colleagues at Vanderbilt, to prepare for his upcoming wedding, put his condo up for sale, and to finalize getting his affairs at the plantation in order.

"I want to thank both of you and your friends at the island who came to help us fight the fire that threatened Indigo. It was a great kindness I won't forget."

Hudson smiled. "You would have done the same if the Maybank Plantation were threatened, and it could have been our place next if the arsonist hadn't been arrested. I hear through the grapevine you had something to do with that, so we owe thanks to you, too."

"Mostly thanks to Levi Jessup and Percy," Edward said, telling them the story of how Percy smelled the accelerant on Ambrose in the crowd at Swallow Bluff.

"What will happen to the boy?" Raymond asked, remembering Edward had talked with him at an earlier time about Ambrose, concerned he might be experiencing abuse at home.

"I'm not sure where Ambrose was taken after the arrest," Edward answered. "Lonnie said his family was unsupportive and unwilling to provide any legal defense for him. Raymond, I would like to take care of his legal fees if you would consider taking his defense. We know how harsh the boy's life has been. I want to see he gets the best help he can. I know personally about abuse and how hard it can be when you're young, although my experiences and homelife were never as harsh as Ambrose's. With good counseling help, Ambrose could have a shot at a full rehabilitation. I want to do anything I can to see that happen."

"I'll call Lonnie and check into it," Raymond said. "If I learn I wouldn't be the best defense in this situation, I have a lot of contacts to see that Ambrose gets the best defense he can. From our earlier checking we already know he holds no previous criminal charges or school problems—in fact, his grades are good. Tommy Lee says he always shows up for work on time and does what he's asked to do competently. Those are good points in his favor."

"I'll help in any way I can," Edward added "My guess is Ambrose would be hostile toward me working with him personally. He'll realize I caused his arrest. I doubt that will put me on his favorites list."

"I don't know if we can get Ambrose off without any time," Hudson put in. "But there are some good programs for troubled teens around the Charleston area and some therapeutic boarding schools. Personally, I'd hate to see the boy released back into the custody of the Fleenor family at any point. A therapeutic boarding school, where he could stay to get the emotional support and treatment he needs and where he could get help to encourage a long-lasting recovery, might be the best option for Ambrose. Several I know of have a full academic program he could get involved in until graduation and they have good transitional help toward continuing education and work afterward."

"I'll pay any expenses needed for him to get a chance for a better life. I only wish we could have gotten to him with help in some way before this." Edward sighed.

Raymond reached out to pat Edward on the shoulder. "Son, you know well we can't solve all the problems in this world, either as attorneys or as men. All we can do is our best, and we'll reach out and do our best for Ambrose. Don't carry guilt that you exposed his crimes. Think how much worse it might have been if you hadn't discovered his part in this, if in future someone were killed in another fire he set or if more historic homes were burned."

"I know you're right," Edward said.

"Don't ever regret having a caring heart though," Hudson added. "And we'll all be praying for that boy, too."

CHAPTER 23

Over the next days, Lila had the fun of sharing her engagement and wedding news with her other two sisters. Celeste immediately suggested they share a sisters' weekend again in Charleston so they could look for bridal clothes.

"There's a wonderful bridal shop on Church Street," Celeste said as they chatted on the phone. "I know we'll find the perfect dresses there. Have you decided on colors?"

"I have some ideas Edward and I both like," Lila replied. "We want our colors to be magnolia white and evergreen, echoing the colors of the magnolias that will soon be thick with blooms at the plantation and also blooming on the date set for the wedding in July."

After a few moments, Celeste said, "Actually, Lila, I think that theme and those colors will be stunning and elegant, perfect for the wedding at Trinity and for the big reception you've planned. I'm impressed with that idea."

Lila giggled. "Well, I'm glad for that, and I know emerald green for bridesmaids' dresses is an excellent color for both you and Gwen, both 'winters' by color personality."

"Hmmm. You're already beginning to sound thoughtful and wise like a lady-of-the-manor should." Celeste laughed.

"Please know that this lady-of-the-manor's planning is being orchestrated primarily by the gifted wedding planner, Angela Weston," Lila replied. "Mother knows her and recommended her. We've met with her once already at Indigo and she is simply buzzing with glorious plans. She also really listens to our ideas. I do like her."

"I'm glad. When can we schedule our girls' night to go shopping?" Celeste asked.

"How would Friday night work for you?" Lila asked. "I'd like all of us in the wedding party, plus Mother, to share dinner at the inn on Friday evening. You, Reid, Gwen and Alex, can stay overnight. Edward thinks a fishing trip for the men would be fabulous on Saturday, while we girls go to Charleston to shop. What do you think?"

"It's a wonderful idea. I can get off work with no problem at my shop if Alex can get off at Trescotts."

"I'll call and talk with Gwen next," Lila said. "I hope Friday will work for everyone."

"I'm sure your days and time are getting busy now with wedding plans. What else are you doing this week?"

"I have a meeting with Morgan Richards in Charleston to talk about my ongoing work for his book. Edward is going with me, and then we plan to go visit his mother at his Aunt Eula's place in downtown Charleston."

Celeste snorted. "I'm sure that will be fun."

"Actually, I hope it will be a good visit. We're believing and praying for that. I want to start off on a good foot with Edward's mother, despite problems of the past. I'm hoping she might feel the same at this point and be ready to move on from hurtful memories herself."

"That sounds kind, Lila, and if anyone can orchestrate that with grace and understanding it would be you."

"Why, thank you," Lila said.

As Edward and Lila drove into Charleston two days later, Lila repeated that hope, that their meeting might be positive.

"We'll see," Edward replied, obviously a little apprehensive.

Lila glanced out the window, as they crossed the Ashley River Bridge into Charleston, before adding, "I think it's nice that your Aunt Eula will be there, too. I've never met her that I can remember."

"She rarely came to Edisto, disliked my father. I heard they never got along. Eula lived in Spartanburg after she married. Her husband Peter Heyward was a professor at Converse College. Eula finished school there and worked in the library at the college, even after Peter died. When her parents were killed in a wreck, she moved into the family's old home in Charleston. I think the house was left to Eula and Clarice jointly. I have no memory of visiting there, but I've been told that I was taken to visit my Alston grandparents when small."

Changing the subject as they drove into town, Lila said, "I'm excited about seeing all the family this weekend, aren't you? I'm so pleased everyone could arrange to come to the island. It will help Burke that we're hosting our sisters time at the Inn, with Drew so small. I want to thank you, too, for planning a fishing day for all the men so we girls can go shopping."

He grinned at her. "No need to thank me for a day I look forward to. The guys are excited about getting out in the Pursuit on the ocean and the weather report is good for the weekend. That boat is a beauty and Waylon knows all the best places to fish and good spots where we can pull up for a break on the bank to scarf down some lunch."

Edward slowed to pull into the parking garage near Morgan's office at the college. "I look forward to getting to know Reid and Alex better." He smiled at her. "They will be my family now, like your sisters. I'm happy about that. As an only child, I never had much family except for the Jessups. Aunt Eula didn't have children; my father had no brothers and sisters. I've always envied people with big families to enjoy."

Their meeting at the college didn't take long. Morgan was pleased to meet Edward and to hear more about their wedding plans, promising to make time to come. He seemed pleased with the new work Lila brought to show him, the sketches and paintings she'd completed at Crawford Plantation, and he was full of new ideas about the upcoming work to be done at Trinity Church next.

"I'm really glad you want to continue with the work on the book and that Edward is so supportive," Morgan said, shaking hands with Edward as they left. "Congratulations again, too, on your engagement."

After walking back to the garage, they started toward Aunt Eula's home not far away.

"What time are they expecting us?" Lila asked.

"Eula suggested we come between three to four when I called. Mother wasn't there when I phoned, but Eula said she felt sure that time would be good for mother, too." He sent Lila a smirk. "I hope so or we'll be visiting with Eula alone."

"Where did you say they live?"

"Eula lives by Colonial Lake in the Alston family home on Rutledge Street, a beautiful old place. You'll see it soon," he said, turning off Calhoun onto Rutledge.

A few minutes later, Edward parked his car on the street in front of a stately two-storied white Antebellum house with crisp black shutters and a graceful entrance. The front door, centered on a pillared, semi-circular porch, was reached from either side by curving staircases.

Lila looked up at the fine house. "This is a gorgeous old place."

"It's been here on Colonial Lake since the 1800s." Edward glanced toward the big lake across the street from the house. "I've always liked the wide promenade that circles the lake here, and the trees, flowers and benches. It should be pleasant to live by this lake."

"Yes, and strolls around the park would be nice, too, wouldn't they? I imagine your mother and aunt enjoy that."

"Maybe," he answered. "I don't know."

They were met at the door a short time later by a somewhat full-figured woman with the same blondish looks and brown eyes as Edward's mother, but without Clarice's beauty.

"Well, Edward," his Aunt Eula said, looking him over, before jutting out a hand to shake his firmly. "It is good to see you again.

I think you were in short pants and not much taller than my hip the last time you visited here. Do you remember any of those early visits when your Alston grandparents still lived here?"

"No, ma'am, I'm sorry I don't," he answered, with a regretful look.

"Well, you haven't missed much not remembering them. The Alstons were always a stuffy bunch."

Lila tried not to grin at the comment.

She turned toward Lila. "Who is this pretty thing you've brought with you, Edward?"

"This is my fiancé, Lila Deveaux. We've only recently become engaged, and I wanted to come and share the news with you and Mother about our wedding."

"Well, that is news indeed. Come in. Come in." She ushered them into the house's entry. "Your mother went to check on the tea we've been working on. We employ a sweet little Thai girl, Ami Tham, who comes in daily to 'do for us,' and she's been helping your mother create a little Afternoon Tea for your visit. It's an old South custom, as you know, and still popular in many places. She and Ami had fun working on it."

Eula led them on into the main parlor of the house, a spacious high-ceilinged room filled with antiques and graceful old furniture, a fine room like one would expect in a house like the Alston place, all arranged cozily around a fireplace with a chandelier hanging in the middle of the room.

Clarice came into the room then, dressed much more fashionably than Eula, her hair and makeup impeccable. "Edward," she said, nodding and offering him a small smile, her tone formal. "How good go see you again."

Lila tried not to wince at the formal greeting, more suitable for visiting guests than family.

Clarice put out a hand to politely shake Edward's as if they were just meeting.

She turned to Lila then. "I believe this is Lila with you," she added, offering her a polite hand, too.

"Edward, did you introduce Lila to Eula yet?" Clarice asked.

Eula snorted. 'He did. He did." She gestured them to the sofa. "Let's all sit down. This is only Edward, after all, Clarice, and his little fiancé, not the mayor of Charleston stopping by. Edward came to share with us that they've just gotten engaged."

"I see," Clarice said, seating herself neatly in a small wing chair by the old fireplace across from them. "I would say congratulation are in order to you both."

Eula rolled her eyes, settling herself in the matching wing chair on the other side of the fireplace, creating a cozy circle.

A young girl appeared in the door between the living and dining room then, wearing a simple black dress with a white collar and a white apron, her dark hair pinned back neatly. She smiled politely. "Would you like me to bring the tea in now?" she asked.

"Yes, dear. Thank you," Eula replied.

She rolled in a cherry wood tea cart a few minutes later, with a floral tea pot, cups, saucers, spoons, plates, and napkins on the upper shelf, and a three-tiered tea tray, full of sweets and small sandwiches, on the second shelf.

Clarice got up to help, moving the tiered tray, filled with scones, finger sandwiches, and sweet treats, to the coffee table between their seating area. "I think we can serve ourselves a plate better from the table here," she said. I will be happy to pour tea for everyone, too."

Eula stood. "Guests first," she gestured.

Lila went to take the plate Clarice offered, putting a few sandwiches and sweets on it, plus a cup of tea, then sitting back down to balance the plate on her lap.

"This is so nice," she offered as Edward followed suit, sitting back down to put his own plate and cup on the coffee table in front of them.

"I haven't enjoyed Afternoon Tea for quite some time," Lila continued. "My mother often serves it for special groups who come for meetings or events at the lighthouse inn where I live. I always love it when I get to join in."

They made polite chit-chat then as they enjoyed their tea, sharing a little about their upcoming wedding plans. Eula asked polite questions about Lila's family and sisters.

"I do hope you will both plan to come to the wedding and reception," Edward said after a time. "You are my family, and it will mean a lot to me and to Lila if you'd come."

"That sounds very cordial and certainly not like your father," Eula said. "I'm sure you know I haven't been to Indigo since you were practically a baby. Your father and I did not get along, which is an understatement at best. I wasn't allowed to visit Indigo nor did I allow your father Sam to visit here." She glanced at Clarice. "I assume your mother has told you, Edward, that I wasn't allowed to visit you either at Indigo or here. I regret that fact and I'm so pleased you decided to come to see me here today."

Clarice glanced away, her posture tensing at the more personal discussion ensuing.

Eula shook her head. "Clarice, I can see you never told Edward this from your expression. Honestly, don't you think it's time for all this pretense to come to an end? Sam Calhoun is dead. The gracious behavior of Edward and Lila coming here today to share their engagement news with us and to invite us both to their wedding, should show you that your son is nothing like his father. Obviously, he is trying to make a healthy, clean new beginning here."

Eula put a hand on one hip and leaned toward Edward. "I assume you've decided to stay and run Indigo now and work at the law firm from your comments earlier. Is that correct?"

"It is, Aunt Eula," Edward answered. "And Lila and I do want to put old hurts and bad memories away and create a fresh new life and future together at Indigo."

"That sounds very sensible, Edward." Eula looked at Clarice. "How much of your past have you shared with this boy, Clarice?"

Clarice sat up straighter. "Eula, I don't think we need to air our personal laundry with our guests. All families have their problems and we do the best we can to get along in the lives we're given."

Eula laughed. "That sounds just like something our mother

might have said. It was her way of dealing with the controlling bully we had for a father. He may have owned half of Charleston, a real estate mogul like he was, but Selwyn Northcliff Alston, our father, was a mean man and our mother, Louise, was a weak, distant parent, shuffling us off into the care of servants, cowed by her husband, playing roles with all her socialite friends, a huge phony."

Clarice flushed. "That is not kind, Eula."

"It's the truth. I came to understand a lot of needed truths about my past while married to Peter Heyward, a steady, normal man I was blessed to marry, and through good counseling." She turned to Edward. "Our family here in Charleston may have been rich and well thought of, but ours was an incredibly dysfunctional family. Our father was overbearing, controlling, and often verbally abusive, and our mother lived timidly in his shadow, not emotionally available to either Clarice or myself. The textbook term is insecure attachment."

Clarice tried to open her mouth to protest but Eula continued, "That pattern of mothering, all Clarice had known, she carried over in the way she raised you and, also, Sam Calhoun was a virtual clone of our father. I know Clarice wasn't available to you as she should have been, Edward. She was literally fearful of mothering well and didn't know how either. Your father was no help with any of it either, which comes as no surprise. Our father chose Sam for Clarice to marry when she was a young debutant, and in her way, she loved Sam. We need to give her credit for that, and it's well-known Sam had his strengths, just as our father did. I always felt Clarice replicated the home life we'd grown up in with in her own married life."

Clarice put a hand to her mouth and was struggling with tears. "Eula, please …"

Eula turned to her. "The boy has a right to know why his childhood was the way it was, Clarice. His heart has to be full of questions, as ours once were, and you know Sam bullied Edward as he did you. It's no surprise to me he wasn't eager to return home."

Clarice tried to regain her composure. "I apologize for Eula. She has a tendency to be somewhat outspoken," she offered the words as if in apology.

"The truth needs to come out, Clarice," Eula shot back.

Lila could sense Edward tensing beside her, and when he leaned forward to speak, she put a hand on his knee and said, "Life often gives us many problems and challenges. Sometimes the hurts are so deep we don't understand them and don't really know how to talk to others about them. I'm sure Clarice did her best in the situation she was in, and I think it will help Edward to understand his own childhood with what you've shared, Eula. Thanks for your honesty. I do believe it will be a help to Edward, who wants so much to move past any old hurts and difficult memories he holds."

She turned to Clarice. "It sounds like you had a lot of problems to work through in your marriage and not a lot of loving warmth in your home growing up. I hope this will be a time now for new beginnings for you. Eula shares your experiences and obviously loves you. As you talk and pray together going on, I'm sure the Lord will help you both toward more healing and to new happiness. We all yearn for peace and happiness. Edward and I will pray for both of you."

Eula shook her head up and down. "You are marrying a wise woman, Edward, who carries peace in her soul and a strong faith. I shall look forward to seeing how you both get along in the future, and I hope you both will feel welcome any time to come back to Alston House to visit with us."

Ami came into the room then to retrieve the tea things, breaking the somewhat tense and volatile moments they'd passed through.

Eula pointed to a portrait on the wall. "That's our mother Louise Whalen Alston. As you can see, she was a beautiful woman like Clarice. I wasn't a beauty, more the bookish one. I was ten years older than Clarice, too, gone from home and married by the time Sam came courting with the urging and approval of our father. Sam was a charismatic charmer. Most who knew him admired him and never saw or knew he had a dark side."

She sent Edward a studied look. "You know of that cruel side of him and, if you think on it, you'll realize how hard it was to oppose your father. Your mother faced that problem, too. I'm sure you think, as an adult, she should have been stronger. But I will tell you, she was a sweet girl and your father didn't do much to nurture her."

Clarice lifted her chin. "I tried to do my best for you, Edward, and I tried to be a good wife to your father. I know I had my failings but I did try. I tried hard, too, but I never seemed to really please your father most of the time, and I simply wasn't strong enough to stand up against him in the hard things. Perhaps I should have been but I simply wasn't."

"Now, there, those are some honest words," Eula added.

After a few minutes of quiet, Clarice looked across at them. "I hope you will have a happy marriage and life." She hesitated. "My life is much happier here. I know I told you I want to move here to live with Eula. Our parents left the house to both of us. It will be a help financially to Eula for me to be here, too. She works at the library, and perhaps she will find it easier to retire from that later if she wants to."

"Maybe, we'll see. I'm not much for idle hands," Eula put in.

Clarice sent her a little smile. "I might surprise you and find some useful things to do myself. I've never had a chance to try my wings before."

Eula laughed. "Well, if you meet another man, I think I'll get him psychologically examined before I let you marry again."

Edward tried not to laugh. "Good idea."

Lila was grateful the heavy mood had shifted a little. She smiled at Clarice. "Life is always filled with the chance for new opportunities, and God has His Purposes for us all, even after heartaches."

"Here, here," Eula said.

Edward stood. "Lila and I appreciate your kindness and hospitality today, but we do need to head back to the island. Again, we hope you will come to the wedding in July and sooner to see us if you wish."

As they left, driving away, Lila said, "You know, they never did mention the fire. I wonder if they really didn't know about it."

Edward shook his head. "With all those revelations dumped on us I never even thought to ask."

"Did it help you to learn more of your mother's past?"

"It did," he admitted. "I still don't admire her but I understand where she was coming from more now than I did before."

He grinned then. "Gosh, I really like my Aunt Eula though. Wasn't she something? I'd like to have been a fly on the wall sometimes when she went at it against my father. I imagine she told him exactly what she thought, too."

Lila considered his words. "I think Eula will be a help to your mother, too, who still has a lot to work through."

"I suppose. Maybe she'll get her to go to counseling as she did."

"Well, we know more how to pray for them both now."

He sent her a smile. "I am marrying a very nice person, Lila Deveaux. I am blessed."

CHAPTER 24

In mid-July, two days before their wedding, Edward walked Lila back to her new studio to put away her art supplies from her day's work. She'd been doing initial sketches today at the new plantation next on Morgan Richard's agenda.

Edward followed her up the steps to the second-floor apartment, pleased to see her pause to look around the big sunlit room in delight.

"I still can't get used to all this huge space to work in." She gazed around with pleasure. "I am so blessed, and your architect friend built in so many little nooks and crannies, work areas and shelving, to make this studio cozy and special. He even created a little seating area to rest in with a fireplace and a small kitchenette."

She walked over to settle onto the small sofa, arranged with two chairs near the fireplace. He followed.

"If you remember, Lila, the apartment already had a fireplace and a small kitchen area. Barton just utilized well what was already here." He leaned over to kiss her. "But be assured I will find ways to make you want to come back to the main house often."

"I imagine you will." She traced her fingers along his face. "It isn't long until the wedding now. I'm getting eager, aren't you?"

"Yes, definitely." He kissed her at length, counting the hours in his mind. His cell phone rang, interrupting them.

He glanced at it. "I need to take this. It's Isaac."

"Hey, Bro. Is Lila back?" Isaac asked.

"Yes, she just got home."

"Good. Tanya and I are at the event barn with Angela Weston and her crew. They have questions for you. Can you walk over?"

"Sure," he agreed, seeing Lila nod, who'd heard the conversation. "We'll be there in a few minutes."

They soon headed around the main house and out the circular drive, to start down the winding side road leading to Indigo's horse barn and on to the plantation's event barn.

As they walked along, Lila said, "Annamae told me the event barn was once a stable earlier and built at about the same time as the horse barn. That's why they look so much alike."

"That's true. The event barn originally stabled the work horses used at Indigo, before so much machinery replaced the need for them. Race horses and pleasure horses were stabled in the other barn, many valuable and bred for extra profit. Charleston was a big seat for racing in those early years. As times changed and Indigo kept less and less horses, only one barn was needed, the other used for storage." He paused. "When my father was young, long before I was born, my Granddad went to a wedding held at an event barn at another plantation. He loved what they'd done to convert their barn and decided to replicate the idea at Indigo."

"They did a beautiful job converting it," Lila added.

"The old barn was always a pretty structure, but it's been updated and renovated several times over the years. It now has restrooms, heat and air, better lighting, a stage for entertainers and good electrical hookups. We keep tables and chairs in the storage area, but most event organizers bring their own. They like to use those big round tables that seat eight, like Angela is using."

She smiled at him as they passed the horse stable. Walking on, they followed the road to its end, where the event barn stood. The graceful white barn, with its cupolas high on the gray roof, had long windows marching along its sides where the stall doors used to exist. A covered pavilion sat to one side, as well as several parking areas. A picturesque barn door stood wide open today in invitation.

"Oh, look!" Lila pointed. "Angela has strung lights all around the outside of the barn and put big pots of ferns and flowers around for decoration already. Everything looks beautiful, doesn't it?"

"Yes, it does," he agreed, loving the animated excitement he saw on her face and pleased she was happy about their upcoming wedding.

Angela Weston, their wedding coordinator, came to meet them as they reached the door. "Hello, hello. Here's our happy couple. Come in and let me introduce you to my staff."

She gestured them inside. "Isaac and Tanya helped us this morning, but I'm happy you are here now for some needed input. I sent them off for some lunch and a break, knowing you were on your way."

She gestured to a small group of people gathered around a big round table. "Weston staff," she announced, "this is our bridal couple, Edward Calhoun and Lila Deveaux." She began to introduce her staff to them in return. "Lila and Edward, this is my assistant Ruthie Harris, our chef Daniel Miller, our photographer Harper Rothman, who will be doing your pictures, and our florist Iyla Chin. Please know this is a very gifted group I have been working with for years, and I assure you they, and their assistants, will make every aspect of your day this Saturday memorable."

"Nice to meet you all," Edward said, Lila parroting similar words.

Angela gestured to two empty chairs. "If you would sit down with us for a short time, we want to go over a few things with you."

Edward and Lila settled into chairs, as Angela turned her laptop computer to show them a layout sketch of the barn room they sat in. "The event hall will be set up in this way, with round tables on each side to seat all your guests. You indicated you expected about 140 to 150 at most from your RSVP returns. Our twenty round tables, seating eight each, will accommodate up to 160, so we should be good for numbers. Daniel has planned, based on that count, for the dinner. He'll tell you about that in a moment."

She pointed toward the end of the long event barn. "On the stage there, we've brought in a piano, and all the hookups for the small band that will play later."

As Angela paused for a moment, Ruthie jumped in to add, "I have to tell you we are all so excited, Lila, that your sister Celeste will be performing throughout the dinner hour with her pianist Marcus McClain. I am sure your guests are going to be thrilled to enjoy a special performance like that at your wedding."

Lila looked pleased. "Celeste offered to sing, and Edward and I were excited to say yes. My sister also arranged to bring in some of her band members from Nashville to play afterward for dancing. I know it will make the evening memorable for everyone."

Angela winked. "We're all so excited we get to be here for that." She turned to Ilya, the florist on their team. "Do you have anything to add?"

"I think your deep evergreen and white color scheme is a simply beautiful choice," Ilya put in. "As you asked, Lila, we're incorporating white magnolias, a few with a touch of yellow or pink, white roses, and other small filler flowers and mixed greenery into the wedding bouquets and arrangements for the tables at the reception. I know you wanted things to be simple but lovely. What do you think?" She turned her computer now to show them more pictures.

"I like those very much," Lila said. "Don't you, Edward?"

"I do." He nodded. "Do you also have pictures to show us of how you're going to decorate all these tables you've already set up here?" He gestured around at the tables already in place with gold chairs around them.

"The tables are going to be fabulous, as well," Angela laughed, obviously loving her job. "Look at these pictures and see what you think." She clicked to another picture on her computer, showing tables fully decorated, draped in cream cloths, the white dinnerware and pretty stemmed glassware gilded in gold, the cutlery golden to match. Each place setting sat on emerald green placements with cloth napkins to match beside every plate. Greenery and white candles decorated the middle of each table.

Lila put her hands together. "Oh, my. Everything is going to be simply beautiful."

Edward and Lila looked at photos then of the wedding cakes being prepared, a lavish three-layered white cake, with magnolias and greenery decorating it, and a second three layered groom's cake in chocolate, sprigged with green leaves and berries. On the cake table would be decorative trays and fancy tiers of green and white mints, and hand-created edibles and sweets of different types.

At that point, Angela gave Daniel the stage to tell them about the dinner planned that he and his staff would serve, a mixed green salad with butter lettuce, tomatoes, dried cranberries and feta cheese, and, for the main course lovely stuffed chicken breasts over rice pilaf, with sauteed haricot green beans and mushrooms, followed by a dessert plate with wedding cake and a side selection of mints and sweets. Drinks would be sweet tea, tinged with peach flavoring, or water, with no alcoholic beverages served, as they'd requested.

Tanya and Isaac came back into the barn then as Edward and Lila were finishing their talk with Angela and her staff. Tanya, tall like Isaac, and slim, her long legs tucked into white capris today, had her black hair pulled back behind her neck, and she wore her usual big smile that Edward had always loved.

"We have a surprise to add," Isaac said, as he and Tanya pulled up two more chairs. "While we were working with the architect and that crew sent in to renovate the carriage house apartment for Lila's studio, Edward asked us to clean out the carriage garage underneath, as well, so the workers could do needed repairs and paint to spruce the place up. We discovered the old white wedding carriage there that we used to use for events in the past and we got this great idea."

Isaac laid an old photo on the table. "This was taken at a wedding here a long time ago. You can see the wedding couple are riding in the carriage, with our white horses Maddie and Lex pulling it."

As Edward studied the photo, Tanya said, "If you'll look closely, Edward, you'll see it's Levi driving the carriage. We showed this to him, and he wants to drive you both from the big house down the road to the reception after the wedding, so you can make a grand entrance."

Isaac laughed. "I offered to drive, but Levi wants to do it himself. He says he still has the suit, or livery, he wore back then and that it still fits. He got really excited about doing this. What do you think? Will you make an old man happy, Edward?"

Edward rolled his eyes. "I suppose."

The photographer snatched up the picture. "This will make great photos, too. Look at this old carriage, open and graceful with the wheel spokes even painted white. It's fabulous." He looked at them with appeal. "Say you'll do it."

Lila giggled. "Well, it would be hard to resist after all this persuasion, so I say yes, too."

Isaac and Tanya left with them to walk back to the main house then. "Stop by our place for some iced tea," Tanya suggested. "My mama took the kids to a movie today. She likes to spend time with them in the summer when she can."

With Lila agreeing, they cut down a side road with Isaac and Tanya to their house where they sat on the porch for a time, drinking tea and looking forward to the wedding to come.

"Everything's going to be so pretty at the wedding at Trinity Church," Tanya said. "I had fun going with you, your mother, and sisters to shop for our dresses in Charleston in May. I love the simple, dark green dresses in that satiny fabric you chose for your sisters and me to wear. Your dress, in that same satiny white fabric with its full floating skirt looks so beautiful on you."

She laughed. "Your sister Celeste said it wasn't fancy enough for a big plantation wedding, but I disagreed. Celeste changed her mind, however, when she saw it on you, especially with that soft drifty veil you're going to wear."

Isaac laughed. "Tanya says you get to lift that pretty thing, to drape it over her hair down her back after you say the I dos, before you kiss her. You better be careful not to mess that up."

Edward grinned. "I plan to practice that at the rehearsal at the church on Friday evening. And remember, we're having the rehearsal dinner at the plantation in the big dining room. The Hughes brothers, that own the Edingsville Grocery Restaurant, are catering it."

"Della told me she and Annamae had to argue with you to be the ones to serve."

Edward shook his head. "The restaurant had people to do that."

Isaac laughed. "Yeah, but Mama didn't want anybody else in her kitchen messing around and moving things so she couldn't find stuff. She's possessive about Indigo."

"I know, but I wanted all your family to simply enjoy this wedding without having to work."

Tanya giggled. "You ought to know all the Jessups well enough to realize they'd never go along with a wedding of yours they didn't help with in some way."

"Well, you can't say I didn't try," Edward said.

"Listen," Tanya leaned toward him. "How is your mother going to feel about Isaac, me, and Tommy Lee being in your wedding? I've worried about that. You know how she thinks of us as the help. Have you talked to her about it?"

He scowled. "No, and I have no intention of doing so. My life and how I choose to run it now is my concern and Lila's."

Lila leaned forward. "I imagine Edward's Aunt Eula will elbow Clarice if she tries to act up in any way. Have you met her? She is a force to be reckoned with." Lila giggled at the thought. "Anyway, no matter what she says or how she acts, don't pay any attention to it."

"I admit we don't have a good past with Clarice," Isaac added. "She all but ignored us when we came back after Big Sam died."

"Well, that's the past," Lila said. "We're leaving it back there in the past where it belongs and moving on. Let this weekend and all the days and years to come be happy ones."

"Here, here," Isaac agreed. "Tanya and I will do that, and we're glad you two are back here at Indigo. Life will hold some good times ahead for all of us."

The next two days skimmed by fast, the rehearsal and the dinner with family and friends at Indigo a time of joy and fun. Edward loved seeing his old home opening its doors to people again, happy to hear laughter and warmth in its rooms.

He stood in his bedroom on Saturday afternoon, dressed in his black wedding tux, vest, crisp white shirt and emerald tie, that all the men in the wedding were wearing. As he'd opened the closet to get his shoes out, he'd caught a whiff of the soft cologne Lila always wore drifting out from her clothes hanging there now.

Glancing around the bedroom, he saw other touches she'd brought to the room they soon would share—framed photographs. a robe hung behind the bathroom door, jars and bottles on the bathroom shelves. He'd found a silky nightdress in a side drawer while searching for dark socks earlier that drew his mind to the big bed in the bedroom they would soon share. They would stay in his old room, a large one with its own bath adjoining, rather than moving to the big master bedroom at the other end of the hall that had been his parents. Their room still didn't feel like a happy place to him, although Lila was determined to redecorate the space and turn it into a guestroom.

How blessed he was that life had brought him home when it did and brought Lila back to him. Perhaps it was all coincidence how it happened, but Edward thanked God for it anyway.

At four, later in the day, he stood at the front of the church watching Leah and Rose, Gwen's daughters, come down the aisle of the church tossing rose petals out left and right, thrilled to be in the wedding. They wore matching dresses with flouncy green skirts and white sparkly tops, and no one seemed to mind their overly-enthusiastic behavior or that they waved to people they knew. They were only six, after all.

Chase, at nearly nine, was serving as the ring bearer, or junior groomsman, a term he preferred. He looked spiffy in his dark pants, emerald green suspenders and bow tie, carrying their rings on a pillow. Near the alter, he tripped and almost dropped the pillow, but grabbed it just in time, and yelled out, "Got it, Mom. Don't worry."

He saw Gwen roll her eyes as she stood waiting to walk down the aisle. She, her sisters, and Tanya soon made their way to the front of the church with his four groomsmen.

As they walked down the aisle, passing the pew where his mother and Aunt Eula sat, Edward heard his mother gasp at seeing Isaac, Tanya, and Tommy Lee in the wedding party. He'd already seen his mother swivel her head around a few times at all the members of the Jessup and George family in the church audience. His mother started to hiss something at Aunt Eula, but his aunt jabbed at her with her elbow, leaned over and told her to shush. Standing near their pew, Edward heard her, but he only smiled at Eula when she looked his way.

Edward, however, forgot everything then as the congregation stood and Lila came down the aisle in a drift of white, that thin, sheer white veil over her face, looking like a white angel. How had he become so blessed that this beautiful woman had agreed to marry him and spend her life with him? He hoped with all his being he could make her happy. God had claimed her once, but Edward had thanked Him profusely many times for gifting her back to him.

After their vows were said, Edward lifted that sheer veil artfully and kissed Lila with perhaps more ardor than she'd expected. But he was happy, and he led her down the aisle with a huge grin on his face that everybody smiled at.

Their big wedding reception afterward would never be forgotten at Edisto. They arrived and left in that big white carriage with Levi proudly driving. Edward loved every moment of standing at the door to welcome all their friends before they moved into the event hall to be seated. As they turned to enter the hall, twilight had begun to fall making all the lights outside and inside the old barn twinkle and shine.

"It's like magic," Lila whispered, and it was.

Celeste sang, with Marcus playing the piano and some of her band members joined in, too. She'd even written a song for the two of them about deep Indigo love enduring through the ages.

As dinner ended, Raymond Maybank took the floor and picked up the microphone on stage to congratulate him and Lila and to welcome Edward into their firm. Several others stood to give toasts or make announcements, too. All meaningful to him and to Lila.

Surprisingly his Aunt Eula was one, saying how happy she and his mother were that he'd come home to step into his Calhoun legacy. Clarice looked a little embarrassed as people glanced her way, but she nodded graciously as if Eula standing to speak had been her own idea.

"At least they came," Lila whispered to him again. "It's a beginning."

Raymond looked around the room. "Does anyone else have any announcements or words to give?" he asked.

"I do," Chase called out.

Gwen gave him an alarmed look, but Raymond said, "Well, come on up, young man."

Chase walked up front, took the mike and grinned at everyone. "I get to announce that I got a brand new Uncle tonight, Uncle Edward." Everyone laughed. "I also get to announce that my Aunt Celeste and Uncle Reid are going to have a baby!"

Gwen gasped and then started to hurry to the stage to get him, while every head swiveled toward Celeste.

Celeste rolled her eyes "Well, it is true," she admitted, trying not to laugh. "Chase must have heard his mother and me talking earlier. Reid and I are blessed to tell you we are going to have a baby, even though the news hasn't been formally announced yet."

Gwen frowned at her son as she moved closer to the stage. "You need to come and sit down right now, Chase."

He looked down at her. "Aren't people having new babies good announcements, Mom?" He gave her a hurt look.

"Well, of course," she said, but before she could say more, he added, "Then you should announce you and Dad are going to have a new baby, too."

The entire room erupted in laughter, but Gwen burst into tears. "What's wrong, Mom?" Chase asked.

She sniffed. "I haven't even told your father yet."

"No kidding?" His eyes searched for Alex in the room. "Well, congratulations Dad. You get to be a new dad!"

More laughter roared around the room as Gwen finally got Chase off the stage.

"I think Chase really stole the show tonight," Edward said to Lila, after leaning closer to her.

"I think so, too," she said, trying to brush away tears.

Celeste signaled to the band she'd brought to start the dancing a few minutes later, covering over the awkward moment.

Edward had asked for the first song to be "The Way You Look Tonight" for a slow dance number for him and Lila to lead off. He pulled Lila close as they danced to whisper, "I'll always remember the way you looked tonight, Lila Deveaux Calhoun."

Eventually, the lovely evening ended, and Lila and Edward loaded into the old horse-drawn carriage again for Levi to drive them back to the main house. They were spending their first nights there before starting on a honeymoon trip.

As everyone prepared to toss rice on them as they drove away, Rose and Leah called out, "Can we ride with you in the pretty carriage?"

"Yeah, can we?" Chase echoed. "I can ride up high with Levi."

Before Alex and Gwen could start to protest, Edward looked at Lila, who grinned in response, and he said, "Sure, come on."

The newly married couple then drove away with Chase on the livery seat with Levi, waving to everyone, and the two little girls in the carriage on either side of them, throwing their rice at the crowds as they were showered with rice and good wishes, too.

In their bedroom a little later, Edward smiled at Lila. "I'd say no one will forget our wedding for more reasons than a good time."

"No." She laughed. "But oh, Edward, everything was simply glorious and beautiful, wasn't it? I'll never forget a minute of it."

"Yes, I agree." He moved to take her in his arms and kiss her, the moment soon progressing to rapid breathing and rising passion.

"Can I help you out of your dress, Sister Anne?" he whispered against her ear. "I don't think you're going to be able to keep those vows of chastity any longer."

"No, I don't think so," she answered softly, giggling and loosening his tie. "Let's discover a new adventure, Edward."

"I'm all in," he replied, already starting to unbutton the satin buttons down the back of her dress. "Welcome to our forever, Mrs. Calhoun. We're going to have a wonderful, happy life."

RECIPES from *The Light Continues*

Burke's Baked Chicken Chimichangas

Ingredients:

2 cups cooked, shredded chicken 1 cup salsa
1/2 tsp dried oregano leaves   1 tsp ground cumin
1 cup shredded cheddar cheese   1/4 cup chpd green onions
6 (1 in) flour tortillas   2 Tbsp melted butter
Plus: diced tomato, sour cream, guacamole, more salsa and
shredded cheese for topping after baked

Instructions:

Pre-heat oven to 400 degrees. In bowl, mix chicken, salsa, cumin,
oregano, cheese and onions. Place appx one-third cup chicken mixture
in middle of each tortilla. Fold sides of tortillas over filling, then roll
up tortillas and place seam-side down on a baking sheet. Brush tops
of tortillas with the melted butter. Bake at 400 degrees for 25 minutes
until crispy and golden brown. Garnish with your favorite toppings and
serve with extra salsa and yellow rice on the side.

Lila's Grape Salad

Ingredients:

1/2 to 1 lb green seedless grapes   1/2 cup sugar
1/2 to 1 lb red seedless grapes   1/2 carton 4-oz sour cream
1/2 of 4-oz block cream cheese   Brown sugar & chpd pecans

Instructions:

Mix cream cheese and sugar, then adding sour cream. Stir in grapes
until well coated. Sprinkle with a little brown sugar and pecans.
Refrigerate until ready to serve.

Novaleigh's Sicilian Meat Roll

Ingredients:

2 beaten eggs   1/4 tsp salt and pepper
3/4 cup bread crumbs   1 small clove garlic
1/2 cup tomato juice   8 slices boiled ham
2 Tbsp snipped parsley   1 1/2 cup shrd mozzarella cheese
3 slices mozzarella cheese (each cut in half)

Instructions:

Combine in large bowl all ingredients but ham slices and cheese. After mixing well, spread meat out in 10 x 12 piece of foil. Sprinkle meat mixture with cheese. Start from short end and roll up meat and cheese loaf. Peel away foil while rolling. Put meat roll on greased baking sheet seam side down and bake at 350 degrees for one hour and 15 minutes. Remove and add cheese slices on top and bake 5 minutes more to slightly melt cheese. Cut in slices and serve.

Etta's Chocolate Chip Cake

Ingredients:

1 plain yellow cake mix   1 cup Hershey's chocolate syrup
8 oz sour cream   1 pkg instant chocolate pudding pie mix
6 oz chocolate chips   1/2 cup oil
1/2 cup lukewarm water   3 eggs

Instructions:

Mix cake mix, pudding mix, oil and water at medium speed about two minutes. Add syrup and sour cream. Then beat in eggs one at a time. Hand stir in chocolate chips. Pour batter into a greased and floured bundt pan and bake 1 hour at 350 degrees. Remove cake from pan when slightly cooled so it doesn't break up. Drizzle cake with an icing glaze of 1/4 cup confectioner sugar with 1 Tbsp milk. Can add a drizzle of chocolate syrup, too.

A Reading Group Guide

THE LIGHT CONTINUES

Lin Stepp

About This Guide

The questions on the following pages are included
to enhance your group's reading of
Lin Stepp's *The Light Continues*

DISCUSSION QUESTIONS

1. As this last novel in The Lighthouse Sisters series begins, Lila, her sisters, and her family are getting ready for Easter services. What events have happened since the following year for Lila and her sisters Gwen, Celeste, and Burke? What changes happened in Lila's own life, as well, that brought her back home to the island? What did you think about Celeste's advice to Lila at the end of Chapter 1, encouraging her to be open to new opportunities and changes for her own life and to be brave enough to explore them?

2. What has brought Edward Calhoun home to Edisto this Easter? Where has he been? Why has he delayed returning for so long to his family home? With his father's death, Edward has inherited Indigo Plantation. Why is he not happy about this inheritance and eager to enjoy it? What does his mother want him to do about the plantation and what does she want for her own life now?

3. As you begin to follow Edward's story, what did you learn about his parents, Sam and Clarice Calhoun? What was Edward's father Sam like? What did you think of his mother Clarice? Edward has been raised with great wealth at Indigo but do you think he has experienced a warm and happy childhood? How is Edward's family acquainted with the Deveaux family and how are the two families interlinked in their past? How is Lila's family different from Edward's?

4. Edward and Lila, close in age, were friends as children. How often have they seen each other in recent years? Why is Edward so surprised to see Lila with her family at church on Easter?

Where did he think she still was? What are his thoughts in seeing her again and how does Lila act toward him?

5. Lila is surprised to see Edward again, too. How does she feel about running into him at church? How did her sisters Gwen and Celeste make that unexpected meeting even more awkward? Later when Lila's sister Burke comes to talk with her at her house, what does Lila admit to her about her relationship with Edward in the past? What more of her feelings does she later admit to herself while walking alone on the beach?

6. Edward's family has left him painful memories to grapple with on his return home. How have the Jessups been more like a loving family to Edward than his own mother and father? When did the Jessup family in past first come to Indigo? What did you learn about the history of both of these families and the past of the plantation? Isaac Jessup had been like a brother to Edward growing up. How was Edward able to talk Isaac and his wife Tanya into coming back to Edisto?

7. Sam Calhoun was a powerful and brilliant man but not a morally righteous man. What were his strengths and weaknesses? What were his worst behaviors that brought hurt and shame to others? Have you ever known wealthy, powerful men like Sam, with many strengths and advantages, who were also unkind and flawed in how they dealt with others?

8. How do the Jessups help Edward with the harsh memories of his past? How was Della kind and helpful to him when he found it hard to clean out his father's office? What advice did she give him about holding resentment toward the house and the places all around him? How did Levi offer him good advice and counsel, too, on several occasions? Early in the book, Levi advised *"Let the past and its bad memories go. They'll only keep hurting you if you keep holding on to them."* Do you think that's true? Do you

find it hard to let go of old hurts? How did time and good counsel help Edward toward healing?

9. When Isaac Jessup learns Edward has seen Lila again, he asks, *"Are you going to try to get something going with Lila Deveaux again?"* What does Edward answer? When Lila comes to work on her art drawings at Indigo, how do Edward and Lila talk candidly about their past and its problems? Does this talk help them? Being with Lila again fires Edward's old romantic interest toward her, but Lila is not as quick to respond. Why does she not want to return to more than friendship with Edward?

10. Lila has become a gifted artist over time. How did her early interest and talent in art grow into a career? Did her family and friends recognize and encourage her gifts at a young age? How did Lila's time at college and at St. Mary's help to develop her gift? What type of art does she create and how is she helping to develop and market her work? What does Lila help the most with at the family's business at the Deveaux Inn and Lighthouse? What ongoing project is she involved in with Morgan Richards and his story?

11. How and why was Edward pressured by his father to study law in college? Although angry and determined to later pursue a different career after college, how did Edward's feelings about studying law change while at Vanderbilt? How were his professors there and his friend Ryan Markman a help to him? What legal work has he been doing since graduation? Why is Edward reluctant to take his place in the Maybank-Calhoun Law Firm?

12. What does Edward learn about his father, as a professional attorney, in visiting with Raymond Maybank at the firm's legal office and at lunch? Edward can't help wondering how they got along with his father in the firm. What does he learn about that

from Raymond? What are his legal expectations at the law firm? How is Raymond kind and gracious in presenting options to Edward about coming into the firm?

13. Lila and Edward have always enjoyed riding horses at Indigo. What horses does the plantation keep in the book? When Lila and Edward go riding, how does she act about wanting to ride to the old folly on the river, a special spot they've always enjoyed? As the book unfolds, what do you learn happened there that makes Lila want to avoid the folly? How do Annamae and Della, and later Edward, help Lila to confront her old memories of that painful time? How does she later also share about this time with her family? How do they act?

14. Where did Indigo Plantation's name come from? What did you learn in the book about the early cultivation of Indigo on plantations in the South? Over the years, since its earliest days, Indigo Plantation has experienced many changes. What are some of those? How does the plantation sustain itself now financially? What crops do they grow and what outside enterprises do they gain income with? How is the Indigo Plantation Market a help? Who manages most of the everyday business of the market and what is it like?

15. A series of small fires, occurring around the island, soon escalate and become a concern. What does Edward learn about a new fire probem when he goes to meet with Lonnie Culler, with the Edisto Police Department, at Waylon and Burke's place? What did you learn about arsons and arsonists in reading this book? What big fire later threatens Indigo Plantation and even the Deveaux Lighthouse island? How was the fire stopped and what damage was done? How was the arsonist finally caught? What part did Edward and Percy play in that? What were your feelings about all that you learned about the arsonist Ambrose Fleenor?

16. How did the fire help Edward and Lila realize the extent of their feelings for each other? How did Edward propose? What sort of wedding did they plan? How did the fire also help Edward with his decisions to stay at Indigo and join the family law firm? How did the fire make Edward want to plan a big reception after the wedding at the plantation? What sort of reception did they plan and who helped to plan it?

17. After becoming engaged, Edward and Lila drive to Charleston to tell his mother about their engagement and to invite her and his Aunt Eula to the wedding. What happens at that visit? What do you learn about Edward's mother Clarice's past? Do you think that knowledge helped Edward to understand his own past better? How had Eula and Clarice, as sisters, dealt with their past differently? Did you like Clarice better after learning about her past? What did you think of Aunt Eula?

18. Edward and Lila's wedding in July is a joyous time of new beginnings for them. What events made the day humorous as well as happy? What do you imagine the future might be like for Lila and Edward? Did you enjoy these books about the Lighthouse Sisters? Which was your favorite of the four novels and why? Did these South Carolina coastal books make you want to visit Edisto Island and places in Charleston and Beaufort featured in the stories? Which of those places have you already visited?

Books by J.L. and Lin Stepp

The Afternoon Hiker
Discovering Tennessee State Parks
Exploring South Carolina State Parks
Visiting North Carolina State Parks
Coming next - *Traveling Georgia State Parks*
And a devotional - *A Journey Of Words*

Books by Lin Stepp

The Smoky Mountain Series

The Foster Girls	*Tell Me About Orchard Hollow*
For Six Good Reasons	*Delia's Place*
Second Hand Rose	*Down by the River*
Makin' Miracles	*Saving Laurel Springs*
Welcome Back	*Daddy's Girl*
Lost Inheritance	*The Interlude*

The Mountain Home Books

Happy Valley	*Downsizing*
Eight at the Lake	*Seeking Ayita*
Shop on the Corner	*The Red Mill Bookstore*

Christmas Novella
A Smoky Mountain Gift
In *When the Snow Falls*

The Edisto Trilogy
Claire at Edisto
Return to Edisto
Edisto Song

The Lighthouse Sisters Series
Light the Way
Lighten My Heart
Light in the Dark
The Light Continues

About The Author
Lin Stepp

Lin Stepp is a native Tennessean, businesswoman, and educator. A *New Your Times, USA Today, Publishers Weekly,* and Amazon bestselling author, Lin has twenty-six published novels out now, including her twelve beloved Smoky Mountain novels and six Mountain Home books, all set in different Tennessee or North Carolina mountain locations, a novella in one of Kensington's Christmas anthologies and seven South Carolina coastal novels, including her three Edisto Trilogy books and four in the new Lighthouse Sisters series.

Lin and her husband J.L. also write regional guidebooks, including a published Smoky Mountain hiking guide and four state park guide books for TN, SC, NC, and GA, all filled with hundreds of color photos. Writing and adventuring are her joys and more novels set in the Smokies and at the beach are on the way, as well as more colorful regional guidebooks. Lin's title *Claire At Edisto* was the *2019 Best Book Award Winner in Fiction: Romance,* sponsored by American Book Fest and her novel *Welcome Back* a finalist in the *2017 Selah Awards.* Lin enjoys speaking for events, festivals, libraries, and book clubs. She also loves reading, hiking, exploring out of doors, and keeping up with her readers. Look for her pages on Facebook and Twitter and follow her monthly blog and newsletter, too, that you will find on her website at: *www.linstepp.com.*